ROCK STAR'S HEART

Kella Campbell

TIED STAR BOOKS

Rock Star's Heart
CONTEMPORARY ROMANCE

©2018 Kella Campbell

TRADE PAPERBACK EDITION
ISBN 978-0-9921152-1-0

BOOK TEXT TYPESET IN ZAPF RENAISSANCE ANTIQUA BOOK
WITH HEADINGS IN INKED GOD PRO & LOVE LIGHT
COVER PHOTOGRAPHY BY TIFFANY JOHN
EDITOR TANYA OEMIG

TIED STAR BOOKS
VANCOUVER, CANADA
WWW.TIEDSTARBOOKS.COM

Once there was a musician who worked at a coffee shop
where I used to write, and when it was quiet,
he talked to me about guitars...

chapter

I

CRYS SAT IN THE SEMI-DARK OF THE ARENA, UP IN the nosebleeds with a couple of girlfriends, clutching the arms of her seat. She hadn't expected to feel vertigo, but she'd never been so high up in an arena of this size; the steep elevation of the seats and the distance to the stage below were having a funny effect on her. With white knuckles, she told herself that she would not, could not possibly tip out of her seat and freefall down the endless rows, off the balcony and down to the stage.

All around, people rustled into their seats, juggling plastic drink cups and neon glow sticks, squirming into brand new Smidge tour t-shirts or moaning over the photographs in their glossy souvenir programs.

"Oooh, look, Crys, Debbie, look at this one of Angel!" Leah's words almost came out on a squeal as she thrust her program toward them and jabbed a finger at one of the pictures. Soaking wet and with shirt ripped half off, the lead singer appeared to be in the process of unbuttoning his jeans, with a devilish smirk on his handsome face. Water droplets glimmered in his bleached-platinum crew cut and along high cheekbones – narrowed green eyes held an invitation.

Debbie leaned across Crys to have a look. "Pfft! So fake." She craned her neck for a better view of the suggestive pose and the vocalist's semi-revealed muscular chest.

Crys looked too. "I like this one of Blade best," she said, pointing to another picture which featured Smidge's guitarist, dark in shadow and leather, pinpoint light glinting on his lip and eyebrow piercings as he cradled his guitar with a hint of bitter tenderness.

Leah laughed. "You've got creepy taste, Crys – Blade's too hardcore for me. Angel's the hottest for sure, but some of these pictures of Dice are kind of yummy too." Dice's poses weren't quite as openly sexual as the others – the drummer was the youngest of the Smidge boys, a cute kid-brother joker with an appealing half-innocent grin.

"Okay, so maybe Angel technically has the best cheekbones and abs, but that doesn't make him the sexiest or the best date." Debbie turned her program to a shot of the bass player, a fallen seraph, all golden curls and the bluest eyes. "I'd go for Easy in a heartbeat, if I had the chance," she said, with a hint of a blush. Crys's eyes met Leah's, and their lips twitched – Debbie was a dead sucker for any nice-guy-gone-bad, and it never ended well.

"Honey, can we get by?" asked an athletic man with spiky hot-pink hair, touching Leah on the shoulder to get her attention. His two friends crowded behind him, shoving good-naturedly and balancing plastic cups of beer. All three wore t-shirts with the acid-green logo of the opening band, and sported gelled-up hair and facial piercings. They fit in with the crowd, much more so than the girls did. "Our seats are next to yours, I think," he added. "I'm Johnny, and these are Rhys and Adam."

"Leah, and my friends are Debbie and Crys," she said, hopping up to let them squeeze by, maybe squeezing a little closer than absolutely necessary. Her hair snagged on a button of Adam's denim jacket, and he laughed, untangling her as he wedged past. Adam had young-Lenny-Kravitz dreads and an attractive smile. "You girls want something to drink?" he asked, with a diffident shrug to show that it didn't much matter either way. "No strings – just drinks, you know?"

Leah glanced at Crys and Debbie. After almost four years of university, they were used to having at least some tenuous connection with guys they met – a shared class, a mutual acquaintance, familiar territory – and these were completely unknown quantities, with nothing in common but concert tickets in the same row. Attractive, though...

Leah's eyes begged her friends to agree, to keep the conversation going.

"Well, I'd love a beer," said Debbie, prodding Crys with an elbow to say yes as well.

Although her mother wouldn't have approved, and she wasn't sure she felt comfortable taking drinks from strangers, Crys nodded. "Sure, please." She liked the look of these men, with their gelled hair and piercings – easy enough to imagine them in rock star makeup, a bit of eyeliner and sparkle, like the Smidge boys in their beefcake photos.

Leah giggled, her cheeks pink under her freckles. "You won't be able to carry all that, Adam; I'd better come down with you."

Adam shot his friends a look that plainly said four cups was hardly a challenge, but he wasn't going to turn down a pretty girl's company. "You bet," he agreed, with another wide smile, gesturing for her to precede him along the row of seats toward the aisle.

Crys and Debbie stood and squeezed back against their seats, as Johnny and Rhys pushed past, checking them over with interested eyes. Crys looked downward to avoid their assessment – and the vertigo hit her again as she took in the drop to the stage. With an inadvertent moan of distress, she sank back into her seat, groping for the armrests.

Rhys turned toward her, concerned. "Hey. You okay?"

"I'm fine," Crys said, shaking her head, though she could feel the blush rushing to her cheeks. "It's stupid. I've never been so high up in an arena before. I get... kind of dizzy when I look down." She gazed at her feet, eyes fixed on her shoes, hair falling forward as though she could hide behind it.

"It's not stupid," Rhys assured her. "They call these the nosebleeds for a reason, but it's ridiculously expensive to sit further down. We couldn't afford better seats either."

"Shut up," said Johnny. "None of anyone's business what we can or can't afford."

Rhys just laughed. "Come on, Johnny, who'd be sitting up here if they could be down there?"

"That's true enough," Debbie agreed. "Still, I guess they can charge whatever people are willing to pay. It's unreal how popular Smidge has become – did you guys see them on their first tour here?"

"Nah," said Johnny. "Didn't know much about them then. I mean, I heard 'Skanky Treat' on the radio, of course – who didn't? But it was impossible to get tickets, and then they didn't even come here on their second big tour. Anyway, I didn't really get into Smidge until *My Tainted Baby* was released."

"I've liked Smidge from the beginning, but I couldn't get tickets to the *Skanky Treat* tour either. Nobody could." Rhys shook his head. "Their stuff has gotten more and more commercial, though. It's a shame. Even *Human Lollipop* had more original material on it than they're doing now."

Debbie squeaked an indignant protest at that. "But they're on the radio and TV all the time, and selling out every arena on their tour! They're bigger than... anything!" She held up the glossy souvenir program in illustration.

Rhys and Johnny both laughed. "That's kind of my point," Rhys said, "but... I'm here, aren't I?"

Crys only smiled. Men always pretended to know so much about music, were so quick to fling around words like 'commercial' and 'generic'. Surely it was all subjective in the end – you either connected to it or you didn't – mostly a matter of taste. And, as Rhys had said, they were here.

On the stage below, the opening band had started, to general disregard from the crowd waiting for Smidge. The seats filled up, and excitement built as a murmur circulated throughout the arena that the Smidge boys had arrived in the building. Leah and Adam returned with the promised beer, and when they shuffled down the row and Crys and Debbie stood to let Adam by, Leah gestured to her friends to move one seat along, saying to Adam, "Why don't you sit with me? The girls can move down."

"Sure," Adam agreed easily. So Crys shrugged and moved down. Then Johnny told Rhys to swap with Debbie, and Crys found herself next to Rhys, while Johnny chatted up Debbie down the row.

As the fog machine began to fill the arena with rolling clouds of powder-scented white mist, and the spotlights focused down on the stage, Crys's feeling of vertigo subsided. Maybe it was the fog, filling up the space that had threatened to overwhelm her, or maybe she'd become acclimated to the height and vastness of the arena. Or maybe it was the man sitting beside her who put such trivial considerations out of her mind. She glanced over at him, Rhys, who had reacted so considerately to her distress, who spoke with a gentleness that seemed unconnected to the tough look of his piercings and spiked hair. As she observed him, he turned his head and met her eyes.

"You have a lot of piercings," she blurted out.

Rhys smiled, touching the ring in one nostril ruefully. "Most of these are fake," he admitted with a laugh. "Clip-ons and magnets. I'm an actor, so I know how to... look the part, you know? A couple of the ones in my ears are real, but that's it."

Crys laughed too. "Wow! I'd love to be able to, well, look the part like that too," she said. "I suppose I'll always look like the good little girl I am, though. I don't know how to seem tough; I always feel like an underage schoolgirl at concerts and bars. So pathetic!" *And worse, to babble on like that about it,* she thought, but something about Rhys invited confidences.

"My friend Amy has the same problem – a young and innocent face." Rhys looked at her with professional consideration. "As an actor, it's a career advantage for her, and she gets lots of work because of it, but she also gets typecast. Going out, though... okay, she plays it up, makes it work for her. Knee-high socks, you know, short schoolgirl skirts and pigtails and a lollipop – she gets tons of attention!"

Picturing herself in a pleated plaid miniskirt, Crys wondered whether maybe her babydoll face was less of a liability than she'd thought. Her mother always said that a nice cashmere sweater and good jewelry would give her some sophistication, but embracing the innocent look sounded like a lot more fun.

Rhys must have noticed her brightening at the notion, as he took on a serious expression and added, "Of course, Amy isn't young *or* innocent, so she can handle it. Don't... er... get yourself into a situation based on what I've said. I probably shouldn't have suggested it."

"I won't try it, really," Crys agreed, "but it's a lovely idea." And Rhys was a lovely gentleman, she thought, someone who took her frustration seriously but also worried about what might happen to her if she did tart up and go out like jailbait. Wouldn't it be wonderful if he asked for her number, if he wanted to see her again? On her right, Leah chattered away at top volume while Adam nodded in agreement, and on the other side of Rhys, Johnny leaned close to Debbie, his mouth close to her ear, saying something that made her laugh.

The opening act finished playing, and with a blast of electronic thunder, the entire arena was plunged into pitch darkness. A voice seemed to roar from everywhere at once: "Ladies and gentlemen, please welcome... SMIDGE!"

The stage exploded into a mass of light and dazzle. Pyrotechnics blasted and strobes flashed, lasers whirled. Slowly rising into the spotlights from trapdoors in the stage came the Smidge boys, Jumbotron screens lighting to show their ascent in close-up. Rock gods they were, made up in glitter and flash, hair sprayed stiff with blue and silver stuff, glorious in artfully ripped dark denim, studded leather, black mesh, rhinestones and LED lights.

Angel, of the satanically elegant face, actually wore a pair of white-feathered wings as he rose to the stage – Leah reached across Adam's lap to squeeze Crys's hand in excitement. The thundering sound effects were much too loud for conversation, but the hand-squeeze told Crys that Leah found the wings effective. Reaching the stage, Angel picked up his guitar and strode forward to the stand that held his mic, raising one arm in a salute to the crowd. Behind him, Dice in a jester's cap jumped up onto the drum riser and lifted his drumsticks with an impish grin, and Leah squeezed Crys's hand again. Then Easy, with his blue-and-silver-streaked fair hair glowing like a halo in the spotlights, took his bass from its stand and held it aloft in greeting to the crowd like the lover-boy he was, basking in the shrieks of response as he stepped up to flank Angel. Blade, though, paid little attention to the screaming fans as he collected his guitar – he seemed focused inward as he lifted up the instrument and settled it into position, adjusting the strap. All in black, he wore a spike-studded dog collar around his neck and leather cuffs around his wrists; a sleeveless vest showed off the ink on his arms. He moved into position, and magnified on the jumbotron screens he gave a sharp nod to Angel – saying without words, *I'm ready, let's do this thing.*

Music filled the arena, drums like gunfire, heavy bass and power guitar, a rock anthem that had most of the audience up on their feet. As Angel gripped his mic close and began to pour his passionate words into it, a raw moaning noise swept around the arena, thousands of delighted voices responding to him in appreciation.

Rock gods weren't for falling in love with, Crys knew; they were for daydreams and fantasy, for wishful thinking in between boyfriends. But as she gazed down at the stage, irresistibly drawn to the Smidge boys in their stage makeup and punk hair – especially Blade with the metal in his face – she wondered if she'd ever find a regular guy to date who attracted her in that way.

Next to Crys, Rhys sat watching the concert, absorbed in the music. As an actor, he looked the part because he'd chosen to do so for the night. Presumably, he could also look the part of a nice, appropriate, sane-and-normal boyfriend if he wanted to. Not that he'd said anything about wanting to see her again. Crys wondered if, in some imaginary perfect world, he could be convinced to wear his fake piercings for her – if, and she felt a bit hot in the concert darkness at the thought, he would wear them to make love to her. Rhys the actor must be well used to stage makeup, too; it wasn't such a stretch to think of him with a bit of eyeliner darkening around his eyes... would he do that too, for her, if she asked him?

"God, I'm such a fool," she muttered to herself, her words eaten up by the concert sound all around. How could she be thinking these thoughts about someone she'd just met?

On the stage below, Smidge segued into a power-ballad duet – Angel singing the part of a relationship-bound man longing for sexual freedom, with Blade taking up a second microphone to sing the contrasting part, the promiscuous adventurer longing for love. "For every night when the bedsheets burned / For every night when thunder rolled / I've longed to find a princess / One love to have and to hold," Blade sang, his raspy deep voice a counterpoint to Angel's more melodic one.

Rhys hadn't given any sort of clue as to how forward he was in that direction.

A fragrant skunk-ish smoke drifted over them. Crys glanced around to see if she could see where it was coming from; more particularly, she was curious to know whether the three guys they'd met were responsible for the smoke. Rhys noticed her curious eyes – he laughed. "None of us do it," he said into her ear. "I used to, but I've given it up. So has Adam. And Johnny never did."

"I'm such a child, sorry," said Crys. She had to speak up for him to hear her, but with the loud ambient sound it had the effect of a whisper.

"Don't be sorry. You're curious. You don't know us. It's natural." Rhys reached over and took her hand. "Let's enjoy the concert, huh?" As the band on the stage far below shifted into one of their fast-paced club hits, he squeezed her fingers and didn't let go.

When the lights finally came up at the end of the concert, after the last of the fog from the machines and the smoke from the pyrotechnics had faded, Crys had the strange feeling of emerging from a dream, ears ringing and aching from the barrage of sound. While the others put on their coats and gathered up programs and purses, she looked down at the bare distant stage – the vertigo long gone – where workers unplugged and carried away instruments, packed equipment into large black cases, swept up glitter and assorted debris. Had Smidge even really been there? The dream-world of laser lights and silver confetti, spotlights and swirling fog, had disappeared under the bright arena floodlights, and all over the building the chattering crowd swarmed outward, while the black boards of the stage stood abandoned.

"Come on, space cadet! It's time to go!" Leah said, gently prodding Crys's shoulder. "Don't forget your coat."

But before she could bend to get it, Rhys had scooped it up and was holding it out for her to slip her arms in. She turned to thank him, and he smiled. Then they were filing out, an inch at a time, stuck in a human traffic jam as the sold-out arena emptied itself of occupants. Leah and Adam made their way along the row of seats and into the aisle to start the trek down the stairs, and people from other rows wedged themselves into the gap before Crys and Rhys could catch up. Debbie and Johnny had been right behind them, but again, the sheer press of numbers had created separation, and in the midst of all the people Crys was alone with Rhys for the first time.

"I don't like to do this," he said, with the first bit of hesitation he'd shown, "but your girlfriends should know that Adam and Johnny aren't exactly... standard date candidates."

"Oh?"

"Mm-hmm. Adam's in what you might call a complicated relationship, and Johnny – well, Johnny's bisexual and prefers open relationships, and most girls get kind of intense about that when they find out."

Crys took a quick look back in startled curiosity, but didn't immediately see Johnny, though his hot-pink hair should have made him visible, even among all the people on the stairs. And Rhys hadn't said anything of himself. "What about you?" she asked. "Are you a complicated date too?"

"Well, I'm an actor," he said, with a wry smile. "But if that doesn't scare you off, I'd like to get your phone number."

Crys wrote her number on the back of his ticket stub. "There you go."

"Crystal Murphy. That's a pretty name," Rhys said, looking at the ticket stub.

"What's your last name, then?"

"Davies."

"Davies. I like that," said Crys. He couldn't possibly know that she was trying herself out as Mrs. Davies in her head, could he? "I really do hope you call me," she added.

"I will call you, Crystal Murphy," said Rhys Davies, "believe me, I will."

At the bottom of the steps, they found Adam and Leah, and waited for Johnny and Debbie. When the pair turned up, Crys couldn't help eyeing Johnny in semi-shocked fascination. She couldn't put what Rhys had said out of her mind. Had Johnny made love to both men and women? Did he have them both at the same time, or one at a time? Debbie, who was deeply into exclusivity and promise rings and relationship status conversations, wouldn't be able to cope with an alternative arrangement. Then Crys had to wonder how she herself would handle it. Not that she was even interested in Johnny. But a lover who had other lovers, who didn't buy into the one-boy-one-girl-forever model of things... Could she be strong enough, open enough for that? And there was Rhys, watching her watch Johnny, with an odd half-smile on his face. *Oh, good God, he knows I'm thinking about sex!*

And then they were saying their goodnights in the main concourse of the arena, standing to one side of the herd of bodies flowing outward. "We could walk out together, help you flag a taxi?" Johnny offered, but Leah and Crys shook their heads, and though Debbie looked tempted to drop all caution and abandon her friends, Leah jabbed her in the ribs with an elbow until she agreed with a regretful moue.

"That's kind of you, but we're taking the train home," Leah said, looking around for signs to direct them to the station connected to the arena. "So... I guess this is goodnight."

Crys saw Adam kiss Leah on the cheek, but there was no promise in his body language. Debbie, on the other hand, had lost the lipstick off her lips on the journey down the stairs, and Johnny had a hand resting intimately on her lower back as he murmured something in her ear. Crys couldn't meet Rhys's eyes.

"Crys," he said softly. She raised her eyes, and he was looking straight at her, telling her without words that he wanted to kiss her, asking without words whether she wanted a kiss goodnight. And because she didn't know the answer to that, he didn't press her. "Next time, then." A promise.

♥

The queue for the women's washroom was staggering. "Are you sure you have to go, Deb?" Leah asked. "We'll be back at our place in less than twenty minutes. Or you could use the ladies' in the station; it's bound to be less crowded..."

"Absolutely not," replied Debbie, wrinkling her nose. "Gotta go; you know what I'm like after drinking beer, there's no way I can wait the whole way home. And I'm not going near the station washroom – disgusting."

"You shouldn't drink if you can't hold your pee," Leah muttered. "Fine, go and get in line, then. We'll wait for you at the exit." It was one of those washrooms with inflow and outflow doors, allowing the herd of women to file in at one end to use the toilet stalls, then move on to the rows of sinks, then out by the other door. Debbie, clearly too content with her night to be offended by Leah's sourness, waved cheerily in agreement and scooted off to get in line before the wait grew any longer. Leah rolled her eyes at Crys. "Honestly, Debbie's bladder is the size of a toddler's!"

Crys raised her eyebrows – it wasn't like Leah to be so negative. "What's the matter, Leah?"

"If you have to know, Adam didn't make any move to see me again. No phone number, no hint that we could connect online, nothing."

"His loss." Crys thought for a moment, and then decided that, as much as she disliked passing on hearsay, her friend deserved to know what Rhys had said. "Listen, it wasn't you. Rhys told me that Adam is in a complicated relationship of some sort. I think he meant for me to let you know, so you wouldn't feel bad – I mean, Adam obviously enjoyed your company, he just isn't single."

"That's my usual rotten luck. Why do I always get the unavailable ones?" Leah cursed under her breath. "At least Debbie might get laid sometime soon. She clearly had a bit of a grope on the stairs, huh? I wonder if that Johnny asked for her number..."

Crys sighed. "As to that, you might as well know what Rhys said about Johnny, and I don't think he was kidding; apparently Johnny, um... goes both ways, you know?"

"Eww, that's nasty – Debbie would freak if she knew – and she let him kiss her, too!" Leah shook her head. "And she thought she'd catch something from the subway washroom!" The scandal in her voice was tinged with relish, and her expectant expression said she was waiting for Crys to agree, to validate the horror and deliciousness of it.

"I... don't think we should, um, judge him like that. Sure, it's... different, and Debbie won't like it, but... he and his friends seem nice. I expect he, well, you know, practices safe sex and all that."

Leah snorted in disgust. "Oh, come on, Miss Vanilla Virgin, don't pretend like you're not as squicked out by it as I am – or is this some churchy 'love the sinner, hate the sin' thing?"

"Wow, Leah. You know me better than that, don't you? Try 'his body, his choice,' okay?"

They looked at each other, uncomfortably silent.

"Fine, whatever." Leah crossed her arms and contemplated the remains of the crowd with a scowl. Crys shrugged outwardly at Leah's grumpiness, but couldn't help hearing the hurtful words over and over in her mind, wondering if her friends really thought of her as a churchy vanilla virgin. To pass the time, she too watched the shifting masses of people.

A man in a dark suit was moving through the crowd, with a clipboard and pen in hand and a security earpiece in his ear. He didn't look like a member of the security team, though – those wore yellow jackets with silver reflective stripes and SECURITY in big letters across the back. This man seemed out of place among the concert-goers, an executive sort, and the suit looked expensive. He observed the crowd intently, occasionally checking his clipboard and speaking into what had to be a microphone clipped to his lapel. He had to be either looking for someone or watching for some sort of activity or behavior. His eyes connected with Crys's, and his gaze sharpened. She looked away at once, trying to appear nonchalant, but she could feel her cheeks reddening at the thought of having been caught watching him – whatever his purpose was, she'd no call to stare at him like that.

Moments later, Debbie emerged from the washroom. "Come on, let's go!" Crys said at once. "Do either of you know where we are in relation to the subway entrance?"

"Well, it's by the northwest gate, and I think I saw a sign–" Debbie began.

"Debbie, you won't believe what Crys told me about your new friend Johnny, you'll be absolutely sick–" Leah interrupted.

"Excuse me," said the man in the expensive suit and security earpiece, right there at their elbows, making them jump. "May I ask you ladies a few questions? It will only take a moment."

He appeared to be conducting some sort of marketing survey – had they enjoyed the concert, had they purchased a souvenir program? Looking at the program, could they show him the photos they liked best? Which Smidge boy did each of them find most attractive? Were they speaking as single girls or did they have boyfriends? They answered the man's questions and pointed at pictures, and just as they were beginning to eye each other with a touch of impatience, he smiled in a pleased but slightly calculating way and thanked them for their time and assistance.

"It was no trouble, we're glad to have helped," said Crys with a polite smile; Leah and Debbie nodded in agreement, eager to be on their way.

But the man reached into his jacket and extracted three laminated tags. "No, really, your answers are much appreciated. In return for that, let me do you a favor: you'd like to meet the Smidge boys, wouldn't you?"

"You've got to be kidding!" Leah said.

The man shook his head. "Not at all, young lady; part of the promotional activities they're contracted for includes meeting individual fans backstage after the concert. In this case we're... using that access as appreciation for assistance with our survey." The explanation rang slightly false, as though there had to be more to it, but the tags he handed them were actual backstage passes with serial numbers and holographic seals of authenticity, and he spoke into a microphone clipped to his lapel, summoning an assistant to escort them in.

The assistant appeared almost immediately, a tough-looking woman who looked like she could be in her late thirties – or maybe she was younger and lived and partied harder than most. She wore what might have been a power suit if it hadn't been made of black leather, and a black satin shirt unbuttoned rather too far. Diamond studs gleamed in her ears.

"Marigold will take care of you," said the man. "Thanks again."

The leather-suited woman spoke into a two-way radio: "I'm bringing three more in for photo op and autographs, alert to one possible, authorized by Mr. Kinney." A static hiss and an assenting response issued from the radio's speaker. "Right this way; follow me. Please refrain from touching anything in the backstage space, and immediately obey any instructions given to you by the backstage public relations manager or any member of the crew for your own safety and comfort." She recited the string of directives without pause or inflection; she must have given the same spiel hundreds of times. "You will have a brief opportunity to speak with the band members. They will sign your programs, if you'd like them to do so. We ask that you not take any personal photographs or recordings of any sort in the backstage space." Her patronizing look suggested that, given the privilege of breathing the same air as the Smidge boys, no one would dare to find these arrangements less than satisfactory.

She marched along ahead of them at a brisk pace, exuding a strong aura of being much too busy and important to escort little girls around to meet the band.

Crys patted her hair anxiously, wishing she'd brought a hairbrush – why would she have brought a hairbrush to a concert? – and wondering if she might get a chance to touch up her lipstick. She saw Leah straightening her shirt, and Debbie undoing and then doing up the top buttons of her denim jacket.

In silence, the three of them savored tingles of anticipation as Marigold led them through a steel door and down a long concrete ramp, up a short flight of stairs and along a carpeted hallway, stopping at a door with a plaque that read "Lounge A." Pinned to a corkboard below the plaque was a paper notice with the words "Guest Holding Lounge – No Admittance Without Passes." Marigold spoke into her radio, and the door was opened from the inside.

"Hello, ladies, please come in and have a seat," said a tall man in a Smidge Crew t-shirt and dark jeans, with a skull-patterned bandana covering his head. Freestanding banners with images of the Smidge boys in concert brightened up an otherwise bland room – a couple of basic beige sofas matched the industrial wallpaper. The crewman turned to Marigold. "Goldie, could you tell Kin that this has got to be it for tonight; the boys have had enough." Marigold shot him a withering look, but he shrugged it off. "Hey, not my doing, I'm just passing the word along."

"Whatever."

"So, introduce me?" He inclined his head toward the girls.

"Leah, Debbie, and this one is Crys," snapped Marigold, pointing them out. "Jed is the crewperson in charge of backstage public relations, so he'll take care of you." And she turned on her heel and walked out.

"Busy lady," said Jed, with a look that suggested he didn't think much of her. "Now, have some snacks, make yourselves comfortable, and I'll need you to fill out these waivers before I take you in." He handed them each a small clipboard. "Legal stuff, you know. Personal liability waiver, in case you slip and hit your head, and there's also a photographic model release in there – I think Goldie told you that you can't take personal photos?" The girls bobbed their heads. "Management doesn't want random cameras popping off all over the place, so our photographer takes the pictures, and our guests get autographed prints in the mail. But we need you to sign a model release form so we can do that. Sound good to you?"

The girls sat there, gazing at the waiver forms in their hands, half reading the legalese and hardly taking it in as they thought about what Jed had said. Photos with Smidge after all, and something better than a blurry phone-camera shot.

Crys signed her waiver form, printing her address and phone number as instructed. When she handed it to Jed, he asked to see some ID, then peeled a barcode sticker from the back of her backstage pass and stuck it onto her waiver form, then stuck a fluorescent green star on the front of her pass. He repeated the process for Leah and Debbie, although they got orange stars instead of green. Jed's assessing look as he handed back the passes gave Crys the idea that the green star was somehow significant.

Uncomfortably aware of her most-likely-rumpled hair and lack of lipstick, Crys finally cleared her throat and asked, "Is there a mirror I could use somewhere around here? I'd kind of like to fix myself up before..."

"Don't worry about it. Sally will be – ah, you'll... have a chance at a mirror before you go in." Jed smiled, and gestured at the table. "Have some snacks, have something to drink."

Crys obediently took a can of Dr Pepper from the ice bucket and cracked it open. The sweet liquid fizzed on her tongue and slipped down her throat, and she tried not to worry about what one should or should not say to famous people on meeting them. Leah reached for a diet Sprite, and clunked it against Crys's Dr Pepper, saying, "Here's to meeting the hottest band on the planet; let's hope we have better luck than we did in the audience."

"What do you mean, 'better luck'?" Debbie asked. "I don't know about you, but I had a great time, and what's more, Johnny asked for my–"

"Well, crap," said Leah. "We were about to tell you, when we got interrupted by that PR man."

"For the love of God, now is not the time, seriously," Crys interrupted. "We're about to go and meet Smidge. Can we talk about this later?"

"But—"

"Let's just leave it 'til we get home," Crys said. "Come on, girls, please – help me figure out what to say to the legends I've been daydreaming about for the past year, okay?"

"That's right, we might actually have to say something to them." Debbie let out a little gasp of excitement. "I still can't believe we're really going to meet Smidge."

Leah grinned, widening her eyes and putting on a love-struck expression. "How about, 'Hi, I've been fantasizing about you for the past year, you're hot, can I have your autograph?'"

Jed, watching them, laughed. "You don't need to worry, ladies," he said. "You say hello, they'll ask you if you enjoyed the concert and what your favorite song is, you answer them, then the photographer will arrange you for pictures. Afterward, they'll tell you it was nice meeting you, and you'll tell them it was an honor; that's it. You don't need to have a speech prepared or anything." The girls laughed too – put like that, it sounded pretty straightforward.

And yet, remembering that she'd dreamed of Blade naked, dreamed of touching his bare skin, Crys didn't see how it could be simple to come face to face with him.

The two-way radio on Jed's desk bleeped and chattered, and he jumped up to open the door for a woman with slicked-down electric orange hair, whose Smidge Crew t-shirt stretched over an impressively stacked chest. She carried a square silver case, which she set down and opened to reveal neatly arranged trays of brushes and tubes and tins. "This is Sally," said Jed. "She's going to touch up your hair and makeup, and they'll be ready for you in the lounge by the time she's done."

"I won't need to do much, I shouldn't think," added Sally, with a calm smile that immediately put them at ease. "All three of you have lovely skin. A dab of powder and some highlighter should do it, okay?" She hooked a chair with one foot and dragged it over, positioning it in front of Crys before she sat. "You got a lipstick you want me to use, honey, or should I choose one of mine?" Sally's efficient hands moved over Crys's face, buffing, dusting, dabbing, and then she was done, and Crys sat looking into Sally's hand mirror while Sally moved on to Leah. It didn't look like makeup, what Sally had done – only a general impression of matte healthy skin and freshened lipstick. Crys passed the mirror along to Leah, and in no time at all, Debbie was inspecting herself in the mirror and Sally was packing up her kit.

"Thank you so much," Crys said to Sally. "Do we, um, give you a tip or anything?"

"Not at all, honey, but you're sweet to offer – and listen, just be yourself in there, okay? He likes natural girls, not too much makeup and flash, so you'll do fine. Luck and love to you." And with a wink and a wave, Sally was out the door with her case. *He likes...? You'll do fine...?* What had Sally meant? Jed saw Crys's puzzled face and gave her a thumbs-up sign, which puzzled her even more, just as a bleep sounded from his radio.

"On our way," said Jed into the radio. "Okay, ladies, they're ready for us. Follow me." Out into the hall they went, down and around a corner to another door – Lounge B – with a security guard sitting at a table outside and a paper tacked to the door's corkboard, reading: "Meet & Greet – passes MUST be scanned by Security prior to admittance – please leave ALL cameras & phones with Security before entering."

The security guard nodded to Jed and solemnly scanned each girl's pass before holding out a basket labelled "Cameras & Phones." Crys fished her phone out of her purse and powered it down before dropping it into the basket without hesitation, but Debbie looked at hers reluctantly before parting with it. "You'll get it back," said the security guard with an expression of utmost patience. "Pardon me, you with the red hair, do you have a phone to turn in?"

"Nope. Lost it last week and I haven't got another yet," said Leah, holding her purse open to show its lack of contents. A lipstick tube, key ring, and change purse lay forlorn at the bottom of it, along with her driver's license and debit card and a couple of crumpled-up receipts.

"Very well." The security guard picked up his radio. He pressed a button, and someone on the other side of the door pushed it open.

chapter

USIC REACHED OUT TO DRAW THEM IN, ANGEL'S voice growling and crooning through the lyrics to "My Tainted Baby" – drums pounded an infectious rhythm, and Jed waved the girls forward to precede him into the room. They paused on the threshold and glanced at each other, suddenly shy, and then Blade's guitar solo moaned and soared out to them, as Jed took Crys by the arm and led her through the door.

The walls were obscured by black velvet backdrops, and black matting with a huge Smidge logo covered the floor. Bored-looking bodyguards stood in the corners, semi-alert, arms folded. Big speakers pulsed out the music. Photographic floods lit four black leather couches arranged in a square, with the Smidge boys lounging on them. Crys closed her open mouth, and tried to take in the reality of four such glamorously sexual men sitting there, pierced and tattooed and clad in leather and denim and mesh, waiting for her to say something.

"Hello?" She smiled tentatively, trying to neither gawk at the Smidge boys nor look down at her feet like a schoolgirl.

"This is Crystal Murphy, accompanied by Leah Tucker and Debbie Frangelli," said Jed. Leah and Debbie crowded up beside Crys, all but drooling as they reacted to their first sight of the band at close quarters. "Ladies, I'm sure you recognize Angel, Easy, Blade and Dice?"

"Ooh, yes," Leah agreed, almost wriggling with enthusiasm.

"Did you enjoy the concert, then?" asked Angel, his voice as rich and caressing in person as from the stage. It was surely a rote question, but he asked it with such a sinful smile that he had all three girls nodding and giggling like teenagers.

Easy looked up from his sprawling position on one of the couches. Seen close up, he looked a little less sweet and a lot more dangerous than he did on stage and in photographs. "So, which are your favorite songs, girls?" he asked them, with poorly masked ennui – fed up with public relations, and not bothering to hide it.

"'My Tainted Baby,' of course," said Debbie at once.

"From this album, sure. But 'Star Shot Down' is my all-time fave," Leah added, "it's got a great rhythm and that drum solo, and I love the bit that gets all quiet and is just the vocals and then smash on the crash cymbal..."

"Cool, a girl who knows what she's talking about," said Dice. "How about you, ah, Crystal? Which song is your favorite?"

Crys felt her cheeks flushing at the attention. "You have so many great songs, but if I have to choose one, it's 'Love Bound'..." The duet, in which Blade sang of bedsheets burning. Blade, who sat before her now with a quizzical look in his eyes, silver rings in his lip and eyebrow and studs in his ears, a spiked leather dog-collar and black mesh top under his leather biker jacket, black jeans slashed across his long thighs.

"Are you already somebody's princess, then, or are you looking for a sinner to turn saint?" His raspy deep voice melted her, and she bit her lip, unable to form an answer.

The photographer gave her an excuse to look away. "Hi, there. I'm Scott, pleasure to meet you." A plain-featured man with a receding hairline, he stepped forward to greet them each with a firm handshake and practiced setting-at-ease smile. "Welcome to your Smidge photo moment. I'm aiming to get one good individual shot of each of you with the band member of your choice," he said, "but I'll be taking several frames each time to be sure of getting a good print, so bear with me. We'll do a group shot last. Now, if I could ask you ladies to each pick your crush for the evening, we'll get started."

"Great. Thank you, Scott." Jed adjusted his bandana, then jammed his hands into his pockets. "Crystal, why don't you choose first – who will it be?"

Short of denying herself forever the chance to have a photograph taken with the rock god she dreamed of at night, this was the moment of confession. The others were more socially acceptable, but it was Blade who attracted her beyond sense. She flicked a glance at him, trying to discern whether he'd welcome her admiration. His eyes met hers, but she couldn't read his expression.

"Crystal?" Jed asked again. "Which of the guys are you going to sit with for your picture?"

"Blade, please, if he doesn't mind," she whispered, her face on fire.

A cynical half-smile curved Blade's lips, causing the silver lip ring to catch the light. "It'll be my pleasure," he told her. "Come and sit with me, then."

Crys stumbled over to the couch where he sat, and perched on the edge of it, but the leather was unexpectedly slippery underneath her, sliding her toward Blade's weight, so that she wound up with her hip against his thigh, which burned like white-hot steel. "So sorry," she murmured, trying to shift away, but the comfortable couch fought her.

"You've no need to be sorry, or shy," he murmured in response, sliding an arm around her shoulders. "Just relax."

As she eased herself back against the leather-jacketed arm around her shoulders and the hard warmth of his thigh alongside hers, Crys was astonished to find that the whole interchange had taken only moments. Debbie had claimed a seat next to Easy, gazing at him with unconcealed adoration, and Leah was looking back and forth between Angel and Dice, unable to decide.

"Hey, could I... do you suppose I could have my picture with Angel *and* Dice?" she asked. "See, you're both so hot, I just can't decide, and I'd hate to leave either of you out." She shot the two of them an ingenuous grin which made them both laugh. They shrugged their agreement, and Jed said he didn't see why not.

Angel patted the seat beside him, saying, "Come on over, sugar," and Dice got up from his seat opposite and joined them, hooking a leg over the arm of the couch as he plopped himself down on Leah's other side.

The photographer adjusted some of the lights, and snapped off a few frames of the three of them, then turned and photographed Debbie listening in adoration as Easy talked – bragging of some fabulous exploit – with her hand resting on his arm in a pose of overt worship. "Raise your chin a bit, please, miss," he asked softly at one point. "Tilt your shoulders toward me, Easy, that's it, and drop your right elbow a little. Nice."

Crys sat in silence at Blade's side, overwhelmed by proximity and at a loss for words. A rock god, after all; an international star. How could she have a clue what to say?

"Do you know, then?" he asked her quietly, after a while. "Did someone tell you?"

She looked at him, completely puzzled by the nonsense question. "Do I know what?" she replied, startled into meeting his eyes – a beautiful hazel color, blending deep green and amber, which she hadn't realized from his photographs, in which they usually appeared just dark. The black eyeliner he wore had gone a bit splotchy after the concert, but Crys thought it was actually sexier that way, slightly smeared and imperfect.

Blade laughed, an odd bitter laugh. "Did you know that no one ever chooses me? At these photo-op meet-and-greets, I mean – it's always Angel or Easy. You're doing all the right things, sweetheart, and I was wondering if someone told you to be nice to me."

"Good God, no!" Crys said, utterly shocked that he might think her only being kind. Blushing madly, her hand shaking, she reached up and softly touched his silver lip ring with one finger. "I like... this... very much."

The popping brightness of a flash startled them both, the moment caught on film. Crys snatched her hand away, clasping it with the other in her lap. "Good, good," the photographer muttered to himself. "Let's see what else we can do with this, hmm..." He eyed the pair of them closely, then cleared his throat. "Little lady, d'you think you could see your way to sitting in Blade's lap for a shot?"

"Sure she will," said Blade, before Crys could even get her mind around the request. "Climb on up, sweetheart!" He patted his knee in invitation.

Crys shook her head, nearly frozen with embarrassment. "Oh, I couldn't!"

"Why not? You're a tiny little thing, bound to be light as a feather... and I want to know how you'd feel on top of me – unless you're a missionary kind of girl?" he added with a grin. Crys's mouth opened, but no sound came out. And before she could form a single word, his big strong hands slipped around her waist, and he'd scooped her up onto his lap in one smoothly powerful motion. "Hmm, now, does that feel as good to you as it does to me?" he whispered into her ear. "You're trembling, Crystal."

"Crys; everyone calls me Crys," she corrected him, wanting to change the subject, to buy some time until she could control her reaction to him.

"Crys. You're still trembling – you're not afraid of me, are you?"

A tense giggle escaped her. "I'm a little out of my league here, that's all."

"You're doing fine." Blade laughed softly, in genuine amusement; not at all a bitter laugh this time. "Just pretend we're alone." He pulled her close against him, stroking her shoulder in a motion that was both soothing and sensual, until her tremors subsided.

"That's very nice, Blade," the photographer said, "but tilt your head slightly toward me. Hmm... little lady, why don't you lay your head against Blade's shoulder, nice and relaxed, and look up at him...?" He waited, and Blade squeezed her upper arm with his long guitar-playing fingers, encouraging her. Because Crys didn't know what else to do, she did as they expected: she laid her head down against Blade's black-leather-clad shoulder and just breathed, smelling the leather-smell of the jacket, and clean sweat mixed with a hint of soapy citrus, and underneath that a faintly spicy masculine scent. She looked up at the angular smooth-shaven curve of his jaw – felt suddenly, urgently hungry – wanted to lick it.

And the photographer's flash popped bright white around them. "Great. Okay," he said to the room at large, "I'm taking the group shot now – no one needs to move, but turn your heads this way and give me a smile." The flash popped again. "One more." Flash. "And I'm done. Thank you kindly," he told them, "I've got everything I need now. Have a great evening, gentlemen, I'll see you tomorrow. Ladies, it's been a pleasure, I hope you've enjoyed meeting Smidge." Unscrewing the lens from his camera as he went, he walked across to the door and slipped out.

Feeling awkward in such an intimate snuggle once the excuse of photographs was gone, Crys moved to sit upright, preparatory to wrenching herself off Blade's lap altogether. Had she imagined his reluctant sigh as she pulled away? She couldn't be sure. "I... I should go," she said. "I know this was only a public relations thing for you, but it's been... special for me. So thank you."

"Wait a second–" Blade pushed up one sleeve of his jacket and unbuckled a silver-studded black leather wristband, then took her hand and fastened the wristband around her much smaller wrist; he had to force the tongue of the buckle through the never-used hole at the inner end of the strap, and she could see the worn place where the buckle had rubbed during his wearing of it. The leather against her skin was warm from his body heat, slightly damp with concert sweat. "There," he said. "Don't forget me, huh?!"

"As if I could!" Crys looked down at the black leather band on her wrist, metal studs glinting in the light. Something to remember him by.

The lights flickered twice, and Jed was standing by the door with his hand on the switch. "All good things must come to an end, ladies," he said, with what could only be interpreted as a satisfied expression on his face. "If you'll say your goodnights and come with me, I'll escort you out of the building."

Blade wrapped his hands around Crys's waist and boosted her off his lap, again giving her that same sense of physical strength as before. He stood as well. "Take care, sweetheart," he said.

"And you," Crys replied. "You take care too." Then, before she could do some incredibly foolish wanton thing – like reach up to kiss that lovely pierced lip of his, like offer him her body for the night – she forced herself to turn and walk to the open door. Once there, safely out of reach of all that she might desire, she remembered that there were other members of Smidge in the room. "Thank you all so much for giving us the chance to meet you; it's been such a treat to be here, I'll never forget it."

"You've been lovely guests, ladies," said Angel in that melting-chocolate voice, which Crys couldn't help comparing in her mind to Blade's deeper, grittier tone. "Thank you for joining us." Dice stood and bowed to them in elaborate courtly fashion, but Easy only raised a hand in farewell without getting up.

Crys allowed herself one final look and smile at Blade, and then dragged her feet out through the doorway.

The girls didn't talk much as they walked – one look at the fluorescent lighting and dirty tile of the station platform, one look at each other and they'd known they didn't want to go home, not yet. The train home meant a return to reality, and all three of them were still half in the glittering world they'd just visited.

"Coffee," said Leah.

Crys nodded. *Yes. Coffee.*

"Princess," agreed Debbie. Thankfully, there was a 24-hour doughnuts-and-coffee dive not too far from the arena – and a brisk walk in the clear night was just, maybe, what they needed to clear the stardust from their eyes.

Walking along with her friends, looking up at the faint stars above the downtown lights, Crys could not calm her spinning mind. It was shock she felt, mostly; first from the dawning recognition that she'd been chiefly attracted to Rhys for his temporarily punk appearance, and then from the intensity of her reaction to Blade. She couldn't conceal from herself any longer that her taste – kink, maybe – for guys with facial hardware and makeup was stronger than any desire to date a socially acceptable husband-candidate. And then there was that hungry ache, that desire to lick along the vulnerable line of his jaw, the urge to find out what the silver ring in his lip would feel like in a kiss, and worst of all, the mad impulse to offer her body to him for the night. Groupies did stuff like that; he probably wouldn't have been surprised, might even have accepted. As she walked along, safe with friends and morality intact, she shivered with the awareness that she could have been lying in his hotel bed with answers to all these torturous questions – and, sweet God, how the idea of it burned in her mind.

Princess Donuts was fairly quiet for a weekend night, with only a few groups of post-nightclub revelers sobering up with coffee before heading home. There was no line-up at the counter, where a tired-looking older woman served up coffee and doughnuts on automatic pilot. "Chocolate glazed?" Leah asked, looking at Crys's tray as they walked over to an out-of-the-way table. Crys usually had a chocolate-dip doughnut.

Crys blinked at her plate. "Oh. Um. I guess I'm having chocolate glazed today."

"You didn't notice that you got the wrong kind of doughnut?" Debbie smirked. "Lost in space, are we? Does it have anything to do with sitting in your favorite rock star's lap for fifteen minutes?"

Leah grinned conspiratorially. "Kind of handy, the photographer posing you like that. So, did Blade have a hard-on? Could you tell?"

"Good God, Leah!" Crys said, but couldn't stop the hot blush from rising to her face.

"Oho, look at you! He did, didn't he?" Leah insisted, her eyes avid.

27

"Well... yeah, pretty much," Crys confessed in a low voice, torn between embarrassment and fascinated recollection. The few guys she'd dated had all been so tame in comparison; she'd never sat in anyone's lap before, never met anyone so unashamedly sexual. *Does that feel as good to you as it does to me?* Blade had asked her, without a shred of awkwardness. Lost in memory, she missed a bit of the conversation; something dirty, to judge by her friends' snickering.

"–what Easy mentioned, it sounds like they're all generally, erm, ready for it after a concert," Debbie was saying in a hushed tone. "Which sort of explains the whole groupie thing."

"I can't believe we're discussing this. We are so not discussing this." Crys shook her head, unwilling to think about Blade being with a groupie as they sat there. *God, I'm such a fool!*

"So, what's going on, Crys?" asked Leah, eyeing her friend with genuine concern. "You're not acting like yourself. Is it Smidge, or are you thinking about Rhys?"

"Rhys?! Oh, no, not at all. Nice guy; he asked for my number and I gave it to him, but I don't know how that's going to go." She shrugged, trying to look as though the whole situation was no big fuss to her – better that they think her unsure whether he'd call, or unsure whether she's interested. *I can't tell them,* she thought. *I can't explain that I don't know whether he'll indulge the twisted bit of me that wants... oh, a kiss from a pierced lip, a lover with stage makeup around his eyes.*

Debbie perked up. "Speaking of those guys, weren't you going to tell me something about Johnny?"

Leah's eyes gleamed. Crys suppressed a groan of regret, and as she reached clumsily left-handed for her doughnut – keeping her right hand down in her lap to conceal the wristband she wore – she managed to knock over her coffee. Leah jumped out of the way of the spreading liquid and grabbed a handful of napkins from the counter. "Come on! First the glazed doughnut, and now you knock over your coffee. What's wrong, Crys?" she demanded. "And don't tell me you're just tired or something – confession time – what's on your mind?"

"So I knocked over my coffee – big deal," Crys muttered. Then, irritated and embarrassed, she said the only thing she could think of to change the subject. "Johnny's bi, okay, Debbie? Rhys told me. Can we please not make a big drama of it anymore?"

Leah drew in a hissing breath of anticipation.

For a split second, Debbie's eyes were wide and appalled, and then she laughed. "Gosh, Crys, you almost had me there!" She took a drink of her coffee and shook her head in disgust. "I can't believe I almost believed you for a moment."

"But..." Crys said, and then her voice trailed off into uncertain silence at the sweetly stubborn disbelief on Debbie's face – she'd seen that look before – Debbie wasn't going to change her mind. Leah stood blinking, her hands full of coffee-stained napkins, equally unsure what to say.

"Okay, that was kind of funny," Debbie conceded, "but let's get back to Crys spilling coffee and getting the wrong kind of doughnut, hmm?"

It wasn't meant to be funny, Crys thought, as she took an enormous bite of her chocolate glazed doughnut to buy some time. Chewed thoughtfully, licked a bit of sugary glaze off her lip. Saw the funny side of it all and started to laugh. "It's so stupid," she said. "I finally meet a perfectly nice guy, who actually asks for my phone number... and yet I can't stop thinking about sitting in Blade's lap and..."

"And feeling his hard-on pressing into your butt?" Leah filled in, grinning.

Which at least put to rest the subject of Johnny and his choice of bed partners, for the moment.

❤

When they got back to their apartment, Crys took her phone from her purse and saw that she hadn't turned it on after getting it back from security. There was a message from Rhys.

"Hi Crys," he'd said. "I guess you're already asleep, sorry. I'm so glad I met you at the Smidge concert tonight, I wanted you to know that, and I meant it when I asked for your number. I should have told you I'm going to be out of town for the next couple of weeks, but when I get back I'll call you; we can go out for coffee or something." Rhys had paused for a moment, then, and the voicemail recording had picked up some domestic background noises – the whistle of a kettle, maybe, and the static chatter of late-night television. "I... I do wish I could see you again sooner, sorry – this is the part where actors make bad dates – but I *am* going to call you when I get home, okay? Uh, okay, bye."

Crys saved the message so she could listen to it again later. "I guess Rhys meant it about calling," she told Debbie and Leah. "That's something, anyway."

chapter
3

EN DAYS LATER, ON A SUNNY TUESDAY, DEBBIE RECEIVED a thick packet by registered mail. Inside the large bubble-padded pouch were two foil-printed cardboard folders and a limited-edition Smidge t-shirt. The first folder Debbie opened contained a glossy 8" x 10" print of the group photograph – sprawled across the couches, smiling up at the camera: Debbie snuggled up against Easy, Crys in Blade's lap, Leah sandwiched flirtatiously between Angel and Dice – signed by all four band members in silver marker. The other folder held Debbie's individual portrait with Easy, also a glossy 8" x 10" and autographed by him in the same silver marker.

Leah got her packet the following day. "Yours'll probably come tomorrow," she said to Crys, as she tried on her new t-shirt. "It's got to be the most amazing thing ever to happen to us. We just happened to be in the right place at the right time. I suppose we should thank Debbie for having a small bladder, huh?"

Crys did not receive anything in the mail the next day, but she did get a phone call from Rhys, inviting her out for a coffee date Saturday afternoon. *That's my future,* she told herself, and agreed to meet him at the Starbucks near the museum.

♥

Friday morning, Crys's phone rang as she and Debbie were on their way out the door to go to class – they took a ten-o'clock Shakespeare lecture together, their earliest on Fridays, while Leah had long since left the apartment for an eight-o'clock biology lab. "I'm ignoring it," said Crys, as she fished in her backpack for her keys to lock the door behind them. "We're already going to be late."

"Wait, what if it's Rhys calling? You have to! I'll answer it for you." Dropping her bag on the floor, Debbie snatched Crys's phone and answered with a breathless, "Hello, Debbie speaking!" Moments later, crestfallen, she said, "Oh! ... Yes, this is her phone. ... We were on our way out – is it urgent? ... Okay, just a moment." She held the phone out to Crys. "It's for you. She says it's urgent."

Crys took the phone, shaking her head. Whatever it was could have gone to voicemail, and as it was they'd miss half the lecture. "Hello, Crystal Murphy speaking..."

"Good morning, Ms. Murphy," said a woman's voice. "This is Marigold Hendon calling from Kinney Wicks Public Relations."

"Oh?"

"We met briefly at the Smidge concert on the fourteenth – I escorted you backstage to meet the band."

Crys had a sudden memory-flash of a black leather suit and satin shirt, streaked hair and a sharp-featured, hard-partying face. "That's right; yes, of course," she agreed, waving at Debbie to go to class without her. Whatever this Marigold wanted, it wasn't worth them both missing it. "I'll copy your notes," she mouthed to Debbie, who nodded and dashed off.

"I'm sure you'll recall that you were promised one photograph of yourself with the Smidge boy of your choice," Marigold went on, "and in general we simply mail our guest packages out, but in this case we have a number of good shots of you with Blade, and Mr. Kinney, uh, thought you might want to select your favorite one."

"Sure," said Crys. "That's very kind of him. How do I go about doing that?"

"We're in town today and tomorrow," explained Marigold, "so you can come by our hotel to look at the prints – we have an executive suite at the Fairmont." She laughed sharply. "You're probably wondering why I told your roommate this call was urgent."

"Not at all, Ms. Hendon," Crys said politely. "I'm sure it's more convenient if I'm able to look at the prints while we're in the same city."

Marigold laughed again – it sounded forced. "We also have a potential, uh, marketing application for the photographs, and while the original waiver covered... it would require some cooperation on your part, and Mr. Kinney would like to discuss that with you in person."

Crys wasn't sure what use they might have for the photographs, but she'd thought the waiver covered commercial usage. "You can use the pictures however you like; I don't mind at all," she told Marigold. Her friends might tease her for not negotiating some extra financial compensation, but she didn't want her precious memory of the night spoiled.

"I think you'll find Mr. Kinney more than generous," Marigold assured her. "What time can we expect you, then? Mr. Kinney has openings at two o'clock and five o'clock today, but if neither of those works, I can shuffle a few things around to fit you in."

"I'll be in a lecture at two," said Crys, "but I can get to the Fairmont by five."

"Very good," replied Marigold. "I'll meet you in the foyer, shall I?"

Without waiting for confirmation, Marigold ended the call.

Should she try to catch the tail end of the morning's lecture? Then a glance in the mirror made Crys question the Fair Isle sweater and jeans she had on – perfectly appropriate for the university campus, but her mother would judge the outfit as too casual for a nice hotel. Dropping any last thought of going to the lecture, she headed for her bedroom closet instead.

Twenty minutes later, she was still poking through her things in frustration. *It's not like I wear a uniform to school anymore.* But she'd never before noticed how much of her wardrobe was made up of sweaters and blouses, jeans and cords. She had a couple of evening dresses for the college's formal evenings, and a few nice wool skirts for church and faculty receptions.

She grimaced at a floral-print blouse, thinking it babyish compared to Marigold's black leather suit. At last she settled on a black denim dress with silver-thread overstitching – while she'd still stand out from the business crowd, it struck her as being closer to the right kind of thing to wear. It made her feel pretty and confident, and she wanted to look good for this meeting, as she'd be seeing someone who must actually speak with Blade and the other Smidge boys on occasion. If by some random chance Blade should ask about her or the public relations man should mention her, Crys wanted the report to be flattering.

Before leaving the bedroom, she reached under her pillow and drew out the leather wristband Blade had given her. She buckled it around her right wrist, as he had done on that wonderful night, fingering the worn place on the strap that bore testament to his wearing of it.

It suited the black denim and silver stitching of her dress. *Leah and Debbie had better not see me wearing it, though.* They still didn't know she had it, and would be hurt and offended that she'd concealed it from them. If they knew she slept with it under her pillow, she'd never hear the end of it, and the fact that she was wearing it today – in case this Mr. Kinney might notice and tell Blade she'd worn it – would lead to unbearable teasing.

Leah will be home for lunch soon. Crys grabbed her backpack and jacket, and slipped out of the apartment. *I'll get something to eat at the cafeteria in the library.*

♥

Bright autumn leaves drifted red and gold on the sidewalk, floating down with every breath of wind from the trees lining the downtown street. The air held the crisp bite of the changing season, but it was still warm enough in the sunlight that Crys took her jacket off and carried it as she walked. She reached the hotel on time, even a few minutes early, and touched up her lip gloss outside before going in.

She saw Marigold immediately; the scarlet satin pantsuit would have been immediately noticeable in any room, and more so in the elegantly conservative hotel. Marigold recognized her at once and jumped up from one of the Edwardian sofas in the grand lobby area. "Ms. Murphy, I'm glad you're here," she said, holding out a manicured hand for Crys to shake. "Please follow me; I'll take you up at once." She whipped out a phone as she walked and rang someone, presumably Mr. Kinney, saying, "Ms. Murphy is here – we'll be right up."

The elevator rose quickly and smoothly, and in the soft lighting and the flattering mirror panel, Crys was pleased with what she saw. The hotel corridor was as elegant as the public spaces downstairs had been, with thick footstep-muffling carpet.

Stopping abruptly at an imposing double door, swiping a key card through the electronic lock, Marigold ushered Crys into the executive suite.

As she stepped into the room, the first thing Crys saw was a large rectangular frame propped on an easel, a small spotlight rigged up to light the pictures to best advantage – there were two of them in the frame, one above the other. The photographer had somehow captured everything Crys had felt that night: in the top image, she was reaching up to touch the silver ring in Blade's lower lip, her face in the portrait reflecting every bit of the tenderness and fascination in the moment, and his face full of strangely vulnerable surprise. And then – *oh, sweet God in heaven* – the image underneath showed her with her head against Blade's shoulder, gazing up at the delicious line of his jaw, with a look on her face that laid bare her urge to lick and taste him. And the blatant desire on his face, the obvious chemistry between them, should have incinerated the paper on which the photograph was printed.

"Beautiful pictures, aren't they?" asked a man's voice. "Scott's a photographic genius, knows his stuff like no one else I've ever met, and Blade can really work the camera – but then, clearly so can you." Crys looked up, startled, to see the public relations executive from the concert crossing the room toward her. "It's a pleasure to see you again; I'm Curt Kinney, public relations manager for Smidge. Please do come and sit down."

"Thank you," said Crys, feeling faintly diminished. *Blade can really work the camera, indeed.* But the pictures were beautiful.

The main room of the suite had been divided up into clusters, a desk and working paraphernalia in one area, couch and chairs grouped around a coffee table in another. Two doors, one on either side of the room, had to lead to the suite's bedrooms. Meekly, she followed as Mr. Kinney led her to the sitting area, and she sat down in the seat he indicated. "Please call me Curt," he told her smoothly. "And may I call you Crystal?"

"Crys, please," she corrected him automatically.

"Crys," he said, as though testing the sound of the name. "That's cute, I like that." She raised her eyebrows, feeling slightly offended and trying not to show it. Would the man get to the point, already?! He turned and beckoned to Marigold, who approached with a gift basket in her hands, which she handed to him. "Thank you, Marigold. You can take a break now; I'll call when I need you."

"Thank you, Mr. Kinney," Marigold murmured, and departed from the suite with a brisk step.

Mr. Kinney – Curt – held out the gift basket to Crys. "We've put together a few small things for you," he told her. "I think you'll like what you find in there; a couple of special edition t-shirts, a limited-release album that's nearly impossible to find in stores, a Smidge crew hat, and a few other little goodies. And I want you to know that it's yours to keep, no matter what you decide today – and that goes for the framed photographs too."

"What I decide today?" Crys asked.

"Yes." Curt Kinney smiled and ran a hand through his thinning hair. "Crystal, er, Crys, what it boils down to is this – we have a job offer for you."

A dead silence filled the room. "A... job offer?" Crys asked at last, completely puzzled. "I don't understand. What sort of job? What skill or trait could I possibly have that a million other girls don't have twice over?"

"Forgive me, Crys, but... we weren't completely honest with you at the concert. The post-concert survey and photo shoot with the band were, well, really a job interview – and I must say, you did very well indeed. Impressed all of us."

"I still don't understand. What kind of job are you offering me? What are my qualifications?"

"We were simply searching, at the outset, for a wholesome-looking and photogenic young lady who would be able to form a good rapport with Blade," he explained. "The fact that you're intelligent and well-spoken is a plus, and your courtesy to the crew and the band was also noted with pleasure. You're not a screamer or a fainter; in fact, Jed reported that you appeared fairly calm throughout the whole process, even when you were asked to sit in Blade's lap – adaptability and equanimity were high on our wish list. So we're very happy to invite you to join our team."

"But what would I be doing?" Crys asked again. "What would the job be?"

"It's essentially a public relations position. You'll probably be aware that Blade has had some, er, media image issues?"

Crys nodded. Though she paid little attention to celebrity news as a rule, she'd have had to be blind to miss Blade's tabloid-fodder exploits: public nudity, fighting, excess and debauchery of every kind, and an endless string of high-profile groupies and starlets. He was always in the news. "Sure. But..."

"Yes. It's been getting worse lately." The public relations executive cleared his throat, letting her see that he was a bit put off by his client's antics. "We urgently need to, shall we say, put a positive spin on things. The media, as an industry, tends to have a soft spot for romance. And that's where you come in – what Blade needs is, ah, a professional girlfriend."

Crys stood up, dropping the gift basket like poison and picking up her purse. "A professional girlfriend is a whore," she said, with all the frost she could put into her voice. "I'm done with this freak show."

Kinney looked momentarily nonplussed, but in a heartbeat he'd recovered himself and raised a placating hand to stop Crys from walking out. "Please sit down and hear me out," he asked, with an almost pleading quality to his voice. "I had no intention of implying that you should be... that sort of companion for him."

"Oh?" Crys was neither convinced nor satisfied.

"I can promise you separate, private sleeping arrangements at every location, even chaperonage if you insist," he promised, nodding to emphasize his sincerity. "You'd really be a sort of embedded media relations handler for him – Blade is what you might call resistant to an actual committed romance, so we need to manufacture one for him, all very much on the surface." He smiled. "It should be a lot of fun for you – plenty of nice dinners, red carpet events, social stuff. All you'll need to do is look sweet for the media... and try to keep Blade out of trouble."

Crys raised her eyebrows. "So you want me to be his pretend girlfriend? So that he gets into the tabloids for giving jewelry to me instead of to groupies?" That had been one of his more recent exploits – buying diamond earrings for several of his professional girlfriends.

"That's a part of it." Kinney sighed. "We're also hoping that if you're out with him – clubbing, and such – that you might be able to steer him away from the worst of the troubles he gets into. Especially drinking too much, getting into fights, and taking his clothes off in public." He rubbed at the back of his neck as if to combat a tension headache. "It's hard to build the band's image when we're fighting such an uphill battle all the time."

"But... aren't rock stars supposed to get in that kind of trouble?"

"A bit of trouble is good," he agreed. "Getting a bit drunk. The occasional wild incident. But cross the line too often and... then it's not so good. Fans will forgive most of what they'd like to dare themselves, but push them too far..." What constituted *too far*, exactly?

Crys hesitated. "I can see that. Still, I... I wasn't looking for a job. I've got school."

"I'm sure the university can be persuaded give you a year off from your studies; people do it all the time, and you'll be back next fall, with work experience, and money saved – you'll be well paid, you know."

"It's not..." She took a deep breath, and tried again. "It's more than deferring classes or earning money; you're asking me to walk away from my whole life!"

"I know." Kinney nodded, taking a folded document from an inner pocket. "Here, at least have a look at the contract and see what you think of it." As she unfolded the sheaf of papers, he kept talking, his voice low and convincing, a hypnotic murmur of advantage and sense. "It's just for a year, and you'll never see a chance like this again – we've got the rest of the current tour to complete, and then the boys'll be starting work on their next album almost right away, so you'll get first-hand experience with touring *and* recording. Plus, they'll probably go to Hawaii or Aruba or somewhere for a break around Christmastime... doesn't that sound nice? And we've got some European concert dates next spring, too – only a mini-tour, but you'll see London and Amsterdam and Paris and Berlin. So you'll get to travel, all expenses paid, and you'll learn enough to work in music or public relations for the rest of your life. You don't want to turn that down, do you, Crys?"

She scanned the contract he handed her, trying to tune out his voice and focus on the printed words; truly enough, it guaranteed that sexual favors were not included, implied, or expected in her performance of the job, and asserted that no penalties would be applied to her if Blade should attract negative media attention despite her best efforts to avert it. Fair enough. Salary and benefits were mentioned; she would be on the books as a personal public relations assistant. She blinked as she took in a requirement that she refrain from dating or otherwise becoming involved with other men while she was under contract to Blade – which of course stood to reason, though she felt a shudder of doubt at the idea of signing away her right to romance and intimacy for a year, even in theory. *Only in theory, Miss Vanilla Virgin.* She'd never even had her pants off with a boy; she had no business thinking there would be anything to give up.

Then she reached the confidentiality clause. "Confidentiality clause?" she repeated aloud in surprise.

"Of course," Kinney said. "You're a bright girl, Crys; I'm sure you can see how damaging our little fiction would be if it got out. Now, I personally feel confident you'll respect that, so the clause is merely a precaution, but anyone who knows of the true situation is a liability to us, a potential leak. Naturally, we need to limit that risk." He laughed conspiratorially, making light of it, but the legal penalties printed out in the contract didn't look like much of a joke.

"But... what about my parents? I'll have to tell them something. And my roommates – I can't walk out of the apartment and disappear without saying anything. I don't want to lie to them..." As she spoke, Crys remembered something else, and her heart sank in earnest. "Oh, and I have a coffee date tomorrow, too!" She thought of Rhys, expecting her to meet him the following afternoon... she'd been imagining a possible future with him... what could she tell him after this?

Kinney nodded. "I understand," he said. "I'll have Marigold prepare a statement for you to give anyone who absolutely needs to know the actual situation. But they'll have to sign a confidentiality agreement first, and there are stiff legal penalties even for accidentally revealing the information it covers."

"Sure. My parents, and Leah and Debbie. And I think Rhys deserves the truth from me, since I'll only be seeing him tomorrow to say goodbye." The enormous weight of that struck her, and her face must have fallen a little, because Kinney's expression turned sympathetic and he laid a comforting hand on her shoulder.

"It's only for a year," he assured her. "If this Rhys is special, he'll wait for you. And Blade – and all of Smidge, really – needs you right now. We're a bit worried about him; he'll fall apart if he doesn't slow down some, and that would tear the whole band up." Crys met Kinney's eyes, and saw genuine concern there. She thought about the hopeful interest she'd felt with Rhys, and then the intense awareness that had come over her with Blade.

"Fine," she said, and held out her hand for a pen, putting her doubts behind her. "I'm in."

The door opened and closed behind her, presumably Marigold returning from her break, but Crys kept her eyes focused on the contract in her hands, determined to sign the legally binding document at once, before she lost her nerve. Kinney glanced up; his eyes flickered in greeting, but he said nothing, and handed her a pen from the inside pocket of his designer suit jacket.

It was a Montblanc fountain pen, fat like a cigar and banded with gold, the ink thick and black, a pen of wealth and power. Crys signed and dated the contract, and handed it and the pen back to the public relations executive.

"I'm really glad you're joining us, Crys," he told her. "The boys and most of the crew call me Kin – I'd like it if you would too."

"Thank you, Kin," she said.

"Damn, these are sexy pictures," came a man's deep voice from the room behind her, an unmistakable raspy drawl. Crys twisted around to confirm with her eyes what her ears had already told her. Blade stood there in front of the easel, studying the pair of photographs. His long lean body looked amazing in a trashed pair of black jeans and a skin-tight black-and-silver Mötley Crüe t-shirt. Even without the full concert get-up he was incredible. "I hadn't seen these, Kin – get me copies, okay?" He looked over at her and smiled, an instinctive sweet smile of greeting and delight. "Hey, sweetheart," he said softly. His eyes went to the leather band at her wrist, and the gratified expression on his face made Crys feel warm all over.

"Blade – I'm glad you've arrived. Crystal here has just signed the contract, so you can start getting to know her while I break out the champagne." Kin vacated his seat, fingers flashing over his phone even as he was moving over to a sideboard which apparently housed a full bar and wine cooler.

Blade strode across the room and lowered himself onto the couch next to Crys, touching fingers to forehead in a mocking salute. At Kin's mention of the contract, Blade's easy smile had been replaced by a far more guarded expression. "So, they've convinced you to sign on as my babysitter, have they? Think you can keep me out of trouble?"

"I haven't a hope in hell of doing that," Crys said, "but I'll do my best to limit the damage." *And that was the one question I never thought to ask,* she told herself; *I should have asked how Blade felt about this whole bizarre arrangement.* Apparently, he was taking it as some kind of personal challenge – to prove that she couldn't keep him out of trouble.

Kin returned to the seating area with a bottle of champagne in an ice bucket, and three crystal flutes clutched in his other hand. "Do the honors?" he said to Blade, who stripped the foil off the bottle top with a sidelong look at Crys and proceeded to pop the cork up to hit the ceiling. Bubbles foamed up and over the lip of the bottle, flowing down onto Blade's hands and the carpet.

Kin frowned. "That's rather a waste of good champagne, don't you think?"

"There's plenty left for drinking," Blade said, not at all repentant. He took one of the flutes from Kin and filled it to the brim before handing it to Crys.

Kin shook his head and took the bottle, pouring a full glass for Blade but only a half glass for himself. "You don't have to drink all that," he assured Crys.

"Sure, she does. I'm not known for dating temperance types, Kin – who's going to believe I've lost my heart to a baby-girl who can't even–"

"Now, Blade, you let me handle the details, okay?" He held up his champagne flute. "Here's a toast to Crys joining our team, and to Blade's new media-friendly romantic image. It's going to be a good year!" He took a big gulp of his champagne, and rubbed the back of his neck again. Raising her glass, Crys thought Kin needed ibuprofen more than he needed alcohol. She took a sip, astonished to find that she liked the taste of it – nothing like the cheap sweetish fizz she'd had before – bubbles bursting across her tongue with a crisp fresh aftertaste as she swallowed.

Blade must have seen the pleased surprise in her face, because he laughed. "So you like decent champagne, do you?" he asked. "That's a good sign."

Kin raised his hand warningly. "Blade, you cannot get the poor girl drunk right now – you'll have to take her out to dinner shortly, and she can't be staggering or sick."

A trapped and claustrophobic expression came over Blade's face at Kin's words. "Dinner tonight? It's starting already?" he asked, his voice cold. It was like a storm building inside him, and Crys began to feel a little bit frightened. *I guess he's really not okay with this,* she thought with an unhappy shiver.

She turned to the public relations executive, drawing up her spine straight and firm, sitting as tall and strong as she knew how. "Kin, could you give me a moment alone with Blade, please?" she asked.

Kin nodded and got up, going to the desk for a packet of cigarettes before heading to the door. "I'll just have a smoke, then," he said, and left the suite.

Her courage melted as soon as she was alone with Blade, but she forced herself to look up at him, hoping he'd see the sincerity and remorse in her eyes. "I am so sorry," she said. "I should have thought to ask; I would never have agreed to this if I'd known it was against your wishes."

"Not your fault," he muttered, his face like stone.

"But now that we're into this," she continued, "I'll do my best to make it as easy as possible for you, okay? Whatever it takes. I... I'll even get drunk for you, if that would make you happy?" Even as she made the offer, she knew it was a mistake – she wasn't used to anything but the cheap beer served at campus events, and had never in her life crossed her personal limit of two drinks – but unwilling to back down, she took a rash gulp of her champagne, and then another.

Something passionate flared in Blade's eyes. "Would you give me your body, then?" he asked, his voice a barely audible rasp. "Would you spread your legs and take me inside you, sweetheart – to make me happy?"

Crys choked on her mouthful of champagne.

Blade said a few extremely bad words under his breath, then his eyes met her shocked ones and all the anger and desire and rebellion drained away from him. "I'm sorry, I shouldn't have said that," he told her. "Forget I said anything. I'll see you at dinner." And he got up and left the suite.

♥

Crys left voicemails for Debbie and Leah, saying only that she was going out for dinner and would be back late. The rest of it had to wait until she could hand them Marigold's carefully crafted statement – and the ominous confidentiality agreement with all its threats. It would have sounded like a joke, in any case – *I'm waiting for the limousine to arrive, the guitarist from Smidge is taking me out to dinner so the press can see me.* She switched her phone to do-not-disturb and slipped it back into her purse.

Marigold had been keeping Crys company in the suite's sitting area, coaching her on what to do and expect for the evening, and going over the legal information in the four thick envelopes wedged into Crys's purse. "So I can give my roommates their envelopes tonight?" she asked.

"Yes, but you have to make sure they read and sign the confidentiality agreements before opening the inner envelopes," Marigold warned her. "We don't play around with our legal work – believe me, none of you wants to find out what would happen if somebody blabbed about this."

"I'll make sure they understand," Crys said.

"Great." Marigold looked at a text message on her phone. "Blade's on his way down. I'd better call the car service; they should be here by now." She stood up and walked over to sit at Kin's desk, phone at her ear – on hold with the car service presumably – and began methodically organizing the paperwork on the desk as she waited.

Kin came in from the hallway, taking off his coat, pungent with cigarette smoke. He sat down next to Crys with an apologetic look on his face. "Crys, I want you to know – to be sure – that Blade will not cross the line with regard to his, er, physical behavior with you. He regrets what he said earlier; he spoke in anger, and knows he shouldn't have tried to shock you." Kin paused, thinking out what to say next. "Look, Blade's a grown man, and no saint, but I can assure you that he has never... well, never taken any sexual favors that weren't willingly given, if you follow me... and he's never been inclined to get involved with, shall we say, the innocent type of girl. So you're quite safe with him."

Crys blinked, unreasonably disappointed at the thought that Blade had just been trying to shock her with his proposition. She thought of how he'd cursed at the look in her eyes – had it only been because he'd realized that she was too inexperienced for him to take to bed? Too virginal to appeal to him after all? "That's all right, Kin," she said at last, because he was waiting for her to say something. "I wasn't afraid; I can take care of myself."

Kin nodded, slightly disbelieving, but accepting it nonetheless. "I knew he wasn't totally in agreement with our plan, but I believed – and still believe – that he understands the necessity of it. I am sorry you had to experience his, shall we say, short fuse before you could get to know him better."

"I'll survive." Crys shrugged, resigned to whatever the coming year might bring, even if it was all storms and thunder from an angry Blade. "I signed your contract, Kin – I'm in this with the rest of you, no matter what."

A sharp double rap on the door to the hall gave them a moment's warning, and then the door swung open and there was Blade, looking very much the rock star in an open-necked silk shirt and hip-length black leather coat, his long legs encased in silvery grey stovepipe jeans. Crys saw that he'd darkened around his eyes with inky black eyeliner; she didn't understand how she could find that appealing on a man, but there it was: she only had to glance at the eye paint and piercings to awaken a hot and squirmy feeling inside her. She wished she'd had something better to wear than her silver-stitched black dress, even though Marigold had praised it – compared to Blade's glamour, she felt a bit plain. "Hi," he said, to the room in general. He looked, if possible, slightly abashed – the look of a man who knew he'd crossed a line.

Marigold's phone rang, startling them all. She snatched it up. "Yes? ... Thank you. Your passengers will be right down." Ending the call with a tap of one manicured finger, she turned to Blade and Crys, saying, "The car's here. You'd better go."

Without a word, Blade waited by the door as Crys gathered up her purse and jacket. "Be sweet to each other tonight, you two," Kin reminded them. "Don't forget that you're giving the fans – and the media – a romance. So be romantic. Laugh. You might even have fun."

Blade glowered, and Crys stood by the sofa, waiting for some cue as to what she should do. Then Marigold scurried up to Blade, holding out a slim ticket folder. He took it, tucked it inside his coat. Held out his hand to Crys. "Come on, then," he said. "Come hold my hand. We might as well get this started right."

Crys crossed the room to him, her feet dragging as if through molasses. Halfway, she stopped to put her jacket on, buying time, just a few moments to compose herself before she closed the gap between them and cautiously placed her small hand into his large one. His strong fingers closed around hers, warm and callused, and the contact thrilled her. With an unexpectedly gentle tug, he pulled her out the door and down the hall.

A man in plain dark clothes followed them at several paces' distance, but Blade paid him no attention beyond a brief nod. "Who's that?" Crys asked softly.

"Ryan. Bodyguard. Just ignore him," Blade told her, without making any introduction. The unfortunate bodyguard hung back respectfully, and took a separate elevator to descend – as the elevator door closed, his lips turned up slightly in response to Crys's apologetic smile.

They got a few glances in the hotel foyer, people saying, "Hey, isn't that..." and "Ohmigod, it's Blade from Smidge!" and the like. Blade didn't seem fazed by it; he raised his hand in greeting and acknowledgement, and kept walking with a firm grip on Crys's hand. Then they were through the doors into the valet parking and car service driveway, a tunnel though the inside of the hotel that allowed guests to get into their cars and taxis without going outside. A gleaming black limousine awaited; it seemed a vast amount of car for the two of them.

Blade spoke briefly with the driver, ignoring the bodyguard who had taken the shotgun seat, and then the dividing panel slid up, and he and Crys were alone. "Hell, sweetheart, I'm sorry about what I asked you earlier," he said, awkwardly fingering the silver ring that pierced his eyebrow.

"It's okay," she replied. "It really is okay."

He fished something from his pocket, held out a little box for her to take. A jewelry sort of box. "To make up for it," he said, pressing the small velvety thing into her hands.

She opened the box as though it might contain a bomb, but instead she found a pair of dazzling splashes of light. He had given her diamond earrings. "They're beautiful, but... I mustn't..." A thought struck her. "Don't you give these to – oh, God!" She blushed.

"To groupies who've pleased me?" he completed the thought for her. "Sure. All women like diamond earrings. But you're not a groupie, and these are much nicer earrings than those were. Come on, you can't tell me you don't want them." The earrings sparkled like ice, like stars, against the deep midnight-blue velvet of the box.

"They *are* lovely," she agreed. And did it matter so much if he had given earrings to easy women who had... pleased him? She removed the small silver hoops she was wearing, and dropped them into her purse. "Thank you."

She unfastened one of the glittering earrings from its velvet bed, and fumbled a bit at her ear, trying to insert it without the benefit of a mirror. "Let me do that," suggested Blade, shifting closer to take the earring from her. His fingers brushed her ear, her neck, and she could feel the warmth of his breath on her cheek – sensual tingles ran all over her at this slightest contact. The white-gold post of the earring pushed through the tiny hole in her ear. And then he deftly repeated the task, slipping the second earring into her other ear. "Crys," he said softly, his lips next to her ear, "you – you're a virgin, aren't you?"

"Oh. Um, well, yes-s-s, as a matter of fact I am. Not that it's any of your business," she muttered. He straightened up, pulled away from her, slid across to the opposite side of the car. Obviously, the man was seriously not into virgins. "Thank you for the earrings, Blade," she told him, forcing the words through lips that felt numb with – what? – disappointment?

"I'm too used to being around groupies," he said, looking out the car window. "Women who've done everything and will do anything. I don't mean to shock you, Crys, and I don't want to hurt you without meaning to – I play dirty, sweetheart, and things would go too far."

"It's okay," she lied. "It really doesn't matter. Whores, groupies, that's your thing, that's fine. I don't totally love the idea of looking like an idiot in front of the world next time you get in trouble with one of them, but hey – it's a job, right?" The diamonds felt heavy in her ears.

Neither one of them spoke again, icy faces looking out the windows, until the car stopped and the driver lowered the partition. "We've arrived at the Ballroom, sir, miss," he said. "I hope you've had a pleasant ride. Let the valet parking attendant know when you're ready to leave; he'll know where to find me."

"Great – thanks, man!" said Blade, with his signature half-grin. He took Crys's hand firmly in his, and if the cheerful look he turned on her was a little bit forced, at least he was trying. "Smile," he reminded her; "it's show time for Romeo and Juliet!"

Limousines always drew a few curious glances, but otherwise there was no initial reaction on the street as the bodyguard opened the door for them and Blade got out, turning back at once to assist Crys as she emerged. The moment Blade straightened up, though, and became clearly visible under the streetlamp – lip and eyebrow rings glinting harshly in the light, his famous face unmistakable – someone waiting in line outside the Ballroom recognized him and called out his name. Moments later, the line-up had erupted in screams and waving and camera flashes. The club's security staff kept everyone in line, and Blade – waving and smiling as he had in the hotel lobby – led Crys up to the entrance, reaching into his coat for the tickets

Marigold had given him. Crys thought she heard someone shout, "Who's the girl, Blade?" – but she could easily have been mistaken in all the noise. The manager of the club rushed up to personally escort them to their table.

Inside, the dance floor on the lowest level was already filling up. Tables and chairs were accommodated on two stair-stepped levels on either side of the dance floor, allowing lucky seated patrons to watch the band onstage over the heads of the dancers and standing crowd. A section of the first riser had been roped off near the stage for Blade and his guest. A waitress hovered, smiling as the manager introduced her. She handed them menus with stars in her eyes, and then retreated to stand against the back railing until called for.

Blade eyed the equipment on the stage, checking out the setup with professional interest. "Nice!" He paused, and turned to Crys, explaining, "That's a Strat – a Fender Stratocaster. Looks vintage. A sweet guitar."

"Is that what you have?" she asked, seeing his enthusiasm, the way he brightened and looked almost friendly.

"No..." He looked at her, possibly trying to gauge her interest in what he played, what he thought. "I've got a Firebird, and a Telecaster as my backup. Actually, I do have an old Strat at home too, but I don't take it on tour. My Firebird is the one I keep with me, what I play most onstage. Angel prefers a Les Paul. You probably don't care about this shit..."

Crys shook her head. "You're so wrong – I do! I'm living in your world now, and I want to learn about everything. Otherwise, what on earth is the point?"

"True enough. You know, Crys, I thought this... going out thing would suck, but you're pretty cool. If you're interested, I'll show you my guitar next time we've got a chance – maybe even teach you a few chords, if you'd like?"

Hearing this, she nodded, brightening with eager anticipation. "Maybe I'll learn properly and even have my own guitar someday. Of course, I might be terrible at it... and then you'll laugh at me."

"Nah. Trying it is the thing. We should have some downtime in Seattle or Portland, and definitely in San Diego – it'll be fun..."

His face looked genuinely happy, and he seemed relaxed in a way that Crys hadn't seen before. *Maybe we can survive the year ahead,* she thought, *if I can just keep talking to him about guitars and music.* She looked around at the rapidly filling dance floor and the packed tables on the risers around them.

"Yo, Blade!" shouted a group of young guys, hanging over the railing of the riser above them, holding out pens and random bits of paper. "What about some autographs, man?"

"Piss off, guys, I'm on a date!" he shouted back, but seemed more good-natured about it than Crys would have expected – for good measure, he then draped an arm around her shoulders, giving her a conspiratorial wink.

The manager of the Ballroom, approaching, had observed the exchange and appeared concerned. "Are those gentlemen harassing you, sir?" he asked. "I can have them removed, if necessary."

"Not at all," said Blade. "I told them I don't do autographs when I'm on a date, that's all."

"Very well, sir. Tonight's performers are aware that you're here, sir, and – please forgive the imposition – they requested that I ask you if you'd be willing to go on and play a song or two with them. Only if it suits you, naturally... of course, with the young lady present, they – and I – would quite understand if you'd rather not..." The manager blathered on, torn between the prestige of securing Blade's presence on the stage and the risk of irritating him with the request.

But Blade grinned. "Sure," he agreed. "I can show off for my girl, huh? Just let me know when they'd like me to join them."

"Absolutely, sir. They tell me they've done covers of 'Star Shot Down' and 'Skanky Treat' in the past, if that suits you. In the meantime, can I have Nancy bring you something to drink?" He gestured toward the waitress standing in the shadows by the railing, ready to dash over and take their order.

Blade nodded. "Crys, what are you drinking?" he asked. "More champagne? Wine? Gin and tonic, or a martini or something?" When she looked a bit flustered at the all the sophisticated choices, he continued, "Or you could have a beer with me?" He glanced at the beer list in its plastic holder on the table. "What do you like? Looks like they've got a local honey ale on tap, might be decent."

Ah, there was something familiar. "That sounds good," she agreed.

The waitress suggested burgers to go with their beer, and Blade shook his head. "I can't eat before I go on stage," he explained with a shudder. "Crys, you go ahead if you're hungry – no? Okay, beer for now," he told the waitress, "then you can bring the burgers after I've done my set. I'll be hungry then."

As the house lights were going down, and the band was filing on stage, the waitress brought their beer. She also brought a dish of pretzels. Blade looked slightly green at even the sight of the snacks – which Crys hid behind the plastic stand holding the beer menu – and took a few rapid gulps of his beer. "Stage fright?" she asked in amazement.

He looked ready to deny it, then laughed. "Hell, you might as well know. You'll learn soon enough – I always feel a bit queasy before I go on, big stage or small, whatever. This is a bit worse than usual," he admitted, "since I've never played with this band and I don't have my own guitar... but I'll be fine the moment I get on stage... you must think me the most complete dork..."

"No, actually, it makes you more human." She smiled, so much more at ease with him now, able to talk about guitars, and stage fright, and beer. She took a sip of her beer, nodding in appreciation – of the beer, of the band on stage playing their first song of the night, of this growing rapport with Blade which she had begun to doubt was possible. "Decent music, this... Will you enjoy playing with them?"

He nodded, his eyes focused far away, and she realized that he was thinking about chords and fingering, drifting into the music, barely present next to her at all. It was as if a whole other world existed within the music, one into which he could slip at will, an internal space where he couldn't be followed.

With a shrug of acceptance, Crys turned her attention to the band on stage, sipping her beer and sneaking pretzels from the hidden bowl. She grooved to the band's pop-rock sound, and waited until Blade would be called to play.

A few songs into the set, someone slipped out of the wings of the stage and, with a nod to the lead singer, headed down the stage-steps into the crowd, where he was joined by a security guard. The two moved purposefully toward the riser where Blade and Crys were sitting, as up on the stage, the lead singer took up the microphone and announced, "Ladiiies and gentlemen, we are lucky enough to have a gen-u-ine rock god in the house with us tonight – Smidge guitarist Bla-ay-de!" As the crowd roared, a spotlight flooded their table with white light, and Blade stood up and waved. "We are deee-lighted to be able to tell you," continued the lead singer, "that Blade has agreed to join us for a song or two – let's definitely make that two – Blade, please come join us!" More roars from the crowd. Blade downed the rest of his beer in one long swallow, plunked the glass onto the table, and followed his escorts as they cleared a path to the stage for him. The spotlight followed, leaving Crys in darkness.

Blade was welcomed onto the stage, the band members reaching out in turn to clasp his hand in greeting, as eager to touch him, it seemed, as any other fans. The lead singer lifted the strap of his Strat over his head, handing the instrument over to Blade. Would he tell all his friends, later, that the Smidge guitarist had played it for a couple of songs? As casually as if he were alone and not on stage, Blade settled it across his body, adjusting the strap, strumming his fingers across the strings, testing a few chords and listening to the sound. Then the band's guitarist stepped back to play rhythm, letting Blade take the lead part as they swung into Smidge's hit "Star Shot Down."

It was a little faster, a little lighter than when Smidge did it. Blade's guitar stood out more without the power of Angel's vocals, and it had more of a pop-rock feel without Dice's hard-rock drumming. Crys watched with a growing sense of admiration as Blade adapted himself to the different sound and unfamiliar musicians, speeding up to match the vocals and drumbeats, glancing back at the other guitarist playing rhythm, his face intent as he felt his way through the song like a familiar room crossed barefoot in the dark. The second song, "Skanky Treat," was the title track from Smidge's first major-label album and still one of Crys's favorites. Blade relaxed into it, taking his cues from the others on the stage, as though he'd played with them a hundred times before.

"Hey! Hey!" called a female voice somewhere near to Crys, and she looked around to see who was shouting. The voice came from below her on the dance floor, on the other side of the riser railing near which Crys was sitting. A girl, who looked to be about the same age as Crys, waved and shouted in an attempt to get her attention. Puzzled, Crys leaned over the railing, trying to hear what the girl was saying. "Are you ... him?" When Crys cupped her ear to show that she hadn't heard, the girl shouted again: "ARE YOU WITH HIM? ARE YOU DATING BLADE?"

"Well... yes... I suppose I am..." Of course, the girl down on the dance floor couldn't hear anything at normal volume. Crys nodded, exaggerating the motion, and called down as loudly as she could, "YES! I AM!"

The girl held up her phone and snapped a picture.

Sated, full of burger and fries and beer, full of good music and intense company, Crys stumbled out of the limousine. Blade peered after her. His lip and eyebrow rings stood out sharply against a face white from tiredness. "D'you want me to come up with you?" he offered, rubbing his eyes blearily and preparing to step out of the limousine.

"Thanks, but it's fine," she told him. "They're probably asleep anyway, and you're jetlagged beyond belief, not to mention slightly drunk. I'll see you tomorrow afternoon."

"Cool. You're slightly drunk too, you know."

"Funny new job I've got – working nights, getting paid to go to clubs and drink and stuff..."

"Yeah. Best PR girl I've ever had."

"Goodnight, Blade."

"Sleep well, sweetheart; you'll be jetlagged with us soon enough." He raised a hand in farewell, and she raised a hand in reply before pushing the car door closed.

As she climbed the stairs to the apartment she shared with Debbie and Leah, she knew there was little chance they'd be sleeping. Dark hours of the morning or not, her cryptic voicemail would have them waiting up to quiz her on where she'd been.

chapter

4

*A*LTHOUGH THE WEATHER WAS STILL FINE THE NEXT DAY, it was colder, and windy – leaves whipping about rather than drifting, white-cotton clouds scudding across the sky playing peek-a-boo with the sun. Crys wrapped her jacket tightly around her as she walked, wondering whether she'd arrive at the Starbucks first or if Rhys would already be waiting for her.

She hadn't gone to bed until after sunrise. Through the dark hours of the night, she and her roommates had stayed up, wrapped in their dressing gowns, red-eyed and nursing cups of tea as they talked. Unable to think of how to explain, when she'd walked in to face the pair of them sitting at the kitchen table waiting for answers, she'd simply taken two of the heavy cream envelopes from her purse and handed them over, in silence. She'd watched as Debbie and Leah had opened the outer envelopes and discovered the confidentiality agreements, shooting doubtful looks at Crys as if to say that her idea of a joke wasn't funny at two in the morning.

"Read them carefully, and then sign them, but you'd better mean it because they're binding and no joke," Crys had warned, and both of her roommates had signed. Then incredulity and disbelief had set in, as the two girls read Marigold's assiduously impersonal statement about Crys's new job. Why had Crys been chosen, and not one of them? Who would take over Crys's room and share of the rent, or could they manage between the two of them without Crys for a year? Was Crys out of her mind, or had she been drunk, to agree to such a thing? What would her parents say? Crys told them about Kin and Marigold, and about Blade's distaste for virginity, and how she might learn to play the guitar a bit, if he remembered his promise. When the shadows had begun to fade, and the rising sun cast a rosy glow through the kitchen window, the three of them finally dragged themselves off to bed.

Even sleeping until noon had not been enough to refresh her after that, and now, walking along in the chilly wind, she felt achingly tired – and worse, slightly hung over.

Crys arrived at the Starbucks, hauling open the door against the wind and gladly diving into the coffee-scented warmth inside. She glanced around the packed coffee house, trying to spot Rhys, hoping she'd recognize him without the spiked hair and facial hardware. She wondered whether she would need to give him the envelope, or if the conversation would flag naturally, and she'd be able to make some excuse not to see him again. After all, she wasn't honor-bound to tell him anything.

Not seeing him immediately, she joined the line-up at the counter, and ordered her usual non-fat latte. She moved down to the end of the counter to wait for her drink to be ready – and there was Rhys, at a table stuck away back by the washrooms, hidden from general view by the counter and the espresso machine and the sign advertising toffee mochas and pumpkin spice lattes. He was less striking in appearance without the false piercings he'd worn at the concert, but still handsome: a nice-looking clean-shaven man with slightly tousled dark hair and a fisherman's sweater.

He looked up and saw her, and his face was full of surprised disappointment. She hadn't thought he'd been drinking heavily at the concert – was she so unattractive to him in the daylight? And then he stood and dropped the tabloid newspaper he'd been holding, and she understood. The girl who'd taken her picture at the Ballroom, who'd asked if she was really dating Blade, must have sold the image – because there it was on the front page of the rag, under the headline "SMIDGE GUITARIST'S SECRET SWEETIE!" Unmistakably Crys, leaning over the railing from the roped-off VIP area, with the rock star's diamonds sparkling in her ears.

"So, were you planning to tell me about your boyfriend, or was I just supposed to figure it out on my own?" he asked, hands in his pockets as he walked toward her.

"Rhys, I–" She fumbled for words to fix things, explain, take the hurt look from his face – and then she remembered the confidentiality agreement in her purse, which he had to sign before she could tell him anything.

The barista at the counter called out her non-fat latte and she turned to collect it, glad of the moment's interruption.

"Come and sit down, anyway," Rhys suggested, heading back to his table, where he took the offending newspaper and shoved it into a nearby garbage bin. With her hot cup clasped in both hands for comfort, she followed him to the table and sat down. She gave him a tentative smile, which he met with a half-smile and shrug. "I don't really know what to say, Crys... unless the girl in the *Star* isn't you?"

She sighed. "Oh, it's me, all right. Look, it won't make anything right between us, but I do have something that will explain it to you a little. There's a catch, though; read it carefully, okay, because I wouldn't want either of us to get in trouble." She fished the thick cream-colored envelope out of her purse and placed it on the table in front of him. His eyes widened as he read through the confidentiality agreement.

"Is this for real?" he asked, though Crys could tell by his face that he believed it was.

"Yes... whether fortunately or unfortunately, I'm not sure. It's up to you whether you want an explanation badly enough to sign the agreement."

"You got a pen?"

She handed him a pen, and he signed, a flowing swirl dominated by the tail of the R and the curve of the D. "Go on, then," she prompted him. "Open it and you'll know."

Rhys ripped into the inner envelope, pulled out the single sheet of paper contained within it. Crys watched his face as he read the brief statement, and couldn't be sure what he was thinking; he didn't seem incredulous or angry or even impressed. If anything, he looked concerned. "Well," he said at last. "Well. That does explain... the gossip rag, at any rate. I imagine you'll be fielding a lot of that in the days to come."

"I guess so. Probably."

The concern on his face deepened. "At least I understand now." He looked into her eyes, and she saw that he was troubled for her. "Hey, if you ever... need a friend... I know we can't date while you're doing this, but..."

"Yeah. Friends would be good," Crys agreed. "I'll be fine, you know, but friends would still be good." She sipped her latte, stifling a wistful sensation. Rhys was a rare kind of man: handsome, kind, understanding. He hadn't asked her why she was doing this senseless thing, or asked her to give it up for him. He offered friendship when no other option was open, and showed concern for her though they'd only just met. He was clean and well-groomed, had told her at the concert that he didn't smoke pot, he would make beautiful babies and be an amazing father. *Am I a fool to turn my back on this, and for what?* Crys sighed, answering her own question. *A pierced lip that I ache to kiss, a guitar god's hands that leave stardust on me when we touch. A daydream.* She met Rhys's quizzical glance, and smiled. "Who knows?" she told him. "Maybe when this is all over..." Maybe she'd want to settle down, or something.

"Friends for now, then," he said, with a grin to show he meant it, no bitterness or games, straight honest friendship until Crys should be free to pursue more. "Surely your new bosses will let you have email access wherever you are, or social media? We can kind of hang out that way, if you'd like."

"Sure, that would be nice," Crys agreed. *Nice.* Her own word echoed in her mind. Yes, it would be nice, just as Rhys was a nice person, and Crys was always seen as a nice girl. Fitting into expectations. But one could never have too many friends, and an online buddy could prove a comfort if things on the Smidge tour got difficult. "Staying in touch would be fun."

"Good," he said. "I didn't feel like eating before, but I'm kind of hungry now. Want something with your coffee? A muffin, or one of those oat fudge bars? My treat."

"Mmm, I like those." Crys hadn't so much as eaten a slice of toast before rushing out of the apartment, and her hung-over stomach needed some ballast. "But... you don't have to pay, you know, since..." She gestured at the newspapers in his hands.

"A guy can treat a girl without expecting something in return," Rhys said, gently reproving. "And we're friends, aren't we? You can buy me coffee next time."

♥

"Crys, you're finally home!" said Debbie, leaning out the door of the apartment as Crys came trudging up the stairs. "You've got a visitor."

"Oh?" Crys pushed past Debbie and headed for the living room, where she found Marigold sitting in slightly inappropriate splendor on their ratty old couch. Marigold had obviously made an effort to appear inconspicuous for her visit to their apartment, but her jeans were so far beyond skin-tight that they appeared painted on, and the closely fitted burnt-orange leather jacket couldn't be mistaken for anything but an expensive designer piece, probably custom-made. She'd slicked down her streaked hair a bit, but still looked like she'd just escaped from a rock concert, and Crys nearly laughed at the sight of her – Marigold couldn't be anything but herself, no matter what she tried. Several boxes and bags were heaped on the couch beside her, more on the floor. It must have taken several trips up and down the stairs to bring all of them in.

"Come on, Crys, we've got to get you ready," Marigold told her. "You have to see Blade off, and we haven't a lot of time to spare, since I'll need to get you back to the hotel so you can ride with him to the airport." She waved a hand at the bags and boxes. "I brought you some clothes."

"But I can't afford–"

"Don't be silly. PR expenses, all taken care of. Try these on."

Crys felt a bit like a dress-up doll as she tried on pair after pair of jeans, trying to find something she felt comfortable wearing that also met Marigold's standards for tightness. The pair she ended up choosing had a faded-vintage look and were tighter than any jeans she'd ever worn. She had to admit that they flattered her hips and legs, and even agreed that Marigold was right to insist on thong underwear – which wasn't as uncomfortable as she'd expected, either. A sleeveless grey Smidge t-shirt matched Crys's eyes. Then Marigold drew out a black leather jacket, and Crys felt her mouth falling open in amazement, saw the same expression reflected on Leah and Debbie's faces. The finest ink-black butter-soft leather was accented by shining silver zippers, the exquisite design and materials matched by exquisite workmanship. Crys couldn't stop herself from reaching out to touch it, stroke it. "Wow! That's a gorgeous jacket!"

"I'm glad you like it," said Marigold. "Put it on now, and we'll try on some boots. I think you said you wear a six-and-a-half, right?" She chose a box from the stack on the floor, and opened it, lifting tissue paper away. The boots were sexy, on the edge of kinky, black leather dripping with steel buckles and D-rings; they made Crys's feet and ankles look tiny, somehow both graceful and tough.

Crys looked in the mirror and saw a rock-and-roll princess looking back at her.

"I thought I was supposed to look wholesome?" she asked, with more than a hint of doubt in her voice. The wicked boots, the leather jacket and the curve-hugging jeans looked like they belonged to a beautiful stranger.

Marigold laughed. "Crys, I don't think you could look unwholesome if you tried. But don't worry. We'll keep your hair and makeup sweet, so you'll look just like what you're supposed to be: a little angel dating a rock star." Marigold fluffed Crys's hair up with hot rollers and hairspray until it floated like a halo around her face, and powdered away any hint of tiredness. "Pink or peach?" she asked, holding out two tubes of lip gloss.

"Crys, you look amazing," said Leah, looking with awe at her dolled-up friend.

Crys laughed. "Don't be silly – it's the glamorous clothes, that's all."

"No, really, Crys." Debbie nodded seriously, adding her voice to Leah's. "You look awesome. That rock-babe leather look suits you."

Marigold inspected her work, with a satisfied expression on her face. "You look fabulous – which always helps when you're about to meet the press. Now go and put on your diamond earrings, and that wristband you were wearing yesterday." At Crys's astonished gasp, she continued with a knowing look, "Yes, I recognized it the moment I saw it on you. I have no idea why he gave it to you, but we can spin it nicely into the story."

Leah and Debbie's eyes were agog with curiosity, all the more so as Crys went into her bedroom and came out with the black leather band buckled around her wrist. The diamond earrings they had already seen and exclaimed over, but she'd managed to conceal the wristband from them. "Where did that come from?" they asked. "Did Blade give it to you? When? Why?!" Crys just shook her head.

"If you're all set, we should go," Marigold insisted, all but tapping her foot in impatience. "This is going to be tricky enough without being late on top of everything."

Glancing into the mirror one more time, Crys nodded.

From the underground parking garage at the hotel, Marigold hustled Crys up a flight of emergency fire stairs, and then into a service elevator behind the kitchen, and from there – at last – into the suite where Kin waited. "Let's get her up to Blade's room," he said, the moment he saw the two women.

"I thought you were going to have him come here to collect her," Marigold said.

"Changed my mind. We'll have her leave from there with him – get a bellhop sent up for the bags to witness it – gives the whole thing authenticity." Kin smiled at Crys. "Hello there, Crystal. Are you ready for this?"

"Uh, I think so?"

"There's nothing at all to worry about. Basically, you're going to ride with Blade in the limo to the airport, stay with him until boarding – we've arranged a gate pass for you – get seen doing the tender farewell thing as he leaves."

"Sure," Crys agreed.

"Once Blade is off, the security team will get you out of the airport and into the limo – be prepared for a lot of media interest at that point, they're going to want to interview you," Kin warned her. "If you can possibly manage it, give them something to quote: tell them 'he's just so amazing...' and 'it's all so new and wonderful right now...' Do you think you can do that?"

"Do you really want me to say those bad-soap-opera lines?" Crys asked, with a skeptical lift of her eyebrows.

Kin smiled. "Trust me," he said, "that's exactly what they want to hear. Don't say anything about sex – blush if you can manage it – and don't use the word 'love' yet. You'll be fine. Then you'll be done for the day and the limo will take you back to your place. You've got the rest of the evening and all day tomorrow off, but you'll need to pack and do whatever else is necessary before leaving town, because we're flying out to join the boys first thing Monday morning. Have you spoken to your parents yet?"

Crys shook her head, no. "I'm having dinner with them tomorrow," she explained.

"You might want to take care of that tonight," said Marigold. "Before they see tomorrow's papers – if they didn't already see the *Star* today."

"Oh, good God! I hadn't thought of that... no, they never read the *Star*, and they'd have called me if someone had shown them–"

"Not the moment to be thinking about that now. We're out of time; you've got to get up there. Up one floor, directly above us, room 904." Kin paused, and clapped her on the shoulder with a hearty hand. "Good luck, Crys; I know you'll do a great job! I'll see you at the airport on Monday."

Marigold hustled Crys over to the door, practically pushing her into the corridor. "I'll call him and tell him you're on your way up. Off you go!" The door clicked closed, and Crys was alone.

She hurried down the hall and pressed the button for the elevator, fidgeting with tension until the up-arrow glowed green and a soft chime announced the elevator's presence. In the elevator, she caught sight of herself in the mirror panel, and barely recognized the leather-and-denim-clad stranger who posed there. The soft lighting highlighted her floating halo of hair, and cast her eyes into shadow. The elevator moved smoothly up one floor and chimed as the door slid open; glancing warily about, Crys stepped out into the hallway of the ninth floor.

Evidently, this was an extra-luxurious floor. A side table with fresh flowers stood in the open space around the elevator, and a jewel-toned Persian carpet lay over the cream wall-to-wall, further muffling footsteps in the high-traffic area. Everywhere she looked, touches of gold-leafing and crystal-hung chandeliers told her that she'd entered the domain of the privileged few. *Room 904,* she reminded herself. Hurrying down the hall, her boots sinking into the plush carpeting and making no sound, she darted glances at the number plates on the doors. *908 ... 906 ... 904!*

Crys raised her hand to knock, then froze in sudden trepidation as it struck her that Blade was in there, alone. A shiver of dread and anticipation flowed over her. *Don't be a fool,* she told herself, and knocked softly.

The door opened at once; he'd been waiting for her. Throat dry, she swallowed hard, trying to summon some sense, standing there in the doorway like an idiot. "Hi," she said at last. "Hi, Blade." A nervous giggle escaped her, and she clapped a hand over her mouth.

"Hey, Crys," he replied, looking her up and down with evident admiration, from halo hair to sexy boots. "Suits you." He raised the Jack Daniels bottle he was holding in a toast.

"Oh. Thanks. Marigold dressed me." *God, I'm pathetic.* She struggled with the awful feeling of wanting so desperately to say and do the right things, knowing that she was tripping over herself trying. And there was maybe a foot or two of space between them, and he hadn't so much as touched her hand.

Blade stepped back from the doorway, saying, "Well, you'd better come in." He paused, and took a slug straight from his bottle. "Want a drink?" Something in her face must have reminded him that Jack straight from a shared bottle wouldn't be in her range of normal, and he added, "I don't mean... There's champagne and beer in the bar fridge, and sodas..."

"No, thank you." As Crys moved past him into the sitting room of the suite, she saw the lone suitcase by the door. "Don't you have more stuff than this?" she asked, glancing around for more luggage. "I would have thought you'd have, I don't know, another bag at least."

He laughed. "I'm a guy. But yes. My guitar and carry-on are in there – I'm carrying them myself." He nodded his head toward an open door, and Crys took a few curious steps so that she could peer in. It was a bedroom – the bed where he'd slept was unmade, rumpled sheets and blankets flung half onto the floor. A black guitar-shaped bag with a shoulder strap was propped against the bed, and next to it rested a scuffed black leather satchel. "Do me a favor, sweetheart, and have a quick look-round to see if I've forgotten anything in there. I'm supposed to call for the bellhop right away, now that you're here."

Crys edged into the bedroom, looking around cautiously. She found a lone sock hiding half-under the bureau and a guitar pick on the bedside table. Then she approached the bed, touching the blankets gingerly, lifting and straightening as she checked to see whether any hidden items should appear – and she did find an empty beer bottle and a ball-point pen tangled in the sheets, and a black leather-bound notebook under one of the pillows. *This is where he slept,* she thought. Did he sleep naked? *Oh sweet Lord!* The thought was dizzying. The sheets smelled faintly of citrus soap – his soap – and a trace of spice and clean sweat, a musky skin-scent.

Feeling flushed and trembling, Crys retreated into the main room, clutching the sock and guitar pick in one hand and the pen and notebook in the other. Unwilling to trust her voice, she simply held up her finds. Blade dropped the pen case he was holding and snatched the notebook from her. "Where did you find this?" he asked, looking oddly shaken.

"It was under the pillows in the bed," she told him. "But you've got it now. Is it something important?"

"My song-writing notebook," he muttered, still a bit white-faced.

"It's okay, you've got it now. No harm done," she said, trying to reassure him. "Would you like me to put it in your carry-on for you?"

He shook his head, no. "I'll do it," he said, his fingers tightening on the notebook. As he disappeared into the bedroom, there was a knock on the door. "Can you get that, sweetheart?" he called out. "It's probably the bellhop."

She was still holding the sock and guitar pick, so she put them down on the desk next to the pen case that Blade had dropped. Took a deep breath, tried to feel glamorous, and crossed to open the door.

The bellhop waiting there eyed Crys with fascinated curiosity, presumably making all of the assumptions that Kin and Marigold had intended. "I think it's just the one bag there," she told him, indicating the suitcase.

"Sure thing, babe," he said, but didn't immediately take the bag. He looked her up and down with openly salacious speculation; the wink he gave her made her feel uncomfortable and dirty. "So, how much does a girl like you cost? Or do rock stars get it for free?"

And then his face paled and his expression dissolved, and Crys turned to see Blade in the bedroom doorway, radiating raw violence. Something flew past the bellhop's head, hit the wall with a crunch and slid down in a mess of broken glass and dark liquid – had Blade thrown his bottle? A few furious strides brought him to crouch protectively in front of her, squaring off for a fight with menace in two knotted fists as he stared down the hotel employee with lethal intent. "You keep your sick thoughts to yourself, scumbag," he snarled, "and don't make assumptions where you don't know shit!"

The bellhop backed away, raising his hands in a placating gesture. "Don't hit me, you don't want another assault charge, do you? I wasn't thinking anything, didn't mean anything by it..."

Crys, knowing that she was supposed to avert exactly this sort of incident, placed a tentative hand on Blade's arm, gasping at the barely-restrained force she could feel in the taut muscles under her fingers. "Please, Blade... no harm was done, and we don't need any trouble today, do we?" she asked. For a moment, she thought that it wasn't going to work, that he would haul off and floor the bellhop. But then he blew out a long breath, and the tension in his frame eased a fraction.

"Whatever. Okay, clown, we'll pretend I didn't hear anything and you weren't thinking disrespectful thoughts about my *girlfriend*, so I won't have to hurt you. You can take the suitcase down to my driver, and then get lost – if I see you when I get down there, I'll–"

"Absolutely, sir." And the bellhop retreated without dignity.

Crys stared at Blade, not sure what to make of this aggressive, hard-drinking stranger, wondering if it had been a futile hope that they could get along and maybe even forge some kind of friendship over the year ahead. He seemed unable to look at her, and at last he turned with a muttered profanity and gathered up his pen case and guitar pick and sock from the desk. "Excuse me," he said, still without looking up, and almost slunk through the bedroom door; she heard the door to the en suite bathroom slam.

She waited an awkward ten minutes before he emerged, all tension abated, the controlled rock star once more in the ascendant. "I owe you an apology, sweetheart," he said. "I've been a cranky bastard over this plot of Kin's, and it's just been proved to me that he's right – obviously, I do need a handler, a babysitter, whatever you want to call it. So I'm sorry, and... thank you."

Crys smiled. "That's all right. This is kind of a weird situation we're in."

"Yeah." Blade shot her a rueful grin in return. "I can't promise I'll make it easy for you, but I'll do my best." He glanced at the time display on his phone, and at the open door. "Come on – we'd better get moving. Are you ready for this?"

No, I'm not, Crys wanted to say, but she nodded anyway. "Sure."

♥

Crys peered out the window as the limousine carried them smoothly up the ramp to the departures level of the airport. Directional signs for domestic and international flights flashed past, logos of the airlines for the different check-in areas.

"Here," said Blade, cracking open the bottle of champagne that had been provided for them in the vehicle – no wild popping of the cork this time, just a businesslike twist, and he splashed a little bit into the bottom of a glass.

"Why–?" Crys asked as he handed it to her. The limousine was pulling up to the curb now. Surely this was no time to be drinking, and in any case, he'd poured barely a sip or two into the glass she held.

Blade gave her a cynical glance. "The vultures. They'll try to get a look inside the limo, so they oughta see we've been having a good time in here. Rock star lifestyle, and all that. Go on, get a bit of lipstick on the rim of that glass." He splashed a token bit of champagne into the second glass, and then sipped thoughtfully from the bottle. "Too bad. It's pretty decent stuff."

"If I were really your girlfriend, I wouldn't be sitting here sipping champagne like I'm at a tea party," Crys pointed out.

"That's right, sweetheart; we should mess your hair up a bit, shouldn't we?" With a grin, he scooted closer to her on the limousine's bench seat and slid his hands into her hair, massaging her scalp. Crys nearly moaned out loud, it felt so good. "You like that, do you?" he asked, seeing the pleasure on her face as her eyes drifted closed. *Oh, yes!* His fingers stroked, rubbed, soothed – and her whole body writhed against his hand in a sudden involuntary spasm of desire. "Are you so responsive all over?" he asked, his voice low and rasping. Her eyes flipped open in shock, and he jerked his hand away as though her now-thoroughly-rumpled hair could burn him. "Sorry, kid... it's just habit." He grabbed the champagne bottle from its holder and took another swig, held it out to her. "Want some?"

She could have used her glass, of course, but she drank from the bottle as he had, her lips touching it where his had touched. Such a schoolgirl-crush thing to do – but really, wasn't that all this was? "Shouldn't we go?" she asked, giving him back the bottle smudged with lipstick. "I mean, we've been sitting here for a while, haven't we?"

Through the mirrored windows of the limousine, they could see a crowd of shadowy figures gathered around the open space between the vehicle and the automatic doors to the airport check-in area. A pair of larger shadows hovered, the extra security detail that Kin had promised. "You're probably right," Blade agreed, muttering a few vicious words under his breath. "Man, I hate dealing with this freaked-out media circus all the time."

"Maybe you shouldn't do so much to make yourself into a meal for them, then." The words popped out before Crys could censor herself, and then she couldn't hold in a gurgle of laughter at the blend of affront and guilt that crossed Blade's face.

"Yeah, whatever." He punched the intercom button. "We're ready; Ryan, you'll open the door for us?" He saw Crys looking at him, and added, "Uh, please. And thank you, driver."

"My pleasure, sir," came the driver's reply.

"Coming around now," said the bodyguard, and they felt the slight percussion of the car door opening and closing up front.

Blade slung the strap of his guitar bag over his shoulder, and reached for the handle of his satchel. He held out his other hand to Crys. "Come on, sweetheart – hold my hand, smile, be sweet and follow my lead."

With a brief warning knock on the window, the bodyguard pulled open the door, and a barrage of camera flashes caught the interior of the vehicle – the open champagne bottle, the couple holding hands, and Crys's tousled hair.

Voices shouted as they stepped out onto the curb. "Blade! Blade! Look over here!" "Who's the girl?" "What's your name, baby?" "Give us a smile, Blade!" "Where did you meet her?" More camera flashes washed over them – Crys felt a little bit disoriented by all the shouting and lights, and tightened her grip on Blade's hand as he pulled her forward – and the pair of security men flanked them, fending off the determined photographers and reporters as they moved toward the airport doors, mere steps away.

In comparison, the inside of the airport was beautifully quiet. Blade's bodyguard brought in the suitcase that the driver had unloaded from the limousine's trunk, and then the group was able to proceed directly to the first-class check-in desk. Blade autographed a couple of blank boarding passes for the agents. They gazed at Crys with interest, sensing a fairy tale, and produced the gate pass Marigold had arranged for her.

At Security, even Blade had to take his shoes off and walk through the metal detector – no one was exempt from that – but the security staff were so eager to please, and so thrilled with the autographs they got, that it didn't seem like much of a hassle. And then a 'courtesy transport' was waiting for them.

Crys had seen the fancy little golf carts scooting about the airport before, but she'd never been near enough to touch one. It was something of a thrill to ride on the cart, clinging tightly to Blade's hand and smiling until her face ached as random flashes kept surprising her – she didn't know if they were members of the press, or ordinary travelers wanting a photograph of a celebrity, but he'd said happy and sweet, and she was determined to do her best.

They arrived at the gate, where only a couple of people were showing their boarding passes and heading down the jetway to the airplane, though a cluster of photographers and reporters waited, perking up as they saw the Smidge guitarist and his girl. Cameras flashed. "We've already boarded; we've been holding the flight for you," explained a harried-looking gate agent, whose face had lit up with relief the moment she'd recognized Blade. "Please board as soon as you possibly can." An equally tense flight attendant waited at the entrance to the jetway.

"How do they get in here?" asked Crys, looking at the paparazzi who hovered like the vultures Blade called them.

"They buy tickets to the cheapest flights they can get, the bastards, and use them to get through security," said Blade, with a snort of disgust. "Then they chuck the unused tickets and walk out with the pictures they wanted – worth the price of admission, to them."

The gate agent touched Blade hesitantly on the sleeve. "I'm very sorry, sir, but could you consider boarding... er, at your earliest convenience, of course!"

"Yes, ma'am," he said, putting one arm around Crys's waist in a tender and possessive gesture that made Crys want to lean into him. "Could you give me a moment to say goodbye?" The gate agent turned a bit pink and nodded, retreating toward her desk. Then Blade lowered his guitar case and carry-on to the ground at their feet to free his other arm.

Crys looked up at him. He had just a hint of eyeliner darkening around his eyes today – not the full stage-makeup treatment, but enough to give him that rock star look. Her breath catching in her throat, she looked away from his knowing hazel eyes... only to find herself staring at his mouth, at his pierced lip with that sexy silver ring. "Well, I guess you'd better go, then," she said, trying for firmness, but coming up with a wistful little smile.

"You know we've got to do better than that," he said, cupping her face between his hands as though he were saying something romantic. "Our friends over there will be expecting a kiss."

Crys blinked. "You... you're going to pretend to kiss me so they can take pictures..." Surely that was all he'd meant, that he'd lean over her and pretend.

"Can't fake it this close to those cameras. Just lean into it like you mean it." He shot her a quizzical look. "You've been kissed before, right?"

Oh sweet God! With a mute jerky nod, she tilted her face upward in his hands, trembling a little.

Blade smiled with wicked tenderness, his lip ring glinting in the light of a camera flash. "Come on, sweetheart," he murmured, his voice rough and urgent, "I want to taste you... give it to me, just a little bit, let me know you want it too..." Closing her eyes with a soft helpless moan, Crys gave herself over into his hands, and his mouth covered hers.

Electricity zapped and sparked between them. Her lips parted under his. She felt the steel of his lip ring press against her lip – licked at it – expected a metallic taste but found only a hint of champagne. Devastating bliss rolled over her in a dark wave. With a groaning curse that she felt more than heard, he slipped his tongue into her mouth, a sweet invasion that heated up fast and overwhelmed all conscious thought in its fire.

They both came back to their senses at the same moment, dazed and breathing heavily as they drew apart, looking into each other's slightly shocked eyes.

"Oh..." said Crys.

"Fuck," said Blade. "Oh, fuck." He stepped back, raising a hand in salute, first to her and then to the press contingent, before turning to follow the flight attendant down the jetway. He didn't look back.

"I... I'll see you on Monday..." Crys whispered after him, knowing that he couldn't hear her. "Have a safe flight..."

♥

Afterward, Crys could never remember getting home from the airport. She learned, from the newspapers the next day, that she'd performed admirably for the media – she'd apparently told them how amazing Blade was, blushing and lowering her eyes when asked if they were lovers. She'd apparently gushed that it was all so new and wonderful, like an ingénue in a bad B-movie. The quotes on the tabloid pages the next day made her cringe, but the headlines and photographs were everything that Kin and Marigold could have wanted: "BLADE'S SWEETHEART" and "TRUE ROMANCE FOR SMIDGE BAD BOY" over shots of them holding hands in the limousine, Blade cupping Crys's face in his hands, and that damned kiss – which instead of being a relief had made everything that much harder to cope with. Impossible to cope with, really, because of how unhappy Blade had looked as he'd turned away.

♥

Crys sat in her parents' front room, staring at the pattern of the carpet and thinking that her luck couldn't possibly get any worse. With everything that had been happening, she had not after all managed to get up to see them earlier, to give them the confidentiality agreement and explain. Nor had she called them – she'd meant to call them, to warn them that they might see her in the papers and ask them not to jump to conclusions, but had put off making the call over and over until it had been too late.

"What have you been up to, Cryssie?" her mother had asked her as she'd opened the front door, adding, "And you needn't try to come up with a story about it, the papers have already been quite clear."

Now, settled on her mother's overstuffed rose-velvet Victorian sofa, with a cup of tea in her hands and the *Star* and the *News* lying on the coffee table in front of her, she tried to ease into an explanation. "Things aren't... quite the way they look..."

"Well, it's pretty clear that you know the boy, kitten," said her mother with a reluctantly sympathetic smile. "Which part isn't the way it looks? Isn't he planning to see you again?"

Grimacing, Crys took the envelope from her purse. "It's more complicated than that. I'm flying out to join him in the morning," she confessed, holding it out for her mother to take. "But this will explain." *Sort of.*

Mrs. Murphy squinted at the confidentiality agreement, and took the reading glasses from her apron pocket. Those reading glasses made Crys smile; her mother had carried them around for years, a pair in every pocket, it seemed. They were never quite strong enough; even wearing the glasses, Mrs. Murphy tended to hold whatever she was reading at arm's length and squint – as she did now, peering at the dense legal text. "So, Cryssie, what's all this about?" she asked with pursed lips. "It doesn't look like a joking matter to me."

"No, Mum."

"I'll need a pen, I suppose..." Mrs. Murphy got up and dug in the sideboard drawer for a pen, unearthing assorted bits of ribbon, twine, rolls of tape, old keys and felt markers before she found what she wanted. She sat back down in her armchair and signed the document, her cramped signature wandering down off the line, and then tore open the inner envelope. Her lips pursed even further as she read the statement it contained. After a dreadful endless silence, she looked up at Crys, her brow creased with anxiety and disapproval, and said, "If you want a year off school to work, that's fine, but I wish you'd talked it over with us first. You'd be better off taking a job in Daddy's office, if it comes to that."

"It's not – I didn't go looking for a job."

"Then tell them you have to finish your studies. Traveling around with a rock band isn't the sort of thing nice girls do, is it?" The pursed lips again, and the wide, expectant eyes that meant Mrs. Murphy was waiting for agreement.

"I already signed the contract, Mum. I can't back out of it now. But at least I'll get to see a lot of cities that I've never seen before, and I'm learning lots of stuff about public relations and the music industry."

"Cryssie, kitten, you don't want to work in the music industry. I know you better than that – you're doing this because you've gotten fond of the boy, haven't you?" Mrs. Murphy shook her head, concern and sympathy warring in her face. "You may say it's just pretend, but I can see the truth in those pictures. All the chaperones and promises in the world–" she gestured toward the legal papers "–won't mean anything if you're lusting after him in your heart."

"Good God, Mum! Lusting?!"

"Is it necessary to be profane? I'm only concerned that you'll get caught up in this boy's temporary charms, instead of waiting for a meaningful relationship with a husband who respects you."

If someone's respect is contingent on my body being untouched, is it worth having? But debating that point with her mother never brought anything but grief, so Crys let it pass. "I have a bit of a crush on Blade, sure. But it won't matter; he's not interested."

Mrs. Murphy blew out a long breath, and narrowed her eyes at Crys in resignation. "Well, maybe I'm seeing with a mother's eyes, but it looks obvious enough to me that he fancies you. Does he at least treat you decently?"

"He doesn't know me, really. I'm just someone the PR people hired for him. And he doesn't like – oh, Mummy, he looked so unhappy after he'd kissed me!" Crys's voice cracked, thick with holding back tears.

Mrs. Murphy came over and sat next to her daughter, wrapping her arms around Crys's shaking shoulders, comforting her as the sobs came. "Hush... hush, kitten... hush now, Cryssie... all will be well in the end..." she murmured over and over, stroking her daughter's hair, until at last Crys quieted and wiped her eyes.

chapter

5

A T DAWN, CRYS WAS ON HER WAY TO THE AIRPORT.
Rain had blown in overnight, with heavy grey clouds that made the early morning colder and darker than it might have been. Marigold had arranged for an ordinary taxicab to collect Crys and deliver her to the airport discreetly in the hope that the tabloid stringers would leave her alone. Debbie and Leah had offered to accompany her, but she'd told them that it would be less painful for her to say goodbye at the apartment – in truth, she wanted to sleep in the taxi. Insomnia had plagued her for the past two nights, endless wakeful hours during which she couldn't stop thinking of Blade's face after he'd kissed her, how unhappy he'd looked, how he'd only said 'oh fuck' and walked away without a farewell. Torturous dozing periods were punctuated by warped dreams, which woke her again. And so, after tearful hugs for her two best friends, amid promises to stay in touch, she'd climbed into the car and leaned her head against the window. Her eyes had drifted closed the moment Leah and Debbie were left behind out of sight.

The driver woke Crys as they approached the ramp to the departures level. Bleary-eyed, she struggled for alertness as he pulled in to the drop-off area, and fumbled in her purse for the taxi voucher Marigold had given her. Then, pushing open the cab door, she scrambled out into the rainy morning. The driver came around to unload her duffel bag from the trunk, and she lugged it onto a handcart – glad to find one available, even if it was slick with rain.

Marigold had told her not to bring much luggage – an appropriate wardrobe would be arranged for her. But Crys had panicked at the thought of uprooting her life and crossing the continent without a few of her own familiar things, and the old duffel bag held an unglamorous selection that Marigold would no doubt disapprove of, including two pairs of flannelette pajamas. She longed for the moment when she could put them on and crawl into a soft clean hotel bed... still hours away.

Crys took a firm grip on the slippery push-bar of her handcart and headed toward the automatic doors out of the rain.

As soon as she got inside, she pulled out her phone and dialed Marigold. "I'm here, in the airport, near the top of the central escalator," she said. "What do you want me to do?"

"Stay right where you are," Marigold ordered. "I'll come and find you."

As usual, Marigold Hendon was unmistakably herself from miles away, this time in an enormous faux-fur coat in a leopard pattern shot with hot pink and gold. Only Marigold could get away with wearing such a glamorously weird thing, Crys thought, a stab of amusement cutting through her anxiety and fatigue. *Oh, good God, I'm getting used to Marigold!* She nearly laughed out loud at the notion, and then swallowed the laughter, saying instead, "Good morning, Marigold! Isn't Kin with you?"

"He's already in the business class lounge having coffee; I waited on this side of security so we could walk down together – but shit, Crys, you look like crap! What happened to you?"

This time Crys did laugh out loud at Marigold's bluntness. "I haven't been sleeping so much," she admitted.

"Well, I hope no one with a camera sees you until we can get you fixed up. You've got to take better care of yourself, girl." Marigold whipped open her purse and pulled out a powder compact, dusting the shine from Crys's face as a first step to general improvement. "That'll have to do for now. I've got some blusher and bronzer that'll give you a bit of color, as soon as we can find a washroom, but first we'd better get you checked in."

Fumble-fingered with exhaustion, Crys managed to drop her purse in front of the check-in counter. "Sorry," she muttered, bending to collect her lip gloss and keys and change purse. "I'm just so very tired..."

Marigold retrieved a roll of breath mints and a tube of mascara and handed them to Crys. "I can see that. You're taking a sleeping pill on the flight. Come on, now." Marigold took Crys's boarding pass from the check-in person and tucked it inside her fluffy jacket with her own. "I'll take care of everything." She hurried Crys along to airport security, prompting her to take off her shoes at the appropriate moment, making sure that she didn't lose her purse.

At last they reached the lounge for business class passengers. Marigold vanished and returned with coffee and doughnuts. *Oh, yummy!* Crys sipped the hot liquid gratefully, alternating with bites of doughnut. As Marigold had no doubt intended, the coffee and sugar-laden treat together perked Crys up enough that she was able to board the flight without raising eyebrows, and a judicious application of concealer and powder hid the exhausted circles under her eyes well enough.

Crys had never flown business class before. As she boarded the plane, she discovered that her seat was only four rows from the front, a window seat, with Marigold beside her and then Kin across the aisle – the seats were wide and comfortable, with plenty of leg room.

"Did you want the window seat?" Crys asked Marigold, thinking that the woman might have given up her preference for Crys's benefit. "I don't mind either way."

"That's very sweet, Crys, but no," Marigold said. "I might want to get out of my seat or talk to Mr. Kinney – and you, on the other hand, will be sleeping. So, sit down and make yourself comfy."

As soon as Crys was buckled into her seat for the flight, Marigold took a small enameled tin from her purse and shook out one gel caplet – such a tiny harmless thing; smaller than the tip of Crys's little finger, it looked like Tylenol or a vitamin. "Here," said Marigold. "Can you swallow it like this, or do you need a sip of something?"

"I don't know..." Crys said, not liking to take a strange pill from an unlabeled container, no matter how much she might trust Marigold.

"It's only diphenhydramine – you can buy it in any pharmacy – Unisom, Sominex, you know? You need to take this pill and get some sleep, girl," Marigold insisted, impatient with Crys's qualms. She pushed the little capsule into Crys's hand. "We can't have you making yourself ill. D'you need some water with it?"

When Crys didn't answer, still looking at the pill in her palm with misgivings she couldn't set aside, Marigold waved over a flight attendant to ask for a cup of water.

"Sparkling or still?" the flight attendant asked.

The next minute, Crys found herself with a glass of Perrier, complete with ice and a wedge of lime. "Just swallow it already," Marigold said, nearly snapping with impatience, and Crys gave in, lifted the pill to her mouth and washed it down. The cool, fizzing, lime-flavored water tasted so good that she kept on sipping it until the glass was nearly empty and her hand felt too heavy to hold anything anymore.

Crys woke up in the dark, groggy, surrounded by clean sheets and fluffy pillows – in bed, then. There was none of that uncomfortable sense of sleeping in one's clothes, and she became aware that someone must have removed her cargo pants and hoodie and put her into her pajamas. Jerking upright in a panic, she fumbled around for any sort of bedside light – knocked something onto the floor – tried to calm herself, to feel around more methodically. At last she located the shape of a lamp, walked her fingers upward and found the switch – turned it – welcomed the soft warm light with relief.

The hotel room was done up in an ultra-modern style, with granite surfaces and cherry wood furniture and cabinets, and mirrored panels everywhere. A box of tissues lay on the floor next to a granite-and-cherry nightstand – that must have been what Crys had knocked off in the dark. The king-sized bed in which she lay dominated the room, but there was a desk and chair by the window, and a couch – on which someone was sleeping, wrapped in a blanket. The sleeper must have been awakened by the light, because the blanket jerked in a convulsive motion, and the person inside it flopped over and sat up, coming untangled from the blanket and pushing strands of electric orange hair out of her eyes. It was the makeup artist from the Smidge concert, which now seemed so long ago.

"Hey," the orange-haired woman said. "I doubt you'll remember me... my name's Sally; I do makeup and wardrobe for Smidge. Didja sleep okay? Is it okay if I call you Crystal, or would you rather I say Ms. Murphy?"

"Hi, Sally – I do remember you, and you can call me Crys."

"Coolness." Sally glanced at her watch. "It's, like, five in the morning local time, but I'm so used to being on the road, I'm adaptable. D'you want to sleep longer, or are you ready to get up?"

Crys blinked and checked the digital clock radio on the bedside table – it read 5:07 AM. "Sally, at the risk of sounding like an idiot... how did I get here, and how long was I asleep?"

"Yeah, that knock-out pill really hit you, huh? Goldie says you did walk off the plane yourself – kind of zombie-like, though – then Kin carried you, smuggled you up the service elevator from the back entrance." Sally scratched her head, then twisted a strand of hair, looking slightly embarrassed as she indicated Crys's clothes, draped over the back of the desk chair. "I... I hope it was okay that I put you in your jammies? I figured you'd probably sleep better without your gear on."

"That was kind of you... thanks very much," Crys replied, relieved to find that it had been Sally taking care of her. *Marigold would have put me into lingerie of some sort,* Crys thought with a grin, *just in case the world's press should somehow get into the room.*

Sally kicked her legs free of the blanket and stood up. "I won't normally sleep in your room," she added. "Goldie and Kin told me I should last night, in case you were disoriented when you woke up or something. Plus, if you'd woken in the night, you might have wandered across the hall, and that could've been ugly." The orange-haired makeup artist shook her head, the thought bringing a dismal look to her face.

"Oh?"

"Two-room suite, of course," Sally explained. "Blade's sleeping it off in the room across. He's been... a bit messed up for the last forty-eight, poor fucked-up smackhead. I guess you might as well know – all the crew knows – we thought we'd be making a trip to the ER Sunday night. Luckily, he came around on his own, this time. And Jed's in there watching over him now."

"Holy God!" Crys whispered, her hands involuntarily rising to her mouth in shock. She hadn't seen it, hadn't realized.

Seeing the expression on Crys's face, Sally said, "Oh, honey, I'm sorry! You... you *did* know he struggles with a heroin addiction, didn't you?"

"Well, I... I guess... no, it never occurred to me..." *Stupid,* she told herself, *so stupid of me not to see it, not to know.*

Sally sighed, sitting back down and looking at her fingernails as though she could find some answers in the blue nail polish she wore. "It used to be really bad, but he did go to a rehab center while we were prepping for this tour, and things have been better since then; still, there's always the temptation for him. This time was... pretty bad... worse than I've ever seen him. Dunno if he'll wanna go back to the clinic, or if he can get clean by himself, or what – it'll mess with the tour, though, if he needs to go away again."

"Maybe there's something I can do to help?" Crys offered, focusing on sympathy, trying not to let disgust and fear overwhelm her. *Heroin.*

"I think that's what we're all counting on – that he won't do it in front of you, that he won't want to corrupt you – so you'll be helping just by being around him. You're such a nice, decent, innocent girl; you've probably never even seen someone strung out on smack, hmm?"

Crys shook her head, feeling naive. "If I have, I didn't know it."

"Don't look so sad, honey. You're lucky not to have experience with this shit. And Blade's fine this time, honestly; he'll just feel like crap for a bit." She wrinkled her nose and shuddered. "Better not to think about it. Are you hungry, Crys? Marigold said we should call room service; she doesn't want you seen eating with the crew."

"A cup of coffee would be great, honestly."

"You should eat something too." Sally got up and took the menu from the desk, flipped it across to the bed where Crys still sat. "Have a look. Muffins, fruit salad... a bagel with smoked salmon and cream cheese... do you good."

Crys smiled. "You're probably right." She hopped out of bed and collected yesterday's clothes from the back of the desk chair, carrying them to the bathroom to dress, while Sally picked up the hotel phone and asked to be connected to Room Service.

♥

Hours later, Sally having gone off to a crew meeting, Crys lay on the bed in her hotel room reading the current issue of *Cosmopolitan*, which Marigold had brought for her. She flipped from article to article without paying much attention to the content. Playing sudoku on her iPad had long since paled as entertainment, and though the hotel claimed to have wireless internet access, she hadn't been able to connect to it. She couldn't go out – Marigold had asked her not to go out alone until she'd had a bit more practice dealing with the media – and she had nothing to do.

She rolled off the bed and stood up, deciding that she needed a change of scenery. *Even if it's only from my bedroom to the sitting room of the suite,* she thought, *it's still better than being trapped in here another minute.* Cracking open her bedroom door, she peeked around... all was quiet. White plush carpet muffled her bare feet.

The sitting room was decorated in much the same way as the bedroom, with granite and cherry wood and mirrors. Here, chocolate-brown leather couches with chocolate velvet cushions matched the bedcovering in her room, everything modern and chunky. As in the bedroom, a plasma television on one wall disguised itself as artwork, with a slideshow of impressionist paintings eternally cycling. Muted lighting concealed in the ceiling washed the room in a soft pale glow. The room gave an overall impression of being unoccupied – a space that no one was using.

In the silence, Crys heard a faint noise. It sounded – did it really? – like someone retching. Because the noise could not have come from anywhere else, she glanced at the door to the other bedroom, and saw that it was slightly ajar. *He's in there – Blade is in there.* Crys hadn't seen him since he'd walked away to board his flight after that earth-shaking kiss. Sally had said he wasn't feeling too well. *I mustn't go in there.* And then she heard more retching and what sounded like swearing. With Jed at the crew meeting – Sally had said she'd walk down with him – Blade had to be alone. *No one should be feeling like that alone,* Crys thought.

She crept to the door, pushed it with one cautious fingertip. It swung inward a few inches; no resistance. She couldn't see anything; the room was dim, unlit, drapes closed. "Blade?" she called, keeping her voice soft. "Blade, may I come in?"

"Fuck off," his voice snarled, thick as though he'd been crying or had a cold.

"You don't sound too good. Is there anything I can do to help?"

Dead silence for a moment. Crys turned to creep away, and then she heard him call to her. "Come in if you must. You might as well see what a fuck-up I am."

With a deep breath, she gathered up her nerve and pushed the door all the way open. The room stank of vomit.

Blade was not in the bed, or on the couch; Crys had to scan the room to locate him. He sat in a corner, on the floor, his back against the wall. He held a slime-smeared hand towel, and between his knees was a plastic tub into which he had evidently just vomited. As she drew near, she saw that he was shivering, eyes and nose running, as though he were suffering from some kind of terrible flu. His inner arms were covered with neat squares of gauze, held in place by surgical tape. "Pretty, huh?" he muttered, with a weak attempt at a smile.

Steeling herself against the smell, she reached out to take the bowl from him. "Are you going to be sick again, or can I take this and dump it?" she asked.

He shuddered in revulsion. "I'll be okay. Nothing left to sick up, anyhow."

"Just sit there. I'll be right back." Crys held her breath as she carried the bowl to Blade's en suite bathroom and dumped the contents into the toilet before washing the bowl out in the bathtub – ginger and honey scents from the fancy hotel soap did a little, at least, to replace the unpleasant odor. She snagged a fresh bath towel from the vanity counter, and headed back into the bedroom.

Blade had risen to his feet while she'd been out of the room, but it seemed to have made him light-headed, because he was leaning into the wall with his eyes closed. "I'm... so sorry," he said in a low voice, so low she could hardly hear him. He swayed alarmingly.

"Good God, Blade – you're going to fall down, then where would we be? I wouldn't be able to lift you." He cracked a slight laugh at that, and Crys came over and took his arm. "Come on, you should get into bed."

"Got some nasty shit on my t-shirt," he said, looking over at the clean bed and then down at himself with distaste.

"Take it off, then. I'll find you a clean one." Jed, or someone, had unpacked for Blade; his suitcase was empty in the wardrobe, and Crys found a stack of clean t-shirts in one of the dresser drawers. There were also a few pairs of silk boxer shorts printed with wild designs. Face flaming, she picked out a pair with lipstick kisses printed all over – by far the tamest of the lot – and took the neatly folded grey t-shirt from the top of the stack to go with it. When she turned back to Blade, she found him sitting on the edge of the bed, shirtless, the long line of his bare back and firmly-muscled shoulders awe-inspiring even in such a currently shaky state. *I can't possibly want to... to touch him... not while he's sick like this...* Crys fought the urge to stroke that long back, massage those powerful shoulders, caress the smooth musculature of his chest. *I'm warped,* she thought, *and such a fool.* "Here's a clean shirt, Blade. Better wipe your face first, though – hold on a moment."

She darted into the washroom and dampened a washcloth with warm water. Returning to the bed where Blade sat, she held the washcloth out to him, and then – when he didn't immediately take it from her – she began with hesitant gentle strokes to cleanse his face for him, wiping away snot and tears and vomit, tenderly running the edge of the washcloth around the steel rings in his eyebrow and lip to be sure no foul matter remained caught there. Blade's eyes drifted closed with a sigh of relief as she worked; he appeared to be enjoying the caressing warmth of the rough cloth. Greatly daring, she worked right down the long column of his neck, touching his collarbone and the top of his spine, making certain that all the unpleasantness was washed away. And then she knelt in front of him and took his strong beautiful hands, first one and then the other, and scrubbed away the slime and smell from them too.

Feeling a tingle of awareness at the back of her neck, she glanced up to find his eyes open – puffy and bloodshot but still gorgeous – gazing at her with the most incredible expression of vulnerability and sorrow. "Thank you, Crys," he murmured. "You're a saint."

"No, I just... you looked pretty miserable... I couldn't leave you like that." She snatched up the clean grey t-shirt, which had fallen to the floor, and held it out to him. "Here, put this on." She tried not to stare as he pulled it over his head, with a strange sense that watching a man dress was somehow more intimate than just seeing him bare-chested. The front of the t-shirt read 'Free Love'.

Blade saw the look on her face as she took in the words, and a shaky laugh bubbled from his mouth. "You're such an innocent kid," he said. "It's kind of sweet."

"Then you won't mind if I turn my back while you take your jeans off. I, ah, found you a pair of boxers in the drawer." She pointed to where they lay on the bed, feeling too shy to pick them up and hand them to him.

"I didn't get anything on–"

"You'll be more comfortable. Really. I don't know why you were dressed and out of bed, anyway."

"All right, then." With an effort, Blade got to his feet and began to unbutton his jeans – at once, Crys whipped around to face away from

84

him, her eyes squeezed closed as an extra shield against the rustling noises of his undressing right behind her. She gritted her teeth against a terrible desire to turn and look, to see more of him than she had any right to see – which would be so wrong, especially with him in this weakened state. Resolutely she waited with her eyes glued shut, until she heard him say, "You can turn around now, sweetheart."

She opened her eyes, but didn't turn. "Oh, no. You hop into bed first." The mental image of Blade in a pair of silky boxers was not going to make it easier to stay professional and friendly with him, and she knew that seeing him without his jeans on could only make things worse.

"There. I'm all covered up."

"Good." Crys turned, and truly enough, Blade was sitting upright in the bed with a corner of the duvet drawn across his lap. "You're supposed to get comfortable, silly!" Going over to him, she propped up the pillows for him to lean against, and gave the top sheet and duvet a tug so that they covered his long bare legs properly. Passed him tissues for his nose, which was running again, and moved a garbage pail to a convenient spot for disposing of used ones. Touched a hand to his forehead and found it clammy, noticed goose bumps and a dampness of sweat already on his t-shirt. "Are you feeling queasy again?" she asked, reaching for the plastic basin she'd cleaned out earlier, placing it next to him on the bed with the clean towel under it.

"A little," he admitted, mopping his eyes and nose with a tissue. "Mostly just achy and restless, though. It's... kind of like having the flu. I want to sleep and can't, and it's no good trying to get up either. It'll pass; I... I've been through this before."

Crys sat down on the bed next to him. "Blade, I don't want to pry... but if you want to... well, talk about stuff, I'll listen," she offered, hoping he wouldn't take offence at the suggestion.

He shrugged, a wry smile passing across his face. "Not much to tell. Went to rehab before the tour started, got straightened out. But touring's kind of deadly – rocking out on stage one minute, killing time in a hotel room the next – and then... well, there was Kin's fake-girlfriend plan freaking me out too. None of the guys knew I'd started using again, though, and it was just a little; I had it under control. Only I got kind of fucked up on the weekend."

"Is it... over?" Crys asked, trying to keep the sadness and sympathy she felt out of her voice. With all her heart, she just wanted to hold and comfort this unhappy man until the horrors passed.

"I hope so," he said, with a rueful grimace. "I'm trying."

"You said Kin's plan was freaking you out..." Crys spoke slowly, trying to think of some solution – any solution – other than the one she was about to give him. But there could be no other choice. "If... if my being here, my role in Kin's plan, is making things tougher for you... I'd understand if you wanted me to... to just g-go home. I don't care about the contract penalties – I won't be a part of making you go back to doing h-heroin." She choked out the words, her throat tightening, but she meant it. It would be better to spend the rest of her life without his glowing presence than to feel that he might overdose and die because of her.

Blade looked appalled at the thought. "Crys, the one thing I never imagined was that Kin would find me a sweet little friend to nurse me back out of hell. I don't want you to leave... though you might not care to be associated with a smack-head junkie freak like me, now that you know."

"Don't call yourself names," Crys told him firmly. "Sure, it's a little scary, but... I'm not a quitter. I'll stay as long as you want me to." Their eyes met, and it suddenly wasn't clear whether they were talking about that room and that night, or Kin's plan and the Smidge tour, or something greater and more cosmic than that.

Blade opened his mouth, about to say something, and then closed it again.

Seeking a distraction, Crys stood and picked up the soiled t-shirt and jeans and hand towel, taking them to the closet where she guessed she would find a hotel laundry bag. "No, sweetheart; can't have those going to the hotel laundry," he said when he saw what she was doing. "No one's supposed to know I'm going through this again – a stupid fuck who can't stay clean." He groaned, whether in discomfort or self-disgust Crys wasn't sure, and wiped his tearing eyes with a tissue. Blew his nose again.

"I'll just put them in the bag for now to get them off the floor."

He nodded acceptance of that. "Jed will sort it out. Nothing fazes him – bet you didn't know he was an ER nurse – Kin found him for me when... when things were... well, Jed's saved my life at least three times now. He's a good guy."

"Yes." Crys smiled, pulling the drawstring tight on the laundry bag. "I'm glad he saved your life. Sorry he needed to, but glad he did."

Distantly, a door opened. The sound of conversation drifted in to them, Sally's laughter and Jed's deeper voice. Crys dropped the bag of dirty clothes and spun around to face the open doorway, just as Jed came striding in, saying, "Blade, how're you doing, buddy? Hey, you got back into bed, huh? I've got your meds!" He tossed a paper pharmacy bag to Blade, and then caught sight of Crys standing by the closet. "Crys! I didn't figure–"

Embarrassed though she had no reason to be, Crys ducked her head. "I was... just leaving anyway. Excuse me." She headed for the door.

"Jed, Crys isn't in her – oh!" Sally, bursting through the door, nearly crashed into Crys. "There you are!"

"I..."

"Come on, I've brought you some lunch," said Sally, linking her arm through Crys's and hurrying her out of Blade's room and back into her own across the hall. "Sorry to rush you, but Goldie wants to see you as soon as you've eaten, and anyway Jed has his work cut out for him getting Blade sorted before sound check – best to leave 'em to it!"

"Sound check?" Crys asked, and then it hit her – they must have a show tonight. To hide the fact that he was detoxing, Blade would have to play.

♥

Marigold had been shopping. Standing in the doorway, Crys stared in amazement: the PR woman's suite overflowed with bags and boxes from various stores. Upscale ribbon and tissue paper peeped from most of the bags. A garment rack stood in the center of the room, and a heap of padded hangers filled one corner of the couch. An impressive-looking garment steamer sat next to the rack, hissing softly to itself, as Marigold drew a pale pink satin slip and matching robe from one of the many bags, pushing aside tissue paper and ribbon. A quick pass with the steamer appeared to satisfy her critical eye, and she hung the elegant lingerie on the rack, fingering the dainty ruffled-lace trim with a privately appreciative smile.

Sally cleared her throat. "Maybe you'd rather be handling Smidge's wardrobe," she commented, then added, "Crys is here."

"I only like dealing with women's clothes," Marigold said, in a tone that suggested it was an ongoing line of conversation between the two of them – which one might expect, given Marigold's acid-green low-rise jeans and cropped teal-sequined sweater compared to Sally's baggy jeans and t-shirt. Of course, Sally didn't need any extra special effects with her bright orange hair and spectacular boobs. Marigold turned to glance at Crys, which became a sharper look at the cargo pants and hoodie Crys wore. "Well, I suppose you're comfortable. But it's important to create a habit of being image-conscious all the time; cameras are everywhere, and I don't want you to learn the hard way that nine times out of ten it's the ugly pictures that end up in the tabloids and on the gossip websites. Always ask yourself: would I want to be all over the internet looking like this? And if the answer is no – fix it!"

Crys ran a hand through her hair, trying not to feel irritated at Marigold's coaching – if looking like a proper rock star's girlfriend was all she could do for Blade right now, she told herself, then she ought to just cooperate. "I can do that."

"That's what I like to hear." Marigold bent over her shopping bounty, hunting through the bags until she found what she was looking for. "I've found you some fabulous things; check out what you're wearing tonight!" She moved three of the bags onto the couch.

"Marigold, can I leave Crys with you for now?" Sally asked. "I need to make some wardrobe adjustments to hide Blade's monitor." When

Crys looked up in alarm, Sally shook her head. "It's no big deal, Crys – the clonidine can cause low blood pressure, so we need to know if we have to get him off the stage."

"Right, no big deal," Crys said, and tried to believe it.

Marigold nodded. "I'll make sure Crys gets into the boys' limo to go to sound check. I won't be down until showtime, got some other business – but buzz me if there's an incident of any sort."

"Good stuff. See you at the show." Sally raised a hand in farewell, and headed out the door.

"Right, let's get straight to business." Marigold tossed Crys a small pink bag. "Get these on to start with." When Crys looked around for the washroom, Marigold laughed. "Don't be shy, girl! What you've got, I've got too – just get changed, already." Marigold turned away, working through the bags and boxes of purchases, hanging up assorted items of clothing as she went, steaming out creases as necessary.

Inside the pink bag was a black lacy push-up bra and matching thong, and a pair of fishnet thigh-highs. *Stripper gear.* Crys poked dubiously at the delicate lace. "I thought I was supposed to look like a good girl."

"Just trust me," Marigold replied. "You need to fit Smidge's look, and Blade's look. That's what I'm doing. Your face tells the good-girl story without my help."

"Okay. I'm dressed... undressed, that is."

"Good. Oh, cute – I thought those would work nicely on you!" The tops of the black fishnets had pale pink ribbon threaded through the black lace trim, tied like old-fashioned garters with little bows. Matching pale pink ribbons adorned the bra and thong. Then Marigold took a second bag from the couch, larger and heavier this time. "Here's what I've picked out for tonight; put these on." 'These' were a black leather miniskirt and a shimmery top, black shot through with silver, so that it shifted and changed with every movement.

Crys's eyes lit up, and she wriggled into the splendid top at once – it fit her perfectly, clinging and flowing like dark liquid metal. The miniskirt felt frighteningly short, but it covered the essentials, and she had to admit that it suited the outfit. "Will I wear the same boots from before?"

Marigold nodded approvingly. "Good choice." She looked at Crys, considering the total picture. "Oops, I forgot the belt! Here you go." From yet another bag, she drew out a rhinestone-studded belt, all flashes of white light, and buckled it low on Crys's hips. "Very sexy. You can wear the diamond earrings with this outfit again, and your wristband too. Run back to your room now, and get your boots and accessories on. The boys'll be ready to leave for sound check in about half an hour, and – shit, Sally's probably left for the venue already; I'll have to do your face for you. Go on, be quick."

❤

A sharp knock sounded on her door, and a voice that Crys recognized as Jed's called out, "Time to go, Crys!"

"Coming!" she answered, jumping up in what was almost a panic. *Why am I feeling shy? This is ridiculous!* She grabbed her leather jacket and pulled it on. Hurried to the door on nervous feet. Opened it.

Jed waited there with Blade, both of them in leather jackets, ready to go; Jed carried a small black bag in one hand, and steadied the guitar case slung over Blade's shoulder with the other. Blade's eyebrows rose as he took in Crys's outfit, and she wished that she could hide her lower half from his eyes – what must he think of his 'sweet friend' now, tarted up like a stripper off to work?

"The rest of the boys are already in the limo," said Jed; "we'd better go down. How are you holding up, Blade?"

Blade groaned. "I'll manage," he said, "but it's going to be a rough night."

"Sure you don't want me to take your guitar?" Jed asked, and Blade shook his head in an irritated negative, although he looked as though the weight of it would overbalance him. As they headed down the hall to the elevator, Jed passed the black bag to Crys. "Here. You'd better take the babysitter bag, since you'll actually be with him in the limo."

"Babysitter bag?"

"Barf bags, tissues, decongestant for the runny nose, ibuprofen and heat packs for the muscle aches. Lemon drops for dry mouth. I've got an extra dose of clonidine on me if it's absolutely necessary, but... it's a sedative, which means he's coping on the lowest possible dose to control the worst of the detox symptoms. Not comfortable, but hopefully functional."

Crys looked over at Blade, whose slow unsteady walk suggested aches and general unwellness. He didn't look functional. She reached out and took his free hand, wanting only to give support and comfort, and was gratified when his large hand curled around her small one with a squeeze of appreciation.

As the elevator dropped smoothly toward the hotel lobby, Crys saw that Jed kept his eyes focused on the display counting down the floors. When they had mere seconds left before the elevator would reach the lobby and open its doors, he turned to Blade. "You're on your own now, buddy. I'm riding down with Phil. I'll see you backstage, okay?"

Blade nodded, shifting the guitar more firmly onto his shoulder just as the elevator doors slid open. "Okay." And they were walking through the hotel lobby, people watching and waving, cameras flashing, and Blade straightened his spine and waved and smiled as though nothing at all was wrong. Crys, learning, smiled too as though she were thrilled that all these people were watching them. Blade's hand tightened convulsively on hers, and she saw him grit his teeth against a wave of nausea – but it passed, and then they were at the limousine.

With a murmured "thanks" to the bodyguard who opened the door for them, Crys bent and climbed in, glancing around to see where she should sit. But that was solved for her as Blade climbed in behind her; he caught her around the waist and pulled her down beside him, so that she landed between him and the drummer Dice, with Angel and Easy sitting across. Blade's guitar rested between his knees, with his free arm curled protectively around it.

"Those are cute," said Dice with a grin, his eyes on her lap – and Crys looked down in dismay to see that as she'd sat down, the ribbon-trimmed tops of her fishnet stockings peeked into view from under her suddenly-way-too-short leather skirt. She tried to tug the skirt down, and when that didn't work she did her best to fold her hands over the offending ribbons.

Easy laughed, clearly enjoying the view in a way that made Crys uncomfortable. "Don't be shy, baby doll," he said. "We're enjoying the show."

She felt Blade tense up in the seat beside her, but before he could say or do anything, Angel lifted a calming, warning hand. "Show a bit of respect, Easy – Miss Murphy is here to do a job and doesn't need your crap." His laid-back voice like melting chocolate had an instant effect on the others – Easy snorted contemptuously, but he stopped eyeballing her thighs, and Blade relaxed against the limousine's comfortable seating.

"Please call me Crys," she said. "I'd find... all this... a lot easier if you'd just let me fit in and help out where I can."

Angel laughed, as the limo pulled out of the hotel driveway and into traffic. "You want to help, Crys? You'd better get out a barf bag. Car rides aren't pleasant when you're detoxing." He turned to Blade, asking, "How're you doing, dumbass?" Despite the appellation, he spoke in a tone of utmost sympathy verging on tenderness.

"Been better." Blade's eyes were closed now, his face white. Crys realized that Angel hadn't been joking, and fumbled at the drawstring-and-toggle arrangement holding the babysitter bag closed. She got a white motion-sickness bag out and opened just in time, as he reached for it in desperation, bringing it to his mouth and retching. Disgusted, Easy pulled headphones from his pocket and hooked them into his ears, turning away to stare out the window and groove to a beat no one else could hear.

"That's gotta be hell, man," Dice commented, averting his gaze to give Blade the illusion of privacy.

Angel smiled, eyes serious with a bitter memory. "It is." When Crys looked at him in puzzlement, he met her eyes without flinching. "I was the one who gave Blade his first hit of heroin – tied the rubber tubing around my best friend's arm and stuck the needle into his vein myself," he confessed, his face bleak and sad. "I'd discovered heroin first, you see, while he was still fooling with pot and cocaine. I just wanted to share that amazing feeling, but... it got out of control." The pain on Angel's face became so pronounced that tears welled up in Crys's eyes in sympathy. "The first time he overdosed, the guilt hit me – I checked into a clinic the next day and came out clean. And I've watched him struggle with it ever since."

"Not your fault," Blade rasped, hands fumbling as he tried to twist closed the sick-bag in his lap. Crys took it from him and sealed it properly, dropping it into a waste container hooked to the limousine's built-in bar. She looked inside the babysitter bag, to see if she could find anything that might give him some relief.

"There are some lemon drops in here, if you'd like...?" she asked him, holding out one of the cellophane-wrapped candies. At least it would freshen his mouth.

"Thanks, sweetheart – d'you think you could find me an ibuprofen to go with it?"

Crys found the ibuprofen too.

The limousine fell silent, each one of them lost in thought, until they arrived at the arena where they were to play. "Should I take the sick-bag out of the limo?" Crys asked Angel, mindful of how Blade had told her that the hotel laundry mustn't see his soiled clothes.

"Better leave it – there's a chance the limo people will go through our garbage, sure, but it'd be much worse if someone photographed you carrying it."

"Right."

And then they were out of the limousine and hurrying toward the arena's staff entrance – cameras flashing all around them – Crys with her arm linked through Blade's, Angel walking close on his other side to make sure he didn't stumble or drop his guitar, Dice and Easy flanking them like an honor guard. It felt like an eternity, walking up the concrete ramp to the door, smiling and waving and hoping so hard that nothing untoward should be caught on film. Press stringers shouted for quotes and comments, but only Dice called back, "No time, guys, sorry." As they filed through the door, away from the press, Jed waited, and Crys was able to relinquish Blade into his care. Jed, looking the same as he had the first time she'd met him – skull-patterned bandana on his head, Smidge crew t-shirt and all – ushered Blade away down the hall, leaving the others to follow.

Dice, walking next to Crys, told her with earnest sincerity, "It pays to be polite to those press guys. You never know when you're going to need some good karma. See how they're always looking for mud to throw at Blade, because he hasn't been civil to them – they'll crucify him if they catch on that he's detoxing again."

"We can protect him, though – can't we?" she asked.

"Depends." Dice shrugged. "Not much we can do if he passes out onstage or is too zonked by the clonidine to play decently. But short of that, yes, we can hide the evidence. Angel and Jed are good at this stuff – and you're being a little superstar about it all."

"That's for sure," agreed Angel, overhearing them. "When we heard that PR wanted to bring a fake girlfriend on board to give Blade a better image, we thought we'd get stuck with some airhead chick who'd need babysitting all the time – and here you are handing out barf bags and propping him up in front of the cameras. Makes me proud of you, kid, I can tell you that!"

Crys looked up at Angel. "I only wish there was more I could do for him."

"Just be there for him, Crys – that's all any of us can do."

Afterward, all they remembered was that the concert had been a nightmare. Twice the boys had needed to find a way to get Blade briefly off the stage when his blood pressure had dropped dangerously low. Three times, he'd rushed backstage himself to vomit. At sound check, they'd decided to strike any songs with more challenging guitar solos from the set list – even so, on a couple of songs toward the end of the night, Angel had been forced to take over as lead guitar, all of them hoping no one would notice that Blade was just playing rhythm.

"We've done all this shit before," Sally had said to Crys as they watched from the side of the stage – Sally watching for any summons to run up and take care of a makeup or wardrobe issue, Crys just watching Blade. "Smidge has played with Blade either high or detoxing more times than I can count. There was a little while when both Blade and Angel were high all the time; those were scary concerts..."

"No doubt," Crys agreed, her eyes wide. If this was a disaster obvious even to her untrained eyes, how much worse might it have been if Angel were unable to take over the lead guitar on those songs, or joke and talk with the audience while Blade sat offstage with his head between his knees until the dizziness passed? *Please, God, just let us get through this night,* she thought – and then she wondered how and when Smidge had become 'us' instead of 'them' in her thoughts and her heart.

♥

Immediately after the concert, Jed upped Blade's medication to a dose that would actually give him some comfort, and he was staggering with the sedative effect by the time they reached the hotel.

Easy didn't wait to lend his assistance – the moment the car door was opened, he was out of there and off upstairs, winking and waving to any adoring fans who might be watching. The lone bodyguard who'd ridden back with them in the front of the limousine was left looking back and forth, unsure whether to follow Easy or stay with the others, though ultimately his loyalty was to the larger group.

Angel and Dice got Blade inside and into the elevator by draping his arms around their shoulders and helping him walk between them, trying to look like they were just drunk and having a good time. The bodyguard hovered protectively. Crys followed, holding Blade's guitar with utmost care: the lucky girlfriend getting to carry her famous boyfriend's instrument. Although in truth she carried it only because he couldn't, she did feel lucky – she'd seen how he always chose to carry it himself, and knew that she was holding something infinitely precious to him.

Upstairs, Angel and Dice stopped trying to fake it and just plain carried Blade the rest of the way to his room, whisking him in so quickly that Crys barely caught a glimpse of his shoulder and the top of his head before he disappeared. She was still holding his guitar. Feeling that he might miss his instrument if he woke in the night and couldn't find it, she tapped on the door.

It opened at once. "Yes?" Jed asked, looking slightly forbidding at any further disturbance of his patient.

"I'm so sorry to interrupt," she said, holding out Blade's guitar case. "But I... sort of think he'd worry if he woke up and his guitar wasn't there."

Jed and Angel looked at each other with an odd expression on their faces – sharing some thought that didn't need to be put into words – surprised and speculative and thoughtful all at once. "You're right, kid," Angel said at last, taking the guitar case from Crys. "Sometimes it's his sanity and salvation, and he doesn't like to be parted from it."

Crys smiled, liking the way Angel respected his friend's quirk rather than making fun of it. She caught Jed's impatient glance at his watch, and at once backed toward the door, saying, "Well, I should be getting to bed... Goodnight." Angel and Dice said their goodnights as well, heading out of the suite and down the hall to their own beds.

"I hope today hasn't been too distressing for you," Jed said with a hint of concern, as she was turning toward the doorway of her own bedroom. "I've got some mild sedatives in my kit, if you're going to have trouble getting to sleep."

"No, thank you. I'll be out the moment I close my eyes," she assured him, not wanting anything to do with drugs of any sort after what she'd seen that day.

"Sleep well, then," he said kindly, vanishing back inside Blade's room and closing the door.

chapter

6

O N WEDNESDAY MORNING, THE ALARM ON CRYS'S PHONE woke her far earlier than she would have liked. Even as she swung her tired legs out of bed and stretched, she could hear a commotion in the hall, and Jed's voice snapping, "Keep it down, you idiots."

"Where d'you want them?" came another man's voice, not one Crys recognized.

"Line them up next to her door, they can go inside once she's up," Jed ordered. Line what up in front of her door? Crys hopped off the bed, reached for whatever nearest clothes she could find, and stopped – Marigold had been clear about never leaving her room in something she wouldn't want to be photographed in. *Not last night's concert gear, not at this unholy hour.* She rummaged in her duffel bag for the vintage-faded jeans she'd worn to see Blade off at the airport back home, and the grey sleeveless Smidge t-shirt. Dug out a pale grey cashmere cardigan of her own – a gift from her mother – and laced up her old sneakers, for lack of a better early-morning choice. Dashed into the bathroom to wash her face. *I'll shower later,* she thought, *as soon as I figure out what's going on.*

Heeding Marigold's advice, Crys spared a few precious seconds for moisturizer and mascara, and a dab of lip gloss. Tied her hair back, with a bit of hairspray to keep the wispy bits in place – checked everything in the mirror. *Oh, good God, I look about seventeen!* But at least decently covered and not looking like she'd just rolled out of bed, she walked

97

over and opened her door, curious to see what mysterious items had been lined up next to her door.

A luggage set, evidently. Two huge suitcases, three medium-sized ones, and a matching carry-on bag were neatly lined up along the wall between her door and the suite's main door. *Empty?* She tried to lift the nearest large suitcase. *Not empty.* The shopping bounty she had previously seen in Marigold's room must now be packed away inside the mammoth array of luggage.

Jed popped out of Blade's room, and saw her. "Oh – you're up and dressed! Good. Could you come and sit with Blade while I run down to coordinate with Zachary and Phil? He's pretty much sedated, but I'd rather not take any chances, so if you don't mind..."

"Sure, but... Jed, what's going on this morning?"

Jed laughed. "Didn't anyone tell you? We're moving on to Portland today, time for the next stop on the merry-go-round." He gestured for her to proceed into Blade's room. "You don't need to do anything, just sit by the bed and – on the off-chance he wakes up – don't let him leave the room. I'll be right back." With that, he hurried out the door to the hall, whipping out his phone as he went.

Crys tiptoed into Blade's room, blinking as her eyes adjusted to the low light. What little light there was filtered in, dim and grey, from around the edges of the closed drapes, and some light did bleed in from the open door behind her. The duvet from the bed had been thrown on the couch, and only a sheet covered Blade's long body – Crys registered that much, and jerked her eyes away, cheeks burning although Blade appeared to be oblivious and no one else was there to observe her reaction. A chair had been pulled up to the side of the bed, and a magazine lay open on it, with a flashlight on top – Jed must have been reading by flashlight to pass the time, after he'd finished packing for Blade – a pair of suitcases waited by the wardrobe, ready to go.

After cautiously transferring the magazine and flashlight to the bedside table, Crys sat down on the chair, keeping her eyes averted from the bed. A minute passed, maybe. She looked at the toes of her shoes, at the white-carpeted floor. Over at the drapes, at the suitcases by the wardrobe. It seemed wrong, somehow, to let herself watch him as he slept – an invasion of his privacy, an intimacy that he hadn't granted her.

She wouldn't have looked if he'd stayed quiet, as comatose as when she'd first walked in. But Blade groaned, a noise of distress and dark dreams, and it startled her into looking without meaning to – he lay spread-eagled on his stomach, face turned into the pillow, dark hair rumpled with sleep; the sheet had slipped down to expose his bare shoulders and did little to conceal the rest, clinging to the lines of his back and legs, the curve of his buttocks. *Oh sweet God!* The perfect shape of him gave Crys the strangest feeling of being out of breath. *Is he even wearing anything under the sheet?* He lay there, so strong of body and yet so vulnerable in sleep, and she sat on her hands to control the powerful urge to touch him. And then he groaned again – writhing in the grip of some nightmare – and twisted over onto his back with a jerking motion, fighting the bedsheets as he did so.

Crys's eyes widened as he thrashed about, first muttering curses, then whimpering in pain, bare bruised needle-marked arms and hair-roughened legs now free of the sheet which had become twisted and tangled around him. *I can't bear this,* she thought, and leaned forward to touch a soothing hand to his forehead. "It's just a dream," she told him gently, softly. "It's just a dream. You're okay."

His eyes opened, his beautiful clear deep hazel eyes, gazing up at her dream-dazed and haunted. "Hold me," he whispered, his voice a barely audible rasp. "Stay with me, Crys. Hold me." And he reached for her, pulling her down into his arms, cradling her against him as he pressed his lips against her forehead and eyes.

Lying against him, touching bare skin and feeling his needful kisses all over her face – the steel of his lip ring contrasting with the gentle pressure of his mouth – Crys felt herself falling, shifting from desire and bedazzlement into something deeper. A fragile new feeling unfurled itself inside her, a bright tenderness so powerful it made her shiver. No holding back. *Why deny what I'm aching for?* And when his mouth finally found hers, she opened herself completely to him, drowning mind and body in the absolute sweetness of the moment.

A dry cough behind her brought Crys suddenly back into awareness. Blade's head fell back against the pillow, his eyes drifting closed, the brief tension and hunger fading from his face and limbs, replaced by a look of peaceful sleeping bliss. Jed stood by the side of the bed, looking at her in complete surprise. "Well, I didn't know it was that way between you two," he said, as Crys peeled herself off the bed and stood to face him.

"It... it wasn't, before... I don't know why..." She stumbled over the words, not even sure how to explain the urgent intimacy that had overtaken them in that earth-shattering kiss – from which Blade had just drifted back to sleep.

Jed sat down on the edge of the bed, gesturing for Crys to take the chair. "Do you want to talk about it?" he asked.

"What's to talk about?" she said. "Unless you want to hear me confess that I'm an idiot?"

"You're not an idiot. But he's half-sedated; he wasn't operating with his conscious mind, and I doubt he'll remember it, unless to think he dreamed."

"A lovely dream, then." She tried to keep the sadness out of her voice, and knew as she spoke that she hadn't managed it.

"Crys." Jed placed a comforting hand on her shoulder, and waited until she met his eyes. "He has a long struggle ahead of him. I would wish for him, that he did have a loving partner to help him through it, and you've already shown that you don't run from his dark side."

"What are you saying?"

"Nothing." Jed smiled kindly, patting and then releasing her shoulder. "Just making general observations." Then, more briskly, he suggested, "I suspect that you haven't had any breakfast – you'll feel much more the thing with some solid food in you – can I order you something from room service? I was just going to call for something myself anyway."

The band had originally been scheduled to fly from Seattle to Portland first thing in the morning, to take advantage of a full twenty-four hours' rest before gearing back up for the Thursday night show, but Blade was in no fit state to board a plane. "The airport's a bad place for him right now," Marigold said, and Kin agreed. It would be too risky to try to sneak him aboard, with the flight plan filed in advance and any number of vultures with cameras sneaking around.

Traveling by road was the most sensible solution – so Marigold and Kin boarded the jet in the usual manner, along with the flight crew and Scott the photographer, but it took off while the paparazzi were still waiting for the band. Meanwhile, Blade was quietly assisted onto one of Smidge's crew coaches.

Smidge's road crew traveled alongside the tour's fleet of massive eighteen-wheelers in luxury sleeper coaches with tinted windows, and it was easy enough to double up some of the crew in the other coaches to clear one for the band. Easy grumbled about how rough it was to have to go by road, but the trip took barely over three hours, with an entertainment system and a kitchenette stocked with all the usual drinks and snacks the boys were accustomed to having on their flights.

Blade slept through the entire trip, waking only briefly to use the washroom and drink some water.

Crys sat in the dressing room in Portland, watching Sally work her pre-show magic on the Smidge boys – and secretly reveling in her own transformation. Leather skirt and leather jacket, a black Smidge t-shirt with a low scissor-snipped neckline, slouchy metal-studded ankle boots. Hair sleek with gel. Sally had dusted a brush full of glitter over her eyelids and hair. *I sparkle,* Crys thought. *I shine. I fit this world – I belong.*

Dice's joker makeup turned out to be a mixture of black eyeshadow and superfine silver glitter. Sally paused to adjust a strap on one of

Angel's wings, gave an extra squirt of spray to stiffen Easy's hair. Found Blade's dog collar and buckled it on for him. She'd also pulled out wicked-looking sleeves for him made out of black leather and steel grommets – going from just above his wrists to just below his armpits, they laced up the outsides of his arms, leaving his shoulders bare, and covered the still-bruised inner arms that bore witness to his heroin binge. Sally called them 'smack sleeves' and told Crys that Angel had worn a matching red pair during the bad days when the drug had ruled the days and nights of the two band members who made up the core of Smidge. Easy played good bass and his image worked for Smidge, Crys learned, but he didn't write songs or contribute to the creative direction of the band. And Dice was slightly younger than the others, a fantastic drummer but still developing his strengths beyond the drum kit; Angel and Blade had been encouraging him to try out some of his own ideas, and he'd collaborated on one song for their latest album, but he still didn't constitute a major part of the artistic force that made Smidge what it was, and certainly hadn't back in those dark days.

Blade was starting to look better; Jed had cut down his dose of clonidine, making him so much more alert and functional compared to the train wreck he'd been. And the detox symptoms themselves were lessening a bit, the chills and muscle spasms hardly noticeable to a casual observer, the nausea mostly controlled. Crys could tell that he was still quite ill – she'd see his jaw clench, his eyes close, and she'd know that he was fighting a wave of awfulness – but he'd started to take an interest in things around him again, talking about the set list, insisting that he could manage the guitar solo in "Empty Girl" and his half of the vocals for "Love Bound."

And he didn't remember their intimacy of the night in the hotel while he'd been zonked on the clonidine. He'd greeted her easily, playfully punching her shoulder with a gentle fist as one might with a younger sibling. In a way, it was almost a relief for her that he didn't remember – nothing needed to be said, she was still just his sweet little friend.

But Crys had trouble meeting Jed's eyes for a while, knowing that he'd seen what should have been a private thing.

The concert was a good one, the band on fire, the audience responsive. Crys watched with Sally from the side of the stage again, but this time – instead of being overcome with gut-twisting anxiety for Blade to the point that she could hardly pay attention to the music at all – she could enjoy it. Standing with Sally behind one of the huge panels that formed the stage, Crys was hidden from view, but could watch the concert with a perspective that no one in the audience could ever have. On the one hand, she could see how the magic was made: she could see the straps of Angel's wings, the trap doors and taped marks on the boards, the mechanics behind the pyrotechnic effects that lit up the stage like magic. On the other hand, she was close enough to see another kind of magic: the interactions and cues the Smidge boys passed between them as things changed and unfolded throughout the concert – a wink and a grin after a near-screw-up, a mouthed curse, eye contact, inside jokes. She saw how Sally and her team supported them, always ready with beer and bottled water, chocolate bars and Red Bull. Jumping into action to accomplish wardrobe changes in the flat seconds available between songs, ready to do whatever necessary if anything went wrong. Crys thought it was fabulous. She wondered if they would let her help, in the future – she could hold a water bottle, couldn't she?

And then Angel flicked two fingers behind his back – the signal for Blade to come up and join him for the "Love Bound" duet. As Angel crooned that he wanted his freedom, the sea of fans screamed for him, though as far as Crys knew he was single anyway – the song told a story about a fictional situation. But when Blade sang about looking for his princess, a collective sigh swept around the arena, a wistful noise – every girl wanted to be somebody's princess. And Blade turned to where Crys stood hidden from the audience, and when he sang the part about bedsheets burning and one love to have and hold, his eyes met and held hers. And she didn't know what that meant at all.

♥

After the concert, Crys expected that she would sit in the dressing room while the boys took off their makeup and changed from their stage wardrobe into street clothes, before riding back to the hotel in yet another limousine. But when she followed Sally down from the stage and through the tunnels that honeycombed the non-public areas of the arena, Crys came instead to a room that reminded her of the one where she and Leah and Debbie had waited before meeting Smidge back home. The couches and carpet were blue, the walls grey, but the same Smidge banners stood in the corners, and – even as he stifled a jaw-wrenching yawn – Jed was setting out bowls of chips and candy. A bucket full of ice stood mid-floor next to a couple of flats of soft drink cans.

"Crys, honey, we've got a bunch of radio call-in winners coming through tonight, and we were thinking you might be able to help Jed out here in the guest lounge," Sally said.

Crys nodded. "Sure, that sounds like fun," she said. What else could she say? *I wanted to watch Blade take off his makeup? I wanted to be with him?* She summoned a bright smile. "Tell me what I can do to help."

"You could unpack those and put them in the ice bucket," Jed suggested, indicating the flats of cans.

"That's great," said Sally. "I'll leave you here then, Crys – I've just got to go and touch up the boys' makeup before the first guests start coming through." And with that, Sally was out the door. Crys took off her leather jacket and tucked it out of the way under Jed's desk, then knelt by the flats of soft drinks and tore away the plastic. Two by two, she lifted the cans and lowered them into the bucket of ice.

On the desk, Jed's radio buzzed an alert, and he turned to Crys, saying, "This will be the first lot. You ready?" When she nodded, he crossed to the door and opened it. There stood Marigold, in her black-leather power suit and stiletto heels, surrounded by gaggle of eager-looking girls dolled up in going-out finery, all with sprayed-up hair and big earrings. They looked to be about seventeen, and made Marigold seem that much older and more ravaged by comparison.

"Jed here is the crewperson in charge of backstage public relations," Marigold was saying to the girls, "so he will be taking care of you. Jed, this–" she indicated a freckled redhead with gold sparkly lipstick "– is Amber, the winner of KTAB 102.5FM's Smidgemania contest, and the five friends she's chosen to bring with her. Enjoy your visit with Smidge." With a nod, Marigold turned and left, radio already in hand as she headed out the door.

Crys finished putting the soft drink cans into the ice bucket and stood up.

"Welcome backstage, ladies," said Jed. "There are snacks on the table for you and drinks in the bucket here, so please help yourselves. I'll just need you to fill out these waivers before I take you in to meet the Smidge boys..." Jed's spiel, sounding all too familiar to Crys, ran on, explaining about the ban on personal photos, the professional photos that Scott would take instead to preserve the memory for them, and so on.

Jed nodded to Crys to hand out the waiver forms and ballpoint pens. Then, as the girls finished reading and signing them, he had her checking their IDs – drivers' licenses and high school student cards. Meanwhile, he used the scanner gun to zap their backstage passes and transferred the barcode stickers to their waiver forms. Amber, the contest winner, got a fluorescent yellow star, and her friends got orange ones.

The next group arrived while the first lot were still waiting. These were less glittery, more goth, and though they seemed slightly more mature than Amber's party, they were equally overexcited and worked extra hard at appearing cool to hide it. In their first year of college, maybe? "Rachel has won the KURN 97.3FM Backstage with Smidge contest," said Marigold, with a displeased look as she realized the first group was still in place. "Those boys have got to hurry it up," she grumbled to Jed. "There's a third group coming, and given that they haven't even let the first group in..." She stomped out of the room, stiletto heels clicking, radioing to Sally to find out what the problem was.

Jed began his spiel for the new group. "Welcome backstage, ladies. Crys will hand out your waiver forms. Please help yourselves to the snacks and drinks–" His radio bleeped and chattered, interrupting him. "Okay. Amber's group, I can take you in now. Rachel's group, please go ahead and fill out your paperwork, and if you have any questions, I'll answer them as soon as I get back." Then he turned to Crys, asking in an undertone, "Do you think you can manage to process them for me? Just zap the bar code on the front of each pass with the scanner gun – all you have to do is point it and press the trigger – then peel the sticker off the back and attach it to the form... you've seen me do it... pretty straightforward, right? Then a yellow star for Rachel and orange for the rest."

"I... I think so," Crys said.

"Great. Amber and company, please follow me." Jed swept the glittery girls out the door, leaving Crys in charge of six goth-looking girls maybe two or three years younger than herself.

"Are you Blade's girlfriend?" asked one, a skinny thing with blue-streaked hair.

"Y-yes," said Crys.

"Oh." That was Rachel, the contest winner, a bit chunkier than her friends, with a ring in her nose like a bull, and badly-dyed black hair. "Why are you working in here, then? How come you're not hanging out in there with him?"

Crys took a deep breath. "Well, Jed – that's the backstage PR host you met just a moment ago – he asked me to help him out tonight, because there are so many guest groups coming through..."

"Oh." Rachel thought for a moment. "Oh. Well, I suppose that's nice of you."

"You're lucky," said the blue-haired one. "Blade is so-o-o hot!" A general murmur of agreement followed.

"Yes," Crys agreed. "He is, isn't he?" They all looked at her, bug-eyed, full of questions they didn't dare ask.

The blue-haired kid blushed. "Is he, like, scary in bed?" she blurted, unable to hold the question back.

What do I say? Crys searched her mind frantically for possible responses. "Scary isn't really the right word," she said at last. She

106

thought about what it had been like when he'd kissed her, both the explosive heat of the first time and the tender sweetness of the second time. "He's... a very strong and passionate person," she said slowly, "but he does have a sweet side, though he doesn't show it often." All six girls looked absolutely awed at the thought. *Time to change the subject, before this gets way too weird.* "Okay, let's get your forms processed before Jed gets back. You want to be ready when the call comes for you to go in, right?"

"Oh, yes!" Rachel nodded, handing over her waiver form at once.

"Good. Let's start with you then, since you're the contest winner. First off, can I see some ID?"

Crys was nearly done with processing the waivers before Jed got back. She was just sticking the barcode label on the last accompanying friend's form, and reaching for the sheet of orange stickers, when he whipped through the door, holding up his radio. "That was Goldie," he said to Crys. "She's got the next group on their way now, and Scott's almost done photographing the first group. We've got to have this lot ready to go. Are those forms done?"

"Here you go." She handed him the stack of papers. "Hey – Sally isn't coming in to do makeup tonight?"

Jed shook his head, with an amused grin. "That was special for the job interviews, you might say." Then his radio buzzed, and he said, "Damn, that's the third group here already." He opened the door, and Marigold ushered six more women into the room.

These women were older, maybe in their mid to late twenties. "Jenny and her friends are here courtesy of the RockOut nightclub," Marigold was saying. *Jenny and her friends look like sluts*, Crys thought – an unusual gut reaction for her, since she was generally more than open to people with different tastes and tended to give people the benefit of the doubt. These women were pretty enough, certainly, in a hard-edged knowing way – artificially perfected bodies tarted up for Smidge's viewing pleasure, minimally wrapped, with lots of makeup and wild just-out-of-bed hair. A marijuana odor clung to them – they must have smoked a little something during the concert – and in contrast to the bouncy overexcitement of the other groups, they seemed entirely too laid-back and confident. Even as Crys was noticing these things and trying not to draw conclusions in her mind, Marigold was still talking. "Jenny, this is Jed, in charge of backstage public relations; he'll be taking care of you. Enjoy your backstage visit." And with that, Marigold was gone again.

Jed, responding to the crackle of his radio, left the waiver collection in Crys's hands again, as he led Rachel and her party down to meet the boys. At first Jenny and her friends paid no attention to Crys, too busy comparing spots on their bodies where they apparently planned to ask the Smidge boys to sign, with the goal of getting the signatures tattooed on permanently. Crys couldn't help noticing that a few scrawled signatures were already in evidence – perhaps a regular practice, a kind of collection? "Excuse me, ladies," she said at last, "I don't like to interrupt, but I do need to process your waiver forms. It'll just take a minute, if you could start by reading and signing them?"

Jenny turned. "You look like – yes, you must be Blade's new girl!" she said, with a condescending smirk. "Seen you in the papers, I know I'm right – jaded guys like him often try the innocent bit for a while; I guess it's something new. So cute, really, helping out the crew while your guy is busy meeting other girls..." She laughed, a sharp nasty laugh, but she did glance over and sign the waiver form, which she then slapped into Crys's hand. "There you go, baby doll."

It stung, enough that Crys wanted to sting back. "Helping out the crew while my guy is *working*, you mean? It's part of his job to make women like you feel special for fifteen minutes while Scott takes a picture. But maybe you didn't realize that. Could I see your ID, please?" The sour look on Jenny's face soothed Crys, and eclipsed the small bit of guilt she felt for not turning the other cheek as she probably should have. She dealt with the waiver forms in record time, zapping with the scanner gun, peeling and sticking – they were ready in a tidy pile, well before Jed returned. Finished with that, and looking for something to keep her hands busy, she straightened all the papers on Jed's desk, wiped and tidied the snack table, and mopped up the condensation wetness that had soaked the floor around the ice bucket. She tried very hard not to listen to Jenny and her friends' conversation.

Finally – and it had seemed like forever – Jed returned. He gave Crys a cheerful thumbs-up sign, which Crys took to mean that things were going well and that this group would be in and out before much longer. His radio crackled and chattered, and he summoned Jenny and her friends to follow him down to the band lounge. Crys, having already tidied up, looked around the room and picked up the two stray pretzels and one crumpled napkin that she noticed on the floor, now that the room was empty. Then she sat down on one of the couches, to wait until it was time to go.

She had a long wait.

Eventually, Sally popped her head around the door and smiled wearily. "Hey, Crys! Long night, huh?"

Crys nodded, feeling as exhausted as Sally looked.

"If you're ready to head back to the hotel now, Phil and I are taking the van – you can ride with us, if you like," Sally offered.

"That's very kind of you, but I should probably wait until the boys are done and go with them. Isn't that what Marigold would expect me to do?" Crys asked, assuming she was intended to be seen leaving with Blade. She'd been looking forward all night to the chance to sit next to him, even for just the short limousine ride back to the hotel.

Sally seemed almost uncomfortable. She came into the room and sat down on the couch next to Crys, her expression kind and even tentative – the kind of face one wears to deliver bad news. "Marigold already left. You know, it would – it really would be... better if you just came back with us now. I think the boys are... going to be back late tonight."

"But... aren't I supposed to stay with Blade?"

"You could go join them, I guess..." Sally's mouth twisted dubiously. "It's just – they're in a mood to, ah, party tonight, and he's not a celibate kind of guy, honey. Unless you're prepared to..." Her voice trailed off.

It dawned on Crys that Sally might be... was... telling her that she should not stay, that she would not be welcome in the band lounge that night. *Unless...* "Oh. Okay, I... I'll come back with you, then," she said, hoping that her face didn't show too much of what she was feeling. She couldn't help thinking of that last group of backstage-pass-winning guests – Jenny and her gang of friends, with their surgically optimal breasts all but bursting from exhibitionist clothing – hiking up skirts and unbuttoning tops as one by one the Smidge boys would choose their spots and sign themselves on the women's skin. *Sluts. Bastards.* Music pumping, drinks being passed around, maybe a joint shared from lip to lip or who knew what else, and no inhibitions to begin with, anyway. The image of Blade leaning over Jenny, placing his name on her bared hip, nearly made Crys gag. *And he's not even mine – I have no right to mind.*

"Come on, honey," said Sally. "Phil will want to get going." She looked around for Crys's jacket, drew it out from under the desk. "You'd better put this on; it's chilly out there tonight."

Crys followed Sally through the warren of tunnels, trying not to let the tears burning her eyes spill over. *I have no claim on him. This is just a job, that's all.* But it had all become too confusing, and fierce pangs of jealousy and envy stabbed her to the heart. None of the crew they saw would meet her eyes, and she surmised that she was being whisked out of the building and away from Blade and the rest of Smidge as quickly and discreetly as possible.

They emerged from the arena into the loading bay, where the runabout van waited next to Smidge's big transport trucks, with Phil the road manager at the wheel. Sally slid over to the middle seat, making room for Crys on the passenger side.

As the van pulled out into the night, Crys stared out the window, not sure what to think. With Phil and Sally right by her side, she hardly dared to think at all for fear of starting to cry, pouring out all the tension and doubt and frightening desire of the past week – had it only been a week? As they drove down dark city streets, she saw a hooker standing on a corner under a streetlamp, bare thighs above her high boots, coat pulled tight against the cold. *Professional girlfriend.* Had getting involved in Blade's world been a huge mistake altogether?

Phil dropped Sally and Crys at the front door of the hotel. No press waited – of course, the band hadn't left the arena yet – so they entered unobserved and quietly rose to the fourteenth floor, booked in its entirety for Smidge. Crys said nothing, because there was nothing to say and because she thought the tears might break out if she did. Sally made a few deliberately casual comments about how helpful Crys had been in the guest lounge and how nice it was to have a positive show after the disaster in Seattle, but clearly felt awkward about the way the night had gone, and ended up dropping into silence also. When they reached the door to the suite Crys shared with Blade, Sally hesitated for a moment, then said, "If you need anything, or you just want company, Erva and I are in 1412, all right?" Erva was a lighting tech, one of the few female roadies and Sally's usual roommate. "Goodnight, honey."

Crys pulled out her key card and touched it against the door lock – the LED indicator changed at once from red to green, and the soft buzz of the door release sounded loud in the silence of the hall. She turned the handle and pushed open the door.

As in Seattle, she and Blade had a two-bedroom suite. In this case, instead of the bedrooms being across a corridor from one another with a sitting room at the end, the door from the hall opened onto the sitting room, with the two bedrooms side-by-side off the right-hand wall. Crys's room was the second door – the smaller of the two, she guessed, though she hadn't seen inside Blade's room in this hotel.

She looked at the pair of sofas in the sitting room, at the gas fireplace and the stack of complimentary magazines on the coffee table, and thought of waiting up for him – with the main door opening right into the sitting room, he wouldn't be able to avoid seeing her when he came in. But... if he didn't want to see her... if he – *oh, God* – came in with someone... that would be unbearable. She turned and went into her room, but as a concession, left her door open so that he would at least know she was still awake. Going back into the sitting room, she chose a couple of the magazines, and brought them back into her room. Instead of being sensible – closing the door, changing into her pajamas, and going to sleep – she lay on the bed reading the magazines and listening with half an ear in the hope that he might come home soon. *Home?* How pathetic to imagine their hotel suite as home, to think of him coming home to her.

Eventually, she did hear distant noises coming from the hall outside their room, and looked up from her magazine with a sick feeling of tension, waiting. The sound of voices grew louder as the hall door opened – female voices mixed in with the lower male voices Crys recognized as the band's – and Blade's voice called out, "We'll be along in a bit," drawing wolf whistles and shouts of encouragement from the others.

A woman's voice called back, "Don't do anything I wouldn't do!" Which didn't make much sense until Crys realized with a sinking heart that it hadn't been intended for Blade but for someone with him – or for more than one someone, as the voices entering the suite were not two but three, Blade's deep voice counterpointed by a pair of feminine voices, teasing and flirting.

"You haven't signed me yet, lover," said one voice, with an inviting chuckle that made Crys's skin crawl.

Blade's sensuous laugh in response nearly had her crying. "Where did you want me to sign, then?" A pause, some response inaudible to Crys, then, "Really? Well, I think you might need to lie down for me to do a proper job of it... Use my bed, it's in here – got some champagne if you'd like a drink?"

Crys had heard enough. Getting up as quietly as she could, she tiptoed to her own door and pushed it closed. But through the wall, she could still hear voices, half-drunken screaming laughter, and a squeaking protest from the bed frame. Unbearable.

Hurting and angry, she opened the minibar in her room, took out first one little bottle, then two, and then one by one the rest of them, lining them up like soldiers going to die. *I need some oblivion tonight.* With icy deliberation, she unscrewed the top of the first one – drank it straight like a shot, shuddering at the taste. The second didn't taste so bad, and she couldn't taste the third one at all. The laughter and everything else faded, and her fingers grew numb so that she had to struggle with the little screw-tops. She never did remember finishing the last bottle.

♥

Drifting in and out of a numb and painless darkness, vaguely aware that the floor pitched and spun if she tried to raise her head, Crys floated. She didn't hear the knock on her door, or the voice calling her name. Was only vaguely aware of the door opening, heavy footsteps pounding to her side. "Crys? Crys! Wake up; can you hear me?! Shit!" Blade's deep voice, raspy and beloved. The memory of the women's laughter surfaced, and she rolled onto her side and retched. Faded out again.

Hands shook her. "Did you drink all of these, Crys?" Jed's voice this time. "Come on, open your eyes!"

Vomiting again. Dizzy impression that a toilet was there, right where it needed to be. Cool tiles under her knees, gentle hands holding her head, smoothing back her hair. "That's right, honey, bring it all up." Sally's voice.

Sense that someone was undressing her, maybe two people; had she imagined four hands? How bizarre. Shock of cold water – for a moment Crys flashed to awareness in the shower stall, skin and underwear drenched – and a drift into towels and hands dressing her like a doll, first one leg and then the other into the stiffness of laundered denim, the faint scrape against her face as a t-shirt was pulled over her head.

Cold wind, fresh air. Arms supporting her, dizziness and nausea ebbing and flowing. "Try to walk, sweetheart." That was Blade again, his voice kind and worried. Steps, one by one, supported on either side. Pavement under her feet and stars overhead, both shifting and swirling each time she took a lurching step with leaden feet that didn't seem to belong to her.

Missed a step, stumbled, and suddenly the sidewalk was rushing up to meet her. Never connected but plunged instead back into the darkness, pain-free and welcoming. Surfaced briefly, feeling herself scooped up by safe, powerful arms and cradled against a comforting strength. Smelled Blade's citrus soap smell and smiled muzzily. Floated away again into the darkness.

♥

Crys woke to a multitude of unpleasant sensations. Her head throbbed, her stomach roiled, her arms and legs felt like jelly. Sitting up didn't feel too good, and she quickly lay back against the pillows, realizing as she did so that the bed around her was covered with spread-out bath towels, a precaution against continued nausea.

"Crys, you're awake!" Jed got up from his chair by the window and crossed to the bed. He looked tired. "How's the nausea? Are you going to be sick again?"

She thought about it. "I don't think so. I feel kind of queasy, but I don't think I'm actually going to throw up."

"Okay." Jed took a bottle of Gatorade from the bedside table. "Here, drink this."

Crys shuddered. "I hate Gatorade."

But Jed popped open the sport-drink top and handed it to her. "Electrolytes," he said. He waited until she'd choked down a few sips, and then sat down on the edge of the bed. "So. Talk to me, Crys."

"About what?"

He gave her an I'm-an-ER-nurse-don't-play-games-with-me look. "Crys. Come on."

"What is there to say?"

"You're not usually a binge drinker, right? Something triggered this."

Crys just shook her head, mute and sad.

Jed sighed. "Look. I know that Sally and Phil brought you back from the concert last night – you'd been expecting to go back with the boys – and Sally said you looked a little blue when she left you last night. Is it just that, or did something more happen to tip you over the edge?" *Something.* He must have seen a reaction in her face, because his mouth tightened and his expression changed to one of concern. "Please tell me what happened, Crys. I want to help you."

Shamefully, she burst into tears at that, and Jed put his arms around her, holding her as she wept. Through her tears, she managed to stammer out, "W-wanted to b-block out the s-sounds... wassat nas-sty s-slut too-o... c-couldn' b-bear it..."

"Blade had someone in with him after the party last night?" Jed interpreted.

"Two... I th-think..." Crys corrected him, trying to mop at tears that kept flowing against his shoulder.

"Two? And that shocked you, did it?"

Shocked me? Crys thought about that for a moment, tears drying as she considered the situation, realizing uneasily that two, three, four wouldn't have mattered – if only she'd been one of them – and not those nasty low-end tramps when Blade deserved the best the world had to offer. "Not shocked, really. That's... not the word."

"No?" For once, Jed did look surprised; he'd expected her to be shocked. "What is the word, then?"

"Envious," Crys whispered. "Envious and hurt, because I wanted to be in there too."

"Crys," said Jed, and then stopped, at a loss for words. He took a deep breath. "Crys, you don't have to do anything extreme to prove yourself – to Blade or to any of us."

Prove myself? Crys shook her head, wincing as the motion hurt. "It's not about proving myself; I'm starting to doubt everything I thought was proper. My reaction to Blade freaks me out – I shouldn't want him, but I do – that lip ring is so hot, and oh sweet God, I feel sparks at the slightest touch of his fingertips – I can't believe I'm telling you this."

"It's fine," Jed told her. "A bit of infatuation is normal under the circumstances. I won't say anything to anyone, unless you want me to."

"No. But... you think it's *normal* to feel this way?"

"Sure. Not everyone is turned on by white picket fences and Prince Charming."

"But shouldn't I want Prince Charming? Shouldn't I want a home and a garden and someone who'd make a good husband and father?"

Jed laughed. "Crys, darling, do you have any idea at all what makes a good life partner? Safe and conservative have nothing to do with it. And anyway, you're so young; you don't need to worry about the rest of your life just yet. Explore what you want right now, and let the future worry about itself."

"Jed, do you really think it's okay to... to want to..."

"To want to have sex with him? Of course it is." He looked at her kindly, his mouth quirking in sympathetic amusement. "Desire is a natural drive, just like hunger. You eat when you're hungry, don't you? And speaking of biology, let me get Sally to help you to the washroom – you're probably bursting."

Crys nodded in agreement. She didn't feel up to getting out of bed, not with a queasy stomach and legs weak as jelly, but Jed was right. On all counts.

After using the bathroom and brushing her teeth, Crys felt a good deal better. Jed gave her some painkillers, a bit stronger than the average over-the-counter stuff, which made her feel sleepy but effectively cut the aching in her skull.

❤

Marigold showed up later in the morning, displeased and not bothering to hide it. Her acid-green-and-teal outfit made Crys's eyes hurt. "Are you out of your mind, Crys?" she demanded at once. "Sally says they nearly had to take you to the hospital to have your stomach pumped, you stupid child! We're supposed to be repairing Blade's image here, not adding more scandal to it!"

"I'm sorry, Marigold."

"And now you're not fit to travel. The flight is scheduled to leave at two – not that it really matters since it's a private jet, but changing the flight plan is a hassle and I'll have to do it since Phil is already on the road. I'm not impressed."

Crys rubbed her eyes. Of course, they'd only had the one night's concert booked in Portland – time to move on to the next city on the list. She'd known that; when Phil had dropped them off at the hotel the night before, he'd gone to park the truck full of Smidge's equipment in a secure garage overnight, ready for the ten-hour drive to San Francisco the next day. "I don't want to be any trouble, I'm sure I can manage."

Marigold's phone rang, cutting off whatever comment she'd been about to make. "Hello? ... Oh, Mr. Kinney! What– ... yes, I see ... very clever ... yes, of course I'll take care of it ... absolutely ... bye." Marigold smirked as she slipped her phone back into her purse. "You're a lucky girl, Crys," she said. "No harm done; in fact, Mr. Kinney has found a way to work it to our advantage. You're going to stay here with Blade while the rest of us go on to San Francisco today – we'll call it taking some romantic time – and you can both fly down commercial tomorrow morning. It's perfect," she added, "because no one will even question why you're spending all day in bed."

"But–" Crys started to protest that she couldn't possibly stay alone in the hotel with Blade, but she caught Jed's look and fell quiet. Maybe she could. *Maybe I should.*

chapter

7

ARIGOLD HAD LEFT FIRM INSTRUCTIONS — CRYS was on no account to change out of the pale pink satin slip and matching robe – any room service waiter or housekeeping maid who might see her must assume she was there for a romantic interlude.

But she felt too exposed in the clinging silk, and as soon as the others had left for the airport, she scooted into her room to change into her own things: old faded jeans – not the tight sexy ones that were part of her rock-star's-girl wardrobe but her own favorite pair, soft and worn with age – and a much-loved and much-washed grey cotton blouse. She sat on one of the couches in the sitting room, curled up with her feet tucked under her. She was alone.

Angel and Dice and Easy had left hours before, along with Jed and Sally and Marigold. They'd come in to say goodbye, telling her that they'd see her in San Francisco the following day, joking with her about being hung over – making light of it. And since then, Crys had been reading magazines in front of the fireplace, half dozing off from the warmth and the comfort of the couch. Outside it rained, a wet grey day, and she was glad enough of the fire and the cozy sitting room.

At last, a scraping noise and the faint buzzing of the electronic lock at the door alerted her, and Crys jerked from semi-sleep to full awareness as the door opened and Blade walked in.

Her first instantaneous reaction was of delight – pure happiness in seeing him, in being with him for however brief a time, however little the contact between them, however unimportant the words spoken. She saw that his hair and his leather jacket were wet – he must have been outside in the rain. Then the delight was swallowed up by a tangle of confusion, of nerves and desire and memory and hurt and uncertainty, and she looked away, then up again, and didn't know where to look or what to say.

"Hey, Crys," he said, his face full of hesitation and concern, as though he weren't quite sure what to say to her. He seemed almost surprised to see her there; had he expected her to be sleeping it off in her room? "So... how're you feeling?" he asked at last. "Pretty rough?"

"Not too bad," she told him, relieved at least to have a question to answer, a lead to follow. "Jed gave me some decent painkillers for the headache, and everything else seems to have pretty much eased up. Though I don't want to eat anything just yet."

"No kidding. Do you... do this often?"

Crys would have liked to just say yes, to avoid the questions and fuss – but she didn't ever drink herself stupid like that, had never blacked out before, and knew that she didn't lie well. "No," she said. "No, I don't."

"Shit, Crys, I'm sorry." He paused, looked down at his wet shoes and kicked them off. "It was the party last night, wasn't it, and... you probably... heard me come in, right?"

"Let's not talk about it, okay?" Crys asked.

"Seriously, let me explain–"

"Just don't. Really, Blade, I already feel like enough of a sad case."

At a loss for words, he stripped off his wet leather jacket and hung it over the back of a chair. Walked over to the fireplace and back again. At last, he took a deep breath, opened his mouth to speak, and breathed out again. Sat down next to her and tried one more time. "Okay. That's fine. But drinking alone like that is dangerous, sweetheart – I'll get drunk with you any time you like, but please don't get drunk alone, okay?"

Crys thought about that, thought about drinking with Blade until both of their inhibitions came down and all the reasons why they should stay apart disappeared. *Foolish dream.* "I'm never going to drink again," she said, and if the regret in her voice was not for the hangover, no one need ever know.

Then she looked up and their eyes met, and she wondered if he had been reading her mind or at least thinking along the same lines, because his sexy hazel eyes held a far-too-intimate recognition of the chemistry between them. "Hey, you know," he said, "way back, you said you'd like to see my guitar, maybe even learn a few chords. Still interested?"

"Oh, yes, please!" She was surprised at the rush of eagerness she felt, to see and hold something that was so precious to him, such a part of him.

"Just a moment, then." He got up and disappeared into his room, coming out a moment later with his guitar in its padded black bag. "Here." He unzipped the bag and lifted out his guitar.

"It's beautiful!" said Crys in surprise, not to flatter but speaking from her heart. The guitar itself was beautiful, which she had not realized in watching the concerts and seeing Blade in performance mode, whether from the side of the stage or only at a massive distance and splashed across the jumbotron screens – she hadn't been paying attention to the instrument but to the man behind it. The guitar had a shining angular body of polished darkness with a tapered waist like a woman's torso, contrasted by a white pickguard etched with a small firebird design.

"Would you like to try it?" he asked, with an indrawn breath that told her it cost him some effort to extend that trust. Crys nodded. She sat very still on the sofa as he placed the guitar in her lap, the waist of the body curving over her right thigh, the long slender neck cradled in her left hand. It was, oddly, both lighter and heavier than she'd expected. She stroked the body of the guitar with experimental fingers, learning the smooth curves of it.

"What do I do?" she asked.

"Here," he said, "scoot forward a bit." He put a knee on the couch behind her, so that he could reach around to guide her left hand with his. "Let's try a G chord first. Your first finger goes on the second string from the top, on the second fret – there, just press the string with the tip of your finger – that's right."

"Oh," she said. "It's kind of sharp." It wasn't exactly painful, but the string did cut into her finger in an unexpected metallic way, like pressing against the edge of a nail file. Like his lip ring had pressed into her lip when they'd kissed.

Blade laughed, a soft intimate laugh. "Yeah. Steel strings. You get calluses after a couple of weeks... but I sort of remember that first time." Were they still talking about the guitar? She could feel the strength of his thigh against her hip, the firm warmth of his chest brushing against her back as he reached around her, his fingertips lightly guiding her hands. "D'you want to stop?"

"N-no... it's okay... it doesn't hurt, really, I was just... surprised, that's all."

"Right, then. Press your first finger down, and then you're going to put your middle finger on the top string, on the third fret – right here – and your ring finger on the bottom string on the same fret – got it?"

"I think so..." Crys pressed the tips of her fingers against the strings, feeling the cut of the steel, the warmth of Blade's breath on her neck.

"Okay, relax that hand for a moment. You'll need a pick in your other hand – here," and he dug a small black plastic triangle out of his pocket, showed her how to hold it. "Just pinch it – yeah, like that – and what you want to do is bring it down across the strings in kind of one motion, here, between the pickups."

"With my fingers pressing the strings up here?"

"That's right." He adjusted her fingers slightly. "Try to touch only the ones you're pressing down – good – now go ahead with the pick, across all the strings."

Crys brought the pick in her right hand down across the strings, and a softly musical sound rang out. "Wow!" she whispered, thrilled.

"Yeah." Blade grinned. "Music. You want to learn a second chord to go with that?"

"Sure."

"How about a C chord, then." He wrapped his left hand around hers, helped her press her fingers into the right positions. "You'll feel a bit of a stretch, but you can do it."

Her fingers were spread across three frets this time, a stretch indeed for her small hand, but he was right – she was able to do what he asked of her. And that flooded her wayward mind with thoughts of how else she might stretch to accommodate him. Finding it hard to breathe, she shifted uncomfortably – and realized with a shock that Blade was aroused, unmistakably so, the hard ridge of his erection pressing against her lower back. She jerked away at once, but the awareness between them could not be erased.

"W-what now?" she asked, hardly able to choke the words out, and not even sure what she was asking about.

It took him a moment to answer, and his voice sounded rough and barely controlled, as though he were having trouble concentrating. "We're... we're playing a C chord, right? So... when you bring the pick down across the strings, skip the top one. You... you just want to strike the bottom five, okay?"

"Okay. Right." That sounded tricky when he said it – twice as tricky with half her mind on what she'd just felt – but when she tried it, she found it simple enough to avoid the top string as she strummed. Another sweet soft sound echoed from the guitar, and she turned her head to smile at Blade – then gasped at the tension on his face. "Did I do something wrong?" she asked in surprise.

"No! Not at all," he said, swallowing hard, and again she didn't know if they were talking about the guitar or something else. "Of course, the... the real trick is to be able to switch between them," he pointed out after a moment, and Crys tried that too, pausing, fingers fumbling, but doing her best to go smoothly from G chord to C chord, over and over.

"I can do this," she murmured to herself. *G chord. C chord.*

Without warning, he pulled away from his position behind her, moving off the sofa, putting space between them. Shoved his hands into his pockets. "We... you... should probably quit for a bit, sweetheart. Your fingers are going to sting for a while as it is." And as Crys lifted her hands away from the guitar strings, noticing for the first time the stinging, almost buzzing feeling in her fingertips, he turned and disappeared into his room.

"Blade?" she called, but he didn't answer.

After a while, she carefully lifted the guitar from her lap and stood, carrying it over to where the case lay on the other sofa. She settled the beautiful instrument into its case with a reluctant final stroke across the strings, zipping it closed. *Do I leave it here? Or take it in to him?* She looked at the guitar case in front of her, and at the half-open door to his room. *You eat when you're hungry,* Jed had said. Crys picked up the guitar case by its shoulder strap and carried it across to Blade's door. Knocked. Called out to him again, and when he didn't answer, because the door was partially open she pushed it the rest of the way open.

Blade sat on the floor with his back against the foot of the bed, his eyes focused on a box like a pen case, open in his hands. As she stood there in the doorway, he threw something – a folded paper packet – toward her with a desperate angry gesture. "Please, Crys – flush that evil shit before I change my mind!"

Startled, she set the guitar down and picked up the folded paper. "You want me to put this down the toilet?" she asked. "What is it?" And then she understood – he'd been out in the rain, his hair and jacket wet – he must have gone to buy the harmless-looking paper packet she held. "Oh. I see."

"It's hell, sweetheart, I want it so bad... please just get rid of it for me."

Crys ran to the en suite bathroom, holding the small packet like a bomb. Standing over the toilet, she unfolded the paper with shaking fingers to find a small amount of ordinary-looking pale powder. *Is this really heroin? It looks just like flour,* she thought, surprised. She tipped the piece of paper over the toilet and flushed, swirling away the fine flour-like stuff that had nearly taken Blade's life three times.

And then she rinsed the powdery paper in the sink until it was soggy before dropping it into the garbage can.

When she returned to the bedroom, he was standing, still holding the pen case, just looking into it with a shadowed self-loathing face that made Crys's heart ache. She took the case from him – willing her expression not to change as she saw the syringes, the bent spoon, the rubber tubing – and snapped it closed. "You don't need this right now," she said, putting it down on the dresser. "I can... give you something better."

His eyes met hers, shocked and desiring. "No, Crys, I can't take that from you! I don't deserve a gift like that!"

"Shh." She laid a silencing finger against his lips, pausing to touch the steel ring there with a sense of daring and awe at what she intended to do. Guided him gently backward toward the king-sized bed. "You do, but don't worry," she told him. "You don't have to deal with that tonight. I just want to... give you pleasure. Won't you let me be the distraction you need?"

He groaned as she pushed him down onto the bed, her small hands working to unfasten the fly of his jeans. With suddenly urgent hands he helped her, pushing his jeans and boxers down out of the way, and Crys drew in a startled breath. "Damn, sweetheart, have you done even this before?" he asked, his voice shaking.

"Nope," she said. "But I think I can manage if you'll tell me what to do." With a growing sense of awe, she reached out with feather-light fingers to stroke the length of him.

"Oh, fuck!" His curse morphed into a moan as she leaned down and licked where she had touched. Her tongue flickered over him, tasting, exploring, and then she took him into her mouth, eyebrows raised at how big and hard he was and how it felt to have her mouth filled so. His hips jerked, and she swirled her tongue around, delighting in his response to what she was doing. He threaded his hands into her hair, a gentle pressure that taught her the rhythm he craved, his breathing hard and fast, until he gasped out, "Sweetheart, you're too much for me – you'd better stop – I'm not going to last much longer like that."

He tried to release her but she didn't stop, didn't pull away. With a convulsive groan, he exploded into her mouth. Crys swallowed reflexively, surprised more than anything by the flood of salty warmth. She raised her head and saw that Blade had collapsed against the mattress, his eyes closed, his face achingly vulnerable in that moment of satiation. *Oh, my love,* she thought, her heart suffused with tenderness and wonder at the intimacy they'd just shared.

Getting up, she stood on shaky legs. Stepped away from the bed – and it hurt to leave him. But her impulsive gift of pleasure had complicated things between them, and she didn't know what to do or say in the aftermath.

He opened his eyes as he felt her move off the bed – confusion cracked through the daze of pleasure as he saw that she was leaving. "Crys! Please don't go," he called after her. "I'm so sorry, I–"

"It's okay." She raised a stopping hand as she saw him about to get up, to follow. "I'm... I'm going to go... have a nap or something," she said. "I'll see you later."

After a moment, he nodded. "Maybe we'd better... we should... go out for dinner?" he asked. It was strange to see him so tentative, a rock god with metal in his face and ears, looking up at her as though he wanted to say something more.

"That... yes, that... would be wise," she agreed. *I've lit a fuse, and it's burning between us,* she thought. The only thing to do was wait for the explosion.

❤

Crys woke from her nap to the telephone's ringing. She glanced at the hotel phone on the bedside table, and then realized that the ringing was coming from her purse. Thinking that the caller was most likely her mother or else Debbie or Leah, she hopped out of bed and grabbed the phone from her purse, answering it without even glancing at the call display. "Hi, what's up?" she said, slightly breathless from her dash across the room. She blinked in surprise as she heard a man's voice reply.

"Hello, is that Crys Murphy?" he asked. "This is Rhys calling." And when she didn't immediately reply, he clarified, "Rhys Davies. You probably weren't expecting me to call, since we've been emailing..."

"No. Of course. Hi, Rhys – it's... good to hear your voice."

"I'm glad I reached you. Hey, you sound a little shook up, Crys; is everything okay?"

"Sure. Just woke up from a nap, that's all," she said, because that wasn't technically a lie, even though the unease he'd picked up in her voice had nothing to do with sleep.

"Listen, are you still in Portland?" he asked. "I know Smidge played Portland last night, but I wasn't sure if you'd still be there or have moved on already."

"Yes, I'm still in Portland – flying out tomorrow morning," she said, puzzled.

"Because I'm here overnight for an audition, and I was hoping you'd maybe want to meet up and get coffee or something. Not as a date – I know you can't – but we *are* friends, remember?"

The thought of spending even half an hour with someone who wasn't part of the rock star world sounded impossibly sane and normal and nice. "God, I'd love to, Rhys!" she said. "I just don't know what would happen if someone saw us and took a picture. What it would look like, I mean."

"Mmm. There is that. I'd still like to see you, see that you're okay... Well, then, do you think your boyfriend would join us for coffee? All above board and all that?"

Crys thought about that. "I don't know. I'll ask him and call you back. Give me five minutes."

She slipped across the hall to Blade's door and knocked. Waited. Was he sleeping? She knocked again, and finally the door opened. "Hi, sweetheart," he said, a slow smile spreading across his face at the sight of her.

"Hi." She twisted the hem of her blouse around her finger, feeling unbelievably self-conscious. "I... a friend of mine is in town, and he asked me to go for coffee," she began.

"*He* asked?" Blade repeated, emphasizing the male pronoun. "This guy a boyfriend or something?"

"Rhys is... just a friend..." No sense in explaining that she'd met them both the same night, and that she'd walked away from Rhys to take a chance with Smidge and a job as Blade's professional girlfriend. "He wants to know that I'm all right."

Blade's face grew still, his eyes shadowed. "And... are you all right, Crys?"

"I'm fine." *Falling in love, but fine.* She could see that Blade was afraid he'd done harm to her by accepting her gift of pleasure – but how could such a beautiful thing be harmful? "Truly, I am fine."

He reached out to trace the curve of her cheek with one finger, a tender gesture at odds with his hard image. "I don't want to hurt you, lovely Crys," he murmured, and they drifted there for a moment, awash in all the dreamy sensuality that could fill one tiny gesture.

But he doesn't love me. At what price do I want this? Crys shook her head to clear it. "Blade, I... I'd like to have coffee with my friend, but I was worried that someone might take a picture and draw the wrong conclusions. So I was wondering if... you'd be willing to come and get a coffee with us."

He shrugged. "Sure. Will he come here to the hotel? There's a coffee place downstairs, and I'd rather not hassle with walking in public or getting a limo to go for a coffee."

"I'm sure that's fine," Crys said, trying to hide her surprise.

"You go ahead and call this Rhys back then – I'll just change my shirt."

♥

They were alone in the elevator going down, and Crys noticed that Blade had put on what she thought of as his going-out makeup – just a slight touch of black eyeliner – did he wear it because of all the pictures, she wondered, or did he simply like the way it made him look? She also saw that he was wearing a black Ramones t-shirt with nothing covering his bare arms; they were healing nicely, but were still noticeably bruised and scarred if anyone cared to look.

Blade saw her looking. "Your friend wants to know you're all right, sweetheart. He might as well see what I am."

Crys heard the bitterness in his voice, saw that he was openly courting rejection and shame. "Blade, you're so much more than that," she said. "And you're clean now."

"Five days means nothing. It calls to me all the time."

"Every day means something. And I... I'll help, you know... in any way I can."

He laughed. "Damn, I wish you meant that for real."

"But I do!" She blushed, and persevered. "If I can... please you, and it keeps you from going back to the – that stuff... I do mean it."

The elevator chimed as it reached the lobby. Blade reached out and took Crys's hand, clasping her small hand in his large warm one. "You're too sweet for words," he murmured in her ear, just before they stepped out into the lobby.

The stares, the occasional camera flashes – it was all starting to seem normal to Crys, which was almost more disconcerting than the attention itself. Walking across the lobby with Blade, she now responded with a confident smile and wave just as he did. *Any behavior can be learned, right?* She was learning all the tricks. She barely even noticed the bodyguards anymore. She had, without effort, remembered to wash her face and put on some subtle makeup before considering herself ready to go out.

Frosted glass doors led to the coffee lounge, and the overexcited hostess showed them to a cozy grouping of brown-velvet armchairs by a window, where Rhys waited. He stood to greet them, reaching out to shake hands with Blade, saying, "Hi, I'm Rhys – Crys has probably told you I'm a friend of hers from home," in a totally ordinary tone. Just as if Blade weren't the Smidge guitarist or anything but Crys's new boyfriend being vetted by her old buddy.

Blade flashed his for-the-cameras smile. "I'm glad she's got people to watch out for her." Unspoken, Crys could almost hear him thinking, *people to take care of her after I've well and truly fucked her up.* She shook her head, no, but there was no way she could say anything without involving Rhys, so instead she stepped forward and gave the actor a hug.

"It's so nice to see you, Rhys," she told him, squeezing tight. She could have sworn Blade growled.

A waitress came over to take their coffee orders. "Our daily fresh snacks and desserts are in the glass cases over there," she explained, pointing vaguely in the direction of the counter. "You can have a look before deciding. I'll be right back with your lattés."

"Why don't you go have a look and pick something for me, sweetheart," Blade said to Crys.

"Yeah, sure – you can choose for all of us," Rhys agreed.

They seemed to want her to go. As she walked away, she noticed Rhys indicating Blade's inner arm with a subtle finger, and overheard him ask quietly, "Heroin?"

"Yeah." Blade paused, apparently awaiting censure, and yet Rhys said nothing, just listened for whatever Blade needed or wanted to say. "Been clean five days now, but I know that means nothing. Crys believes I can do it, though – that helps."

Crys crossed to the refrigerated counter in a warm glow of contentment. It was little enough, but it was enough, that he should know she had faith in his ability to fight the addiction – it meant so much more that her belief in him could give him strength.

She chose coffee cake for all of them, caught their waitress's eye and paid for the coffee cake and lattes there at the counter, to avoid any awkwardness between the two men she was with.

She headed back to the table, balancing three plates of coffee cake; both men turned toward her as she approached, some tension evident between them. "You have loyal friends," Blade commented with a wry grin, and she wondered what had been said. *I hardly know him,* she wanted to say; *I met him the same day as I met you.* But she'd introduced Rhys as a friend, and it would be too complicated to explain.

The coffee cake was delicious, but she barely tasted it.

As they left the coffee lounge, Rhys turned to Blade and said, "Could you give us a moment?" Blade nodded – a sharp assenting jerk of his head – and, glancing around for options, headed for the nearby men's room, giving Rhys the privacy he'd asked for. When they were alone, Rhys smiled ruefully, saying, "He's a lucky man, Crystal Murphy."

"Don't be silly. It's just a job, remember?" Crys muttered, willing away the blush she could feel rising upward.

Rhys looked at her with knowing eyes. "No, it's not. I can see it in you, the way you look at him, the way you respond to him. He *is* a lucky man, Crys, and I hope he knows it." When her eyes widened at the sincerity in his voice, he only shook his head. "No worries. Just know that I'm your friend – and call me if he hurts you, so I can take him apart for you." He laughed, but she wasn't quite sure if this last was a joke.

"Rhys, I'm so sorry things... happened this way," she began. "I never had any intention of falling for–"

"Shh," he said. "I'm not sorry – how could I ever be sorry for your friendship?"

And then Blade was back, slipping a possessive arm around her waist as he came up beside her. Crys pulled away from him to hug Rhys goodbye. "I guess this is it for a while," she said. "We're going on to San Francisco in the morning. Good luck with your audition."

"Thanks. Take care, Crys; you know you can call or email me any time."

With a wave and a farewell smile, Rhys was off, making his way through the people in the hotel lobby toward the grand front doors. He turned once to glance back, a cryptic expression on his face, before disappearing out to the street.

♥

Blade took her out to dinner, as he'd promised. Fortunately, there was a little black satin dress in her Marigold-provided wardrobe. After the main course, Crys excused herself to the ladies' room; the garlic prawns had been fantastic and the red wine divine, but she was sure the breath they'd given her was neither.

She wasn't sure whether going out to dinner had been such a brilliant idea after all – if they'd stayed in their suite, they could have locked themselves in their rooms, or just watched a stupid movie and laughed about it – this felt like nothing so much as very public foreplay. Every time their feet touched under the table, every time his hand brushed hers, their eyes met with a kind of dizzy awareness.

Opening her elegant black satin purse – it matched the dress – she hunted around for the travel toothbrush she kept there. That had been one of Marigold's tips, to keep a toothbrush and paste in every purse, because you never know when you'll want a sparkling smile.

An older woman with a wealth of pearls around her neck stepped into the ladies' room, and observed Crys brushing her teeth over the sink with amusement. "Hot date, my dear?" the woman asked – she, evidently, did not follow the tabloids, did not know of Blade and Crys's supposed romance or maybe even of Smidge's existence. Crys wondered if she'd noticed Blade in the restaurant, and what she'd thought if she had. Even in a dinner jacket, Blade still looked like what he was – a rock star. The piercings couldn't be hidden even if he'd wanted to hide them, and though he appeared to have washed his face, some traces of black liner remained around his eyes. If anything, she found this more subtle variant of his usual look even hotter.

Crys nodded to the woman, who disappeared into a toilet stall. She finished up with her toothbrush, touched up her lipstick. *I do look elegant*, she thought, observing her satin-clad figure in the mirror, smoothing her hands over her hips. She grinned as she felt the ridges of the garter belt underneath the clinging satin – it felt daring and seductive, and Crys knew that she was flirting with wildfire inside herself. *Who am I?* she asked herself. *Who do I want to be?* She had never felt such a divide between the happy life she'd always pictured for herself – the home and children and loving husband, church on Sundays and PTA membership, domestic tranquility – and the growing attraction of everything that was dark, dangerous and socially inappropriate. Could she – would she really – throw away the good-girl image of herself in favor of darker desires, shedding inhibitions, riding the storm? *He doesn't love me,* she told herself. *But does that matter? Why am I supposed to wait for love? Someone who loves me might not make me ache and tingle all over like this.* And in her heart she recognized that she was fundamentally kinked in favor of facial hardware and a world unlike her own – no nice clean-cut boy was going to make her light up like Blade could, not ever, no matter how long she waited.

Perhaps in part because of the red wine, she slipped off her panties and tucked them into her purse.

The walk back to their table seemed to be the longest she'd ever taken. She felt like a model on a runway, Blade's eyes on her every step of the way as she wove in and out between tables to reach him. Could he tell that she'd taken off her panties? She had no way of knowing.

He'd filled up their wine glasses, and a dessert plate sat in the middle of the table; wedges of what looked like chocolate brownie and scoops of orange gelato were decorated with sugared violets and shavings of white chocolate. "I thought you might want something sweet," he said as she sat down. "I know you like chocolate and orange."

"How do you know that?" she asked. She hadn't thought he paid attention to her likes and dislikes. "Did Marigold give you a cheat sheet?"

He shook his head. "I asked Sally," he confessed. She laughed. "So, was she right?" he asked. "Chocolate and orange?"

Crys nodded. "My favorite combination. Especially bittersweet chocolate and slightly tart orange."

"Let's see if this measures up, then." Blade took his spoon, used it to break off a bit of the brownie, scooped up some of the gelato too. Instead of tasting it himself, though, he reached the spoon across, and Crys realized that he intended it for her. Closing her eyes, she opened her mouth and let him slip the sweet treat between her lips, sighing in satisfaction at the perfect tartness of the icy orange against the warmth of the bittersweet chocolate. She opened her eyes as he scooped up another bite for himself, on the same spoon that had just been in her mouth.

"W-what are you doing?" she asked him, crossing her legs to stop them trembling as he slowly licked the spoon.

"Eating dessert," he said, with a wicked sensual grin, fully aware of what he was doing to her.

She stared at him, puzzled. "But why? You... you don't want this, you don't want... me, so what are you doing?"

His eyes met hers, and playful flirting was replaced by blunt painful honesty. "I do want you, Crys. Almost more than I want to shoot up. But I'm not going to do that either."

"So... what are you doing?"

Blade laughed, and the pain in his eyes disappeared. "Playing with fire, because I can't help myself, sweetheart. So play with me?" He shot her a daredevil look, and inclined his head toward the dessert plate. "It's your turn now."

"Oh." Hand shaking slightly, she picked up her spoon and filled it. Held it out to him. Watched him suck the ice cream and brownie off the spoon.

"I'm guessing you've never let a guy go down on you, huh?" he asked softly.

Crys dropped the spoon. It fell into the dessert plate, splattering half-melted orange gelato across the white tablecloth. "Sorry," she whispered, staring in dismay at the mess.

"My fault," he told her. "But it doesn't matter. I think we're done here anyway." A waiter had hurried over to clear up the mess, but Blade just handed him a credit card.

Moments later, the maître d' brought them their coats, helping Crys on with hers as though she had equal status to any of the pearl-draped old-money ladies in the restaurant. "I hope you had a pleasant meal, sir, miss," he said.

Pleasant! That's hardly the word, Crys thought. "Everything was absolutely delicious," she replied truthfully.

Blade punched his PIN into the card reader and handed it back to their hovering waiter. "Done. Let's go, Crys," he urged, guiding her away with an arm around her waist. As they reached the street, his hand drifted south over her satin-covered hip until he felt the garter belt under the fabric – and didn't feel panties – he jerked his hand away as though it burned.

In the limousine, he sat across from her, about as far away as it was possible to get within the confines of the vehicle. She looked out the window, surprised at his reaction, and wondered if she should just get the wretched panties out of her purse and put them back on right there in the car – then maybe things would go back to the dangerous but tempting state of playful flirtation they'd been enjoying. But she lacked the nerve for that, and anyway thought it could make things worse, so she kept her knees locked together and did nothing. They arrived at the hotel, and though Blade took her hand to help her out of the limousine, he immediately let go again, gesturing for her to walk in ahead of him.

Cold and disappointed, Crys hurried up the steps to the grand French doors of the hotel, which the doorman held open for her. She could hear Blade's footsteps behind her, and though she didn't turn back, she did slow her pace so that it wouldn't look to the world like they'd had an argument. As he caught up with her near the bank of elevators, he laid a hand gently on the small of her back, and whispered into her ear, "Damn, you shouldn't tempt me like that, Crys. You have no idea what you're doing to me."

A soft chime interrupted them, and the up-arrow above one of the elevators glowed green. The pressure of Blade's hand on her back guided Crys into the elevator car. As the door slid closed on the lobby and they were alone, he moved to the opposite side of the elevator, gripped the handrail behind him with both hands, and gazed at her with unconcealed desire in his eyes.

Crys stared back. Licked her lips. Almost moaned aloud at the electricity between them.

"Crys," Blade said, his voice deeper and rougher than usual. "You know I'm going to kiss you, when we get back to our suite."

She swallowed, her throat suddenly dry. "Oh. Okay."

"And then you're going to go into your room and lock the door."

"I... I don't have to, you know..."

"Yes. You have to. Because we've been drinking, and I'm no saint – I told you before that I play dirty, sweetheart, and things would go too far. So let me kiss you once, and then lock your door on me – promise?" His hazel eyes were shadowed and lustful all at once, and she could see the tension and hunger in his face.

"Okay. I promise."

The elevator chimed their floor, and the doors slid open.

Crys walked down the corridor with Blade behind her, his hand resting lightly on her lower back. As she walked, she found it harder and harder to breathe as anticipation overtook her. Her hands fumbled with her purse, and because she couldn't hold her key card steady, she let him unlock the door. And then they were inside their suite, in the sitting room, and he kicked the door closed.

He didn't say anything, just guided her backward until her shoulders rested against the wall beside her bedroom door. His hands tightened on her waist, and he bent his head to hers.

Their first kiss had been a surprise to both of them, and their second kiss lost in a dream – this time, though, Blade was fully intent on tasting her, his lips and tongue urgent and demanding as he took possession of her mouth. A sweet ache began to build within her as his hands roamed over her, tantalizing and caressing – he found her breasts, and even through the fabric of her dress and bra, his touch made her wobbly with desire. And when his hands slid lower, stroking up her thighs, lifting her black satin skirt, she didn't even think to stop him. Helplessly, instinctively, her thighs opened for him, and his long, strong guitarist's fingers found her bare inner flesh. Froze.

"Holy fuck – you really aren't wearing any!" he muttered in disbelief. Kissed her again, hotter than before. He slipped a finger inside her, and she moaned out loud against his mouth. He raised his head to look at her, hazel eyes scorching with need, eyebrows arched in surprise. "You're so wet. For me." He moved his hand in a wicked caress, took her weight with his other arm as her knees buckled.

"Please... oh please..." Crys begged, and she wasn't even sure what she was asking for. But her uncertainty reminded Blade how very inexperienced she was, and he withdrew his hands, setting her down on unsteady legs and backing away a pace or two. She couldn't help the hurt and confusion that rose to the surface of her overloaded senses, and knew that some of it must be showing on her face as she struggled to pull down and straighten her skirt.

"Oh, Crys, if you're aching as bad as I am, it's hell – and I wish I could... ease you, but I'm not strong enough – if I stay, I'll end up..." He broke off, looked away. "Please, sweetheart, just go into your room and lock the door."

I could stay, she thought. *I could stay, and damn the consequences.* But when she didn't at once go into her room, he looked straight at her, his face taut with the struggle to do right, and mouthed the word "please" – no audible sound, but it was quite clear that he was pleading with her to go. *I could stay, and make him hate himself over the outcome, though it be my choice.*

"Goodnight, Blade," she whispered, and did as he'd asked.

chapter 8

*A*S THE BOEING 737 ROARED DOWN THE RUNWAY FOR takeoff, Crys sank back into her first-class aisle seat – third row – and glanced shyly at Blade sitting next to her in the window seat. He had a magazine – *Rolling Stone* – open on his lap, but he was gazing out the window as the plane launched itself into the air with the usual stomach-dropping surge. His face looked distant and hard, the quintessential rock star's face with silver metal in his lip and eyebrow and studding up both ears, and that slight touch of eyeliner darkening around his eyes. Between his stupid magazine and him staring out of windows, she'd hardly met his eyes since they'd woken up that morning, safely locked in their separate rooms, with the memory of the night before between them.

She tried to tune out the annoying flight-safety video, the instrumental-backed instructions about putting on your life vest in the unlikely event of a crash landing over water, the droning about not smoking and how to put on those little masks if the cabin pressure were to drop.

The morning had been awkward, to say the least. Crys hadn't slept well, and she didn't think Blade had either, to judge by his ill-tempered lack of communication. He'd eaten his room-service breakfast in silence, muttered that he needed to finish packing, and disappeared back into his room. In the limousine on the way to the airport, he'd tipped his head back and closed his eyes, either sleeping or feigning sleep until their driver announced that they'd arrived at the airport.

He had not given, would not give her an opportunity to talk to him. *What would I say, anyway?* she asked herself, feeling foolish for wanting to repair the silence between them. *If I could go back to being just his sweet little friend, I would.* But there was no going back.

So Crys was completely surprised when Blade put down his magazine and turned to her, saying, "I'm sorry I've been such a bastard all morning; I've had hardly any sleep."

"I didn't sleep much, either," she admitted, a hot blush warming her cheeks.

A faintly gratified grin crossed Blade's face, and she wondered if it was the recollection of her response to him the night before that pleased him, or the fact that she was blushing over the memory of it right there in front of him. "This damnable chemistry between us," he said. "It's forbidden fruit, that's all – if you weren't... so inexperienced, things would be easier – we could just have a good fuck and relax."

"Chemistry? Is that all it is between us?" Crys asked.

"Of course. What the hell else would it be?"

Love. "Well, then..." Crys said slowly. "Maybe we... should."

Blade shook his head. "Crys, sweetheart, you don't want to throw your first time away on me – weren't you saving it for someone special? Maybe even the man you'll marry someday?"

"Blade, I don't do... white picket fences," she told him. "If it takes a confession, then this is it: I've been a good girl all my life by default, not by choice. And nice corporate boys and engagement rings don't get me hot – musicians with eye makeup and lip rings do."

"Don't you at least want to fall in love first?" he asked, sounding puzzled, as if he found himself playing a game with a lot of complicated rules he didn't quite understand.

"Who says I haven't?!" she retorted, and it wasn't until she saw the stunned expression on his face that she realized what she'd said. "Oh. Um... sorry. I didn't mean to, you know? Fall for you, I mean, when you don't love me back – and that's okay – I'm not asking for anything you can't give. You must have millions of girls crushing on you anyway, so one more doesn't matter, right? And I'm babbling here... never mind–"

and she clapped a hand over her mouth to stop the flood of nervous chatter.

"You're kidding, right? Those *millions of girls* just want a piece of me: money, fame, bragging rights 'cause they fucked a celebrity. You're too sweet to be one of them." His uneasy laugh trailed off. "You've seen me in withdrawal; you can't possibly..."

Crys shrugged. "It's how you look at your guitar, how your music reaches inside me. It's your protectiveness, even when you think you're protecting me from yourself. The world shines brighter for me when you're around, and someone's got to be my first. I want it to be you."

Understanding and compassion dawned across his face. "I didn't know," he said after a while, his voice tinged with awe. "Crys, I didn't know." He turned away and stared out the window again, and very quietly said, "Hell, if it's really what you want, then. Tonight after the show."

Crys could barely speak. "Yeah. Okay," she choked out, biting her lip.

Then the flight attendant came along to offer them champagne and orange juice, and Blade turned his attention to her in relief, smiling and chatting with the woman, who was obviously only too pleased to be working in first class that day. Crys did her best to follow his lead, not wanting the flight attendant to tell her friends that the Smidge guitarist's girlfriend had seemed out-of-sorts and speculate about whether they'd fought.

Faking amiability cut the tension between them, and soon things had shifted back to a semblance of normal. When the flight attendant moved away, Blade clinked the edge of his champagne glass against hers in a friendly toast. "Hey, I never said, but you managed those two chords I taught you pretty well yesterday," he commented. "Impressive for a first try, really. Did you like it?"

Crys sighed inwardly with relief – here was something they could talk about comfortably, without the electrical current between them that had plagued her for what felt like the past two days straight. And playing his guitar had been fun – a whole lot of fun – quite apart from their flirting and touching during the lesson. "Oh, very much," she said, warming up with genuine enthusiasm.

"You should try it with the amp plugged in – we could do that during sound check one of these days."

She giggled. "No way! That would be so amazing – on a real concert stage!"

"It is pretty amazing," he agreed. "Even for me, it's still a bit of a rush – I hope I never completely lose that feeling." He cocked his head, considering. "You know, if you want to learn properly, you should have your own guitar."

"You're kidding!"

He shrugged. "It'd make a good Christmas present."

"Blade! It's not even November yet – you can't be thinking about Christmas already!" Crys protested. *He'll have forgotten all about this by Christmas,* she thought wistfully. But at least talking about guitars was comfortable.

Overhead, the seatbelt light blinked on, and the plane began its descent into San Francisco.

♥

When they arrived at the hotel, they didn't see anyone from the crew or band downstairs, but the front desk had several messages for Blade along with the key cards to their two-bedroom suite. He pulled out his phone, and handed one of the cards to Crys, saying, "I've got to make a couple of calls straight away, so why don't you go ahead and get settled in? We've got the whole tenth floor, so the only people you'll see up there are our people. I'll be there in a few minutes."

Crys nodded her agreement, smiling as she turned to find the elevators. A few minutes alone suited her perfectly. One luxury hotel was much like any other, she concluded as she rode up in yet another mirror-paneled elevator, walked down yet another soft-carpeted hallway. One of the doors was ajar, and she heard voices that she thought belonged to Sally and Erva, but she passed by on quiet feet.

Finding the suite she was to share with Blade, Crys unlocked the door and slipped inside. Once again, it was much the same as the other suites they'd shared, this time a long narrow sitting room with both bedrooms side-by-side on the right. She noticed that in this hotel the sitting room had one couch and two armchairs instead of the usual two couches, cozily grouped around a flickering gas fireplace – someone must have turned it on in preparation for their arrival. She peeked into the nearer of the two bedrooms and saw Blade's two suitcases, a king-sized bed. *The bed. Oh sweet God!* Feeling hot and squirmy, she retreated, went into the second room and found the giant array of luggage which Marigold had provided for her – a good portion of it had been unpacked and hung in the wardrobe – presumably Marigold's recommended choices for the night's concert.

After checking the time, Crys decided to take a bath, even though she'd already had a quick shower that morning. She washed herself extra carefully, scrubbed and shaved and trimmed to be as smooth and flawless as possible. Afterward, she set her hair in hot rollers for as much volume as she could get, and moisturized every inch of her skin to slick perfection with her favorite vanilla-scented lotion. Buffed and polished her short fingernails. Then, wrapped in a fluffy white hotel bathrobe, she investigated the fashion choices that Marigold had set out for her in the wardrobe.

Tight jeans are awkward to get off, she thought, touching the vintage-faded denim with a considering finger. She looked at a pleated schoolgirl-style skirt. *Not the image I want to project, when he still might decide that I'm too inexperienced for him.* Then she noticed the black leather miniskirt from the first concert, and nodded to herself in satisfaction. She recalled that he'd liked the garter belt the night before; it was a 1940s style pin-up-girl garter belt, black with silver garter clips, and had plain sheer black stockings to go with it. Panties were an absolute essential with the miniskirt, though – Blade knowing she'd taken them off in the restaurant had felt risqué, but the thought of Easy and Dice and Angel catching an eyeful made her cringe. She considered a lacy thong but even that seemed a bit much to flash, so she opted for plain black satin bikini panties instead. They matched the garter belt, after all. She thought about the liquid-silver top that she'd originally worn with the miniskirt, but instead went digging through the things still in the suitcases to find her black Smidge t-shirt, hoping it would produce the ideal balance between casual and sexy.

Fully dressed, she examined her reflection in the full-length mirror behind the bathroom door. She didn't know whether Marigold would approve, but... *This looks right,* she thought in satisfaction, buckling the black leather wristband Blade had given her around her right wrist. Not a church-supper good girl, nor a Marigold-clone fashion doll. A balance of soft and hard, subtle and wild – but never again would she let herself feel boring or plain.

Footwear was a little trickier. She set aside the bejeweled sandals she'd worn with her satin dress the night before, beautiful but far too dressy for wearing with a t-shirt. Somehow, she didn't feel up to wearing the sexy boots, which Marigold had placed in the wardrobe – they implied too much knowledge that she didn't yet have – and the slouchy ankle boots sitting next to them were cute but didn't suit her mood. Marigold had also set out a pair of satin ballet flats for her, presumably to go with the schoolgirl skirt, but they didn't seem right either – giving up on Marigold's choices, Crys went back to the suitcases, knowing that she'd seen at least two other shoe boxes among all the fashion goodies. She found a pair of sporty casual shoes, but they didn't work with the miniskirt and garter belt combination. Kept looking. Found a pair of frivolous little punk party shoes, nothing but thin leather straps and buckles, with rhinestone heart details and sexy three-inch heels that would probably kill her to walk in. Beautiful.

A knock on the door startled her. "Yes?"

"Crys, we've got to head to sound check in about ten minutes," Blade's voice called from the other side of the door. "Are you almost ready?"

She didn't feel ready to face him, and instead of opening the door she called back, "Sure, I've just got to do my hair. Take me five minutes, I'll be right out."

Dashing into the bathroom, she pulled the rollers out of her hair with hurried hands. *Oh, wow!* She'd originally intended to use the rollers just for volume, as Sally and Marigold had done for her on a couple of occasions – but then she hadn't been looking in the mirror when the rollers came out, not until after a go with a round brush had smoothed everything into the floating halo she'd grown used to. Now, finger-combed into place, the sex-kitten curls made her into a rock-and-roll Marilyn Monroe.

Instead of opting for her usual pale shimmer gloss, she painted her lips a deep candy-apple red.

Blade banged on the door – time was up. "Got to go, sweetheart!" he called out.

Jangling with nerves, Crys darted back into the bedroom and slipped on her shoes, buckling the straps with shaking fingers. Stood, and took a few careful steps on the high heels – the highest she'd ever worn, and with dangerously pointed spikes too – noticing with delight how her center of balance had changed, how her figure was accentuated by the new posture the shoes forced on her.

Blade banged on the door again, irritated, then pushed the door open, saying, "Crys, we've really got to–" His words broke off as he caught sight of her. "Damn, you look amazing!"

"It's just having cool clothes," she said, feeling awkward, and then decided that honesty would serve her better. "I... I wanted to look nice, tonight. For you, I mean. If... if you meant what you said earlier, that is."

"Holy fuck, yeah!" He grinned at her, with a look in his eyes that made her feel excited and squirmy all over, and so brilliantly, amazingly sexy and desired and somehow powerful inside. "Now let's get downstairs, before I mess up your pretty lipstick."

Crys giggled at that – she never could help giggling under pressure – and teetered over to the door on her high heels. "You might have to hold me up until I learn to walk in these," she said.

"Sure," he agreed, taking her hand and tucking it over his forearm, so that she had his full arm strength to lean on for support. "If this doesn't work, I'll just carry you," he joked, cocking his head at her as though contemplating whether to scoop her up into his arms.

She laughed and leaned away from him, almost tripping on her shoes. "Don't you dare!"

"Let's go, then." He towed her out her bedroom door. "Where's your jacket?" Her leather jacket lay where she'd left it on the arm of the couch in the sitting area – he helped her on with it, his fingertips brushing her neck as he did so, and an electric tingle rippled through her at even such a slight accidental touch. He noticed. "Damn, you are responsive, aren't you!" he muttered. His phone rang and he cleared his throat to answer it. "Blade here... great... thanks, man ... yeah, we'll be right there."

"Car's here?" she asked him as he put the phone back in his pocket.

Blade nodded. "We'd better go. The guys are heading down the hall, we'll catch them at the elevators." He picked up his guitar and slung it over his shoulder, held out his arm. "Grab on, sweetheart."

Because of her shoes, Crys couldn't stride out to match Blade's pace as she would have in lower heels. Clinging to his arm, she had to trot along on her toes to keep up with him.

Easy and Dice were already in the elevator, and Angel was holding the door for them. As Blade strode faster down the hall, almost lifting Crys along on his arm, she swore her toes were only touching the ground every third or fourth step. And then they reached the elevator, and Blade was knocking fists with each of the others in greeting, all of them with wide grins on their faces. First Angel and then Dice clapped Crys affectionately on the shoulder, greeting her too. "How're you feeling, babe?" Angel asked her. "All better?"

"Oh, yes," Crys assured him. "It was kind of nice to have some peace and quiet, even after I got over feeling yucky, but I'm glad to be back with the rest of you now." Though she'd only intended the words as a courtesy, she realized as she spoke that she did mean them. *I am glad to see the band again – I missed these guys, and I've hardly known them a week.* She had the oddest sense of friendship, even of family, with these men whom two weeks before she'd only idolized in posters and in listening to their music. *It doesn't make sense; how could that be?* But they seemed glad to see her too.

"Did you guys do anything fun back in Portland last night?" Dice asked idly, leaning against the wall of the elevator.

Fun. Crys blinked. Fun was hardly the word for it.

"We went out for dinner," Blade said. "That's all." He didn't elaborate, and his tone didn't encourage anyone to ask.

Angel punched him lightly on the shoulder. "Ease up, man. Smiles for the press all around, right?"

The elevator hit the lobby, and they emerged into the usual camera flashes, smiles coming more easily this time without the worries they'd had when Blade had been detoxing. And Crys smiled easily too, this time not feeling like a fraud, because Blade really did desire her. *For tonight at least,* she thought, *I really am his girl.*

The usual crowd of press and fans were waiting when the limousine rolled up to the arena. It was a bright clear day, and sunlight flashed along with the cameras as Blade helped Crys out of the vehicle; she wondered if the boys ever wished for bad weather, to chase away the curious and the mercenary – or would onlookers still gather in a rainstorm? There seemed to be an inordinate number of them, but then, maybe that was normal for a Saturday concert.

A group of punked-out guys in brand new Smidge t-shirts were hanging over the security barrier, evidently a bit drunk, slurredly shouting out, "You rock, dudes!" and "I love you guys!" They waved and made some sort of rock-and-roll gesture with their hands. And then one of the guys tried to climb over the barrier, and security moved in with a warning to back down.

"What does that mean, that hand sign?" Crys asked as she and the band hurried up the steps to the door. "The one where they tuck their two middle fingers down and point with the index and pinky?"

Her question made all of them laugh, even Easy. "It's called the horns, baby doll," he said with a snicker. "It's, like, totally metal." As they were about to go inside, he turned toward the crowd of fans and raised a hand in the same gesture, a mocking grin on his face.

"They were doing it wrong, anyway," Blade grumbled. "With the thumb out like that, it's fucking sign language."

Angel snorted. "Yeah, sign language for 'I love you.' Totally metal, man!"

The heavy doors slammed closed behind them, shutting them into the cool dark of the arena.

♥

During sound check, Blade called Crys onto the stage and held out his guitar to her, saying, "Okay, sweetheart – you wanted to try playing with the amp..."

"Really?" Walking onto the boards of the stage, looking around at the vast space ringed with thousands of seats, she couldn't stop the kid-in-a-candy-store smile from spreading across her face.

"Really." He lifted the guitar strap over her head, helped her settle it into place. She'd been sitting before, and it felt a little different standing up, with the weight of the guitar pulling against her shoulder. "Here you go." He handed her his pick. "These two are volume," pointing out the different little knobs on the body of the guitar, "and these two are tone – you just twist them – and this switch over here is the pickup selector."

"I don't know," she said, suddenly feeling shy as she became aware that Angel was watching with amused interest, and that Dice and some of the crew were also paying attention to the impromptu guitar lesson going on. This wasn't some garage-band amp, either, but the real thing, powerful arena-concert equipment.

"Go on," said Angel, walking over to join them, still wearing his guitar. "I didn't know you were learning to play, Crys. What have you learned so far?"

Crys ducked her head. "Just a... a G chord and a... C chord, I think?"

"That's right," said Blade, moving around behind her, placing an encouraging hand on her right hip while he guided her left hand with his to the strings, his fingertips just touching her wrist, ever so gently. "G chord. Do you remember?"

The memory had been burned into her mind. She pressed down on the strings, the steel cutting into her fingertips. "Like this?"

Blade and Angel both nodded in approval, Angel replicating the fingering on his own guitar and playing the chord in demonstration. "Your turn – go on."

Crys brought the pick down across the strings, and instead of the softly musical sound of the unamplified guitar she'd heard at the hotel, she heard the full electric rock-concert scream – the guitar's true voice. She almost dropped the pick in surprised delight at having made that raw sound.

"Okay, now try strumming it a few times," Blade suggested into her ear.

"I'll play it with you," said Angel. And as Crys brought the pick down across the strings, he did likewise, once... twice... three times. "Good stuff."

"Thank you so much," said Crys to Angel, before turning her head to look at Blade, still behind her.

He bent his head forward, close to her ear. "Had enough, Crys?" he asked.

"Never," she said, meaning it, because this feeling of raw noise in a vast space could go on forever and it wouldn't be enough. "But Mack is giving me the evil eye, so I'd better get out of the way and let you finish up." Hovering nearby, the stage manager was fidgeting with his watch like he had a mosquito bite under it, and looking sourly at the three of them wasting time on his stage.

She started to lift the guitar off herself, and Blade helped her, slipping his hands under the strap to take the weight of the instrument. "I can tell you like being plugged in, sweetheart," he said as he raised the guitar strap over his own head, settled it on his shoulder. "We'll do this again, I promise."

"That was fine, babe," Angel added, and then Crys hurried as best she could to the side of the stage, all but tripping in her high heels, more than ready to be away from Mack's gimlet stare. The man wasn't normally ill-tempered, but with the responsibility of an arena full of sound and technical effects on his shoulders, he could get downright fierce if his sound check didn't go quickly and smoothly, and she didn't want his annoyance turned in her direction.

She watched the rest of the sound check from the side of the stage, as always, fascinated at how the single big wall of sound that the audience would hear was so carefully and intricately managed behind the scenes.

Although Crys had intended to walk back to the band lounge with Blade and the other boys after the sound check was done, Sally rushed up as soon as she saw Crys, obviously glad to see her. And Crys was glad to see Sally too. It was one thing to email or text Leah and Debbie, or Rhys, or even to phone her parents, but none of them shared any familiarity with this world. Worse, she had to assume with every email that it might be seen by unfriendly eyes, and never dared to write anything that wouldn't bear repeating. She even wondered if it were possible to intercept phone conversations, and in the end chose to say nothing that might be misinterpreted. Sally, on the other hand, lived within the concert tour world and understood what it felt like to adjust to that, and knew – or thought she knew – the true situation with Blade.

"Crys! How was the flight down?" Sally asked, squeezing Crys in a friendly hug of enthusiastic arms and voluptuous breasts. "Don't you just hate flying commercial? Oh, you haven't actually been with us on the tour jet yet, have you? Well, you *will* hate flying commercial, anyway."

Crys laughed. "Oh, to get so used to the good life! The flight down was okay – I do know that I'll hate flying coach now I've had a taste of business class."

"Blade didn't get into any trouble in Portland?"

"N-no." Was that a lie? Or at least an evasion? Blade had gone out and bought some heroin in Portland, but hadn't used it. "It was fine. He took me out for dinner. We... we drank a bit of red wine, but... it was fine." Crys hoped that Sally wouldn't notice her blush in the hard fluorescent light of the arena tunnels they walked through.

"So, where did you go? What did you eat? Spill, honey, it's the next best thing to eating there myself!"

Crys didn't have a clue about the name or location of the restaurant – she'd been so caught up in the moment, being out on her own with Blade just like the first time at the Ballroom at home, that she'd paid no attention to the streets the limo had driven through or the name on the restaurant's awning. "You know, I have no idea what the place we went was called, but it was very fancy – I was all dressed up in black satin with my diamond earrings – and the food was amazing."

"Yeah? What'd you have?" Sally, apparently a fan of gourmet food, waited eagerly for the details.

Crys dragged her mind back to the food on the table. It had been amazing, but so much had happened before, during, and after the meal that it was hard to recall exactly what she'd eaten. "Garlic prawns. I had totally heavenly garlic prawns. On a, um, mushroom-and-parmesan risotto. With... hmm... carrots in maple butter."

"That sounds seriously yummy! Did you have dessert?"

"Dessert. Yes. We had dessert." Crys swallowed, finding herself awash in memory. *I'm guessing you've never let a guy go down on you, huh?* The moment when the game had turned into not-a-game. And the spoon dropping into the half-melted orange gelato, splattering across the table.

"Well?" Sally asked. "What did you have – Crys, are you okay?"

Crys shook her head to clear it. "Sorry. I'm fine. You were asking about dessert. We... shared a chocolate brownie and orange gelato. It was... good."

Outside the door to the band lounge, the security guard sat at his table, reading a Michael Creighton thriller. A few feet away, out of earshot, Sally stopped and looked at Crys with narrowed eyes. "Honey, did something bad happen in Portland?"

"Nothing bad happened, not in any of the ways you might mean. It was just... intense, that's all."

Sally nodded. "Sure. You wanna talk about it, you let me know, huh?" When Crys didn't answer, Sally linked arms with her and headed for the room designated as the band's dressing room or green room, cheerfully saying, "Hi, Aidan!" to the security guard as they came up to his table. Then Sally was thumping on the door to be let in, even as Aidan pressed a button on his radio to alert them inside that they should open the door.

Linked to Sally, towed along, Crys found herself amid the usual pre-show chaos. Milk crates and rolling garment racks had been moved in, holding all the gear the boys would need to convert themselves from street personae to their onstage presences – mesh and leather and denim, Angel's wings, Blade's collar, cans of blue and silver hairspray. Easy lay sprawled out on a couch, napping, booted feet up on the cushions. In the matching armchair, Angel sat reading a magazine – was it the *Rolling Stone* Blade had been reading on the plane that morning? – while Blade paced the room, restless and tense. Sally's box of makeup tricks sat open on a folding table; Dice was poking through it, looking for something. "You get out of my kit, Dice! You know I don't like you guys messing it up," Sally scolded him, but she was smiling. "What d'you need?"

"I'm getting a zit," he confessed, bordering on a tragic tone. "Need some of that medicated cover-up gunk."

Sally reached into her kit and found the tube she wanted. "Okay, where's the spot?" she asked, and used a Q-tip to dab a bit of the beige paste onto the tiny blemish Dice pointed out. "There, all fixed."

"Thanks, Sal."

The radio on the table next to Sally's kit buzzed, followed almost immediately by a bang on the door. Crys, still standing near the door, recognized the buzz as the signal to open up; she turned and pulled the door open, admitting Jed with two huge brown-paper take-out bags.

A rich, meaty hamburger aroma wafted from the bags. Blade, immediately gagging at the smell, headed for the door. He turned back briefly to ask, "Anyone in the guest lounge right now, Jed?"

"It's all yours. Sorry, buddy, I should have thought to warn you about the food before bringing it in. Guest lounge has an electronic lock – six-oh-four-three."

"I'm outta here." And Blade was out of the room and gone.

Jed jerked his head at the door. "Better go with him, Crys. He's... kind of vulnerable right before a show." Realizing that Jed meant vulnerable to the addiction, to the temptation of cutting his stage fright with the drug, Crys hurried out and down the hall after Blade.

Hearing her footsteps, he whirled around, snarling, "I need to be alone, damn it!" Then he registered that it was Crys coming after him, and took a deep breath. "So they sent my babysitter after me, did they?" he asked, though not unkindly, more resigned than anything.

"I'm not your babysitter," she told him. "Jed said you'd be... I just want to help, that's all."

"Jed said I'd be what? Wanting to shoot up? He's right – oh, Crys, hell, just leave me, okay?"

"No." She looked him in the eye, feeling stubborn as a cat and letting it show. "Do what you must, but I'm coming with you, and watching. Someone's got to be able to call Jed for you, right?" He turned and walked away without a word, and she tagged after him, not sure what else to do. She wanted to beg him not to do it, though she knew it would do no good. *So am I strong enough to watch him put a needle in his arm?* In her high heels, she had to scuttle forward with small jogging steps, weight on her toes, to keep up with his retreating back. *If I have no other choice, yes.*

She caught up with him at the door to the guest lounge – he punched in the code and pushed open the door as the lock hummed permission, then turned to face her, to stop her. "Go back now, Crys. Send Jed to look after me, if you must."

"Didn't you hear me? No!" She reached out, placed a hand on his arm, asking without words that he focus on her, that he listen. "Blade, you know I... care about you... I'm not going to abandon you to the heroin. If you – if you absolutely have to do this – I'm going to watch you do it. I will be here. No matter what."

He closed his eyes. Moved away from her, sat down on the floor, drew the harmless-looking pen case from the inside pocket of his leather jacket. "I'll only do a little," he said. "Just to get me through the concert." Crys couldn't think of an answer to that, so she knelt opposite him and watched in silence as he opened the pen case, took out a spoon and a folded paper packet like the one she'd disposed of in the hotel in Portland. He tipped some of the innocuous-looking pale powder into the spoon, took a syringe out of his case and squirted water from it into the spoon. He kept his eyes down, fixed on the lighter he held under the spoon, as though he couldn't bring himself to meet Crys's troubled gaze. A small wad of cotton went into the spoon and then he was drawing up the demon liquid into his syringe.

"Blade, is there no other way you can get through this?" she asked softly, sadly.

He didn't answer as he took off his jacket, tied the rubber tubing around his left arm just above the elbow. Brought the needle tip close to the healing skin of his inner arm. "Don't look, Crys," he ordered, his voice raw with self-loathing and need. "Close your eyes, turn away, whatever."

"If you have to do this, then I have to see this – make your choice, show me the dark side of your world if you must, but I won't turn my back and pretend it's okay."

His hand holding the syringe shook. "Hell." He bit his lip, hard, eyes squeezed closed. "Take it." And when she didn't move quickly enough, he snarled through gritted teeth, "Take the damned syringe – now! – I can't make myself give it to you; take it from me!"

Terrified, Crys reached out and closed her fingers around the syringe, lifting it away. She held it in a trembling hand, uncertain what to do with it. In front of her, Blade had drawn up his knees and buried his face in folded arms, shaking in what she thought might be silent sobs. *Jed would know what to do,* she thought, but didn't have a radio to call him. Not daring to leave Blade alone – God only knew if he had another syringe, more drugs – she got to her feet and pulled out her phone, looked at it in desperation. The reception in the lower levels of big arenas often wasn't so good. She dialed Jed, and on her second try the call went through, but he didn't answer. *What now?* She did have Marigold's number, and Marigold always answered her phone. This time it took four tries before the call went through; Crys held her breath as it rang.

"Hi Marigold, it's Crys," she said, as soon as the public relations assistant answered. "I can't explain, but I need Jed to come and find me now. Can you tell him that, please? It's urgent."

"What's wrong, Crys? Is it–" Marigold asked over the phone.

"Please just send Jed now," Crys pleaded, and because she wanted Jed there more quickly than would reasonably be possible, she punched the end button to disconnect the call, even though she could hear Marigold's voice still talking. It went against every rule of courtesy she'd ever been taught, but she hoped that her rudeness would have Marigold calling Jed sooner than if she'd tried to extricate herself politely.

The syringe in her hand scared her, but Blade's near-lapse and misery scared her even more. She didn't know whether to go to him or give him space, didn't know what to do with the syringe full of heroin that she held – was she supposed to get rid of it the way she'd washed the other down the toilet? Squirt the contents of the syringe onto the floor or into the garbage can? Or just hold it until Jed showed up? Gripping it carefully in her left hand, the sharp point well away from her body and his, she approached Blade and laid her right hand on his bowed head, stroking his hair with all the love and sympathy in her heart.

In the end, both Jed and Angel came.

Crys said nothing as the electronic lock hummed and the door swung open, only held out the syringe for Jed to take – utter relief washed through her at his arrival to take over, someone who knew what he was doing, who wasn't petrified of the needle and what it contained. Jed crossed the room in a few quick strides, taking the syringe from Crys's outstretched hand, looking at it once, and then again in surprise. "Still full? Is this a second one, then, or didn't he–?"

Crys shook her head. "No. He... he asked me to take it from him."

"That's got to take strength I hope I'll never need," Jed said, blowing out a deep respectful breath, as he bent to pick up Blade's pen case from the floor and gather the scattered items back into it. "You did a strong thing, buddy," he murmured to Blade, who had not looked up but kept his face hidden in his arms.

Crouching down, Angel put a gentle arm around Blade's shoulders, talking to him in a low voice – Crys could see his lips moving but couldn't make out the words – his face full of love for his friend and the fear of losing him. Believing that his best friend must know best how to comfort him, she lifted her hand from Blade's head and stepped away, intending to leave him to Angel's care. But he raised his head as she drew away, choking out, "D-don't go..."

Angel nodded to her, saying, "She won't go, man, she's right here. We won't leave you alone."

"I'm here," Crys said, reaching out again to grip Blade's shoulder, wanting desperately to comfort him. "I'm here."

Together she and Angel raised him to his feet, linked their arms around his waist in support and affection. "I'm such a fuck-up," he muttered.

"No, you're not," Crys assured him.

Angel spoke almost at the same moment, saying, "Dude, you didn't do it – you're not a fuck-up, okay?"

"But I almost – if Crys had turned away when I asked her to, I would have–"

"But you didn't. And standing around here doing the what-ifs isn't going to get you anything. Go back to the band lounge and have a drink, why don't you?" Jed suggested, waving the three of them away.

"Good call. Blade, let's do what Jed says and go get a drink," Angel agreed. "I know it's not the same, but it can take the edge off a bit."

After a moment, Blade shrugged his shoulders, slipped his arms around their waists on either side of him, completing the linkage. "Yeah. Okay."

The three of them walked down the tunnels to the band lounge, hip to hip, as a unit. And though Dice shot one glance of concern at them when they entered, nothing was said – tacit agreement put the rough moment behind them – the only option with a concert ahead.

♥

The concert was manic, intense – all the earlier emotion rocketing out into the music – the audience sensed the mood, fed on it, and fed it. The atmosphere grew electric, one of those unforgettable concerts where magic happens between the band and the audience. Maybe because of the earlier moment of deep feeling, the interaction between Angel and Blade seemed particularly powerful and connected, almost as if they could read each other's mind.

Crys watched from her usual hidden spot, while the crew around her worked and the band rocked out. And when they played "Love Bound," and Blade sang, "For every night when the bedsheets burned / For every night when thunder rolled," he looked directly at her, and this time there was no confusion about what that look meant. He was promising her burning bedsheets and all the thunder she could handle. It was wicked, and intense, and she nearly fell off her shoes at the heat between them – even with half the stage separating them and an arena full of people watching.

After the final encore, when Blade came off the stage he took Crys's hand and pulled her with him, and though Scott was there with his camera to record the moment, it was not done for the pictures.

When they reached the band lounge, Marigold in her black leather power suit was waiting for them with a list of the evening's backstage guests. "Crys, will you come and assist Jed in the guest lounge like you did in Portland?" she asked briskly, so certain that the response would be 'yes' that she didn't pause for an answer. "Great – we only have two groups of four coming through tonight; an easy night, but Jed still appreciates the help. Come on, I'll walk you down there now," she added.

Crys moved to follow Marigold, but Blade tightened his grip on her hand, holding her there beside him. "Crys is staying here," he said, in a flat tone that warned Marigold not to dispute the point.

"Right," she said, pursing her lips – she was accustomed to being in charge and didn't like being contradicted. "I'm sure you have your reasons; Jed will just have to do everything himself."

"I don't mind–" Crys began, but Blade shook his head.

"I want you with me, sweetheart," he said, stroking the hidden palm of her hand with his thumb, sending electric ripples of sensation through her. She tried to keep her breathing steady, as Blade turned to Marigold, saying, "Look, Goldie, Crys got me through a... a very rough moment this afternoon. I need her to stay near me right now, okay?"

"Oh... I see... of course!" Marigold's pout vanished and was replaced by saccharine concern. "It's no problem; Jed will understand completely. I'm so glad Crys is able to give you the support you need."

Crys bit her lip. *So we're going to hide this thing between us,* she thought, *and still pretend it's just a professional arrangement.* Would that make her a whore, she wondered, a true professional girlfriend? She already had the diamond earrings.

Marigold dashed off. Bottles of champagne were opened, passed around – Dice handed one to Crys and she took it gladly. Sally arrived to touch up the boys, and gave Crys a spot of powder and fresh lipstick too. Scott with his camera adjusted lighting and fiddled with lenses. And Blade kept finding excuses to touch Crys, never obviously, but with clear intent – hands brushing each other, fingertip touches, surreptitious caresses. Easy and Dice noticed nothing, but Angel narrowed his eyes and looked hard at both of them.

Crys hardly noticed as first one group of guests and then the other was ushered in and out of the band lounge. Then the guests were gone, and the boys were back in the dressing room washing the makeup from their faces and changing into street clothes, while Crys averted her eyes and pretended that she wasn't sitting in a room with four half-naked men, one of whom would shortly be taking her virginity.

"Come on, Crys," said Blade abruptly, and she looked up to see that he was pulling on his leather jacket. "Let's go."

"Go?" She glanced at the others – Easy was still cleaning his face, and Dice was shirtless and shoeless. Angel looked at her and shrugged noncommittally, and although he was fully dressed, face clean, he didn't reach for his jacket.

"Yeah. We're... going out. Arranged two cars earlier, so we can ditch these jokers. See you back at the hotel, guys."

Easy turned slightly, said, "Catch ya later," and turned back to the mirror.

Dice laughed and waved them off, and Angel raised his hand too, but more slowly, saying, "Enjoy the night, you two." Crys wondered if he knew.

chapter

9

TWO GLEAMING BLACK LIMOUSINES WAITED OUTSIDE THE arena. As they approached, the driver of the first one got out and opened the door for them – Blade's bodyguard had tried to follow them out as usual but Blade had told him no, unwilling this time to be monitored. Blade helped Crys step inside, his hands on her waist, and climbed in behind her. The driver slammed the door closed behind them, then moments later they felt the muted thump of his door closing.

"So. We're alone at last," Blade said, leaning back with arms behind his head and stretching out his long legs, looking at Crys with unconcealed hunger.

Suddenly feeling shy, she crossed her arms across her chest, locked her knees together. "W-where are we going?" she asked, needing a distraction, a postponement of the reckoning that was rapidly approaching. *Play with fire, you're going to get burned.* Crys was slowly growing aware that she stood in the path of a wildfire, and risked a burn of almighty proportions.

"Well... I had an idea." He watched her as he spoke, with a crooked little half-smile. "I thought you'd want... this is special for you, isn't it? And I can't give you an engagement ring, but... I thought maybe... another kind of ring." He touched the steel ring in his own lip, then leaned forward and ever so gently traced her lower lip with a fingertip. "You like mine – d'you want one of your own?"

Her mouth dropped open. "You're kidding, right?" But to her surprise, the idea sort of appealed to her, and she licked her lower lip experimentally, wondering what it would feel like to have a bit of metal there. "It... it would hurt, wouldn't it?"

He nodded. "It does," he agreed. "But I'd be right there with you." He shrugged. "You don't have to do it – only if you want to."

"Well... how bad is it?" And even as she asked, Crys realized that she was going to do it. *His ring in my lip, marking me. Even after it's over, I'll have that much of him, forever.*

"It's a needle. It feels like a needle." He thought for a moment. "I guess the closest other thing would be a bee sting, I don't know – it's kind of hard to describe."

"Okay," she said, with a shaky deep breath. "Yeah, I'll do it."

"I thought you might." Blade grinned. "Now, come here and kiss me hard, because we'll have to be careful after you've got your piercing."

Crys stared at him, as he sat back and waited for her to come to him. Always before, he'd initiated their kisses; now, he was asking her to take the lead. Cautiously, to avoid losing her balance in the high-heeled shoes and moving vehicle, she moved across to him, placing her hands tentatively on his shoulders. And then there wasn't any choice but to straddle his lap, her knees sinking into the leather seat on either side of his hips, the leather miniskirt no hindrance, the black satin of her panties pressed against the hardness in his jeans, sliding around with every shift of her weight, every motion of the car. *Oh sweet God!* He gripped her waist, but waited still, though his breath came more quickly and his eyes were dark with wanting. "What do I do now?" she breathed, the words hardly audible.

"What do you want to do?" he asked her.

"Kiss you," she whispered, lifting a hand to touch his mouth, his lip ring.

He slipped the tip of his tongue out to lick her exploring finger, drew the finger into his mouth and sucked on it. Released it. "Go ahead, then," he said. "Kiss me."

What do you want to do? he'd asked. She bent her head, brought her lips to his. Felt the metallic hardness of his lip ring. Felt his lips part as her tongue explored, felt rather than heard him groan. And then he rolled with her – winding up on top of her, lying half on and half off the pale grey leather limousine seat – taking control of the kiss, his mouth hard and urgent, a warning that tonight he was not holding back.

A knock on the partition alerted them, prompted Blade to break off the kiss and raise his head, bringing Crys back to awareness of things other than Blade on top of her. The limousine had stopped moving. The driver's voice came through a speaker, saying, "Excuse me, sir, but we've arrived at your first destination."

They broke apart, sitting up and straightening clothing. Crys, knowing that her hair must be a complete mess at this point, did her best to pat the curls into some semblance of order.

"Are you sure about this, Crys?" Blade asked, all joking aside for a moment. "I know it was my idea, but... a facial piercing is a bit of a commitment – are you sure it's something you want?"

My parents will freak out, and I'll never get an office job, Crys thought. And neither of those things frightened her. "Yes."

"You're not just doing this for me?"

"I'm doing it for myself," said Crys. *To never be the good girl by default again.*

A brief knock on the vehicle's door gave them a moment's notice to compose themselves for the world, and then the door was open, and the driver offered an arm to steady Crys as she stepped out of the limousine. Blade got out behind her, took her hand and led her forward toward the door of a very clean-looking, upscale shop – with a sign reading CLOSED on the door. Crys looked at him, wondering if they were too late, if she was off the hook for the night – from the piercing, anyway – but he just smiled. "They're not open this late, but Evan waited especially for you, sweetheart."

"Evan?"

He waved toward the glass door, where a tattooed man in pale blue scrubs was approaching from inside the shop, holding a key to unlock it. "That's Evan. He did my lip way back, and everything I've had done since." Then they were at the door, open now, and Blade greeted Evan with a hug.

"Hey, man, it's been ages," said Evan with a wide smile. "Good to see you."

"Good to see you too, Ev."

"And this is the lady wants her lip done?"

"That's right. Crys, this is Evan Metkin. Evan, Crys Murphy."

Evan offered his hand, shaking hers firmly with a grip that reminded her of Jed's – professional hands – medical hands? "Pleasure to meet you, lovey. Any friend of Blade's is a friend of mine."

"Nice to meet you," Crys murmured.

Evan smiled at her. "Nervous?" he asked, and she nodded. "Let's get to it, then – nothing makes nerves worse like waiting."

There was a little bit of paperwork to fill out, and then the two men led Crys to a curtained-off cubicle, where an oddly reassuring antiseptic smell greeted her. A small trolley with a tray of implements on it sat ready for the piercing process, next to a padded medical exam table covered with a crisp bleached-white sheet. Everything looked tidy and extremely clean.

Evan washed his hands and put gloves on like a doctor would. He gave Crys some nasty-tasting mouthwash to rinse with, then cleaned the outside of her lower lip with an antiseptic wipe – it felt cool and tingly – and marked the chosen spot on her lip with a special pen that came out of a sealed packet. Blade nodded in approval, and when Crys was given a hand mirror to check the positioning of the dot, she nodded too. *Even just the ink looks kind of cool,* she thought. *I do want this.*

"Well, it's time, lovey," Evan said. "Let's get you up on the table – d'you want to do it sitting up or lying down?" Feeling ever so slightly faint now that the moment was at hand, sure that she'd never be able to get her legs to carry her the few steps over to the table, Crys looked to Blade for support.

He understood – he scooped her up in his arms and laid her on the table, then took her hand in his – strong fingers in a firm grip supported and reassured her. "Squeeze as hard as you need to, sweetheart," he told her. "I've got tough hands – you can't hurt me."

"Why am I doing this?" she blurted out.

Blade and Evan both smiled. "You said you were doing it for yourself," Blade reminded her.

"Yes – yes, I am." *To never be the good girl by default again. To remind myself never to settle for a life that's only tolerable, never to just fall into the role I'm expected to play. Not anymore.*

"Good," said Evan. He pinched her lip in a cold metal clamp. "This is for you, then – deep breath, here we go." As he heard or felt her draw in a gasping gulp of air, he pushed the needle through. A brief sharp stab of pain rocked through her, just for a moment, and then it was gone, replaced by a dull ache. Evan turned away from her for a moment, to the tray on the trolley. "Needle's through. I'm just getting your ring now."

"You're doing fine, Crys," Blade murmured, looking down at her, his face and voice full of approval and pride. She looked up at him, feeling warm and glowing inside. *He's proud of me; he thinks I'm doing fine.*

Then Evan turned back to her, saying, "A little pinch now, all right?" And indeed there was a feeling of pinching, an uncomfortable dull soreness punctuated by a series of twinges. "There. You're all done."

Blade helped her sit up. Her lower lip ached, throbbed. Cautiously, she allowed the tip of her tongue to touch the metal ring. *How odd.* Blade was looking at her with a sort of pleased awe on his face, and desire too. "Oh, Crys, you look fantastic," he said slowly. "It really suits you."

Evan handed her a paper cup full of small ice cubes. "Suck on the ice for a bit. You want to keep the swelling down, lovey. Blade knows the aftercare drill; he'll take care of you." They walked out to the front, and Evan reached into a cupboard and brought out a bag with the shop logo and the words 'aftercare kit' on it. "There's all the stuff you'll need," he explained, handing it to Crys. "Mouthwash for the inside, cleanser for the outside, sea salt for soaking, and some ibuprofen. There's a new toothbrush for you too – don't use your old one, and replace it as often as you can during the healing process."

All that sounded a bit overwhelming, and Crys started to wonder what she'd gotten herself into – it apparently wasn't as simple as just facing the piercer's needle. There were chairs in the waiting area at the front of the shop, of course, and Blade gestured at one of them, saying, "Sit here for a second while I settle up with Evan."

Gratefully, Crys sank into the chair, and gazed out the window at the night-time street until Blade came back to take her away. Feeling a bit spacey, she got up and allowed him to guide her – she thanked Evan and said goodbye to him, but it was as though someone else were talking through her mouth. Her lip had already begun to puff up and felt hot and achy.

In the limousine, she began to shake – shivering as though with cold, though she wasn't cold. Blade pulled her close and wrapped his arms around her. "You probably need to eat something, sweetheart," he told her. "It's my fault; you should've been having a burger with the others before the concert, instead of babysitting me..." He shook his head in self-disgust. "Well, we'll get room service to bring us something as soon as we get back to the hotel."

Crys smiled. "That sounds good... I suppose I am kind of hungry – I haven't been thinking about food much this evening."

That made Blade laugh. "No doubt." He stroked her hair, not in a sexual way, just soothing her. "Getting your lip done might have been kind of a shock to your system too, huh?"

"But I'm okay, truly I am," she insisted. Surely a momentary weakness wasn't going to spoil their whole evening?

"I know," Blade said. "Of course you're fine."

Crys leaned her head against him, snuggled into his arms. Closed her eyes. The sensation of his hands gently smoothing her hair combined with the rocking motion of the limousine to send her drifting into a doze. Suddenly she felt something cold against her lip, and struggled to sit up, startled. "Huh?"

"Hush. I'm just icing your lip a bit, so it won't swell so bad." The coldness had been an ice cube – Blade was holding it to the aching part of her lip. "You should take an ibuprofen, too – it's better to take it before you need it, doesn't help so much if you wait until after the swelling sets in." He got out the packet of tablets and tore it open, fished one out and slipped it between her lips. She swallowed, shuddering at the powdery medicinal taste. "There, now. Close your eyes again." And she did, feeling the icy pressure against her sore lip, feeling melting dribbles run down her chin to be wiped away.

♥

By the time room service arrived, Crys was curled up on the couch in their sitting room, with the gas fireplace turned up high. Blade took the trolley from the service person at the door and pushed it into the room himself – Crys could see a bottle of champagne sticking out of an ice bucket, a bunch of covered dishes. "You must be starving, sweetheart," he said.

"I don't know if I... it's going to hurt to eat, isn't it?" Crys asked.

"It's just a question of taking small bites – you won't be wanting a burger for a few days, but this should be easy to eat." He lifted a cut-glass bowl out of its bed of ice, wiped off the condensation with a linen napkin and placed the bowl in her lap, handed her a salad fork. "There you go. Lobster-and-avocado salad – nice easy little bites – go ahead and start while I get us some champagne." Still standing, he placed his own bowl on the coffee table, and reached for the bottle chilling in the ice bucket.

"Sure," she said, watching him pop the cork and pour the sparkling liquid into a pair of crystal flutes.

He turned to her with a grin. "Look what I've got for you," he said, sticking a pink bendy straw into her champagne flute before passing it to her.

"Cool!" She took the glass, sucked cautiously on the straw – on the side away from her new piercing – and closed her eyes in contentment as the tart icy bubbles rushed over her tongue.

"Hey, you're not eating," he said.

"I... I just..." Crys fumbled for words. The salad looked and smelled delicious, but she felt anxious about putting anything like food or a fork near her achy lip.

"Try a bite, okay?" Blade sat down next to her on the sofa, close enough that his knee brushed her leg. He took the bowl from her lap, scooped up a tiny bite of the salad on her fork, and held it out to her. "You've got to eat. Go on, open your mouth just a little, not so much that it'll hurt." Almost against her will, her lips parted, and he slipped the forkful of lobster and avocado into her mouth. It was cool and soothing in her mouth – meltingly tender pieces coated in a creamy lemony dressing – and slid easily down her throat. "That was good, huh?"

"Oh, yes!"

He brought another bite to her lips. This time she opened her mouth at once, without prompting. "Good." He grinned at her, his eyes filling with sinful promise. "You need to eat, sweetheart – I can guarantee you're going to need the energy."

How he was able to turn the ordinary business of eating into a sinful game of teasing and desire, she didn't know, but he did it – feeding her as though what he was putting in her mouth wasn't simply food, licking the fork where she'd licked it, gazing at her with a different kind of hunger. He'd done this in the restaurant in Portland, and now he was doing it again. *Oh sweet God, and he's not going to stop this time.* She moaned out loud, unable to help herself; the look in his eyes was enough to start that sweet ache building inside her.

"Crys baby, I want you so bad," he murmured, and his obvious desire sent lovely tingles of excitement running all over her. "Lip care first, though."

Lacing his fingers with hers, he pulled her off the sofa and – grabbing the aftercare bag from the piercing shop – led her into his bedroom and through to the en suite bathroom. He took the new toothbrush from the bag and peeled off the plastic for her, and she gingerly cleaned her teeth. He cleaned his teeth too: a weirdly intimate moment, standing over the sink together. Once they were done with brushing, he pulled out the bottle of mouthwash and removed the plastic sealing the cap.

She thought it would sting, but the sea-salt-based healing rinse was surprisingly mild, with a fresh lemon flavor. He rinsed his mouth too. And then they stood there, clean-mouthed and waiting.

Raising his eyebrows in a clear question, Blade reached into one of the bathroom drawers and pulled out a box of condoms. Flipped the box into the air and caught it. "Are you sure about this?" He looked straight at her, no hint of flirting or seduction in his suddenly serious eyes. "Please be absolutely sure before you say yes, Crys – your first time is a one-time-only thing, and I don't want you to regret it, ever."

Am I sure? It was such a simple question – to give him this special gift of herself, or to save it for another. *Is it enough that I love him, without him loving me?* And then she realized that if she turned away from this, it would be for all the wrong reasons, all the conventional good-girl reasons that infuriated and stifled her, the expectation that things should happen in a socially acceptable order and with a socially appropriate person. "I want this more than I've ever wanted anything," she confessed, her voice a bare whisper. "I want you. I've already given you my heart – please take my body too."

"Oh, fuck, Crys, you have no idea..." Blade's voice was husky, hungry. He pitched the box of condoms out the bathroom door in the general direction of the bed. Slid his fingers into her hair and brought his mouth to hers, unbelievably gentle as he kissed her tender lip and yet firmly insistent, sliding his tongue between her lips, demanding that she surrender herself completely to him. The ache in her lip receded. Desire flooded her, and she couldn't help moaning. At the sound, Blade drew in a sudden breath, and scooped her up in his arms, carrying her in long strides into the bedroom, to the bed.

She felt the mattress under her back, felt the bed dip slightly as he crawled up beside her. Felt his hands gently stripping off her t-shirt, pulling it over her head. He still had his t-shirt on, and it seemed wrong when hers was off, so she pulled at the hem of it and he helped her, peeling it away to let her eager hands explore his lean torso. He held still at first, giving her a chance to get comfortable with him, and she was grateful for it – although she'd given him a very intimate form of pleasure back in Portland, she'd been fully dressed then, and it seemed that giving pleasure and getting naked were two different things.

Then Blade took control of the situation again, easily unfastening her bra and slipping it off. His strong sexy guitar-playing hands stroked her, caressed her. He cupped her breasts – brushed the nipples with his thumbs, making her arch her back and gasp. And then he leaned down and used his mouth, and a dizzying sweet feeling shot through her, frightening her a bit in its intensity. "Oh, help," she murmured, feeling out of control and beyond restraint.

"You're okay, babe..." Blade's deep voice reassured her, all while he was stroking her with wicked magic hands, tugging down the zipper on her black leather skirt, caressing her inner thighs, playing with the garter belt straps and the tops of her stockings. "It's all about letting go... don't fight it... just ride the wave..." Her black satin panties were slipping down, down, gone, and then his hands lifted and parted her knees. Shock washed over Crys as his intent became clear. *I'm guessing you've never let a guy go down on you,* he'd said – and now Blade was claiming that privilege for himself.

She gasped at the overwhelming intimacy of it, moaned with pleasure. "Please, oh, please..." she begged, unable to put it into words, that desire to be filled, that need for *more.*

He looked up from between her thighs. "Just enjoy this for now, okay? I want to make sure you come – I promise you'll have all of me before the night is over." As he returned to his task, the avid desire on his face made her burn.

"Sweet holy – oh my Lord, I – ohh... that's – oooh!" She squirmed in delight, but he held her firmly, and she dissolved into wordless sounds of urgency and rapture, relinquishing awareness of anything beyond the sensations he was giving her. No restraint, no volume control. She melted, blazed up, exploded into a starburst of earth-shaking bliss.

"You're a screamer, huh?" he asked as she opened her eyes. Even through her satiated haze, she could see his pleased grin.

She felt herself blushing. "I guess so... I mean..."

"You've – you *have* had an orgasm before, haven't you? Surely?"

Crys blushed even more. "Well, only... um... by myself, to be honest, and it... it wasn't like *that!*"

Blade's grin grew wider. "By yourself? You get hotter by the minute, sweetheart!" He got off the bed and stood up. "I'm just going to go rinse with the mouthwash again, okay? Not that I don't love the taste of you

– sweet as peaches, babe – but I'm going to want to kiss you, and that pretty new piercing of yours needs to stay clean." He strode off into the bathroom.

Crys lay on the bed, wearing nothing but her garter belt and stockings, feeling incredibly relaxed and sexy and beautiful. When Blade came back and stood by the bed, she smiled up at him in welcome and delight, saying, "Hey, love..."

He smiled back, replying, "Hey, beautiful..." And his hands went to the waistband of his jeans, popped the top button. "Is... is it okay if I take my jeans off now?" he asked, hesitating, and she thought maybe he didn't want to push too fast and scare her.

"Sure," she said, and then, "oh, wow!" As he slid his jeans and boxers down, a rush of shyness overcame her, but it was impossible for her not to look – and she could have sworn he was bigger and harder than she remembered from Portland. "That's never going to fit..." she muttered to herself, gazing at him in amazement.

He heard her. "It will – trust me, it will fit," he assured her. "You're beautifully wet and slippery." The notion of that enormous rod sliding into her wet and slippery parts sent a wave of desire through her, and her eyes met Blade's, electric with tension and hunger. "I need you too, babe," he murmured, seeing the wanton craving in her face.

"Come on, then," she invited him, reaching her arms up toward him.

"Half a second – this is no time to play Vatican roulette." Glancing around, he found the box of condoms he'd tossed toward the bed earlier.

Crys blushed, realizing that she'd completely forgotten about using protection. "Yeah." She gazed up at him as he tore one of the little packets open, rolled the rubber over his hard shaft – expertly, she realized; he'd barely needed to glance down at himself. He'd obviously done this more times than she could imagine.

He climbed on top of her, taking his weight on arms and legs so he wouldn't crush her, his gloriously naked body moving against hers, his cock like a steel bar pushing into the softness of her belly. He kissed her deeply, tasting of mouthwash – the pleasure-pain of her lip drifted into insignificance. "Crys," he said against her mouth. "I... think I'm going to hurt you a bit, no matter how careful I am..."

"It's okay," she told him, feeling slightly short of breath and on the verge of hysterical giggles. "I can handle it. I had my lip pierced today, didn't I?"

He shifted his body, and the tip of him pressed against her entrance. Instinctively, she spread her legs wider for him, and he groaned, his face tense. The silvery rings in his eyebrow and lip glinted in the light from the bedside lamp. "I... don't think I'll be able to... stop, once I'm... inside you," he said, struggling for control of himself.

"I won't want you to stop," she promised, looking up into his beautiful hazel eyes still smudged with traces of makeup, giving him all of her heart. "Come inside me, love."

With a look on his face that was almost pain, he eased into her – met resistance – drew in a sharp breath and thrust forward. Crys gasped, a little involuntary cry escaping from her. He froze, his whole body shaking with the effort of it. "Shit, Crys, a-are you all right?"

Crys was suddenly finding it hard to breathe, as she adjusted to the strange incredible feeling of taking a man into her body. "Y-yes," she panted. "It's... just... so different from... anything I've ever..."

"I've got to move now, sweetheart," he told her, his voice rough with need, and then closed his eyes and groaned, "Holy fuck!" as he started to slide in and out of her. The delicious friction made Crys tingle all over, and she arched her back and wriggled against him, wanting to get closer, take him deeper into her. "Hell, Crys, I... can't..." he choked out.

"It's okay," she said. "It's okay." His eyes flickered open, and he held her gaze with his as he began to thrust hard and fast, the intensity between them electric. There was something raw and full of soul in his eyes, and it echoed what she was feeling in her heart – an unbelievable, unexpected connection beyond just their bodies. And then he jerked hard against her, ecstasy rippling over his face. Moments later, he'd collapsed on top of her, his body heavily boneless in satiation, his emotion-flooded face buried in her shoulder. Crys wrapped her arms around Blade's lean hard torso and held him, her small hands stroking his back.

After a while, he rolled off her onto his back, staring up at the ceiling in dazed incomprehension. The silence grew awkward. Eventually he sat up, dealt mechanically with the used rubber. "Well, that was kind of a first for me too," he said at last, not looking at her. "I'd never... deflowered anyone before."

"Is it always as intense as that?" Crys asked, without moving from where she lay. It felt safer not to move, just to lie still for the moment.

"No," Blade said, with an odd tone to his voice that Crys couldn't identify. He sat slightly turned away from her, so that all she could see was his back and shoulder, one pierced ear, the angle of his jaw – his face was hidden. "It can be all kinds of things; playful, wild, rough. Mostly, the girls I've known... they don't do tender or sweet. So that was sort of different for me."

Tender. Sweet. Was that how he thought of it, then? Crys had believed she'd seen raw honesty in his eyes and a deep electric soul connection between them. *Wishful thinking,* she told herself. *You knew beforehand that this would be just another night for him – why pretend now?* And if tender and sweet were novelties for him, then maybe he'd remember her a little while longer because of it. Praying that her voice wouldn't waver, she smiled her best smile and said, "A nice sort of different, I hope." The words sounded brittle in the quiet air.

He turned to look at her then, with an apologetic grimace. "Shit, Crys – here I am talking about how it was for me, when... how was... I mean, are you okay?"

A near-hysterical giggle escaped from her, and she pressed her lips together – which was not at all comfortable with the new piercing already feeling warm and swelling. "I'm fine. Getting my lip done hurt a whole lot more," she assured him. Realizing that she lay there essentially naked, still only in the garter belt and stockings that hadn't come off the whole time, she sat up and looked about for her t-shirt. As she leaned to reach for it, she noticed some pinkish smears on the sheet underneath her.

"Yeah. Sorry. You might... want to go clean up a bit," Blade said, seeing her face. He picked up the t-shirt from the floor and handed it to her.

"I... I think that's probably a good idea," Crys agreed, pulling on her t-shirt, wondering whether he meant her to clean herself up in his en suite or go back to her own room and use the bathroom there. *How are we supposed to say goodnight, after what we just did?* She stood up.

He stood too, unselfconsciously naked. "You know," he said, "when I asked if you were okay... I didn't mean just... physically."

"Oh."

"So?" He cocked an eyebrow at her, asking.

She smiled, and this time it didn't hurt inside, though her lip ached. "You were lovely," she said. "I won't ever forget it."

A glimmer of satisfaction shone in his eyes. "Good."

She gathered up her skirt and shoes. "I expect I'll need my toothbrush, and the mouthwash and stuff," she said, and crossed to the bathroom to get it. He pulled on his boxers and followed her, standing by the bathroom door while she collected her things.

"If you're hungry, there's some chocolate mousse from room service we never ate," he suggested. "Supposed to be dessert, but we never got that far. It'll still be on the cart in the sitting room."

Chocolate mousse sounded good to Crys – or eating chocolate mousse with Blade did. "Sure," she agreed. "Will you have some too?"

He shook his head. "I'm just going to crash," he said. "But you go ahead. I'll see you in the morning, right?"

"Right."

"Oh, and make sure you clean your lip damn thoroughly before you go to sleep," he reminded her. "And take another ibuprofen."

Crys nodded, feeling hollow. "Sure, okay. I promise."

"Goodnight, sweetheart," Blade said, giving her a gentle kiss on the cheek, the faint brush of his lip ring nearly making her cry.

She waited until she was outside his door to whisper, "Goodnight, my love."

The lights were still on in the sitting room – neither Crys nor Blade had thought to turn them off earlier. Not sure what else to do, she went over to the abandoned room service cart and found the dishes of chocolate mousse. Took one of them and a spoon, and grabbed the champagne bottle out of its bucket of melted ice. Then she turned off all the sitting room lights and waited a moment for her eyes to adjust to the lack of light before heading into her bedroom.

She left the lights off and crossed in the dimness to the window, drew open the curtains. It was a beautiful clear night, with a sky full of stars faintly visible above the city's night glow. Sighing, Crys peeled off the garter belt and stockings, and then her t-shirt. Naked, she walked into the bathroom and saw a faint outline of herself in the reflected darkness of the mirror. She contemplated turning the light on, but she could see well enough to use the toilet, and would maybe rather not see more clearly as she cleaned herself up. Minutes later, she was back in the bedroom, wriggling with a grateful sigh into a pair of cozy pajamas.

The vastness of the sky and the countless number of stars always made her small wishes and frustrations seem trivial in comparison. *So, no more virginity – am I any different now, because I know what it feels like to have a man inside me?* Cross-legged on the corner of the bed, gazing out the window, she ate chocolate mousse with a carefully-handled spoon and swigged semi-flat champagne out of the bottle. She didn't feel different, physically, beyond a slight ache between her legs. *And he already had my heart.* A warm glow of love enveloped Crys as she remembered the ecstasy on Blade's face as he'd reached his climax inside her – how beautiful to have been able to give him that moment. Not to mention what he'd given her; even alone in the dark, she blushed at the memory of his tongue between her thighs and her uninhibited response. She wondered how she could ever speak to him in the daylight again, in public, in front of people, without going up in flames at the thought of what they'd shared. *This is not the time to think of aftermath,* she told herself. *This is a time to feel blessed, because I had an unforgettable first experience that I will treasure forever.*

When every last bite of chocolate mousse was gone and the champagne bottle was drained dry, she felt better – the comforting effect of the champagne even gave her the fortitude to turn on the bathroom light and wash her lip with the cleanser from the piercing shop.

Remembering Blade's advice, she took an ibuprofen before getting into bed. *I hope my lip isn't too terribly swollen tomorrow,* she thought sleepily, closing her eyes. As she drifted off, one last waking thought crossed her mind: *Oh, good God, what's Marigold going to say?!*

When Crys left her room shortly after noon the next day, she did so feeling hesitant, almost shy. She'd bathed and knew she looked reasonably presentable in jeans and a demure cashmere sweater, her damp hair tidily slicked back, with no trace of a wild night hovering to betray her. The sitting room was unoccupied, and Blade's door was closed, no light showing underneath – either he still slept, or he'd gone out. Not wanting to hang about in their suite alone, waiting until Blade should wake or return, she headed out into the hall intending to look for Sally. Really, anyone's company would have done, but Sally was the closest she had to a friend out of all the Smidge crew.

The hall was empty when Crys stepped out of the suite, but before she could figure out where Sally's room was, Marigold came striding along the hall in a frighteningly gorgeous leopard-print velvet mini-dress, with a shiny gold trench coat over one arm and a clipboard clutched in the other. *She always looks so... so wrong it's somehow right,* Crys thought. No one would ever forget her, or overlook her in a crowd. *She's just... Marigold. She is what she is.*

And Marigold freaked out. "Oh my fucking Christ," she said in disbelief, staring at Crys. "You've gone and pierced your lip."

Crys nodded, a bit taken aback. She'd realized that Marigold might not be too happy about the possible blot on her good-girl image, but the

PR woman's reaction was a bit more extreme than Crys had anticipated. "Yes," she said. "It was Blade's idea, but I think it suits me."

Marigold just shook her head in disgust. "It's all swollen and looks like crap – did you even clean it this morning?! Well, you look like crap, and you'd better get back into your room before someone takes a picture, you dim bitch!"

The venom in Marigold's voice staggered Crys. "I'm sorry," she began – and then it struck her that no one had told her she couldn't alter her image; her contract addressed behavior but didn't mention physical appearance. "Marigold," she said, straightening her spine and looking the older woman right in the eyes, "I'm not sure why my lip is such a big issue for you, but you have no business screaming at me like that. In any case, it's done; if I took the ring out, the empty hole would look worse, I think, and it would still have to heal. So just tell people Blade said I should have some kind of a ring, and this is what he got me."

"Well, now, that is kind of cute," Marigold agreed, still looking sour. "Of course, what you clearly don't realize is that he's gone – we can't fucking find him – he's probably off shooting up somewhere, and you're standing here arguing with me."

Crys felt cold all over. "He's... not in his room?"

"No. Nor with the other boys, nor with any of the crew. Not answering his phone, and Security can't find him."

"Oh... oh, no..." *I did this,* Crys thought. *It's my fault.* She'd kept on offering herself to him, played with a firestorm when she could have stayed away, convinced him to take her virginity – and thereby, for some reason, pushed him back into using heroin. She'd thought he'd enjoyed being with her, but now... "Can I do anything to help?" she asked.

"Hit your room for now, girl – and do all of us a favor and clean your lip good and often, okay? A piercing we can work with, an infection not so much."

"I did wash it in the shower this morning, you know."

Marigold rolled her eyes. "Then go soak it in salt water." Then she sighed. "I'm sorry I snapped at you earlier," she added, in the sort of voice that meant she wasn't really sorry but knew she had crossed a line. "It's just stress. I'll let you know if I hear anything, all right?"

"Sure," Crys said, because she did want Marigold to call her if any news of Blade came in. She still in many ways admired Marigold, but she'd begun to understand why many of the crew seemed to dislike the older woman – volatile bursts of a venomous temper followed by insincere apologies wouldn't exactly endear someone to her workmates. Crys didn't want to request any favors from Marigold after the less-than-pleasant interchange, but – recalling her initial plan in leaving the suite – she asked, "Marigold, since you'd prefer that I stay out of sight, could you ask Sally... that is, tell her that I'd love some company, if she isn't too busy?"

Marigold nodded. "I'll tell her," she agreed, glancing at her watch. "I've got to get going. Go do something about your fat lip."

Refusing to dignify that with a further comment, Crys turned and headed back to the suite she shared with Blade.

She found the door open, and for a moment her heart leapt in relief, thinking that he must have returned from wherever he'd been. But a crash of disappointment followed as she noticed that the room service trolley from the night before had been moved out into the hall – the disappointment was confirmed when she entered the suite and found a pair of young housekeeping maids chattering away in Spanish as they dusted and tidied the sitting room.

They jumped, startled, when they turned and saw her. *"¡Dios, me asustaste!"* one of them muttered, then crossed herself.

Crys blinked, and the second maid giggled, with an eye-roll for her co-worker's fright. "We're done now; please excuse us," she said, stuffing her duster and furniture spray into the janitorial push-cart, then taking her co-worker's things and putting them away also. And the two of them trundled away with their housekeeping cart.

Crys opened the door to her bedroom – they'd tidied in there too: fresh flowers filled the vase on the nightstand, and foil-wrapped chocolates rested on top of the pillows. The t-shirt and leather skirt she'd worn the night before, dropped on the floor when she'd changed in the dark, were now neatly folded on a chair, the rhinestone-heart shoes demurely side by side below. And as she looked at them, Crys realized that something was missing – when she'd gathered up her things to leave Blade's room, had she forgotten anything? Her bra and panties were nowhere in sight.

She could remember so clearly the post-coital awkwardness, after the bliss had evaporated – the unpleasant realization that she'd bled a bit and stained his sheets, the desire to cover herself. He'd handed her the t-shirt to put on, hadn't he? And she'd picked up her leather miniskirt and shoes. What had happened to her bra, and more to the point, her panties? Had she really walked out of there bare? She couldn't remember. *I couldn't have walked out of his room with a bare bum, could I? Surely not!* But if not, where were the black satin bikini panties and push-up bra she'd put on at the start of the night?

The suite was completely empty, except for Crys. No one knew where Blade was – not even his bodyguard, not even Angel – and everyone's focus was on finding him, so even if he returned, it would take him a while to make his way back to the suite and his room. The missing bra and panties were probably in that empty room; all she had to do was retrieve them.

And if I don't go and get them? The question only raised assorted uncomfortable possibilities. Would he give them to Marigold or Sally to return to her? Would he leave them on the coffee table in the sitting room, where anyone might see them? Would he hand them to her next time they met, maybe with some forced remark about an unforgettable memory? *An unforgettable memory – oh sweet God, yes!* Crys knew she'd never be able to erase from her mind the look in his eyes as he'd reached his climax inside her. But it would be a sad moment indeed for him to use those words without truth, when it has been at best pleasant and a bit of a novelty for him – *after all,* Crys told herself in sorrow, *how could I ever compete with the expert lovers he's known?* But the conclusion was inescapable; to avoid the possibility of such a moment, she had to go and get her underwear before he returned. *Damn.*

The maids had tidied his room too. The bed was neatly made, and the crisp white pillowcases suggested that the sheets had been changed – the stains of lost virginity now removed and better forgotten. Standing in the doorway, Crys looked around and didn't immediately see her bra and panties. If the maids had found them, they would most likely have placed them on a chair, just as they'd done with her clothes, Crys assumed. Since the underwear was not tidily laid out on the nearest chair, it stood to reason that it had not been anywhere the maids might have found it. Would Blade have put her things somewhere? In a drawer? Cautiously advancing further into the room, she pulled open the drawers of the dresser one by one – nothing but Blade's folded clothing, reminding her of her first day in Portland, when he'd been detoxing and she'd gotten a clean t-shirt and boxers for him. She saw those boxers with the lipstick kisses, folded and clean. But not her bra and panties.

If they weren't in the dresser, then... Approaching the bed, she pinched the corner of one pillow with a finger and thumb, raised it slightly. Nothing hidden, and definitely clean sheets – they smelled of laundry soap, not the citrus soap and slightly spicy skin-scent she would recognize anywhere as his.

I was on the bed the whole time, Crys told herself, *so where can my things have gone?* Standing there in his room, she relived again in memory how he'd unfastened her bra and slipped off her panties. Dropped them on the floor? Crouching down, she raised the ruffled bed skirt and peered into the darkness under the bed. *Ha!* She could just see a bra strap and the curves of push-up cups, with a second dark satiny shape nearby. They must have gotten kicked or pushed under there somehow. Fishing her underwear out and standing up, she took a last look at the bed where she'd lost her virginity, then made herself walk out of the room without a backward glance.

It wasn't until she was putting the underwear into her laundry bag that she realized something hadn't seemed right about Blade's room – what had it been? The more she thought about it, the more she was sure: something in his room, something about his room, was telling her... what? Where he had gone? What he was doing? She became increasingly certain that Blade had not gone out to get high, but why? What was it that she'd seen, or not seen? Puzzled and curious, she returned to his room – this time not embarrassed but focused, seeking an answer. And then she knew. It was what she had *not* seen that had given her the clue, and she was running for her purse and phone, punching in Marigold's number even as she ran out into the hallway to look for someone, anyone to share her revelation.

chapter
10

A S SHE JOGGED DOWN THE HALL, CRYS PUNCHED Marigold's number into her phone but couldn't get through. *Where is everyone?* The hotel corridor was deserted. She tried Kin's number and couldn't get through to him either. She rounded a corner and ran straight into Angel – literally. She bounced off him and staggered to stay on her feet. "He... his guitar... not in his room," she gasped, waving her hands in her urgency to tell him what she'd realized. "He wouldn't... wouldn't take it with him... to... you know... would he?"

"Calm down, babe," said Angel, grabbing her hands to still them. "It's okay. Now, tell me. Blade's guitar isn't in his room – are you sure?"

"Yes. Absolutely positive. And I... I could be wrong, but it seems to me that – his guitar is so precious to him – he wouldn't take it with him to somewhere he, um, wasn't going to be himself, would he?"

Angel stared at her with sharp assessing eyes. "You're awfully quick, Crys. You see things that took me years to figure out. And you're right; if he's taken his guitar with him, he's not getting wasted. He's just running away from us for a bit."

"Running away from me," said Crys, and Angel nodded with sympathetic eyes.

"I thought things were heading that way for you two," he said. "More than one kind of piercing going on last night, huh? The lip hardware looks good on you, by the way."

"Thanks," she replied, not denying what had happened in the night.

179

"So... are you all right, babe?" Angel asked, and Crys saw that he was not mocking or critical, only kind. Had he known she'd been untouched, and Blade her first?

She nodded, with a blush for the intimate confession. "Blade was... considerate... gentle... it was good." She couldn't find words for the dazzling intensity they'd shared; considerate and gentle seemed such faint praise in comparison – but he truly had been a considerate and gentle lover.

"He isn't always," admitted Angel, with a shrug for the fact of it, "but you seem to bring out the best in him. I'm glad it was good for you."

"I'm just sorry to have made him run off on everyone," Crys said.

He sighed, rubbing his knuckles along one high cheekbone in a considering gesture. "It's not your fault – he takes off when he's stressed, always has – sometimes into booze or drugs, other times literally."

"But I've caused this stress!"

"You alone? I don't think so," Angel said with a gently teasing laugh, then his expression sobered. "Look, Crys, we haven't exactly had much in the way of normal dates in the last few years; there's been too much attention, too much money, too many women throwing themselves at us for all the wrong reasons. Gold-diggers, groupies, obsessed fans – you name it! I think all four of us have sort of forgotten what to do, how to date a regular nice girl, what's expected in terms of commitment and all those rules when we've been living without rules."

Crys felt herself blushing as she shook her head. "There was never any talk of dating. I'm not sure I *am* such a nice regular girl, you know – I never asked for any promises – I... I kept on offering myself to him even when he told me he wouldn't..."

"Babe, it was bound to happen sooner or later – I could see the sparks between you two from miles away. It's just that he doesn't know what to say to you now, that's all. But it will be okay."

"Yeah, sure," Crys agreed, though she wasn't sure, really.

Angel snorted. "Right. Well, we'd probably better tell Phil and the rest of them that Blade took his guitar with him; they can stop panicking now. As long as he's not back on the heroin – and he's not, if he's got his guitar – he's a pro; he'll turn up before the concert." He set off down the hall, gesturing to Crys to walk with him.

"Oh!" Her hand flew to her mouth as she thought of Marigold, and stopped just short of touching the offending lip ring. *Avoid touching your jewelry or the newly pierced area,* the care sheet had said. "I wasn't supposed to leave my room," she said to Angel. "Marigold said not to. I'm all puffy."

"Marigold is sometimes a bit of a nit," he replied, with just a hint of impatience. "The piercing suits you, and there's nothing wrong with a swollen lip – looks kind of sexy, actually. Look, I've got to go catch Phil. If you're worried about Marigold, hide out in your room for a bit, that's fine. How about I ask Sally to head over and see if she can fix you up some?"

Having a good deal of faith in Sally's powers, Crys nodded gratefully. "That would be fantastic."

"I expect I'll see you at the arena later," Angel told her, and strode off down the hall. It hadn't been a question, so Crys merely watched him go.

In the end, Crys did not go to the concert that night.

Sally did her best with dramatic eye makeup and hair glitter, but she couldn't put any lipstick or makeup on Crys's mouth area without risking getting some into the piercing itself – with all the attendant potential for infection – and Marigold ruled that Crys should stay behind.

"Come on, Goldie, she looks fine. And the boys like having her there," Sally said, as she packed up her makeup kit.

Marigold's face took on a pinch-lipped warning look. "Sally, if you want to keep your job, trust my judgment on this and get going. Crys isn't joining us tonight, and that's final."

Sally huffed and opened her mouth to say something more, but Crys held up a hand to stop her. "Don't risk your job for me, Sally. The boys need you. I can deal with a night off."

"All right, then," Sally said doubtfully, still looking concerned.

Crys gave the makeup artist a smile that she hoped would convey some of the gratitude she felt. *The fact that you'd put your job on the line for me makes me want to cry, but please don't. I couldn't bear to be responsible for that.* She kept her smile going strong until Sally walked out the door.

"Thank you for seeing this my way," said Marigold with smug satisfaction, once she and Crys were alone.

I don't want to start a war, Crys told herself. *I don't want to make an enemy of Marigold.* But Sally's willingness to stand up for Crys had given her a boost of courage, enough to refuse the nod and smile that Marigold wanted. Crys waited silently, keeping her face as neutral as she could, until Marigold shrugged and departed.

She had been on tour with Smidge for a week – three different hotels, and the concert she was missing would have been her fourth – they would be in Phoenix by the following evening, and then San Diego and Los Angeles before another week was out. What did one concert matter, really? But Crys hadn't seen or spoken to Blade since she'd left his room the night before, wearing only her t-shirt and carrying her skirt and shoes. And it felt like a punishment, being left behind.

Stuck alone in the suite for the whole evening, she had little to distract herself with. She gave her aching lip a salt-water soak for the first time: an awkward process that involved sticking the lower half of her face into a bowl of hot water mixed with sea salt from her aftercare kit. Afterward, she texted Debbie and Leah, but neither of them answered. She checked her email and social media, surfed the web, and read all the magazines in the sitting room.

Later, she got into her pajamas and curled up in front of the fireplace, thinking that perhaps some time and space to be alone wasn't entirely a bad thing. She flipped from channel to channel on the television, finding nothing but sports talk, celebrity gossip, and bad news – war, disasters, political skullduggery. Just when she was considering turning it off altogether, she flipped one more channel and saw Blade.

"IMPROMPTU TREAT FROM SMIDGE GUITARIST" read the headline across the bottom of the screen. In a grainy cell-phone-at-a-distance video, he sat on the edge of a very small stage with his guitar – behind him, Crys could just catch glimpses of a drum kit and a keyboard, before the camera cut to a shot of a fashionably trench-coated reporter. The woman stood under the awning of a small café, saying, "This afternoon at the Mission's trendy Café Mieke, patrons were treated to a surprise performance by the Smidge guitarist, who apparently showed up without warning and asked staff if he could play a few songs."

The screen flashed back to the video of Blade playing; the sound quality was rough, but Crys knew at once that what he played wasn't an existing Smidge song. "Frozen heart wants to warm," he sang, over the wistful melody. "These arms want to reach for you / But I don't know how." It was hard to see, but she thought he looked peaceful, intent, focused on his music. In his own world, as he'd been at the concert they'd gone to back home.

"So, for the price of a coffee, some very lucky people got to see Blade play up close and personal," the reporter's voiceover cut in, "including his own vocal stylings and a couple of new pieces not yet performed or recorded by Smidge." And then the image faded out. "In other entertainment news today–"

Frozen heart wants to warm. A dangerous bubble of hope formed inside her. *Don't read too much into that; it's just a song.* She switched the television to the hotel's movie listings, chose a light romantic comedy – laughed a bit at the silly predicaments, sighed a bit at the love scenes, and in the end dozed off on the couch before the movie was over.

The doze turned into a deep sleep. She was hardly aware of waking, though she had a dreamlike impression of Blade standing over her, his face full of the song's tenderness and longing – which might actually have been a dream since her waking self later had trouble imagining such an expression on him. But he, or someone, must have entered the suite, because a sensation of soft warmth and darkness settled over her as gentle hands tucked the comforter around her and turned out the lights.

♥

Crys woke with a start, morning light streaming through the windows, and realized that she still lay on the couch in the sitting room. The door to her bedroom stood open, and through it she could hear a familiar pinging from her phone. *My wake-up alarm.*

She scrambled from the sofa, her legs tangling in the comforter from her bed, which had been wrapped around her, tucked under her feet and legs and pulled up around her shoulders like a cocoon – at least some of her night recollections must not have been dreamed. But the thought was fleeting as she scrambled to end the irritating noise from her phone.

Then Sally was knocking at the half-open door, her orange hair tied back by a business-like bandana, her splendid figure straining the bib of a pair of denim overalls. "Hey, Crys – I'm glad you're up – you didn't forget we're on the move again today, did you?" Sally asked, casting an eye over Crys's pajamas and generally rumpled state.

"Ugh, no, I... well, I fell asleep on the couch," Crys explained, "so my phone took a while to wake me out there, and I ran in here like a wild thing to grab it. But I'm almost ready; I never really unpacked. I just have to pack the things I wore yesterday, and my, um, laundry." She couldn't help thinking of the contents of her laundry bag – the t-shirt and undergarments that Blade had taken off her, and the garter belt and stockings she'd worn to lose her virginity.

"Well, where's your laundry bag? In the closet? We'll just stuff it into one of your suitcases and sort it out at the hotel tonight." Sally glanced at her watch. "Honey, why don't you go have a shower – I'll pick out something for you to wear and make sure the rest gets loaded up."

Crys smiled. *Yes. A shower. Please.* "That sounds great, but are you sure you can spare the time? You must be so busy!"

"Nah, I made sure all the show gear was packed up last night. I never like to go to bed without everything done – it worries me and then I kinda don't sleep," Sally explained. "I wouldn't offer if I didn't mean it."

With a murmured thank-you, Crys darted for the bathroom. Was brought up short by the crusty build-up around her piercing, reflected in the mirror over the sink. Remembered with an effort that crusting was a normal part of the healing process. *Ugh! I'm glad Blade didn't see me like that,* she thought, even though she realized that with as many piercings as he had, he would be unlikely to find any part of it all that repellent.

She herself did, however, find it repellent to have a scabby crust around her beautiful new lip ring – and hastened to soak it away in the shower, cleaning it well with the saline spray, because if a bit of natural healing crust made her shudder, she was sure that she wouldn't cope well with an infection. Afterward, feeling clean all over – she'd brushed her teeth and rinsed with the mouthwash as well – she dutifully smoothed moisturizer over her skin and dabbed a tiny bit of brightening concealer under her eyes to hide any hint of slept-on-the-couch tiredness. Then she gathered up the contents of her wash kit; everything needed to go into her suitcases or carry-on bag, and there was no sense in leaving odd small chores for the last minute.

The wash kit would, apparently, need to go into her carry-on bag – while Crys had been in the shower, someone had come and taken away her suitcases. All her things were gone, except for the carry-on bag and one outfit laid out on the bed – a short velvet dress, in such a deep saturated red as to be almost black, not overly tight-fitting or low-cut but the fabric was clingy and somehow more revealing than if it had been skin-tight. A Mary Magdalene dress. Fallen and proud of it. Crys shot Sally a sharp glance, wondering what the orange-haired makeup artist knew and whether she disapproved.

Sally looked back in surprise. "What's the matter, Crys?" she asked. "Don't you like this dress?"

"No – I mean, y-yes, I do like the dress, it's not that – not that there's anything the matter. There's not. Anything the matter, I mean," Crys babbled, looking down at her hands as though stuffing her wash kit into her carry-on bag needed all of her concentration.

"I love this color, myself, but it doesn't go with my hair," Sally said. "Be beautiful on you, though. Did you want the queen-of-hearts tights, or the fishnets? I kept them both out for you to choose, because I wasn't sure."

The queen-of-hearts tights had a pattern of black and white diamonds with playing cards and red hearts – novelty tights, eye-catching and fun. They didn't suit Crys's mood, though, and she wished that Sally had kept out a pair of plain black stockings for her. But it did no good wishing for the moon, and if she were forced to wear red to celebrate her new status as a fallen woman, then she might as well wear the fishnets and look the part entirely.

It really was a gorgeous dress. The deep, deep red gave an appealing glow to her skin, and the soft rich velvet almost begged to be touched. There was a matching hair band too, she discovered – it had fallen to the bed when she'd picked up the dress. And the black fishnet stockings did look right with the dress, in a sin-waiting-to-happen way, with the dark clingy red velvet above and the sexy boots below.

"Thanks for picking this out, Sally," Crys said, as she inspected herself in the mirror. "I wouldn't have known what to wear to fly with the band anyway... somehow I've managed three cities of this tour without once traveling properly with them."

Sally laughed. "That's right – how funny! 'Cause of course you went by road from Seattle to Portland, and flew down here commercial with Blade after your hangover. You'll like flying with Smidge, I think. But here, sit down and let me fix your hair and do your eyes."

Obediently, Crys sat down on the chair Sally indicated and handed her the hair band, saying, "Okay. I already put on moisturizer and a bit of concealer, but that's all." Closed her eyes and enjoyed the feeling of being fussed over, the slick movement of the brush through her hair, the misting of hairspray, and Sally's deft fingers sliding the velvet band into place.

"What kind of eyes do you want today, honey?" Sally asked.

Crys opened her eyes in surprise. "I get a choice today?"

Sally grinned. "You always have a choice, Crys; I'll always do any kinda makeup you're in the mood for – no matter what Goldie's orders are. Anyhow, what's it gonna be today?"

Fallen woman, Crys thought. "You tell me. What suits the dress?"

"Hmm." Sally considered Crys's outfit, thoughtfully, her professional mind at work. "Well, the color and fabric say decadent and sensuous, and contrasts are always good... I'd say we go with the sweet innocent face, just a touch of dark liner around your eyes and a hint of pale sparkle on your lids. A little bit of corrupt-me-please."

Crys giggled and nodded. *I've already been corrupted.* But Sally seemed to think that the giggles were simply a response to her comment, and Crys just closed her eyes and let the makeup artist edge her lashes with dark smoke and brush sheer glitter onto the lids above. It took only a few minutes, and then Sally was handing Crys a mirror and packing away her supplies in the smaller travel case that she carried everywhere. "Thanks, Sally," Crys said. "And... I want you to know how much I appreciated your trying to get me to the concert last night."

"It's what friends do," said Sally, like it was no big thing. "Are you looking forward to the flight? I get to go with you – lucky me!"

"Doesn't everyone?" Crys asked.

"Nope. Flight's for the lucky ones. The rest of the crew get hours of road time on sleeper buses. They're pretty luxurious, mind you; Smidge doesn't skimp out on the roadies' comfort. But it's still being stuck on a bus. I go on the flight with my handy kit to freshen everyone up before landing. Jed flies with us too; it started when Kin found him to take care of Blade, and now we're all just used to having him around, even if no one is high or drug-sick or whatever. Bodyguards, of course. Kin and Marigold, unless they've got business elsewhere. Scott. And any guests the boys want to bring with them, of course." Sally shrugged, and Crys could guess what kinds of companions had joined the boys on past flights. "Phil and Zachary could choose to fly with us if they wanted to, they'd be welcome, but most of the time they'd rather stick with the crew, unless they need to talk show stuff with the boys."

"I'd definitely choose a plane over a bus, any day," Crys said, "even a bus as nice as the one we had on the drive from Seattle to Portland."

"No kidding," Sally agreed. "Now, I called Ev Metkin – that's your piercer, honey – and asked him about lip balm for you."

"Really? How d'you know about him? Did Blade tell you?"

"He did my belly button, on Smidge's first tour. Blade didn't have to tell me; I knew he wouldn't have taken you anywhere else." Sally smiled at Crys's surprise. "Yup, I've known the boys a long time. Back then I was their only wardrobe and makeup person, and general gofer besides, and we none of us had any money, and it was all a hell of a lot of fun. But anyway, Ev's okayed the all-natural beeswax stuff, as long as we put it on with a clean Q-tip every time, and I went out this morning and got you some. Would you like me to put it on for you, or would you rather do it yourself?"

"I'll do it." Crys's lip was still fairly tender, and she figured that she'd be able to judge the pressure she could bear better than leaving it to other hands, even ones as gentle as Sally's. The gloss did give her lips an appealing natural shine, and relieved the dryness from all the washing and salt-soaking.

Sally's phone rang. "Hello? ... Oh, hi Goldie ... You bet, we're all done here – I'll be right down ... Sure, I'll tell her ... See you in five!" Sally clicked her phone off. "That was Goldie – we're ready to head for the airport. You'll be riding in the limo with the boys, of course, so she said to tell you just to wait and be all set to go. Blade will come and get you when they're ready to go down."

"Right, okay," said Crys, forcing a smile.

"I'll see you on the plane, then." Sally dashed out the door, leaving Crys awash in dismay. She'd counted on Sally's presence, on not being alone when she should see Blade again. But the very situation she'd wanted to avoid had become unavoidable.

♥

The knock on the door startled Crys, even though she'd been expecting it, keyed up as she was after sitting for twenty minutes in tense anticipation of the moment. She jumped up, sat back down again, stood again, and called out in a strained voice, "Come in."

Blade pushed the door open, took one step into the room. Stopped, and leaned against the door frame. "Hey," he said, and then, fumbling for something to fill the uncomfortable void, added, "We missed you at the concert last night."

"Sorry." Crys giggled nervously. "Marigold said I mustn't... well, my lip, you know... it's less puffy today, I think."

"It looks great," Blade said. "Are you... are you still glad you did it?" He wasn't talking about the lip ring, was he?

The awkwardness between them grew painful. *We're like survivors after a bad accident,* she thought, *not sure what to say or do. Checking for damage, afraid to ask, to know.* "Yeah," she said at last. And she didn't mean the lip ring either, though she was glad she'd done that too.

"Hell, Crys," he said, his voice rough. "Come here."

She walked slowly toward him, where he stood by the doorway. Last time they'd touched, it had been to make love... "Wh-what d'you want me to do?" she asked, feeling suddenly shy.

"We... we just need to hold each other for a minute, I think." He opened his arms and drew her in, his long lean body enveloping her in warm strength. She leaned into him, her face pressed against his t-shirt, hearing his heartbeat and breathing in his citrus-soap-and-clean-skin scent. And gradually they reached calmness and ease together, just holding each other and breathing. "There," he said at last, looking down at her. "Better?"

"Better," she agreed. And it was.

He stroked her cheek with one finger, his beautiful hazel eyes gazing down at her, his expression both serious and affectionate. "Are you truly all right, sweetheart? You don't regret... any of it?"

She swallowed against a sudden lump in her throat, murmuring, "No... never..." *Why can't moments like this last forever?* In that instant, contentment filled her – even if he could never love her, even if he never made love to her again – friendship and affection were enough. No, not enough, but better than nothing, better than coldness or anger or being sent away. *Oh, my love, if I could hold you like this for eternity, I would!*

"Good. I'm glad." Blade grinned, releasing his hold on her, and she knew that it was time to move away, to not betray how much she wanted to stay there in his arms. "I was worried you might have felt a bit strange about it, afterward."

"No..." she repeated, getting her purse and carry-on bag, smiling brightly to convince him it was true.

"Are you all set to go, then?" he asked.

She nodded. "Yes, everything else was taken away earlier; I've only got these two things."

"Great – we should head downstairs – I'll just call Angel and find out where they're at." He pulled out his phone and dialed, listened for a moment, and put it back in his pocket. "Not answering. Let's just go down."

"Okay." Crys took a last glance around her room, confirming that she had everything and was leaving nothing behind.

In the sitting room, Blade picked up his guitar from the sofa and grabbed his carry-on bag off the coffee table. The door to his room stood open, and Crys couldn't resist looking in. *I'm leaving a memory behind in that room,* she thought. *Nothing in my room, but it's hard to walk away from his when it's my virginity I've left behind there.*

And maybe he caught her looking in – with who knew what expression on her face – because as they stepped out into the hall, he looked at the number plate on the door to the suite and said, "1018 – must be my lucky number. I'll always treasure the fact that you gave me your first time, sweetheart. It's a gift a person can only give once, and that makes it special."

Crys, afraid that too much of the love she felt might be shining out of her face, made herself laugh and say with flippant lightness, "Well, you are a rock star, after all – who better to give me a first-time memory I'll never forget?"

This seemed to reassure Blade that she was taking it all in stride, because he flipped the ends of her hair with his fingers in a lightly teasing gesture – the kind of thing he might do to a band-mate or crewmember – and headed down the hallway toward the bank of elevators, reaching a hand out to Crys to join him. "Remember on the flight from Portland, I told you things would be easier between us if we could just have a good fuck and relax?" When she nodded, he smiled – a wide I-told-you-so smile – and said, "Was I right, or what?!"

Easier between us? When I've fallen for you harder than ever? Crys shook her head in disbelief. But Blade did seem to be relaxed and happy, at ease with her and himself and the world. She just took his hand, and hurried with quick steps in her high-heeled boots to keep up with his long strides down the hall.

♥

The mood in the limousine was quiet. Eighteen minutes into what they'd been told would be a twenty-minute drive, the boys had fallen silent, no sound but the occasional slurp as one of them took a noisier sip from his beer can.

Crys clutched a beer too, though she'd only taken a few mouthfuls – she hadn't hidden the surprise she'd felt when the boys had broken out a case of beer instead of the champagne she'd already seen so much of. Angel had laughed. "Sometimes we get sick of champagne," he'd said by way of explanation, and with Blade's eyes on her she'd accepted the beer Angel had offered. She remembered that Blade had said something early on about baby-girls who couldn't drink, and she didn't want the band to think her a stuck-up princess who would only sip fine champagne. It wasn't that she didn't like beer – she did – but she hadn't eaten anything, and her empty stomach roiled at the malt smell each time she brought the can to her mouth. Plus, the edge of the can knocked her lip ring uncomfortably. She held the can in her lap, and drank only when she felt herself observed.

Easy, as usual on the road, had stuck his headphones into his ears almost the moment the car had started to roll and was ignoring the lot of them. The others had started out in desultory chat, but their remarks became less frequent as the minutes passed. The partition was closed, so they couldn't even hear any conversational noises from the driver and bodyguard up front. Dice flipped through a magazine. Blade stared out the window. Angel took out a notebook and pencil – making a list of some sort, Crys thought.

Every now and again, Angel or Dice would inadvertently catch her eyes, and smile. She'd smile back, and sip her beer, and look away. She avoided meeting Blade's eyes, and Easy paid no attention to her at all.

At last the signs flashing by outside started referencing the airport, with arrows indicating routes to take for domestic and international drop-offs, short-term and long-term parking. Crys expected the limousine to continue toward the airport proper, following the signs for domestic drop-offs, but instead it turned off along an access road meandering along the shoreline on what appeared to be the far edge of the airport. Could the driver be lost, she wondered? Or was this some sort of back route to try to evade the ever-present paparazzi? "Are we going the right way?" she asked at last.

"Private jets fly out of an FBO, not the main terminal," Dice explained with a kind look that made Crys wish she'd never asked.

"That's right, man," Angel agreed, "now tell the lady what an FBO is."

Caught out, Dice reddened. "Jeez, Angel, I don't know – it's where private jets fly out of!" Angel chuckled, and Crys felt much more at ease, though she didn't like to gain her self-confidence at the expense of Dice's discomfiture.

"It stands for Fixed Base Operator, you idiots," Blade muttered; he'd apparently been paying attention, for all he was gazing out the window as though lost in thought.

"How do you know that?" Dice asked in amazement.

Blade shrugged. "I listen when people talk," he said.

Then the limousine was turning into a parking lot, not crowded with cars but milling with photographers and reporters and entertainment-broadcasting personalities of various sorts. An irritated man in an orange traffic vest exhorted the crowd to stay behind a roped-off boundary – he waved the car through, and the driver seemed to know what to do, because he pulled right onto the tarmac where a small turbo-prop plane and two jets waited for their passengers. Another orange-vested worker swung his traffic cone toward the larger of the two jets – unnecessarily, as the wings and tail were emblazoned with the band's name – and the limousine rolled right up to the aluminum steps that led from the ground to the airplane's doorway. The Smidge jet wasn't as large as a commercial 747, but for all that it was big enough to dwarf the car, and caused Crys to draw in a breath at such a reminder of the band's staggering success and the material returns of that success.

"Are you ready back there, gentlemen?" came a voice through the limousine's intercom system – Crys thought it was the bodyguard speaking rather than the driver; the voice sounded mildly familiar.

Angel glanced at the others – everyone nodded – he punched the talk button and said, "Yes, Will, we're all set to go. You know the drill." Then, releasing the button, he turned to his band-mates and added, "Happy faces, kids – I saw a lot of vultures out there." He kicked Easy's ankle, not hard, just to prompt him to take the headphones out. Then a warning knock heralded the door's opening, and they were piling out onto the tarmac.

A cold wind blew in off the water, ruffling Crys's hair and whipping her skirt around her thighs as she stepped out of the limousine. Camera flashes popped all around, and she could only think how cross Marigold would be if a picture caught her with her hair blowing around her face and her dress plastered against her by the wind. "Come on," Blade said into her ear, "smile – show off your pretty lip ring! It's just for a few moments, and then we'll be inside." He squeezed her hand, and that did make her smile. Flash! A white light popped off far too close, and moments later one of the security guys was there, hustling the over-enthusiastic photographer back to a more appropriate distance. Then Blade was striding with her toward the airplane's steps, all smiles, though his grip on her hand was tight and his knuckles were white on the handle of his carry-on bag.

In moments, they were on the stairs, every step taking them closer to being on board the airplane – Crys gripped the metal handrail with cold fingers and concentrated on not slipping; spike heels were possibly not ideal footwear for the occasion, she realized. At the top, they turned and waved to the cameras one final time, and then stepped aboard the Smidge jet – out of the wind and into total luxury.

It was like stepping into a well-appointed office building rather than an airplane. The cream-colored inner shell of the fuselage was accented by varnished wood paneling. A flight attendant with a smart black uniform and startling pink hair took their coats as they boarded, and Crys saw her hanging the coats in a closet as they moved down the passage into what looked like a long narrow living room. Opulent black leather couches and recliners were grouped around chrome-edged tables.

A pair of recliners, occupied by Kin and Marigold, faced each other over a small table – Kin looked up in greeting, keeping his place with a finger on the newspaper spread out in front of him, while Marigold spared them only a quick glance before returning her attention to her computer screen. Across the aisle, Smidge's bodyguards sat talking quietly around another table. A massive L-shaped couch with four reclining segments took up the whole middle section. Beyond it, Sally was playing cards with Scott and Jed – and winning, from the look of things – at a large conference or dining table.

"I'll just go and say hello to Sally..." Crys began, turning to Blade – and realized that she didn't know where she was supposed to sit for the flight. Even as she wondered, she saw that Blade had dropped his carry-on bag onto one end of the big couch, and was lifting his guitar case into a special rack next to the seat, securing it with an elasticized net that would keep it in place during the flight. *Am I supposed to sit with him?* But Angel flopped down onto the seat next to Blade's, and Dice and

Easy settled into the two other places, so Crys understood that those were the band's usual seats, and no special provision had been made for her. There were no vacant seats nearby, and her only option was to walk on past the boys and sit at the big table. "I... I think I'll ask Sally if it's okay to sit with them and watch the card game," she mumbled.

"Sure, sweetheart," Blade said, though she wasn't sure if he'd actually heard what she'd said or if he was just offering a blanket agreement, because he was busy stowing his carry-on bag under the table in front of him and didn't even look up.

Sighing, Crys wandered along to where the card-players were sitting, and there at least she was greeted enthusiastically. "Sit with us, honey!" Sally insisted, before Crys could even ask. "We're playing blackjack, because some of us don't have the brainpower for anything more complicated–" she shot a teasing glance at the two men "–and you're welcome to join in the next hand, if you'd like."

"We won't play Texas Hold 'Em with Sally anymore because she beats the pants off us every time," Scott clarified dryly. "But there's more luck involved in blackjack so we sometimes win a little."

"Okay." Crys nodded her agreement, sitting down in the empty seat, her carry-on bag and purse filling her lap.

"It's only a short flight, but you can still get comfortable, Crys," Jed suggested. "There should be room for your things under the table, but if not, you can put them on the bed in the back cabin – no one's using it today."

"Back cabin?" Crys asked.

"Yes. Back past the washroom and office there's a sleeping suite. It's nice – got a queen-sized bed and a private washroom with a shower – but it doesn't get used much. Flights on tour are usually too short to sleep; you talk, read a magazine, play cards, and you're on the ground again. Still, it's been useful a few times, especially when Blade's been... indisposed. Go have a look if you like," said Jed.

Crys shook her head. "Oh, no, thank you. I'm sure it's very nice, but I think my little bag will fit under the table right here." Bending down, she wedged it into the available space.

A blonde flight attendant came swaying along the aisle, pausing briefly to chat with the band before reaching the card-players' table. "Good morning," she said with a bright smile, reaching out to shake Crys's hand in greeting. "I'm Dizzy. You must be Crys, right? Glad to have you aboard."

"Thank you, it's a lovely plane," Crys said politely.

Dizzy nodded. "We're about to start taxiing to our runway, if you could please buckle up. Matt will let you know over the intercom when we're cleared for take-off, but it shouldn't be long. Cyndi and I will serve drinks as soon as we're in the air."

"Thank you," said Jed.

"Matt's the pilot," Sally explained to Crys, as Dizzy moved off to repeat her message to the others, "and Cyndi's the other flight attendant, the one who took our coats. That's one of the lovely things about Smidge having the plane; we've got an awesome flight crew."

As the plane began to roll, Crys grinned. "No safety video?" she asked, with a bubble of laughter.

"Nope!" Sally grinned back. "It's the same drill as on a commercial flight – but Dizzy or Cyn could go through it with you if you need a refresher – all you'd need to do is ask."

"Right," said Crys. "Now, what about that card game? What are the stakes? You lot aren't high rollers, are you?"

"We usually bet chores and favors," Scott said, "but we could do pennies or points or something, since you haven't got a lot of crew chores and such to bet with."

"She can give backrubs and get coffee, though," Sally pointed out. "Up to you, Crys – points, pennies, or chores and favors?"

"Hmm..." Crys considered the options, reluctant to get into betting chores and favors though she knew that it would cement her position as a member of the Smidge crew if she did. She didn't like the risk of what exact chores and 'favors' might end up on the table, nor did she know whether this game stood a chance of devolving into dares and confessions or worse. Pennies seemed childish, though, and points? Points meant nothing, unless... "How about we play for points, and then the points loser buys everyone coffee when we get to LA?"

"Make it drinks, and I'm game," Jed said with an approving grin, and Sally and Scott nodded too.

"We'll go clubbing after the show – points loser to treat the first round – just the four of us, or the whole crew?" Sally asked.

Crys had only meant the four of them, and she'd only been thinking of coffee, but Scott laughed and said, "Why not? Let's make it a round for the whole crew."

"Sure," Jed agreed. "Crys hasn't been out with us yet anyway – it's about time we show her that the crew can party better than the band, don't you think?"

"Won't the boys come too?" Crys asked in surprise. She couldn't imagine the Smidge boys staying back at the hotel while their crew was out having a good time.

"Oh, sure," said Sally, eyes sparkling, "but we can dance them into the floor and drink them under the table any night of the week!"

Crys shot a glance over her shoulder at the four musicians lounging in their recliners, all of them hard-looking men. They were tired today, the tour beginning to wear on them, and without the leavening of animation, the hardness was easier to see in their faces – determination that would not quit, and the will to succeed no matter what the cost – the fierce drive that had bought them success in an industry rife with failure. Sally's assertion about outdrinking and outdancing seemed unlikely; quite apart from the iron will they shared, the boys drank beer and champagne like water, and the powerful energy of their concerts stood as evidence of their physical stamina.

Melodic chimes rang throughout the cabin, just loudly enough to command attention, and the intercom system hummed softly. "Good morning, y'all," said a man's voice with a hint of a Texan accent, in a pleasant and confident tone. "The tower has just advised me that we're cleared for takeoff, so keep your backsides buckled into those seats because we're about to boogie."

"Thank you, Matt!" everyone chorused, clearly a ritual response before the flight. Could the pilot hear them, then? Crys looked toward the front of the airplane, and by craning her neck could see that the door to the cockpit was open.

Sally gathered up the cards, saying, "We've gotta shuffle and start over anyway, since Crys is joining us. Game starts once we hit cruising altitude and ends when Matt announces the descent into LA – cool?"

Then the jet began its forward motion in earnest, picking up speed, thundering down the runway to make its heart-stopping leap into the air – no matter how many times she flew, Crys always held her breath for that split second when so many tons of metal and fuel and flesh and random matter were translated into an airborne improbability, the aircraft's wheels leaving the runway in a jet-propelled rise into the sky.

chapter

II

IN THE END, CRYS DID NOT LOSE THE CARD GAME —
Jed did, by a matter of ten points and a couple of reckless
hands, which led her to wonder whether he'd tanked his game on
purpose to save her from being the points loser.

Word of a party night spread rapidly through the Smidge crew –
Sally must have called Erva the moment the flight had touched down
in Phoenix, because by the time sound check rolled around, the entire
crew was bouncing around the arena in anticipation of a night out
together. Crys couldn't have put her finger exactly on the difference,
because the sound check and pre-show routine unfolded exactly as
it had in San Francisco and in Portland, but she could sense the extra
energy in the crew's banter, in the light-hearted performance of regular
tasks. The usual perfectly choreographed backstage ballet had become
a club dance – slow, measured movements were made fast and sharp;
the women walked with swaying hips and outthrust breasts; the men
moved with self-assured anticipation.

Blade snagged Crys backstage and drew her aside in the cinder
block tunnels. Maybe even the band was infected by the party mood,
because he stood closer to her than usual, with a hand resting casually,
almost possessively, on her hip. "So, are you going out with the crew
tonight?" he asked her.

"Of course," she told him. "I was playing in that card game – I came
awfully close to owing the entire crew a round of drinks – so there's no
way I'm going to miss out on the fun. Why?"

"Just wondered," he said, with a casual shrug. "You know they can party pretty hard, right?"

Crys laughed – it seemed so incongruous to hear Blade warning her about wild partying. "I'm not surprised. They'd have to, just to keep up with you lot!"

That made him laugh too. "True enough."

"Sally said you guys would probably come along too," she added. Not making a big deal of it. Just an idle comment. *Please come,* she wanted to say, *the evening won't be worth a damn if you're not there.*

Blade looked at her. "Oh? Would you want me there, then?" he asked softly, his eyes dark and intense.

"S-sure, of course," she said uncertainly, "why wouldn't I?" He'd said me, not us – *would you want me there?* – and she wasn't sure why or what that meant, when they could as easily have been talking comfortably about the band as a whole.

"No reason..." He nodded in the direction of the dressing room, saying, "We should probably get down there before security comes looking for me, huh?"

"Okay," she agreed. But she caught a vulnerable look on his face as she spoke, and added, "Do come out with us tonight, Blade. Because I like your company. Because I want you there. All right?"

He smiled, gratified. "All right."

Maybe I'm a fool, she thought as she followed him down the hall to the dressing room, *but for some reason he needed to hear that from me.* The need, the vulnerability, puzzled her. He knew that she loved him, didn't he? But then... could he have thought she'd meant love in a physical sense? Could he have believed that she was only interested in his body, that friendship and affection would evaporate once the physical need had been satisfied?

She shook her head to clear it – no use analyzing these things too closely, and she knew she should just be glad there was no residual awkwardness between them. In any case, it was settled; they were all going out after the show, and Sally had mentioned dancing. *Maybe he'll ask me to dance. Or maybe I'll ask him?*

♥

The floor thumped with a dance beat, colored lights swirled. An immense dance floor was packed with shadowy gyrating bodies. A waitress moved past with a tray full of drinks held high.

Oh, good God, I was getting too used to the campus pub and college parties, Crys thought, a thrill of awe running over her as she filed into the club with the rest of the crew and the band. She stumbled over something – a discarded bottle, maybe – and her attention was drawn downward; in the shifting light, her deep-red dress looked almost black, and the inky cross-hatching of her fishnet stockings was brought into high relief against her skin, standing out against all the denim-clad legs around her. Sally and Jed were just ahead with Angel and Dice, and Blade walked beside her with his arm linked through hers. Easy was somewhere behind her, she thought, though he'd seemed disinclined to stick with the group and had probably already peeled away to pursue his own interests. The bodyguards hovered, as always, and other crewmembers were all around, some she'd come to know quite well and others she hardly knew. The beat of the music ran through them all, bringing with it the urge to dance.

She'd been to clubs like this before, once or twice, but they weren't for the light-of-pocket. Keg parties in a ratty dorm or student apartment were cheaper and had always been good fun – better still when you didn't have far to crawl to bed. And the Duke's bartenders had been willing to serve pitcher after pitcher of half-decent draft beer at reasonable prices, along with giant plates of nachos and all-dressed fries, and never worried too much about checking ID. But with typical student budgets always stretched to the breaking point, that had been pretty much the extent of their nightlife at home.

Sally turned as they walked, shouting happily over the music, "So? Freakin' awesome, innit?"

The colored lights pulsed and Crys laughed. "Yeah!" she shouted back.

A huge VIP area had been roped off for them, with several long tables, and even as they were all sorting themselves into seats, a couple of pretty waitresses appeared with trays full of shot glasses – evidently primed by Jed, who'd apparently decided that his round of drinks was going to be delivered in a particularly lethal form. "Tequila?" asked the red-headed waitress nearest them, handing brim-full shot glasses to Blade and Angel with a flirty wink. "Tequila, honey?" she asked Crys without lifting one from her tray, a doubtful expression on her face.

"Absolutely," Crys said firmly, and took a shot glass from the tray herself, giving the waitress an unimpressed look for her doubt. *Do I still look like such a baby, even now with my lip ring?*

Blade glanced at her in surprise, and even Angel looked slightly taken aback. They'd expected her to refuse the tequila. "Are you sure that's a good idea, babe?" Angel asked. At least, she thought that was what he'd asked – the music was loud. Blade just looked at her quizzically, and she couldn't tell what he was thinking.

"Why wouldn't it be?" she said, grinning as she raised her glass in a mocking toast. She gestured around at their group, and saw no one without a shot glass in his or her hand. "All the rest of the crew are doing it..." And she'd promised herself with the lip ring that she wouldn't take the safe road anymore, that she'd take chances and try things. And she'd never tried tequila.

Then Jed was standing on a chair, bellowing, "All right, Smidge crew! One... two... three... DRINK!" All around her, the crew tipped up their glasses. Angel and Blade clinked their glasses and drank too. *I shouldn't,* Crys thought, but there was no backing out with the boys' eyes on her, and so she brought the shot glass to her lips and downed the contents.

Though she'd expected – from things she'd heard in the past – that it would taste nasty, she didn't find it unpleasant so much as medicinal, with an odd aftertaste that lingered in her mouth until someone handed her a lime wedge. "Bite into that, kid," said Zachary the production manager with a kind smile, then moved away before she could even thank him.

"There – see, I'm fine," she blurted out.

"You sure are, sweetheart," Blade agreed, laughing.

The waitresses were circulating again, taking and serving drink orders. A pitcher of beer was passed down their table, and Dice filled glasses, handing one to Crys before serving the boys. But she only had time to take a few sips before they all heard the club's DJ announce that Smidge and the crew were in the house, and then "Star Shot Down" was playing, and Sally grabbed her hand and said, "Come on, Crys, we gotta go dance. Smidge crew honor. We always dance our songs." Every female in the crew was getting up from her seat and heading for the dance floor. There weren't so many of them, the crew being mostly male – but there was Trish the tour accountant, who looked a little different with her hair loose and her t-shirt tight, and Kimmy the drum tech with her boyish haircut and facial hardware to rival Blade's, actually wearing a short skirt instead of overalls. And Sally and her assistant Lulu, but they looked much the same as always except with even more ultra-glamorous makeup. And Erva from lighting, and Ruby, one of the sound system techs.

They wedged their way onto the dance floor, fighting for space. Then the rhythm of the song they knew so well took over and they just danced, grooving, showing off. The colored lights touched everything with magic, and their possessive pleasure in Smidge's music gave their dancing an extra edge – a powerful sense of 'this is mine' that set them apart from all the other women on the dance floor. And the tequila began to make itself felt, in a warm uninhibited feeling of lightness.

Back at her table afterward, Crys sipped her beer, feeling charged with energy from dancing and yet totally relaxed. Across from her, Blade had taken off his denim vest and was down to a tight black t-shirt with the heretofore-unnoticed words 'willing and able' printed in lime green across the front. The words made her smile, and she remembered her blushes over his 'free love' shirt with retrospective amusement.

"What are you grinning about?" he asked, and she giggled.

"I like your shirt," she replied.

"Willing and able, that's me!"

"Oh, you sure are... able," she said – and though it was hard to tell in the club's lighting, she thought he actually blushed.

A good deal of time later – and it had to be late indeed since they hadn't even arrived until after the concert – when lots of beer and more tequila and assorted other liquids had been consumed by both band and crew, a group of them got up to dance again, and Crys was swept along quite willingly to the dance floor. This time Blade and Angel and Dice came down with them and joined in the dancing, well-watched by their bodyguards and covertly or openly ogled by most of the crowd. And when the song came to an end, a slow song started, and a disco ball in the ceiling began to spin, casting motes of sparkling light over everything. A hand touched Crys on the shoulder, just as she was about to head off the floor.

"Hey. You want to dance?" Blade asked.

"Dance?" Crys repeated stupidly. It was a slow song. Couldn't he see that?

"Yeah. Dance. With me."

And then it hit her – he was asking her to dance. To slow dance.

Nearby, Ryan realized that Blade wasn't leaving the dance floor, and Crys was vaguely aware that he snagged Kimmy to stay and dance with him, within arm's reach of his charge. The others melted away.

Blade waited for Crys's response, light and shadow passing over his face under the disco ball, and she realized that something had changed between them. When they'd first met, he hadn't hesitated to lift her onto his lap without waiting for an answer, with the assumption that she, a star-struck kid, would cooperate. Now he waited – he'd asked her to dance, but he wouldn't just pull her into his arms – he needed her acquiescence. And how could she say no?

Her feet moved her closer to him, almost involuntarily, one tiny shuffled step into his personal space and then another. She couldn't find words, but a sweet smile was enough to tell him yes, and brought an answering smile to his face.

He looked down at her, and she raised her arms toward him, with the instant of hesitation she always felt going into a slow dance, that moment of awkwardness between approach and connection. Then he reached for her, his strong hands gripping her hips and drawing her in, and her arms rose naturally to twine around his shoulders.

As they swayed to the slow rhythm, their bodies pressed together, Crys knew that this dance wasn't just for show, for comfort or as good friends. Tingling with electric awareness, she looked up – Blade was gazing down at her, the desire in his eyes visible even in the lights and shadows of the dance floor. He bent his head, his deep voice rasping next to her ear. "Oh hell, I'd only thought it would be nice to dance, and now I'm aching for you so bad... can you feel how much I need you, sweetheart?" he murmured – as if there were any way she could have failed to notice.

Maybe it was the tequila, but such blatant evidence of Blade's arousal had Crys urgently wanting to find a washroom stall or stairwell and lift her skirt for him. "Ohh, yesss..." she responded, rubbing her hips against him in an uninhibited reaction that would have shocked her former self.

He groaned. "Crys, you're wicked – I won't be able to walk!"

"What're you going to do about it?" she dared him, her eyes sparkling.

"Think of train wrecks," he said grimly, as the song came to an end and the lights brightened. And Ryan and Kimmy were smiling at them, and Scott lurked with his ever-present camera, and Trish and Mack emerged out of the crowd holding hands like shy teenagers.

As Blade released her and stepped back, Crys thought momentarily of acting on her impulse, of dragging him off to some secluded space and abandoning all inhibition. But there was Ryan the bodyguard to consider, sober and on duty, and anyway the moment of opportunity had passed. The group of them was moving back toward the Smidge tables, and an unusually friendly and talkative Kimmy had linked arms with Crys and was asking if she knew whether Ryan dated much and if he might or might not have a girlfriend. Crys did glance over at Blade as they walked, but his face was like stone and revealed nothing of what he might have been thinking.

Sally had ordered another tray full of tequila shots and they sat on the table in front of her with a bowl of lime wedges. "Very important to prove we can outdrink them," she explained to Crys in a confidential tone. "D'you think you can do another?"

"Sally, I'm not really crew, you know..." Crys began.

"Sure you are," Sally insisted, sliding a friendly arm around Crys's shoulders. "And you're my friend. Have another, unless it'll make you puke or something." Crys took the shot glass uncertainly, already feeling more than tipsy and thinking that one more would send her into dangerous territory. Sally passed out glasses to Kimmy and Erva, and offered one to Ryan who refused it. Then she advanced on the Smidge boys, teasing them, asking, "Can't you handle one more, then, boys?"

Blade met her challenge with a flash of recklessness. "I'll do two to your one," he proposed, whereupon Sally handed him a pair of shot glasses with a let's-see-you-try-it look. They clinked glasses and knocked the stuff back, Blade doing both shots with barely a breath between them. Eyes locked on Sally, he took another shot from the tray and placed it in front of her, took another two for himself. They drank.

Unnoticed, or so she thought, Crys looked at the untouched liquor in her hand, knowing that for her it would turn the night from heaven into nightmare. Then Dice came up and touched her wrist with his empty glass, quietly saying, "Here, swap glasses with me – none of them'll notice."

"You sure?" she asked, and he nodded, taking her unwanted drink and placing his empty one in her hand.

"Yeah. Won't hurt me, and you don't want to be sick tomorrow, right?"

"Thank you," Crys said, and then added, "Speaking of hurting, is... that... well..." She gestured toward Blade's four empty shot glasses and the wild look on his face, hoping that Dice would know what she meant, on two levels. Kin had hired her, after all, to help mend Blade's tarnished reputation – surely this was the type of damage she was supposed to prevent. And on a more personal level, even with his legendary tolerance Blade would be incurring one hell of a hangover, and it worried her that their dance, or maybe her forward flirting, had seemed to trigger his reckless mood.

"Yeah, he's gotten a bit out of control tonight," Dice agreed. "At least he's not using again – at least I don't think he is – and maybe you can keep him from getting naked, hmm?" Faint hope, his expression said, and he shot her a rueful smile.

Across the table, Blade was stripping off his shirt. And then he was standing on his chair, shirtless and dangerously inebriated. "SMIDGE ROCKS!" he yelled at full arena volume. "C'mon, get your gear off, people, and let's go DANCE!"

"Dude..." said Angel doubtfully, but Blade had already jumped off the chair and was heading toward the dance floor, with several of the more intoxicated crew following, ditching their shirts as they went. Ryan followed in their wake, trying to stay close to Blade.

"It ain't the booze, just," Dice said, running a frustrated hand through his hair. "He can drink for hours, other times, without getting like this."

Angel came around the table to join them. "Something's set him off again. We'd better go down there." He looked drunk too, Crys thought, but it seemed to have a more mellowing effect on him. "Hey, Crys, you'd better come too," he added. She wasn't sure exactly what she could do to help – Blade in this manic mood struck her as being an elemental force, unstoppable. But she was supposedly paid to prevent situations like this from going too far, wasn't she? She followed, to pick up the pieces if nothing else could be done.

Down on the dance floor, Blade had his arms around a couple of delighted women and was surrounded by a dozen more. If they even knew he was supposed to have a girlfriend, they'd forgotten, or just didn't care. One after another they'd squeeze close to him, taking turns, dancing with their thighs pressed against his, their hands stroking his bare chest.

Seeing Angel and Dice on the dance floor, half the harem detached themselves from Blade and swarmed around their new prey. "Hey

Angel, take your shirt off too," called one of the women crowding around him, and several pairs of hands eagerly helped remove his t-shirt. He let them do it, a slight smile on his face, both flattered and disillusioned.

"You too, Dice," another girl commanded, and more hands turned to divest the drummer of his upper clothing as well. He appeared to relish the attention, willingly cooperating as his shirt was removed.

Then Blade was lying back on a table next to the dance floor, his booted feet propped up on a chair, while a dyed-blonde girl with way too much cleavage tipped the contents of a shot glass into his navel. Shouts and whistles encouraged her as she bent down and lapped up the booze.

Crys looked around, feeling helpless. What should she do? Was there anything she *could* do? Then Sally came up and put a drunken arm around her. "Are you having fun, honey?" Sally inquired.

"Sure," Crys replied. She didn't want to say that it hadn't been a fun night – getting to know the women of the crew better, trying tequila, dancing with Blade – it had really been quite an excellent night, until this moment.

"Right, watching your man get publicly groped by a bunch of wasted bar stars! Strange kind of fun, that is..."

"Oh, he... he's not really my man..." Crys said. *Though I wish he was.*

"Then you're looking gutted for some totally other reason?" Sally asked with a short laugh. "Don't kid me, honey."

"I've gotten... fond of him, that's all, and he deserves better than being pawed by a bunch of girls who are only into him because he's famous and a sex symbol and stuff."

"And he doesn't get you hot? Seriously?!"

Crys blushed. "So what if he does – that doesn't make him mine!"

"Maybe not, but if he *were* yours, what would you do?" Jed asked from behind them, dropping a hand on each of their shoulders and startling them both.

"Jed! Don't sneak up on me like that!" Sally laid a dramatic hand over her heart.

"Last call for alcohol, ladies and gentlemen," the DJ announced. "The bar closes in ten minutes."

Glancing over toward the DJ's stand, a raised pulpit-like thing dominating one end of the dance floor, Crys blinked. Had she just seen Easy emerging from the washroom with a pair of giggling women? Surely not. Then her attention was reclaimed by a touch on her arm; Jed wanted her attention.

Ignoring Sally and last call for a moment, Jed looked straight at Crys, and through all the alcohol and fatigue and club lights, his eyes were full of sympathy. "Go on, Crys – he needs you – get down there!" He gave her a gentle push toward the table where Blade lay, then linked his arm through Sally's, saying, "Didn't mean to startle you, Sal, you just didn't hear me coming. D'you want one more before the bar closes?"

Crys focused her attention on Blade, still being used as a human shot glass. Random flashes from phone cameras did not bode well for the next day's press. *If he were mine, what would I do?* In public eyes, he was hers – these women were willfully encroaching on that – regardless of the true situation. *What would I do?* Pressing her lips together in determination, she was forcibly reminded of her lip ring's presence. Blade's gift to her, on the night she'd given him her virginity. *I've been in his bed; I've had him inside me.* And though he didn't love her and wasn't really hers to defend, she could still stare these trashy sluts down with the knowledge of it. She looked down at herself, glad in that moment for the clingy dark-red dress and fishnet stockings. Wished for a moment that she'd taken that last shot of tequila, then decided she didn't need it. Pulled the schoolgirl band off her head and shook out her hair. *I am no baby doll. I have metal in my face. I am a woman. They oughtn't dare to fuck with me!*

Summoning anger, summoning strength, Crys stormed down to where Blade was the center of attention. A dyed-blonde girl – was it the same one? – was busily working at the fly of Blade's jeans, the top button already unfastened. "Get your skanky hands off my boyfriend's pants," Crys snarled, almost spitting the words. "Do you think that because he's drunk and famous, that it's okay? That it's acceptable?! Would you like me to do body shots off your boyfriend – if you even have one? Would you like me to undo his pants in public? Or would you rather someone took your skirt off for everyone to have a look, 'cause I could help you with that, if you'd like?" The anger was a rush, the stunned looks on their faces a glory. Crys felt ten feet tall and glowing with furious power. The women who'd been manhandling Blade cowered in front of her, and even the ones flirting with Angel and Dice backed off a little in shame.

"W-we were just having some f-fun," stammered the one who'd been undoing Blade's pants, red-faced.

"Like I said, would it be fun if we took your skirt off?" Crys reiterated, narrowing her eyes and feeling quite willing to try it. Then she turned to Blade, who stared up at her, absolutely shit-faced. Her anger cooled a little at his bemused expression – endearingly pleased to see her, maybe a bit relieved, and definitely too drunk to have defended himself from the women or participated much in their shenanigans. *Mine, for tonight at least. Let's make that point clear.* "Get yourself up off that table, love," she told him, running a finger down his bare chest with as much overt sensuality as she could manage, a deliberate challenge both to him and to the women who'd been fooling with him. "I want to dance with you, and then I want to take you to bed."

He rolled off the table and stood, staggering a little and then pulling himself upright. "Oh, yeahh, sweetheart," he slurred enthusiastically, then yelled out, "YO! DJ! SLOW SONG!"

Others took up the shout, until the DJ hollered back, "I hear you, people! All right, last song of the night, in honor of the band's presence, here's 'Love Bound' by Smidge..." Whether by coincidence or not, it was Blade's song. Crossing the distance to the dance floor in a few long steps, he pulled Crys into his arms, no hesitation this time – but then, she'd asked him to dance. And this time he showed no restraint, either; hands openly cupping her buttocks, he slid one long thigh between her legs, grinding with her in total abandon, as though they were alone.

Hearing one of their songs, the Smidge crew poured onto the dance floor, the women quickly pairing off, the remaining guys catching the eyes of available strangers. Dancing to uphold Smidge crew honor. Dancing because the hour was late and the liquor was in them. And the uninhibited lustful mood was contagious – from the corners of her eyes Crys caught glimpses of other couples, known and unknown, locked together, bodies writhing and hands roaming.

When the lights came up, silence settled across the whole dance floor. There was almost collective shame in the way they'd lost themselves in the music and the moment and each other. *Was that really me just now,* Crys asked herself, *grinding with Blade bold-faced in front of everyone, arching into him and running my hands over his bare back?* And in the brief silence she knew that the same stunned question was running through the minds of all those standing on the dance floor, including Blade, who gazed at her with something like brain-fogged dismay.

"Ladies and gentlemen, the bar is now closed," the DJ announced. "Thank you for joining us, and please be safe tonight; do practice safe sex, and don't drink and drive. Goodnight!" In the bright go-home-now lighting, the magic of the nightclub and dance floor had completely evaporated. Crys looked around, seeing for the first time all the debris of the night's end – fallen straws and crumpled paper napkins, discarded bottles, plastic cups, the odd abandoned shoe and worse – littering every surface. The heat of the club had turned to a chill, somehow, though the temperature hadn't changed.

Nearby, Kimmy and Trish were straightening their clothes, while Mack looked smug and Ryan embarrassed, and even Sally emerged from the crowd in a slightly rumpled state, though Crys didn't see whom she'd been dancing with. Then Phil the tour manager and Zachary the production manager – manifestly sober though Crys had seen them both drinking earlier – were gathering the crew together for an organized exodus. "Our transportation awaits, kids, time to rock on out of here," the two more-responsible crewmembers were saying, over and over, herding the stumbling mass of them toward the exit.

Blade dozed off on the way back to the hotel, and staggered groggily inside when they arrived, leaning on Angel and Jed to get to his room. It was for the best, Crys concluded regretfully, as she got into her own empty bed. Much as she'd been curious about putting their uninhibited moods to the test, it would most likely have been paid for in awkwardness and embarrassment the next day. Maybe even long-term misery and a loss of their friendship – it was as well not to have risked it.

♥

The first Crys knew of any fallout from the night's debauchery came with Blade's loud swearing and the sound of his kicking walls and furniture. The crashing and cursing woke her out of a heavy sleep; disoriented and unsettled by the noises. Entirely forgetting about Marigold's dictum against leaving her room in an imperfect state, she dashed out into the sitting room – barefoot, in her lilac flannelette pajamas printed with fluffy white kittens and balls of powder-blue yarn, her hair in slept-on disarray – and stopped short at the sight of a destroyed newspaper strewn about the room, chairs upended, and a furious Blade who'd just put his boot through the drywall.

"Good God!" she said aloud, her unused morning voice coming out as a startled squeak. She cleared her throat and tried again. "Blade! What's wrong?"

Her presence seemed to bring him back to himself. He looked at his drywall-covered boot and the hole in the wall, and muttered, "Shit."

"Blade?" Crys prompted. "Should I... call someone? Jed, maybe?"

He sighed, looked at her – did a double-take at the sight of her. "Damn, don't you look cute in those pajamas!" he said with a half-hearted smile. "No, you don't need to call anyone; they'll turn up soon enough anyway."

"Oh?"

"I'm in the news again." He fished around among the crumpled and torn sheets of newsprint. "Pictures that'll get me in trouble. Can't show you 'cause I kind of shredded them."

"I don't need to see the pictures," she pointed out. "I was there." She hadn't meant anything to show in her face as she spoke, hadn't meant to imply disapproval or distaste, but he looked at her and reddened.

Stung – and reminded of everything that the night had held – he drawled in an almost insulting tone, "Oh, I know you were there, sweetheart: for that dance alone, I won't forget last night in a hurry."

She felt herself blushing at that, reminded of how uninhibited she'd been on the dance floor with him and, though he couldn't possibly know it, how she'd briefly considered letting him have her in a stairwell or washroom stall. In sober daylight, she could hardly believe she'd even thought of it. Her first impulse was to apologize, as always – years of family conditioning to smooth things over and not make a fuss. *Years of watching Mum apologize to Dad for things that weren't wrong, weren't her fault, weren't even within her control.* But saying sorry didn't magically fix everything and restore her perfect lady status, no matter what Mrs. Murphy thought. "My job is to act like your girlfriend in public," Crys reminded Blade in a quiet voice. "I know that was Kin and Marigold's idea, not yours, and no one can force you to play along. I'm doing the best I can with a limited choice of roles, and I... well, I thought you'd prefer 'sex kitten' over 'jealous harpy,' at the time." An unhappy choked feeling surged in her chest.

"Hell, I didn't mean–" he began, only to be interrupted by a knock on the suite door. "Here it goes," he muttered grimly, then crossed to the door, checking through the peephole before he opened it. "Hi, Jed."

Jed carried a couple of newspapers. "Buddy, I just wanted to warn you – oh, you've seen it," he said, as he looked around at the remains of Blade's newspaper, the toppled chairs and the hole in the wall. "Goldie's on her way, and she's not a happy lady this morning."

Blade lowered his eyes, twiddling with his eyebrow ring. "No kidding," he said unhappily. "Can't blame her – it's pretty bad."

Jed shrugged. "Could have been worse." When Blade didn't respond, he elaborated, "You do realize that one of the bitches was about to have your pants off, don't you? Until Crys stepped in, that is."

"Damn, I'd forgotten about that," Blade said, his eyes widening. "It's a bit fuzzy, but – did you really offer to take that chick's skirt off for her?! Crys, you're a goddess!"

"I don't know, it must have been the tequila..." Vividly, she remembered the anger and the rush that unleashing it had given her – and how close she had come to actually ripping the dumb tart's skirt off her. *I wouldn't have... would I?* She couldn't be sure, and felt uncomfortably that she might have done it, if provoked any further. And wound up being sued for assault, most likely. Unable to meet either man's admiring eyes, she looked away, and in doing so was reminded of the room's chaotic state. "Um, guys, if Marigold is on her way... maybe we should tidy up a bit? I don't think a trashed hotel room will add to her general disposition..."

Jed laughed. "Good thought, Crys. But Blade and I will tidy up while you go and dress – you know Goldie has a thing about everyone always looking photo-ready..."

"You're right; there's no sense in adding to her mood," Crys agreed. "I'll be as quick as I can."

As she headed to her bedroom, they were already righting chairs and gathering up the crumpled newspaper. "Not much we can do about the hole in the wall," she heard Jed say, but didn't catch Blade's muttered reply.

Crys meant to be quick, but she'd forgotten about needing to clean and salt-soak her piercing. It was still tender to the touch, and too new for her to be completely familiar with the necessary steps – getting the bits of scabby crust off was a delicate task, and she still had to gather up her nerve to rotate the ring through the piercing. By the time she stepped out of the en suite bathroom, wrapped in a towel and not in any state to emerge from her bedroom, she could already hear the strident tones of Marigold's voice coming from the sitting room, occasionally interspersed with the gravelly rumble of Blade's responses.

She wriggled into jeans and a Smidge crew t-shirt – and, catching sight of herself in the mirror, she realized that she had grown completely used to the snug fit of jeans that had once seemed indecently tight to her, and she'd opted for a thong to avoid panty lines without even thinking about it. Getting used to being a rock star's princess. Hurriedly slicking back her hair with a bit of gel, she did a quick mirror check; no sense in antagonizing an already edgy Marigold by being less than perfect. Her lower lip was still a little bit puffy, but there was nothing she could do about that, and even then with a bit of the beeswax lip balm it looked kind of sexy swollen, as Angel had pointed out. Crys couldn't delay any longer, and opened her door to join Blade and Marigold in the sitting room.

Blade sat on the sofa, his face holding a glazed look, while Marigold paced, tapping her pen on her clipboard. She didn't turn; hadn't heard the door open behind her. The scarlet satin pantsuit meant that Marigold had dressed to handle business, Crys thought – the public relations assistant never wore that particular outfit to concerts or casually around the hotels – which struck her as ominous. "We'll need to address the situation with a press conference, of course – though I don't know when we'll fit it in, since we're flying to San Diego first thing tomorrow – but we need some reason, some justification for your drunken behavior. You wanna get engaged? A last-fling explanation might work, in that context..."

Crys, standing in the doorway to her bedroom, felt her mouth open in shock at the thought. Blade's eyes met hers, and he looked as stunned as she felt. Had Marigold really just suggested...? The travesty of such a false engagement sickened her, even as her knees weakened at the thought of promising herself to him forever. Her heart ached as two worlds collided within her – the electric no-rules chemistry she felt every time she looked at Blade crashed hard into the fairytale she'd grown up on: a white wedding and souls joined forever, a home and children she'd never have with him. *I already have the only ring he'll ever give me,* she told herself, touching the tip of her tongue to the steel ring in her lip. *In memory of one special night.* And the shadowed look on his face confirmed that nothing more could even be dreamt of.

"Don't even think it, Goldie," he said in a flat tone, his face forbidding.

"Right, then maybe we could say–"

"Hi Marigold, hi Blade," Crys said as brightly as she could, to forestall any further horrific suggestions.

Marigold turned, her sour expression lightening a fraction as she saw how tidy and presentable Crys looked. "Not exactly a roaring success, last night," she said. "You're supposed to keep Blade from getting into this kind of trouble."

"He didn't do any drugs, barf in public, lose his pants, or have sex with anyone," Crys retorted, "so I think I did a pretty good job, all things considered."

Blade laughed. "True enough, sweetheart," he agreed.

Grudgingly, Marigold laughed too. "I suppose the situation is better than it could have been," she conceded. "All right, no press conference. Crys, when you're asked about it – and you will be – just say that you don't mind Blade flirting, that you know it's part of his job and you trust him not to cross the line. Got it?"

"Sure," Crys agreed, though she did mind terribly. *Part of the job,* she told herself. Part of his job, and part of hers.

"Great. And we've got a free night tomorrow in San Diego, so you two had better be seen out together – I'll arrange something for you." Marigold didn't wait for their acquiescence; it wasn't a choice. She made a final note on her clipboard and tucked the pen into the top of it, satisfied. Blade stared at the toes of his boots, his face like stone, and didn't respond. Marigold shrugged. "Well, I've got things to do. Please try to stay out of trouble until it's time to leave for the arena, would you? And no more holes in the drywall – I'll have it taken care of, but if word gets out that you're punching walls... it's just the last thing we need right now!" With a controlled nod and tight smile, the public relations assistant was out the door and away.

Crys looked at Blade and didn't know what to say. He seemed so unhappy at times, and there was nothing at all she could do for him. Nothing, except maybe offer her body in comfort. Just as she thought of it, he glanced up and their eyes met – awareness crackled between them like static electricity – they were alone, they both wanted it, they'd done it before...

Her lips parted, as though she meant to say something although she had no words in mind, and Blade just watched her as she stood there, his eyes full of a dark hunger that almost frightened her. *He isn't always a gentle and considerate lover,* Angel had said. Mesmerized, she ran the tip of her tongue over her lips, moistening them.

He closed his eyes. "Go," he said, his voice rough. "Get out of here."

"Blade? But...?" Shaken out of the sensual moment, Crys felt confused, unwanted and hurt. "I thought... I don't understand."

"Just go," he repeated, and he almost sounded angry, his face taut with the effort to control himself. "Not to your room. Leave the suite."

Thoroughly confused, and a bit shocked at herself for wanting this intense angry side of him to overcome his better judgment, she nodded. "I'll go and see if Sally's around, or something," she agreed. "I'll see you when it's time to leave for the arena, right?"

"Yeah. Don't worry. I just..."

And because he couldn't find words, she took pity on him. "It's okay," she said. "I don't really understand, but it's still okay. I'll see you later."

"I'm glad you don't understand, Crys," he said, his eyes dark with bitter self-loathing. And because she couldn't think of anything to say to that, she left.

chapter

12

EVEN THOUGH BLADE HAD SAID NOT TO WORRY, Crys went to find Angel. He was in his suite, reading, wearing a pair of steel-framed glasses – which surprised her, as she hadn't realized he needed them. It was an odd scene, she thought, looking at the lead singer of Smidge sitting on the sofa with his feet in grey woolly socks propped up on the coffee table, wearing an old sweater and ratty jeans, a battered Robert Heinlein novel open on his lap and what looked like a mug of tea steaming on the table within easy reach.

"Crys! Come in, sit down," he invited, seeming surprised to see her. When she'd knocked, he'd only called out for her to come in – had he perhaps been expecting someone else? He removed his feet from the table and stood, waiting until she sat before he too sat back down. "You look concerned, babe; what's up?"

She twisted her hands in her lap, wondering if maybe she was being a fool, imagining disaster because Blade hadn't wanted her company. But she hadn't imagined the darkness in his eyes, the taut distress on his face. "It's Blade," she told Angel. "Maybe I'm blowing things out of proportion, but he... he told me to get out of the suite, and... he seemed unhappy."

"Unhappy? That's one word for it..."

"Sorry. Silly word," Crys agreed. "He looked like he's not liking himself very much, like he... I don't know. He seemed angry, and bitter, and hurting really bad – and he wouldn't let me help, wouldn't let me stay."

Angel nodded, looking troubled himself. "Yeah. He gets that way sometimes."

"I was worried that he might..." And Crys didn't even want to say the words, to voice her fear that the call of the drug might be too much for Blade in such a state.

"He might indeed," Angel agreed with a heavy sigh, fishing a guitar pick from his pocket and sticking it into his book to mark his place. "I'm glad you came to tell me, Crys – we may yet manage to save him from himself."

She shook her head. "But he has to want to save himself first, doesn't he?"

"He does." Angel stood up, then reached for his mug and took a few quick gulps of the steaming tea before abandoning the rest. "Damn. I'll go see if I can cheer him up, then."

"Thank you." Crys got up too, recognizing the urgency and the dismissal, and Angel gestured for her to precede him.

Pausing in the doorway, he rubbed a hand over his bleached crew-cut, thinking. "Look, I don't know how this afternoon is going to play out... maybe you should catch a ride to the arena with some of the crew, or you could go in the limo with Dice and Easy, though that might look..."

"It's fine," she said. "I was planning on trying to find Sally anyway; I'm sure I can go with her."

Angel nodded. "Good. Catch you later."

Then he was off, striding rapidly down the hall in the direction of the suite she shared with Blade. Turning away, Crys set out to look for Sally – or any other distracting company, really – to pass the time until they should have to leave for the arena.

♥

Crys did find Sally, and because the orange-haired woman had nothing urgent to attend to, the two of them had lunch and went shopping. Crys couldn't help, every so often, thinking of Blade and his dark mood, and she wondered how Angel was coping. But she was glad to have a few hours' escape from the endless round of arenas and hotels. Sally proved to be a fun shopping companion, encouraging Crys to buy some beautifully frivolous lingerie and – against the day when her lip should be fully healed – a bold purple-black lipstick like blackberry juice.

All too soon, the escape came to an end, and Crys found herself with an anxiously tight stomach as she arrived at the arena, for the first time doing so anonymously in the middle of a bustle of crew gearing up for the night, of no interest at all to the photographers who waited for the Smidge boys. But she needn't have worried – Blade and Angel arrived without incident, and Angel shot her a small grin and a thumbs-up sign – no heroin, then. Blade even seemed moderately relaxed, drinking and chatting in the band lounge contentedly enough.

He's avoiding touching me, Crys thought. And it was true that he sat where she wouldn't be able to sit beside him, and that where ordinarily their fingers would touch or his hand would brush her waist or hip in passing, he was over-scrupulous about leaving space between them. But he said nothing, so she said nothing. *This will pass,* she told herself. *It must!* No one could keep up that kind of avoidance forever, in the kind of close quarters that a band and crew shared on tour. *And then we'll be comfortable with each other again – I hope!* And so she tried not to mind that he was distancing himself from her as though she were contaminated or would contaminate him.

He didn't look over at her at all during "Love Bound," but she did catch his eyes on her once – when the boys played "Star Shot Down," it brought back a flash of all the crew women dancing in the nightclub, and Crys and Sally danced a little in memory of that fine moment, behind the panel, at the edge of the stage and yet hidden. Then a prickle of awareness made Crys glance out at the stage, and Blade was watching them, just for a moment, with a slight wistful smile on his face. What was it that he wished for, in that moment? Would he have wanted to go back and do that night over again differently? Did he ever wish for a moment that he were just crew, to dance with them behind the panels, to go out and party without press and bodyguards, without all the fame and attention? Or were his eyes on them, on her, for some other reason? Knowing that she was a fool to even dream of it, she couldn't help cherishing a hope that his glance meant something still sparked between them. And then he looked down at his guitar, and out into the crowd, and the moment passed.

He did not look her way again through the rest of the concert, and though she rode back to the hotel in the limousine with the boys, she felt awkward sitting beside Blade with a careful inch of space preserved between them, and his arm along the back of the seat instead of around her shoulders. After four concerts in as many days, they were all tired, and didn't talk much, just stared out the windows as the car rolled along.

Once back at the hotel, the boys decided to have some drinks in Angel's suite before turning in for the night, but Crys cut her losses and went straight to her room, claiming a headache. Angel gave her a puzzled look as she left, but she just shrugged and rubbed the back of her neck as though it ached, and he didn't say anything.

Before getting into bed, Crys dug through her suitcases to find her own black denim dress with the silver stitching, to wear the next day. *Damn, I haven't any plain stockings,* she realized, sorting through the variety in her bags; they were all fishnets, or thigh-highs, or had wild patterns. *The first thing I'm doing in San Diego is buying some plain old normal pantyhose!* Even looking at the black satin garter belt made her feel a bit sad, so she decided on the black fishnet thigh-highs with the pink bows that she'd worn to the concert in Seattle. Even with Blade detoxing and the crazed nightmare feel of the concert, it was a warm and precious memory – for the first time, she'd felt like a part of the Smidge crew, respected by the boys and above all needed by Blade, everyone working together to avert disaster. She added the matching bra and thong since the set went together. Having her outfit laid out for the morning would buy her an extra ten minutes' sleep in the morning.

They had an early flight scheduled for the next day, but it would be a short one – less than an hour – followed by the luxury of an entire free day and night in San Diego, with no concert until the next evening.

♥

"Someone remind me again why we agreed to this goddamn early flight?" Easy grumbled, as they crossed the tarmac in whipping rain to board the jet.

"Dunno. Must have seemed like a good idea at the time, though," Angel replied, glancing around. For once, no photographers had braved the early hour and cold drizzle – they were alone but for the one bodyguard escorting them from the limousine, and one of the flight attendants – Dizzy – waving from the door of the plane. *And thank God for that,* Crys thought, knowing that even the brief exposure to wind and rain was having a less-than-ideal effect on her hair.

The metal stairs were wet and slick, even with the roughened no-slip strips, and the slippery handrails didn't promise much of a grip if anyone should fall. The sole of Crys's boot slid a bit halfway up, and she drew in a startled breath and scrabbled for purchase on the railing, until a strong hand steadied her at the waist. Blade was behind her on the stairs; it could only be his hand steadying her. "Don't worry, sweetheart. I won't let you fall," he said, his raspy deep voice reassuring and wonderful. He didn't draw his hand away, but kept it there, supporting her, until they'd reached the top of the stairs and stepped aboard the airplane.

"Welcome aboard, Blade; welcome aboard, Crys," said Dizzy, taking their coats. "We'll be taxiing to our runway as soon as you've taken your seats, so please fasten your seatbelts right away, all right?"

This time, Crys didn't have to wonder where to sit – Sally was already waving her over, while Jed and Scott looked up smiling, and they had the cards out on the table in readiness. She held up one finger to indicate that she would just be a moment, and turned to face Blade, saying, "Thank you for catching me back there; I thought for sure I would fall."

"I'll catch you any time," he replied with a sexy grin, and she shook her head, unsure what to make of his flirting and the fact that his hand still rested on her hip. And just as she was about to move away, he asked, "Did you want to sit up with us? There'd be room for you in the corner of our couch, if we get a bit cozy..."

"Are you in, Crys?" Sally called at the same moment. "I'm about to deal."

Crys glanced from the card players to the band, and back to Blade. He was smiling his wide beautiful smile, white teeth and silver lip ring gleaming, as though the tensions and avoidance of the previous day had never existed; whatever demons had been plaguing him were banished for the moment. With all her heart Crys wanted to go with him and sit wedged against him on the couch with Angel or Dice on her other side, like a real girlfriend, to listen to them talk or just to sit in silence with his arm around her shoulders and his thigh pressed against hers. But... to declare herself, to choose the band over the crew... it seemed a huge and risky step. If things went back to their previous awkward state, she would be dependent on the crew for companionship and as a buffer – even for card games on flights.

"Crys?" Sally called again, and Blade, seeing Crys's hesitation, shrugged.

"Go ahead, if you want to play cards," he said, though his hand still rested lightly on her hip as if he were unwilling to break the contact. "I don't mind either way."

Feeling herself a coward, Crys mumbled that she had promised the card players a rematch, and moved away on reluctant feet, with a sinking feeling as his fingertips lost contact. "I'm in," she told Sally, sitting down to the game, "but Marigold'll kill us all if we end up going out and getting in trouble again. So can we make the stakes just lunch for the four of us?"

Scott snorted. "Goldie thinks she's the queen of the universe – but all right, lunch for the four of us is fine."

"Works for me," Jed said, and Sally nodded too as she dealt the first hand.

I won't look over there – I won't, Crys told herself as she took up her cards. King of hearts, seven of clubs. Couldn't concentrate. The skin on the back of her neck prickled, and quite without intention, her gaze flicked to where the band sat – catching Blade's eyes on her. Though she jerked her eyes away at once, it had only taken a second to see the look on his face, and a wave of heat washed over her. Sally shot her an odd glance, and Crys realized that she was blushing, her face on fire. "Crys, it's your turn," Sally prompted.

"Oh. Um, hit me," she said, and drew a nine of diamonds, going bust.

Chimes and the hum of the intercom system interrupted them. "Good morning, y'all. I hope you're in your seats and buckled up, because we've just been cleared for takeoff."

"Thank you, Matt!" came the response from all the passengers, and Crys joined in this time, knowing it was expected.

"Why'd you draw on seventeen, Crys?" Scott asked, drawing their attention back to the card game. "Especially when Sal's got a three showing." He shook his head at her folly, and made a note on the postcard where they were tallying points.

Jed said nothing, but his expression was faintly speculative, and Crys wondered just how much he'd observed and what conclusions he'd drawn.

After three more disastrous hands, Crys knew she'd be buying the lunch in San Diego. "I'm so sorry," she told the others, seeing their puzzlement at her lousy playing – she was no card shark, but had kept up reasonably well with the others on their previous flight. They all said it was no problem, but her distraction took the fun out of the game, and everyone breathed a sigh of relief when Dizzy and Cyndi interrupted them to serve coffee and breakfast pastries.

Crys cupped her hands around the steaming hot mug and took a grateful sip – just as the slight clink of her lip ring against the china reminded her that she would have to clean her mouth after eating. She had a toothbrush and toothpaste in her purse, as usual, but remembered with a sinking stomach that she'd packed her bottle of oral rinse into one of her suitcases rather than her carry-on bag. *Damn.* "No, thank you," she said with great reluctance as Cyndi, following Dizzy and the coffee urn, held out a tray of pastries. A warm sweet bakery scent wafted up, making Crys's stomach growl, but she still shook her head.

Without the mouthwash, she didn't dare eat – she'd been warned so strictly to use it every time anything other than plain water crossed her lips.

"What's the matter, hon?" Cyndi asked. "Dieting? We've got grapefruits and peaches and some low-calorie snack bars in the galley, if you like." Whether her voice was naturally loud, or a momentary lull had simply hit other conversations at the same moment, her inquiry was heard by virtually everyone on the flight.

"That's probably wise," Marigold called out from her seat forward, adding, "I'd prefer a half-grapefruit for breakfast, myself. With diet sweetener, not sugar."

Feeling foolish, Crys explained, "Thank you, but it's not that – I've... my lip, I forgot my mouthwash and won't be able to clean it. I shouldn't even be drinking the coffee."

Blade, hearing this, turned in his seat to pay closer attention. "Piercers always talk like you're going to pick up something vile if you break their rules, but honestly, just do a saltwater soak when we arrive in San Diego and you'll be fine." He thought for a moment. "You know, though, I'm pretty sure we've got some mouthwash on board – it's probably in the washroom cabinet. So go ahead and eat."

"There you go," the flight attendant said. "Did you want one of these pastries, or shall I get you something else? A peach, maybe? I'm going to the galley for Ms. Hendon's grapefruit anyway."

"A pastry's fine. More than fine." They looked and smelled delicious – no pre-wrapped airline food here; these treats had evidently been brought on board fresh from the bakery that morning. Crys chose a cream-cheese-filled Danish to go with her coffee; Cyndi lifted it onto a china plate with a pair of silver tongs, and handed it to Crys with a crisp linen napkin folded underneath. Crys accepted it with an appreciative murmur of thanks, all the more heartfelt because she'd been prepared to refuse the food. As she picked it up, the pastry flaked under her fingers and clung to them, sticky and shining with sweet glaze. She bit into it, the decadent creamy filling oozing from within. It tasted every bit as good as promised.

No one spoke for a bit, their mouths full of pastry and coffee. Satisfied that their passengers' needs had been met for the moment, the flight attendants vanished into the forward part of the airplane – Crys assumed there was a crew cabin or at least seats for them somewhere.

She licked a last bit of cream cheese filling from her lip and wiped her hands on the linen napkin. It would be hard to go back to commercial economy flights after experiencing this level of luxury. *I'm getting spoiled,* she thought, a smile passing across her face at the idea. Eating garlic prawns and lobster salad, drinking fine champagne. Flying in a private jet. Sleeping in fancy hotels with nicer sheets than she could afford to own. But then she sobered, knowing in her heart that it was really Blade's presence spoiling her, that all the rich food and surroundings were nice but meant little compared to being with him. That his company, even in the blackest of moods, would be the hardest thing to give up.

With that thought, she put down her plate and napkin, and reached for her purse under the table. "You can go ahead and play a few hands without me, if you like," she told Sally and Jed and Scott, seeing that they'd also finished eating. "I've got to take care of my lip."

"What about the points, though?" Scott asked.

Sally gestured dismissively. "I'll play for her while she's gone." The two men muttered something about it not being fair, but the makeup artist quelled their protests with another wave of her hand. "Just go, honey. We'll see you in a few minutes."

Crys hadn't needed the washroom on the last flight, so she hadn't been past the main cabin area of the jet. Stepping with care, trying to look confident despite the oddly bouncy sensation of walking on a jet in flight, she moved toward the back where she assumed the washroom to be. A bulkhead covered in dark cherry paneling filled three quarters of the fuselage width and featured an enormous flat-screen television; the remaining space formed a narrow hallway into the rear of the airplane. Glancing around, she saw that everyone was seated, no one absent – so the washroom must be vacant.

Venturing down the hallway, she found that the very first door had a small brass plate reading GUEST LAVATORY, and the dial around the handle said AVAILABLE in white letters on a green background, clear and welcoming. She stepped in, closed and locked it behind her. A large and well-lit mirror was positioned over a marble vanity sink; the toilet, with its lid down, looked more like convenience seating than a commode. There was even a shower stall, complete with soap and shampoo, and fluffy fresh towels in a recessed cubbyhole.

Crys looked around for the promised bottle of mouthwash. There was a cabinet under the sink, but she only found cleaning supplies and additional soaps and toilet tissue; not even a tube of toothpaste, or any personal effects. *It's probably in the washroom cabinet,* Blade had said – hadn't he? But then she remembered a conversation from her earlier flight on the Smidge jet, when Jed had mentioned the sleeping suite at the back of the plane. *It's got a queen-sized bed and a private washroom,* he'd told her. That was probably the washroom Blade had meant.

She felt a bit hesitant about going further down the short hall, into the more private spaces of the plane. Elegantly soft recessed lighting gleamed on the cherry-wood finish of the walls, and it reminded her of stately homes in the kind of period movies where all the characters are wealthy and wear gorgeous clothes and butlers and maids are hovering everywhere. She felt like an intruder, a guest in someone's home, prowling about rooms she hadn't been shown by her hosts. *Blade did tell me there was mouthwash in the washroom,* she assured herself, *so he must have meant me to look for it.* But he might have thought it was in the – what had the little brass sign called it? – the guest lavatory. He might never have meant for her to search elsewhere.

A few feet past the washroom door, there was another door, with a brass plaque on it which read PRIVATE OFFICE. Then the hallway ended with a sliding pocket door, and the plaque on that one said STATEROOM; like the washroom, it had an AVAILABLE sign, a small rectangle above the recessed handle.

Stateroom – just a fancy word for a bedroom, wasn't it? *It's been useful a few times, especially when Blade's been indisposed,* Jed had said.

Her hand on the door handle, Crys imagined Blade lying on the bed, pale and ill as he'd been when detoxing, or maybe dreaming under the influence of the drug – she wasn't sure what effect heroin had on its users, wasn't sure how to picture him in thrall to it. And then unbidden, other pictures came to her mind. Sally had mentioned guests that the boys had brought on the jet with them in the past, and Crys had known what kind of company she'd meant, but she hadn't connected it to the bedroom until that moment.

I won't look at the bed, she told herself. *I won't look at anything. I'll go straight into the bathroom.* And she reached out and hooked her fingers into the recessed handle, sliding the door aside.

The door to the washroom was straight ahead of her, and she kept her eyes on her toes as she walked directly toward it. But the queen-sized bed took up most of the available floor space – it was right there beside her, and even with the best of intentions she couldn't help being aware of it, even in only the ambient light from the windows. The bedding that brushed her leg was black satin. *I will not look. I do not want to know.* Head firmly averted, she hurried past the bed and through the open door of the washroom, flipping on the lights.

It was similar to the guest lavatory she'd already seen, though the marble-topped vanity and mirror were larger, and the shower was larger too; the private washroom spanned the entire width of the jet's fuselage – the first thing Crys noticed were the two emergency exit doors, one on either side. There were more cabinets as well, under the sink and on the wall above the toilet, all brightly lit by stage-dressing-room style lighting, rows of round bare globes edging the mirror. Feeling more than ever like an intruder, she opened first one cabinet then another, finding soap and shampoo, a selection of brand new plastic-wrapped toothbrushes, makeup – a vast number of black eyeliner pencils sharpened down to various lengths, glitter dust, concealer and powder, but no mascara or blush. One drawer held a powdery hand mirror and a couple of razor blades, and she slammed that one hastily closed, wishing she hadn't looked. Finally, she found some assorted bottles of contact lens solution, hair gel, and the promised mouthwash.

Hurriedly squirting some into her mouth, she closed the bottle, and with fumbling hands returned it to the cabinet where she'd found it. She swirled the stuff in her mouth around, spat, and rinsed out the sink. Then she caught her reflection in the big beautiful mirror with the bright stage lighting all around, and smiled because the ring in her lip was worth every bit of the trouble it caused her.

A sound nearby startled her – a footstep? Someone coming to use the bed or bathroom, not expecting her to be in there? "So sorry," she gasped in dismay, whirling around and darting out the doorway from the brightly lit washroom into the relative dimness of the stateroom. Just as she moved, the airplane juddered over a momentary air pocket, lurching and sending her staggering off balance. She recognized Blade in the instant before she crashed into him. His strong arms wrapped around her instinctively to keep her from falling, and she caught a breath of the citrus soap he used.

"Oops," he said, his voice rumbling with suppressed laughter as he steadied her. She was overwhelmingly conscious of the bed's presence beside them. Then he released her, his arms falling away as though he'd found himself holding an armful of dynamite with the fuse lit. He took a step backward, moving out of the overly intimate sphere of her personal space. "I didn't mean to startle you. Were you able to find the mouthwash all right?"

"Yes... um... it was in the cabinet in there, like you said," Crys told him, feeling like a fool for her panicked stumbling, and more so for the flash of delight she'd felt at being in his arms. The way he'd moved away from her made it infinitely worse.

He must have seen the desolation in her face, as he looked concerned, and asked, "What's wrong, sweetheart? Why do you look so sad?"

"Oh, I'm not sad, I... just..." Unable to think of a lie or even some way to prevaricate, she shrugged and decided on honesty, with unhappiness welling up inside her. "It... it hurts when you avoid touching me... when you pull your hands away like I'm contaminated or something. Because I – I know you don't love me, I never expected that, but – I wouldn't have slept with you if I didn't think you at least liked me a little. I thought we were friends. And now I feel like a whore."

Blade stared at her, surprised and uncomfortable. "Damn, Crys, I never meant..." Apparently unable to meet her eyes, he looked down at his combat boots, and his hand rose up to fidget with his eyebrow ring. "Look, I..." He cleared his throat. Stuck his hands in his pockets. "Fuck. It's only 'cause I wouldn't be able to keep my hands off you otherwise."

Crys drew in a startled breath. "You're... you're kidding, right?" she asked, full of doubt and feeling very strange.

"Nope." Blade met her eyes at last, and even in the dim light she could see that his face was flushed. Slowly, he drew his hands out of his pockets, and reached out to stroke one long finger down her cheek. The intensity in his eyes and the aching sensuality of that slight caress sent a shiver of desire through her, and she couldn't prevent the soft little moan of pleasure that slipped out, making him raise his eyebrows in gratified surprise. "Oh, Crys, you're so lovely," he said. "And I know it's wrong, but you make me so hungry."

"W-why is it wrong, if it's something we both want?"

"Because you deserve love and commitment, not just a..." His words trailed off, and he sighed, shook his head. "I'm not... I can't..."

Crys understood. "I never asked for any promises," she reminded him.

"Sweetheart, you're too nice a girl to be used like that. I don't want to mess you up." Scrubbing a hand fiercely through his spiky black hair, he turned toward the door. Stopped in the doorway and stood there a moment with his back to her, and the muscles in his neck and shoulders were knotted with tension. Then, instead of passing through the doorway, he slid the door closed and twisted the lock – Crys wondered in a surreal daze whether the lock plate on the other side now read OCCUPIED or IN USE. Blade rested his forehead against the closed door, still with his back to her. "I don't want to mess you up," he repeated, "but hell, I can't walk away."

"Oh sweet God," Crys whispered.

Then Blade spun around, and two long strides brought him to where she stood. He grasped her hips and pulled her against him almost roughly, gazing down at her with reluctant aching need in his eyes. "I've got to... just one more time, I... I need to be inside you... please, Crys?"

"Oh yes..." she breathed, reaching up to clasp her hands behind his neck. And then his mouth covered hers with bruising urgency – her lip was still tender from the four-day-old piercing but she didn't care, opening to his tongue in an immediate surrender that only made it hotter between them.

Always before, he'd been consciously gentle with her – she'd known on some level that he'd been holding back, taking care not to frighten or hurt her. This time there was no gentleness in him, only raw hunger, fierce and wild and barely controlled as he fell with her onto the bed. His hands slid up her thighs, under her skirt. Found her underwear and jerked it down to her ankles with impatient hands. She kicked the scrap of black lace off.

He groaned as her legs fell open for him, and then she gasped and moaned aloud as his long fingers caressed her: not tender, not gentle, but insistent and expertly erotic. For the span of several heartbeats she could not think at all, completely reduced to exquisite sensation, but then it was not enough. She wanted that sense of invasion, of fullness – the surrender of her mouth begged to be echoed by the surrender of her body. She scrabbled at his belt buckle and the fly of his jeans. Her fumbling digits couldn't work fast enough. "Please... I want you..." she murmured, breathless and blunt with her own desire, "I need you inside me, now..."

"I need to be inside you too, babe," he assured her, equally breathless, his hands making short work of the buckle and fly, shoving the denim down over his lean hips with a groan of relief as he was freed from constraint. Driven beyond modesty by the rough urgency between them, Crys spread her legs in wordless wanton invitation, arching her back and squirming in eagerness – Blade groped in a drawer beside the bed and found what he needed, rolled the protection hurriedly into place. Knelt between her thighs.

"Please, now!" she moaned, closing her eyes. And then he was driving into her, filling her, no pain this time, just that awesome intimate sensation of stretching and fullness and then friction as he began to thrust. It wasn't tender; it wasn't gentle. Not cautious or patient at all. *And oh sweet God, I'm going to melt, fall apart, explode,* Crys thought dizzily. "Oh God, Blade, that's so good, oh, don't stop..."

But at her words he did stop moving, holding still, holding back though she could feel the strain of it rippling through him. "Call me Chris," he said, his voice jagged with passion.

"Wha'?" Her eyes flickered open. He lay over her, his weight borne on taut arms, his body joined to hers. She wriggled against him, urging him to move.

"My name. Christopher. Chris," he rasped, sounding almost angry. "You didn't think I was actually fucking named Blade, did you?!"

"Ohh..." Dazed as she was, Crys finally grasped what her lover was saying. "Chris," she said, trying out the name. "Please, Chris – please move now – make me scream for you, love..."

And so he did, riding her hard and fast into a cataclysm of electric bliss, covering her sounds of pleasure with a deep and thorough kiss that reached right into her soul.

Afterward, they lay motionless for a bit, still joined, collapsed together in the warm afterglow of what they'd shared. Some minutes later, Blade raised his head and smoothed a few tousled strands of hair away from Crys's face with a gentle hand, asking, "I... hope that wasn't too rough for you, babe?"

Crys shook her head, blushing, just as the intercom's pleasant-sounding chimes rang out. "It's a lovely sunny day in San Diego," the pilot's cheery voice announced, "and we'll be starting our descent shortly, so please stay seated and buckled up for everyone's comfort and safety." How could the time have passed so quickly?

Blade untangled himself from Crys and sprang to his feet, and though she felt boneless and deliciously exhausted, she too hauled herself up off the bed, pulling her dress down and looking about for her panties.

"Oh, fuck, no," he said, looking down in consternation at himself and the messy bits of latex in his hands, just as she sensed a warm gooey flood of something seeping down her inner thighs.

"W-what's wrong?" she asked, clamping her legs together, though she was pretty sure she knew what had happened – the rubber in Blade's hands didn't look right, and though she'd had to clean herself up afterward the first time, it hadn't felt anything like this.

"Busted condom," he confirmed, his face set and grim as he wiped his fingers with tissues from the drawer by the bed. She pressed her thighs together, looking at the packet of tissues, unable to find the words to ask. He pulled up and fastened his jeans, buckled his belt. Belatedly, it occurred to him that she might need some tissues, and handed them over. Turned his back to give her a bit of privacy. In silence, she tidied herself as best she could, found her pretty lace thong and stepped into it, feeling damp and sticky and frightened.

Crys waited for Blade to say something, anything. *Has this happened to you before,* she wanted to ask; *what do we do now?* But he only sat down on the edge of the bed and looked at his hands. They could feel the airplane begin its descent, a shift in angles and air pressure, and yet he made no move. "Um... sh-should we be going back to the main cabin, do you think?" she asked at last, her voice sounding tentative even to her own ears.

He looked up at her, his face paler than usual, seeming almost white in the half-light so that his eyeliner-edged eyes and the dark arches of his eyebrows stood out in vivid contrast. His beautiful hazel eyes, usually so confident, held a trapped and sickened fear that bordered on panic. "Crys... you... I might have..." He apparently couldn't bring himself to complete the sentence, but he didn't have to – she could hear the words as readily as if he'd said them. *Knocked you up.*

"Isn't there anything I can do? There's a pill... a morning-after pill, right?" she suggested, feeling numb and frozen at the thought. She counted back to her last period; it had started the day Debbie's package came in the mail. *Two weeks ago.* "There were always posters at the college, mostly in the dorm washrooms and the pub. Saying go to any Planned Parenthood clinic–" She'd snickered at the posters, assuming they were aimed at stupid girls who got drunk and didn't take proper care, and she... she'd been the good girl, the one who wasn't supposed to need such things, the one who never did anything risky or foolish.

Blade nodded, but he didn't look happy. "Yeah. It's not a sure thing, though." Crys closed her eyes briefly, with a sinking feeling as his words brought to mind one detail of the posters: optimistically funky lime-green lettering along the bottom, assuring anyone using the toilet that emergency contraception prevented unwanted pregnancy at least seventy-five percent of the time.

"I expect it's still worth taking," she said. "Better than nothing."

"Because anything would be better than carrying a fucked-up junkie's baby, huh?" he muttered, eyes narrowed in bitterness. "Even having the vultures catch you going into Planned Parenthood... shit, that'd be a nightmare! Or any pharmacy; they'd be in there nosing around, asking questions, speculating. Can't buy goddamn throat lozenges without them assuming we've all got the clap."

"Oh. Well. I'm probably not, anyway," she said, trying to sound positive for his sake. But his joke about sexually transmitted diseases chilled her. *Intravenous heroin.* She remembered the needle he'd almost plunged into his arm in front of her, sharp-tipped and gleaming as its point had neared his flesh. What lethal microbes might his needles have carried over time? Surely he of all people could afford clean needles, she told herself. *But...* Then the airplane picked up its descent, and she staggered where she stood, reaching about for something to hold onto. She could feel the air pressure building in her ears, and swallowed. "I, um, don't think it's safe to walk to the main cabin now."

"Sorry, sweetheart," he responded, but in a mechanical tone that made her think he hadn't really heard what she said. Reluctant to go and sit next to him on the bed without invitation, she sat down on the floor, resting her back against the wall – at least that way she couldn't fall down. He stared at the floor, his profile like stone. Without looking at her, he said, "Listen, don't... don't tell anyone, okay? If Goldie thought there was an outside chance I'd knocked you up, she'd... hell, she'd have a sparkly rock on your finger before..."

Yeah. Our little secret. And pray to God that I'm not. Her first impulse was to tell him that it was okay – except that it wasn't okay, and when she'd had her lip pierced she'd committed to herself to never again say something was okay when it wasn't. "Yeah, Marigold had better not find out about this," she agreed. Her mouth felt dry, but she tried to swallow anyway against the building pressure in her ears.

♥

She hadn't thought until that moment of how it would feel, to have all the band and crew know that the pair of them had become lovers. It hadn't occurred to her that the others would notice their combined absence and draw the logical conclusion.

After the jet had finally landed and was taxiing off the runway, Blade had gone ahead out of the stateroom, while Crys stayed back to clean her lip and fix her rumpled hair. When she emerged into the main cabin, for a brief heartbeat she was invisible, observing Blade in his usual seat, with Dice and Easy laughing, and Angel punching him affectionately on the shoulder. The card players had abandoned their game in favor of conversation.

Then they became aware of her presence – first one then another head turned to look. As if there'd be some visible sign on her. *A red S on my forehead, for slut? Or would that be W for whore?* Tense enough already, and wanting to snap at them all to mind their own business, she forced herself to smile blandly around the room as she moved carefully to her seat, mindful that the airplane was still taxiing along to the FBO where they would disembark.

Sally said nothing when Crys sat down next to her, and at first Crys was concerned that she'd offended the makeup artist by not confiding in her. *I should have told her at the club, when she called him my man,* Crys thought. *I shouldn't have pretended.* But as they were disembarking from the plane, Sally grinned and said quietly, "So... I guess he is your man after all?"

"Maybe," Crys replied, but she couldn't help grinning back. *He couldn't keep his hands off me. He tried and couldn't do it.* Even a broken condom couldn't completely dampen the elation that knowledge gave her.

Then they heard Marigold's high-heeled boots clicking along the pavement, coming up behind them as they walked toward the waiting limousines. She glanced at Crys with sarcastically arched eyebrows, and as she passed them, she hissed, "Not so pure now, huh?"

chapter

13

THE POLICE BROUGHT BLADE BACK TO THE HOTEL AT two in the morning. No discreet ride home for the troubled Smidge guitarist this time – peering down from a window upstairs, Crys and Sally saw the long-limbed dark-haired figure decanted from a police cruiser in front of the hotel, in full view of anyone who cared to look; as he swayed on the pavement, two of San Diego's finest took him by the shoulders and escorted him inside. Easy followed, his blond hair all too recognizable as he waved to the few people still out and about like they were a big crowd, appearing – even from an upper-floor window – remarkably nonchalant.

"It doesn't look good," Sally said, and Angel grimaced without surprise – he hadn't expected better news. Dice, ever the optimist, looked disappointed.

"Should we call Marigold?" Crys asked, since no one else suggested it. The police presence, she thought, would require public relations.

"Hell, no!" said Angel at once, with deep feeling.

At the same moment, Dice muttered, "Please don't!"

Blade and Easy had disappeared from the hotel midafternoon, just as the crew arrived with the trucks from Phoenix. They didn't mention to anyone that they were going out – the timing suggested they'd slipped out deliberately. And Blade left his guitar behind.

Angel got up and opened the door to the hall, and remained standing, looking toward the door, visibly steeling himself. Dice didn't get up from the armchair where he was sitting, but he did take his

237

feet off the coffee table and straighten his posture, alert to whatever might come. Sally and Crys waited by the window where they'd been looking out.

They were in the sitting room of Blade and Crys's suite, had chosen to wait there in the hope that Blade would return on his own. Jed had gone to bed, saying that he would grab some sleep while he could since it was anybody's guess what time Blade might come in. But Sally and Crys and Angel and Dice waited.

This hotel was all creams and whites: white marble, ivory carpet, cream brocade on the furniture and eggshell linens on the beds. Elegant, refined. It wasn't the sort of place where Crys could easily imagine anyone being drunk or on drugs, or being escorted in by disapproving policemen. *Oh, Blade! Why?*

He'd dressed up to go out, she saw as the two uniformed officers pushed him forward into the room – his black hair was spiked up, his eyes were heavily ringed with black eyeliner, and he wore a collar of industrial chain. But instead of acting drunk or angry or wild, he seemed abnormally calm, with sleepy eyes half-closed, allowing the momentum from the police officers' hands to carry him forward to the couch where he flopped down.

Both officers looked disgusted. "Your friend is exceedingly, er, lucky that he wasn't found in possession of narcotics when we arrived," said one of them, a youngish and slightly weedy-looking Midwestern type, directing his comments to Angel although he neither made nor asked for introductions. Both he and his partner ignored Sally and Crys completely – perhaps thinking they were just groupies – and Crys was glad of that, feeling a bit frightened and in no way wanting any of the negative attention directed at her. Sally seemed to feel the same way; with a glance at each other, the two women sank onto a pair of chairs by the window and sat there quietly.

"You people will be getting a call tomorrow about some damage to premises, I believe," the other policeman chimed in, also directing his words at Angel, although in saying 'you people' he seemed to include Dice as well. He was taller and stockier than his counterpart, and his tone held more aggression. "To avoid negative publicity, the club is apparently willing not to press charges if a private agreement can be reached – which is the only reason your friend is here and not in a holding cell right now for being drunk and disorderly."

"Drunk and disorderly?" Angel asked, with a skeptical glance at Blade, sprawled on the couch in an attitude of laid-back lethargy. "Really?"

"He had an, er, outburst," the smaller policeman said, with tight-lipped disapproval on his red-cheeked face. "Before we arrived. The manager asked us to, er, remove him."

Angel raised one eyebrow, which looked particularly sardonic on his lean satanic face. "So. Neither of you saw him damaging the property. Neither of you saw him drinking or doing drugs. And he wasn't in possession of anything illegal when you arrived." He narrowed his eyes. "You're lucky you didn't decide to arrest him, all things considered; Smidge has a very, very good legal team." And that was definitely a threat. "Are we done here? I think we're done."

"Yes, sir," the smaller policeman agreed, nudging his partner with an elbow. The larger policeman grunted in what could be interpreted as agreement, and they departed, pushing past Easy in the doorway.

Easy grinned mockingly and sauntered into the room. "We had a great time, dude. Too bad you weren't there. And you ladies too – you could have partied with us, for sure."

"A great time?" Angel glared at Easy. "And what exactly did you two idiots get up to on this great time of yours?"

"Give me a break! We just met some girls, had a bit of a party with them. Hit a couple of clubs. Just a good time, you know."

Angel shook his head. "Don't bullshit me. You came home in a black-and-white. What happened?" He turned to Blade. "Open your eyes, dumbass. You've been using, haven't you?"

Blade's eyes flickered open. He stared glassily at his friend, and then looked away, his eyes coming to rest on Crys. She saw pinpoint pupils and a frightening lack of feeling, as if the Blade she knew had floated away and been replaced by a weirdly calm and untroubled stranger. "It's all good, man," he muttered. "I feel so good now."

"I'll bet you damn well do," Angel snapped back sourly, but there was sympathy on his face and a trace of longing too. "Easy. What happened?"

Easy shrugged, a superior little smile on his face. "We were drinking, and you know Blade. The getting naked thing. A bouncer objected; Blade got a bit out of hand. That's all."

"Come on, Ease, Angel wants to know about the smack," Dice said with an anxious frown, seeing the thunder in Angel's face and the mockery in Easy's.

"Oh, well, he was feeling like crap about something. Wasn't much fun. And getting all aggro with that bouncer." Easy shrugged again, with another cocky smirk. "I was getting something for myself anyway."

Angel stared in incredulous disbelief, looking from Easy to Blade and back again. Even Dice looked disconcerted by the stark fury on Angel's face. "You got it for him?! You gave it to him?! You were with us last year – not to mention last week – or have you forgotten?!" Then Angel shook his head, the fire in him dying as quickly as it had come up. "Just get out of here, Easy. Go to bed. The damage is done."

"Guess I will, then," said Easy, at last seeming slightly uncomfortable, although Crys wasn't sure whether he was genuinely uneasy about what he'd done or just reluctant to face Angel's anger for it.

The bass player was almost out the door when Angel called after him. "Hold on a moment, Easy! Where'd he get the needle?"

"What?"

Angel sighed, looking at Blade sprawled on the couch. "He threw away his rigs last week. Told me he was done for good. Where'd he get the works to shoot up tonight?"

"Oh, the guy hooked him up."

"New needle? Sealed package?"

Easy scratched at the stubble on his chin. "Christ, I don't know. I was busy–"

"Busy snorting happy powder. I know." Angel turned away in disgust. "Just go to bed, okay?"

Scowling at Angel's stiff back, Easy flounced out of the suite, leaving chilled silence behind him. Had it been a dirty needle?

Crys said a silent prayer. *Please let it not have been a dirty needle. Please, if it was a dirty needle, let him be lucky. Please, God, let nothing tragic come of this.* It made the thought of unwanted pregnancy somehow minor in comparison. At least there were options for that. *If someone's got to be unlucky today, let it be me.*

Sally stood up, jamming her hands into the pockets of her overalls. "I'll go get a naloxone kit from Jed," she said. "I dunno if there's anything he can do about a dirty needle, but at least we'll be prepared if Blade stops breathing." She reached out and patted Crys on the shoulder. "Don't look so scared, honey," she added. "He'll be all right."

After Sally had gone, they could do nothing but wait. Angel paced back and forth in front of the couch, and Dice drummed his fingers on his knees.

Finally, Crys couldn't bear the sick feeling in the pit of her stomach any longer and stood up, walked over to the couch where Blade lolled against the cushions. Free of all the stress and pain, his untroubled face looked so very young, even with the makeup and the steel hoops in his lip and eyebrow. Resting her hip on the arm of the couch, she leaned over and stroked his forehead, smiling sadly at the crispy feel of his gelled-up hair. "Oh, my love," she said softly, "oh, Chris... why'd you do it?"

His eyes opened, and he gazed up at her, the lovely deep hazel of his irises too vivid against constricted pinpoint pupils. "Hey... that's my name..." he murmured with a slow happy grin.

"Yeah," she agreed. "Just like mine. Crys and Chris."

He laughed softly, his eyes closing. "Cute... Better not tell Goldie, though... she'll be choked... 'cause no one's supposed to know our names..."

Realizing that he'd drifted into sleep, she looked up, to meet Angel's concerned eyes. "I don't understand," she said. "I thought you guys used to play concerts high, but – he's barely conscious – I can't imagine how he'd even be able to hold his guitar like this."

"He must have done a hell of a lot," Angel explained, with a grimace of knowledge and memory etched on his face. "Usually he's pretty functional; I mean, we didn't even know he was using again until he went on that binge in Seattle." Then something occurred to him, and the dark thoughts faded from his eyes as he said, "You... you called him Chris."

Crys nodded. "Yeah."

"He must have told you."

"Um, he... yeah." *He wanted me to use his real name in bed.* Crys felt her cheeks warming at the memory, but Angel didn't notice, lost in thought.

"It's strange – we haven't used our names in so long," he told her. "Kin went to pretty extreme lengths to hide our real lives and families. Even in private, we use our band names now." When Crys looked puzzled, he added, "There are reasons. It's better like this. But... I'm Andy."

"Dylan," said Dice, with an odd look on his face, as though he'd struggled for a moment to think of his own name.

"Thank you," Crys replied, understanding what great trust she'd just been shown. "I won't use them, of course. But thank you for telling me."

Then Sally came tearing into the room, out of breath, gasping, "I'm so sorry, guys! Goldie's on her way – she was snooping around and saw me go into Jed's room – he's delaying her as long as he can, but..."

"Goddamn!" Angel muttered. In an instant, he and Dice were on their feet, scooping Blade up and slinging his arms around their shoulders. "Come on, dude, we've got to get you into bed," Angel told him, and Blade roused enough to stumble along with them to his bedroom.

Sally looked worried, even more so once the two of them were left alone. "Goldie's really pissed," she said, gripping Crys's hand for comfort. "I've never seen her so mad. This is going to be bad... Look, the best thing to do is, don't say anything – don't try to defend him, don't try to defend yourself if she starts on you – just keep your eyes down and your mouth shut. All right?"

"Sure, but... why is everyone so afraid of her?"

"She's got a lot of power." Sally sucked at her lower lip, and then spoke in almost a whisper, as though someone might overhear them. "They call her a public relations assistant, but she reports to Kin, and he... he goes straight to Magus Horton."

"Who's Mag–" Crys started to ask, but Sally's hand tightened on hers as a thump echoed outside the door, followed by Jed's voice cursing. Had Jed tripped or dropped something on purpose to warn them?

"Angel! Dice!" Sally called in soft-voiced panic, and the two of them came charging out of Blade's bedroom. Dice scrambled to pull the door closed behind him.

"Got your cards, Sal?" Angel asked, and Sally dug in the bib pocket of her overalls for the pack of cards she carried there. By the time Marigold stormed into the room with her phone at her ear and Jed trailing behind, the four in the room were sitting around the coffee table with hands full of cards and cards on the table – a game in progress. And if they had no particular game in mind and the stacks of cards on the table made no sense, Marigold was too furious to notice.

For the first time, Crys thought about how expensively Marigold was dressed for just a public relations assistant, no matter how famous the band. The purple silk blouse and rhinestone-studded jeans she wore were flashy, yes, but visibly of designer quality. Her streaked hair was professionally done, with the indefinably soignée look of a high-end salon. And her ears and neck and wrists and fingers dripped jewelry, all of which had to be real gold and diamonds. But most of all, Crys now noticed the way in which Marigold carried herself – the sense of prerogative, of entitlement, that her whole attitude conveyed – a powerful woman, barely concealed under her wildly flamboyant veneer.

Marigold's eyes were like ice as she looked at each one of them in turn, an expression of disgust on her face. Deliberately making them wait, she finished her phone call and looked at her phone for a moment with grim-lipped amusement. "Where's Blade?" she asked at last, her voice hard. She waited for an answer; none came. "I said, where is Blade?" she repeated.

"He's asleep, Goldie," Angel said as calmly as he could. "In his room. We were just finishing our card game."

"All smacked up again, the stupid little junkie," Marigold surmised with an ugly sneer. "I'm not surprised. He's replaceable, you know – you're all replaceable – it's thin fucking ice!"

Crys bit her lip with the effort to say nothing. *Don't rise to the bait; don't try to defend him.*

Beside her, Angel gritted his teeth. "It was just one hit," he said. "I'll sort Blade out in the morning, I promise."

"Mr. Horton will sort Blade out in the morning," Marigold replied with nasty sweetness. "He and Mr. Kinney are flying in as we speak, and you should know they aren't impressed. There's a lot of damage control to be done."

"There's nothing we can do tonight," Angel pointed out evenly, though his neck and back were stiff with anger. "Maybe we should all get some slee–"

Ignoring him, Marigold turned on Crys. "And you! You're supposed to prevent this sort of thing from happening. Where were you?!"

Don't say anything, Sally had said, but short of outright rudeness it was impossible to ignore a direct question. And Marigold waited with narrowed eyes, expecting an answer. "I've been right here all evening," Crys replied, hardly able to get the words out. "I was downstairs getting a coffee when he, um, left. It was midafternoon; I had no idea he'd–"

"Just forget it. You weren't with him; you screwed up. Mr. Horton won't be happy. You're lucky we've still got a use for you, girl, or you'd be flying home on commercial standby tonight." She scowled. "Now, Jed was needed here for what, exactly?"

Jed stood behind Marigold, watching the fireworks with a frown creasing his forehead. He stuck a finger under his bandana at the back of his neck to scratch a momentary itch, and perhaps camouflage an infinitesimal negative shake of his head: *don't mention Blade or the naloxone kit.*

"Uh, my stomach wasn't feeling good?" Dice offered.

Marigold just rolled her eyes. "Anything else you clowns need to share with me while you're at it?"

Only that Blade might have knocked me up, Crys thought, suppressing an urge to giggle.

"I believe there might have been some damage to property," Angel confessed, "but we won't be able to get any details until the morning."

"In other words, the usual idiocy." Marigold gave a spiteful little laugh. "Well, I'm off to get some sleep. Tomorrow's going to be a busy day." She turned to leave, and then realized that Jed was staying behind with the others. "I expect there's no need for you to stay here, Jed, when your patient is quite obviously asleep," she added pointedly. And Jed shrugged in resignation and followed her out.

Don't go! Crys swallowed against the impulse to call out to Jed, to call him back. *I need you to help me get the morning-after pill!* But there was no way of getting his attention without also drawing Marigold's notice.

"And to think that once upon a time we just made music," Angel said bitterly. He'd spoken to himself, maybe, but loudly enough for her to hear, and Crys turned in surprise to see him staring out the window, his shoulders slumped in frustration and misery. "Now it's all about the goddamn image – we're not a band anymore, we're a fucking brand!"

"Come on, dude, it's not so bad," Dice said with an anxious smile. "We're on tour, right? Playing arenas every other night?" When Angel didn't automatically cheer up, he tried again. "And we'll be back in the studio after New Year's, right? Our fourth major label album? Aren't you looking forward to that, at least?"

"Yeah. Promoting posters and t-shirts and crap. Being told what songs we can and can't play. And sure, I'm looking forward to producing another album of commercially viable bubblegum – can't you see how excited I am?"

Dice flushed. "Sorry – I just thought... I dunno, we're doing what we love, and they're actually paying us... no slinging coffee during the day to play at night, you know?"

"No... instead we've got Marigold Hendon bitching at us, and Magus-Fucking-Horton giving orders from on high." Angel moved away from the window, flopped down on the couch where Blade had been lying earlier.

"But I don't understand..." said Crys. "Why do you let them do it? You're... you're Smidge!"

"I don't know." Angel thought for a moment. "It happened so fast: all of a sudden there was money everywhere, women and champagne, and we were recording in a real studio, being treated like stars. We thought Magus was a gift from heaven, fixing everything for us – we'd hit the big time, and yeah, it did feel amazing... for a while. So we listened to him. We... we got in the habit of it..."

"Who is this Magus?" Crys asked.

"Our manager," said Dice.

Angel laughed, and it wasn't a nice laugh. "We'd been managing ourselves, in between day jobs and gigs and rehearsing wherever and whenever we could fit it in. Our label introduced us to Magus Horton – said we needed him."

"Oh," said Crys, beginning to understand.

"It was just small stuff at first," Angel continued. "He started to coach us on our image, gave us and our band new names, talked up songs he saw as commercially viable and picked the others apart. But, you know, we agreed to everything – he knew the industry, and the rock star life looked awfully nice. Then he got rid of our bass player and found Easy for us. Brought Kin on board to handle publicity. It... it kind of snowballed, and... now they run everything."

He looked so down that Sally and Crys, with a glance at each other, moved to the couch to offer what comfort they could. Crys patted his shoulder with an awkward hand, wanting to cheer him up but not knowing how. "I expect that always happens," she murmured in a reassuring manner, though she had no idea whether such was the case or not, and Sally nodded her agreement.

"I don't know, but it's killing us. In Blade's case, literally – it's just a matter of time." Angel shook his head in bitter sorrow. "He hardly writes music anymore, since Magus either trashes his songs or makes him clean them up, dumb them down... you should've heard the original lyrics to 'Love Bound'..."

Dice nodded. "Yeah. He always had it rough at home and stuff, and he's never really connected easily with people, but... he used to be happy sometimes, like after a gig, or when he'd finished writing something and came to show us, or just goofing around."

"Hell, I used to be happy sometimes," said Angel with a snort of mocking laughter.

Sally wriggled herself onto the back of the couch behind him, and began to massage his neck and shoulders – obviously something she'd done for him many times, as he didn't seem surprised but only relaxed against her hands. "It'll be okay, honey," she assured him. "We'll get through this, and we'll get Blade through this. Somehow." Though her words were strong and positive, a hint of doubt colored the tone of them.

"Yeah." Angel's voice echoed Sally's uncertainty. He stared at his knees for a minute, then gently moved Sally's hands away and stood up. "Well, I think I'm going to head to bed – tomorrow's going to be ugly – don't want to face it short on sleep." He turned to Crys, and added, "I'll bunk in with Blade to keep an eye on him... unless you were planning to?"

"Me?" Crys asked, blushing. "But... no, you... it isn't like that..." She took a deep breath. "We're not really... together, we just, um..."

"No worries, Crys Murphy," said Angel, looking directly into her eyes so she could see that his approval was genuine. "You're good for him. But it's cool – I'll sleep in there tonight."

♥

Crys lay in the bathtub, up to her neck in steaming hot water and rose-and-vanilla-scented foam. She'd shaved and scrubbed and buffed herself to perfection in the shower stall beforehand, and now lolled contentedly in her bath, enjoying the giant tub and luxurious bubbles.

She'd woken before dawn with a feeling of dread. Despite the late night, it had been one of those full and complete inner wake-ups, with no hope of going back to sleep or even dozing. *Might as well get up,* she'd thought. The first hint of sunrise had just begun to color the horizon outside her window – she'd realized that no one would expect her to be awake for at least a couple of hours, and the en suite bathroom had a huge soaker tub and a selection of luxury bath products. She'd decided that a bubble bath would be just the thing. And it was.

Lying in the bath, she told herself that everything would be all right. *I'm probably not pregnant anyway.* A fleeting thought of an infant with Blade's hazel eyes crossed her mind, but she blinked it away. She would get the morning-after pill somehow; she still had more than half of the seventy-two-hour window in which it could be taken, and Jed would help her, surely, if she could just make a chance to talk to him privately. And somehow Blade would be all right too – surely there'd been nothing lethal on that needle, surely one bad night didn't mean the addiction had beaten him. All would be well. In the rose-and-vanilla-scented comfort of the bath, she let her worries go and just drifted.

Some time later, a knock on the door woke her out of a dreamy almost-doze. She didn't think anything of it at first, until the knock came again, and she realized that someone was knocking on the bathroom door, and was thus inside her bedroom. "Y-yes?" she called out, her voice squeaking a bit. "I'm, um, in the bath. W-who is it?"

"It's Marigold, darling; can I come in?" Marigold didn't wait for an answer, but pushed the door open – too late, Crys regretted not locking it – and stepped in, closing the door behind her with one elegantly booted foot. "Oooh, nice and warm in here," she commented, settling herself cozily on the lid of the toilet. "Sleep well?"

"Not so much," Crys muttered, sinking down as far as she could into her bath, hoping that the bubbles covered her decently.

"That's too bad... I've always got some diphenhydramine around, if you're having trouble sleeping. You only have to ask." Marigold smiled kindly, smoothing her hands over the knees of her red satin pantsuit.

Crys stared at Marigold in disbelief, unable to reconcile the sweetly helpful woman in her bathroom with the spiteful harpy she'd seen the night before. The public relations assistant was behaving as if none of it had ever happened, to the point that Crys began to question her own recollection of what she'd seen and heard. Had the threats and nastiness actually been uttered? Had Marigold really been so vicious? *I was a bit stressed at the time,* she thought uneasily, wondering whether her memory could be exaggerated, or if the events of the night had somehow become mixed with her nightmares. Because here was Marigold – the friendly, helpful, trustworthy Marigold – apparently settling down for a nice chat. "Um... Marigold... was there something important? I'm... sort of taking a bath here..." Crys prompted, trying to look as though she didn't mind.

"Well, of course when I came looking for you I didn't know you were going to be in the bath, but it is a perfectly private opportunity to discuss the next phase of Blade's media image management – you might even say, heaven-sent."

No, I wouldn't, Crys thought, but she nodded anyway. "Sure," she agreed.

"Great. So, you're a smart girl; I'm sure you can see that after last night we need some emergency damage control."

"Right."

"And you'll recall that your contract has some flexibility in how we can use you – I think the exact wording is 'willing to take on whatever task or role best serves the public image of the Band' – am I right?" Marigold smirked, catlike, knowing perfectly well that she was right. She'd probably looked it up before coming over.

"Oh, yes," Crys replied. "I remember that perfectly. What is it you want me to do?"

Marigold laughed, a tinkling false little laugh. "So direct! Girl, if you want to be a player in this business, you're going to have to learn a more subtle approach. But Blade got into some pretty serious trouble last night, and the papers this morning are bad. To be blunt, we need a reason for his acting up."

"Oh... why... I don't... um, what makes you think–" Crys stumbled over the words, not knowing what to say. How could they possibly know it was her fault?

"I couldn't care less about the real reason," Marigold said, dismissing Crys's stammering with a brusque wave of her hand. "I meant that we need to give out a public reason. An acceptable, understandable reason. And you, my dear, are going to provide it."

Crys nodded, sensing trouble but not seeing any way to avoid it. "How am I going to do that?" she asked.

Marigold's smile wasn't a cat's smile so much as that of a shark – she didn't just nip, she tore and maimed. "Unfortunately, you're the villain in this soap opera, Crys; you've been dating another man behind Blade's back, you see, and tonight the world is going to find out about it." A flicker of amusement crossed Marigold's face as Crys's mouth fell open in dismay.

"But... I would never..." Crys began, and then realized that Marigold didn't care. *I would never do that to Blade.* But who would ever believe her, once the media and internet had branded her faithless?

"It's for a good cause, girl – just think of it – there won't be a woman across North America without sympathy for poor Blade's broken heart." Crys couldn't think of a single word to say, as Marigold stood up and opened the door. "You shouldn't sit in the bath so long; you'll get all pruney," Marigold admonished on her way out. "And do get a manicure. We're meeting at eleven to work out the details – conference room C on the second floor – so don't be late."

Then the door closed behind her and Crys was left alone, sitting in her cooling bathwater, with her sense of dread returned in full force and nothing good left in the day.

♥

Crys had trouble finding conference room C, and eventually had to ask for directions at the front desk, so she was a couple of minutes late. As she arrived at the imposing double doors, she already felt a bit out of sorts for being wrongly dressed – she had lots of clubby stuff and evening wear, but nothing at all suitable for a business meeting, and though she'd finally settled on jeans and a baby-doll blouse, the effect was hardly businesslike. Being late didn't help.

The doors were closed, so she knocked. Waited, and then knocked again, her knuckles making only a weak little sound against the solid oak doors. No one came; perhaps they hadn't heard her knock. Reluctantly, she reached out and turned the door handle, pushed inward.

There were only four of them, at a conference table for three times that number. Nearest to the door was Marigold in her scarlet satin suit, tapping away at the keyboard of her computer. Next to her, Kin reviewed a folder of printed material, benign and grey-suited, the benevolent executive. Beside him was a man Crys had never seen before. Was that Magus Horton? But she hadn't time to study him, because Blade sat on the other side of the table, the accused facing the jury, and pinned up on a pair of flip charts at the head of the table were the damning front pages of the morning tabloids.

"Crys, you're here!" said Marigold, noticing her. "Come and sit down – oh, I'm sorry, hadn't you seen those yet? They're pretty bad, I know." Despite the apologetic words, she spoke with barely-disguised relish.

"Pretty bad..." Crys echoed, appalled at the full-color, full-page photographs of Blade sitting on the tile floor of a washroom, tourniquet tied and fist clenched, syringe in hand. He looked up and met her eyes, and turned even paler than he'd already been. Defeated, and ashen with shame. She wanted to run to him, to hold and comfort him. *Oh, love, I wish I could have prevented this somehow. I'm so sorry.*

"Please sit, Crys. We have a lot to discuss," said Kin with a sympathetic smile. "First of all, you haven't met Smidge's manager, Magus Horton. Magus, this is Crys Murphy."

"A pleasure, Miss Murphy," drawled the man who sat next to Kin, standing and inclining his head toward her, since the conference table between them prevented him from offering his hand. He was a teddy bear of a man, with greying blond hair in a businesslike cut, rosy cheeks and a genial smile. He looked like someone's uncle, full of good-natured charm. Only his ice-blue eyes seemed cold, and Crys wondered whether maybe she was imagining even that, based on Sally's fearful comments of the night before.

"I, um... please call me Crys," she replied, enchanted by his courteousness despite her doubts of him.

"And you must call me Magus, my dear. Do have a seat, anywhere you like." He remained standing, politely unwilling to sit while a lady in the room remained on her feet. Was it possible that she'd misunderstood what Angel and Dice and Sally had been telling her? Could this well-mannered, charming, avuncular man really be the powerful manipulator that they'd made him out to be?

But then Crys's gaze shifted to where Blade sat, shoulders slumped in defeat, and it struck her how needlessly cruel it was to have displayed the damning tabloids so prominently in front of him, reminders of his failure to stay clean, reminders of the drug he craved. Would any kind person do that? Or permit the painful pictures to remain? And before she even knew what she intended to do, her feet were moving her toward the flip chart stands at the head of the table.

"Now that we've all seen these, does anyone mind if I take them down?" she asked with a defiant tilt of her chin, almost daring them to refuse her as, with shaking hands, she tore the offending pages off and placed them face down on the table.

"Oh. Well. Er, thank you, Crys," said Kin, appearing at once annoyed and relieved. "Not pleasant to look at, are they?" But Marigold pressed her lips together in irritation, and though Magus's expression didn't change, his eyes took on a remarkable chill. Shivering though the conference room was well heated, Crys hurried to take a seat next to Blade, opposite Marigold and as far from Magus as she reasonably dared to be.

The moment Crys was seated, Magus sat too, tapping his pen on the table. "Could we get started, please?" he inquired, waiting with steely eyes until everyone's attention was on him. "All right. It's simple – the public is pretty lenient about drinking and even sexual escapades, but needle freaks are not acceptable. Those pictures will damn you, Blade, and by association Smidge as a whole... unless we act quickly to give your fans an explanation, a route by which they can sympathize with you... and place the blame elsewhere. Right, Crys?" He smiled at her, an orthodontically perfect smile that made Marigold's shark smile look benign. Crys nodded reluctantly, knowing they intended her to carry that burden.

"Magus and I worked all night to come up with a solution," Kin interjected, although neither of them looked short on sleep. "And we do have an answer which might actually increase Blade's fan appeal, particularly with the, shall we say, nurturing-type female population."

Magus nodded. "Blade, you've been a silly boy – the only positive thing here is that one of the pictures shows packaging from a new syringe – but you're going to come out of this better than you deserve. All you'll need to do is act like you've got a broken heart."

"Broken heart?" Blade asked slowly, his expression both puzzled and wary, and Crys's rush of relief at hearing the needle had been clean evaporated.

"Indeed," said Magus. "Because Crys here has been sneaking around with another man behind your back." He leaned back in his chair with a self-satisfied, cat-in-the-cream look on his face. "Isn't that right, sweetie?" he added, with a wink in Crys's direction.

Magus's words had not implied that the story was untrue, and Blade's face went white. He turned toward Crys in disbelief, looking like he'd been gut-punched and muttering, "Oh, sweetheart, no..."

"Never!" she assured him, with a lump in her throat. "It's only what they'll tell people – it's not true!"

"But it *will* be true," Marigold said. "Talk is cheap, and pictures sell papers. By tomorrow morning it'll be Crys's pretty face on the newsstands, and no one will blame Blade that he took something to get over the pain."

"Yes," said Kin. "Crys, you'll need to make sure you're seen, but look like you're trying not to be seen. A drink at an almost-empty bar in the late afternoon – you're more noticeable but it looks like you're avoiding people – then dinner in a small restaurant and we'll make sure you get a window table. Then go to a movie and sit in the back row. Marigold can arrange a discreet leak to some of her press contacts, so they won't have trouble finding you. You'll want to be ready by – hmm... Marigold, what time is the actor getting in?"

"The actor?" Crys asked.

Marigold checked something on her computer screen. "His flight gets in at two. Yes, Crys, we're bringing in your actor friend – the one who already signed the confidentiality agreement? It just made sense, when we realized that he'd listed his profession as acting, not to bring yet another person into the confidentiality circle."

Rhys! Not a stranger, thank God, or someone aligned with Magus. "Yes, of course." Crys tried to keep the relief out of her voice. "I'll enjoy spending time with him."

"You'll have to do a bit more than that." Marigold smirked. "In fact, you'll need to get as hot and heavy as possible without being arrested for public lewdness – it's got to be pretty clear to anyone watching that you're doing the nasty with him, right?" Her eyes flicked to Blade, and she asked with saccharine concern, "Blade, do you need to be excused? You don't look so good."

Blade looked like he was about to vomit.

chapter

14

*T*HE CAR DROPPED HER OFF IN FRONT OF THE PUB WHERE she was to meet Rhys, but Crys didn't go inside. Instead, she hurried up the block to a clothing shop she'd spotted, and bought the first t-shirt she could find – boldly striped in blues and greens, but better than the clingy black lace thing that Marigold had provided for her. "I'll wear the t-shirt," she told the startled teenager working there, "if you could put my blouse in the bag instead." Blouse was too dignified a term for the plunging neckline and barely-there lace of the garment, but she couldn't think of a better word. At least she'd been allowed to wear jeans with it, when she'd protested wearing a miniskirt in the middle of the afternoon.

She hadn't been given a chance to talk to Blade at all – after the meeting, Marigold had hustled her off to the hotel spa for a manicure, pointing out that people were judged by the state of their hands.

"But what does it matter what my hands look like, if I'm just the cheating bitch who broke Blade's heart?" she'd asked.

"Honestly, girl! You need to look *capable* of breaking a rock star's heart," Marigold had explained in disgust.

"Do I need to look capable of cheating, too? Because I'm not sure I can do that," Crys had muttered to herself, but Marigold ignored her. "I need to talk to Blade," she'd said later, when she'd realized that no opportunity was going to present itself.

And for once, Marigold had looked slightly compassionate, if only in a fractional softening of her expression as she shook her head. "Oh,

Crys, you shouldn't have let yourself get so attached to him," she'd chided, her eyes on the two tubes of lipstick she was choosing between. "The red, I think... This is too hard an industry for soft hearts. But it'll all be over soon enough – better just focus on your job for this afternoon." Which apparently meant looking like a prostitute in candy-apple-red lipstick and a bare-it-all blouse. Crys didn't think that she was supposed to be wearing lipstick so soon after getting her lip pierced, but Marigold hadn't listened to any excuses.

In her new striped t-shirt, Crys felt much more comfortable as she walked back down the street to the bar where she was to meet Rhys. She thought about wiping the lipstick off, but worried more about creating a smeary mess and getting it into her piercing. And anyway, she was out of time. The doorway stood in front of her, a double door with long brass handles, and glass panels set in old-style wood. Even in the middle of the afternoon, a neon sign above it cast a sickly greenish light downward, telling the world that this was Frankie's Bar. The door was narrowly set between two retail premises – a bookstore and a shoe store – and inside, a flight of stairs led downward to the below-street-level drinking establishment.

The air was quiet and smelled of beer and fried things, as Crys made her way carefully down the stairs. The lone bartender glanced incuriously at her and then returned to his conversation with two elderly men sitting on stools at the bar. Keno numbers glowed red on the far wall, overtop a small stage – evidently the bar featured live music in the evenings, since the stage held a drum kit and lonely-looking microphone stand. In a corner booth, a quartet of businessmen were drinking beer and watching the muted television screens: hockey, football, racing cars. And there was Rhys at a table in the middle of the room, standing to greet her, looking so wholesome and normal in jeans and the same fisherman's sweater he'd worn for their one coffee date back home.

"Rhys!" She hurried over to him, almost but not quite running, resisting the impulse to throw herself into his arms for a hug – the thought of hidden photographers held her back. He seemed equally uncertain about whether to hug her or shake hands or just sit.

"Hi, Crys," he said, his eyes on her lower lip; "you, uh... you got your lip pierced..." His expression said he wasn't sure he liked it.

"Yeah. It was... just something I needed to do." *And I don't care if you don't like it.*

After an awkward moment, they just sat down without touching, and he smiled. "So... this is weird, huh?" Straightforward, honest and to the point.

"Oh, good God, weird hardly begins to cover it!"

Rhys laughed at her vehemence, and the awkwardness fell away. A small part of Crys had thought she might after all feel some tingle of attraction for him, in this deliberately romantic set-up – a last chance, maybe, at the white-picket-fence family? But he might as well have been the brother she'd never had, and she'd only wanted a hug for comfort.

A waitress materialized from the back of the bar somewhere, and came over to take their order. "What's in the bag?" he asked once the waitress had moved away, indicating the plastic carrier bag that Crys had dropped on the empty chair beside hers.

"The hideous hooker shirt Marigold thinks I'm wearing; you do know that I'm intended to be cheating on Blade with you, right? Apparently scarlet women need to dress the part." She took the shirt out of the bag and held it up for him.

"Wow! Well, I'm sure you'd look cute in it, but... yeah." Rhys shook his head in amused disbelief, and then his expression turned to one of concern. "You're okay, though? You haven't gotten hurt in all of this?"

His kindness gave Crys a choked tearful feeling. "Me? I'm okay. Fine. But they're killing Blade – you have no idea – and even Angel hates what they've become. The PR people and the manager run everything, and when you hear that Smidge is just a pre-fab bubblegum rock band, it's true, but only because they're not allowed to be anything real anymore..."

"Aw, Crys, it can't be as bad as all that..." Seeing her lip trembling, Rhys slid his chair over so that he could put an arm around her shoulders.

She pulled away, snapping out, "Don't!" Her voice was high and tense with stress, and he immediately dropped his arm.

"Crys?" he asked cautiously. "What's going on?"

"I'm not doing it!" she told him. "I'm not going to just meekly cooperate like the rest of them, so scared of Marigold and that Magus creep. And they want nasty amorous pictures of you and me in the tabloids to take the blame off Blade for the heroin that Easy gave him when he – oh, it's just so awful!"

Rhys's forehead creased in puzzlement. "Well, I understand that you have to play the bad girl to save Blade's reputation; that's why they brought me here, to help you do that. But... what d'you mean about meekly cooperating, and why is it awful?"

"It's awful because... I saw Blade's face when they told him." Crys looked down at her lap, seeing again the sickened expression he'd worn. "Believe me, if he'd asked me to do this, I'd be in your lap with that slutty top on, posing for the vultures and doing my best to smile."

"He's not... in favor of this?" Rhys asked. But then the waitress, older and sour on the daytime shift, came up and plunked down the pints of beer they'd asked for. He paid, thanking her and handing over a generous tip that made her crack a reluctant grin. "Why not tip liberally?" he commented, once she'd moved away. "We're on Smidge's tab – they gave me a huge wad of cash. Might as well live like a rock star for once; I dreamed about it often enough."

"You dreamed of being a rock star?" Crys asked in surprise, having assumed he'd always known himself an actor.

He laughed, gently mocking his own youthful dreams. "Oh, sure – didn't everyone? I played bass, thought I'd be just like Flea or John Paul Jones. But our band broke up, and I got into acting." He took a thoughtful sip of beer. "I did always think the big names got to call the shots, though."

"I expect most of them do," Crys said bleakly. "If they don't get too big too fast. If they don't trust others too much. If they don't get addicted to ugly stuff and put themselves into the hands of people who get off on wealth and power."

Rhys looked serious. "Hey. Is it really that bad?" he asked.

She nodded. "Yeah. Please don't say anything to anyone, but it *is* that bad. And I don't know what to do – though I do know I'm not going to hurt Blade by slutting myself out to please Marigold and Kin and that Magus guy." She looked at her pint glass, but didn't really feel like drinking. Her stomach felt too tense, her throat too tight to swallow. *I should have just asked for coffee.*

"Okay, then," Rhys agreed equably. "Much as I'd like to have you snuggle up to me, I respect that. You aren't going to get in any contract trouble, though, are you?"

Crys shook her head, with a small ironic grin. "I don't think so. The contract says I have to do whatever best serves Smidge's public image. Nowhere does it specifically say who gets to decide that. And I don't believe that making Blade look cheated on is good for him or the band."

The conversation flagged, and they sat silently for a while, drinking their mid-afternoon beer in the quiet bar. The businessmen from the corner booth got up and left. The old guys up at the bar kept on with their conversation.

Rhys thought of something, brightened. "You remember Johnny, from the concert where we met? He went on a date with your friend Debbie."

Crys grimaced. That couldn't have ended well. "Oh?"

"Yeah." Rhys grinned back at her. "She went back to his place after the movie, met his live-in boyfriend." He shook his head. "Completely freaked out... I guess you didn't tell her? 'Cause Johnny thought she knew; I'd told him that I'd told you, and he thought you would have told her."

"I did tell her." Crys thought back to that moment in the doughnut shop, with Debbie sitting laughing and sipping her coffee, her face full of stubborn disbelief. "She just didn't believe me."

In the back somewhere, a door slammed, and a slick-looking man came out of the dark hallway that presumably led to the kitchen and washrooms and offices. He was pulling on a coat as he headed across the bar to the stairs when his phone rang – "The Entertainer," which as a ring-tone choice always made Crys giggle – and he paused, leaning on the end of the bar, to answer it. "Yo, Frankie here!" he barked into his phone, loudly enough for the entire bar to hear. "What? Seriously?!" He listened for a minute. "Man, that is seriously uncool. What am I supposed to do?" He listened for another minute. "Damn straight you'll do a make-up show as soon as Timmo's hand is better, but we're still in a hole for tomorrow night – no, I'm not happy! A Friday night with no band... fuck!" Crys could tell that the man, who had to be the bar manager or owner or something, was furious; he jabbed a finger at his phone's screen as though he were trying to break it instead of just end the call. He tried calling someone else, and evidently got voicemail, cursed his way through a message to be called back at once, damn it!

Crys looked at him, thinking of what she'd just heard. *A Friday night with no band.* And then she looked at Rhys. *I played bass,* he'd said, *but our band broke up.* And something clicked in her mind.

"I'll be right back," she said to Rhys, and she got up and walked over to the slick man, stomach clenching at the enormity of what she was about to do. She looked him right in the eye and said, "I think I can get you Smidge."

"What?" he asked, blinking, unsure whether he'd heard her correctly.

"Tomorrow night," she explained, heart pounding. "I, um, couldn't help overhearing that you're in need of a band. I think I can get you Smidge."

The man laughed. "Very funny, young lady." And then he did a double-take and looked more closely at her. "Say... maybe you're not kidding... aren't you...?"

"Yes, I'm Blade's girlfriend. Crystal Murphy. And you are?"

"Frankie Luxton. I'm the owner and manager here. And it's true that I'm short of a band for tomorrow night – the idiot guitarist for the band we had booked went snowboarding at Bear Mountain this morning and broke his stupid hand."

He looked closely at her, his head cocked to one side, assessing. He ran a hand through his slicked-back hair. Crys waited for him to make up his mind, heart in her mouth. *Out on a limb with a saw in my hand,* she thought wildly. *Why am I doing this?*

And then the corners of his lips turned upward in a hint of a smile. "Listen, I must be dreaming, but are you serious? Could you really bring Smidge here tomorrow night?"

"I think so. They don't have a concert on, and... it's been a while since they've had a chance to play a space like this." She looked around at the small stage, the scarred floors, the wood-beamed ceiling; though the place was almost empty in the mid-afternoon lull, she could easily imagine it full of people later in the night, happy, drinking, with her boys on the stage making music without constraint. Luxton still seemed skeptical, and no one stood within earshot, so she decided to take the biggest gamble of all. "They're going to be auditioning a new bass player," she told him in a confidential tone. "Do you want that to happen here?"

Luxton's eyes practically bugged out. "Er, maybe we should step into my office," he suggested. "Does your... friend want to come too?"

"That's the potential bass player," Crys explained. "And yes, he should join us." It would be beyond rude to leave Rhys alone in the bar while she skipped off to the manager's office. She just hoped he would play along.

♥

"Auditioning for Smidge? That's ridiculous!" Rhys's laughter sounded surprisingly loud in the narrow hallway as they followed Luxton to his office.

Luxton turned to glance at them inquiringly as he unlocked his office door, but he must not have heard what Rhys had said, because he ushered them inside with a smile, saying, "Listen, I'm going to grab a coffee from the kitchen; want some?" They shook their heads, and he vanished, with a raised finger to show that he'd only be a moment.

Crys shot Rhys a pleading look in Luxton's absence. "Please just play along for now. I'll explain later," she said softly, and he nodded.

And then they were seated in a pair of comfortable leather visitors' chairs, and Luxton was sliding in behind his desk, setting his coffee mug on a cardboard bar coaster, pulling up a pad of foolscap paper and digging around in a drawer for a pen. "So," he said, with a rather speculative tone. "There's more to this than you're telling me. Why is Blade's girlfriend telling me about this secret audition and saying that she thinks she can bring Smidge to play at my bar? What do you gain in all of this?"

Crys smiled her sweetest smile, knowing that she would be better off dead if everything started to unravel on her. "Can I trust you?" she asked Luxton with earnest eyes. "Really trust you?"

"Er, sure," he replied. "Absolutely."

"Thank you." Crys took a deep breath. "In confidence, then, there are... management issues. The boys need a bit of freedom; you have a stage and no band. I... I know nothing about music management and record labels and stuff, but... maybe I'm at the right place and time to do something for them."

That brought a grin to Luxton's face, and it made him look a lot younger, a lot less slick. "To engineer a walk-out, you mean. Wow!" He leaned forward over his desk, elbows propped, thinking hard. "Okay, contractually it could be sticky, but... if we don't pay them, if they volunteer their time... there's nothing to pay out to management – can't take a percentage off zero. We'll avoid using the Smidge name, just to be safe; recognition will be enough, and the mystery will work from a marketing point of view. So it's just logistics, really." His eyes were bright, enthusiastic.

"Um, yes," Crys agreed in a soft voice, a bit fearful of the consequences now that her plan was under way.

"But you've got to tell me, what's the deal with this bass player audition?" Luxton looked enquiringly at Rhys. Rhys smiled blandly back, his eyes on Crys as he waited for her to explain.

"I'm guessing you saw this morning's tabloids?" When Luxton nodded, Crys continued, "Easy gave that heroin to Blade... when he was too drunk to care about staying clean." Her voice shook a little as she remembered the afternoon in Portland when he'd asked her to flush the stuff he'd gone to buy, and in the guest lounge at the arena in San Francisco when she'd taken the syringe from his hand. The band and the entire crew knew of Blade's struggle to get free of the drug's hold on him – how could Easy have placed temptation in his way like that, when booze and stress had already combined to weaken him? Thoughtless, selfish. Destructive. "Blade's been through so much, detoxing, fighting the urge to use again. To have sabotaged that..." Words failed her at the enormity of it, but no more words were needed. Luxton was nodding in disgusted comprehension; it wouldn't be necessary to explain that the Smidge boys didn't actually know about that aspect of the plan yet. Or any of it, really.

"So. We'd better talk about equipment," Luxton said. "Bands generally bring all their own gear, although... how stealthy does this walk-out of yours need to be? We've got a decent PA, but your boys will need amps for their guitars. And there's a drum kit here, though I expect that, uh, Dice would prefer to have his own snare and cymbals..."

Crys thought for a moment, not liking the idea of bringing too many people into what Marigold would call the confidentiality circle, but seeing the necessity of trying to get the boys their equipment. "I'll talk to Kimmy – she's the drum tech – I'll bet she can snag whatever Dice needs. As to the amps, will the ones they use in the arena do, or will we need something different?"

"Listen, if you can get 'em, your boys'll want their own amps. It sounds strange, I know, but the size of the space doesn't matter – that's down to the PA, not the individual amps."

"Okay. I'll figure out some way to get them. Maybe one of the guitar techs or sound people could claim a problem that would mean taking them... hmm." This was getting more complicated by the minute.

Luxton gave them a thumbs-up. "Not to worry, chickie. We'll be able to swing this. You want to bring a sound guy?"

"Um, I... don't know. I'll have to ask Sally; she knows who was around in the beginning, and who can be trusted." Crys sighed. "I expect there's someone..."

"Great. Here's my card," Luxton said, passing her a glossy black-and-red business card. "Give me a call tomorrow, when you know if you've got a sound person, and to confirm that you can get the equipment, okay?" He flashed her a conspiratorial smile, as he stood. "I gotta get moving, there's some stuff I wanna put in motion – this is going to be awesome!"

His confidence was contagious. Crys and Rhys stood too, shook Luxton's hand. "We'll see you tomorrow, then," said Rhys, when Crys found herself lost for words. She could only smile.

She didn't say anything until they were outside in the street, when the flash of a camera caught her attention. The photographer's face looked smug, as though he'd arrived thinking the worst and found himself right – she wanted to throw something at that smug face, though it would do her no good and only play into Marigold's scheme. But a memory of another day came into her mind: *it pays to be polite to those press guys,* Dice had said, on their way into the arena in Seattle; *you never know when you're going to need some good karma.* And because they needed all the blessings and good karma they could get, Crys raised her hand in greeting to the vulture and called out in the best cheerful tone she could manage, "Don't believe everything you hear, but be here tomorrow night and believe your eyes!"

"Be here?" the man called back in surprise, indicating the bar from which he'd just seen them emerge.

"Yeah. Here. Tomorrow night."

"You going to tell me why?" the photographer asked, his expression no longer antagonistic but curious, friendly. On their side, maybe. "And who's the guy with you? Come on, Crys! Do me a favor!"

"Just show up," she said with a big smile. "Just show up and you'll see." *And I wonder what effect that hint will have on tomorrow's headlines.* Then she turned to Rhys, taking his arm to hurry him along, giddy at how quickly everything was moving. "Come on, we've got a detour to make before our dinner reservation – we need to find a music store – you're going to need some gear for tomorrow."

♥

Crys and Rhys walked down the street toward her hotel, hands in their pockets, looking up at the sky. They'd had some wine with dinner, but no more than that; clear heads would be wanted in the morning. Rhys had a brand-new gig bag slung over his shoulder, with his brand-new bass inside – he'd arranged to pick up the amp the next day. They were glad of that at the moment, as the restaurant Marigold had selected for them proved near enough to both of their hotels that they'd chosen to walk back instead of calling a taxi. It was almost midnight now, and a beautiful night. Romantic. *Wasted on us,* Crys thought, wishing that it were Blade beside her, although Rhys had been a fun companion for the evening. A good friend, a very good friend perhaps, but nothing more.

He'd protested when Crys paid for his new gear, though he couldn't have afforded it himself, but she'd just laughed and held out her credit card to the sales clerk, saying that it had been her idea and they could settle it later. Neither one of them had mentioned that if he did end up joining Smidge, the price of a very average bass guitar and basic amp would no longer be a problem for him. Nor did either of them mention that the audition – and the whole bar gig – was only an idea in Crys's mind as yet, and subject to a lot of cooperation from three very famous Smidge boys and various crewmembers.

A full moon hung overhead, washing everything in clear white light. The full moon could make people a bit irrational sometimes, Crys knew, and she wondered whether its influence could have had anything to do with the outrageous plan she'd initiated. But as she gazed at the moon, her mind was filled with the memory of Blade all messed up on the heroin Easy had given him, and then the deliberate cruelty of the meeting with Magus, the damning tabloids held up to shame him. No matter what phase of the moon, she could not have let that go on. "It just has to work, tomorrow," she said to Rhys, her eyes still on the sky, "even if it's only for one night."

"I still can't believe I might actually get to play on the same stage as Smidge. It's just... hard to even imagine, you know?" he replied.

"Don't say you might – say you will!"

"Okay, I can't believe I will get to play with them." He laughed in disbelief as they reached the hotel, and looked up at the windows, lit and unlit – were the Smidge boys in there, back from their concert? "I hope I can still play; it's been a while." Crys shot him a horrified look, and he pulled a mock-horrified face back. "Don't worry," he said. "I was kidding. I even know quite a few Smidge songs. I'll have a bit of a practice when I get back to my hotel, that's all I need."

She managed a small smile. "I'm not in a fit state to be teased tonight, sorry. It's just..."

"I know," Rhys said. "You love him, don't you?" He spoke lightly, but his eyes were serious and kind. "I knew it wasn't just business before, but you've crossed a line since then, I think."

"Yeah," Crys agreed, with a rueful shrug. *Yeah, I love a drug-addicted, commitment-phobic rock star – but sweet God, the world falls apart when he touches me!*

Rhys allowed a flash of regret to show in his face – allowed, because he was an actor, and knew how to hide what he didn't want to be seen. "I had hoped... that there'd be something more between us, you know? But it's okay."

"I'm sorry," she said, with momentary regret of her own for what might have been. If Debbie hadn't needed to use the washroom after that fateful concert; if they hadn't been waiting where Crys had caught Kin's eye. If she hadn't met Blade... but she could never regret that. "I'd wondered too... but I guess I'm committed."

"Well, maybe not so much in words, but back when we met, I promised you a kiss," he said; "I suppose this will have to do." He leaned over and gently kissed her on the cheek. An almost-brotherly kiss, full of kindness. "A kiss for luck. Tomorrow will be fine. Sleep well, Crystal Murphy." And then he was striding off down the street in the moonlight, the brand-new bass in its gig bag bobbing gently on his shoulder to the rhythm of his feet. Crys watched him for a moment, and then turned and went inside.

In the lobby of the hotel, a thought occurred to her, and she hurriedly stepped into the ladies' washroom to replace her striped t-shirt with the low-cut black lace top in which Marigold had seen her leaving the hotel much earlier. Feeling uncomfortably bare in the revealing scrap of lace, she averted her eyes from the mirror as she left the toilet stall and exited the washroom. She crossed her arms across her breasts as she hurried through the lobby and along to the elevators. There was no sense in telegraphing her rebellion in advance, she'd realized, and the odds were good that Marigold was standing guard to observe her return. It had only been lucky that the public relations assistant hadn't waited for her in the lobby.

The elevator was all mirrors inside – no escape from her reflection. She'd known that, of course; she'd seen her reflected self on the way out earlier. Then, she'd only seen Marigold's intentions in the mirror: the scarlet woman dressed for her part, the whore who would break a rock star's heart – she hadn't really paid attention, beyond resenting it. Now, the full-length sight of herself in the mirrors made her mouth fall open in astonishment: a wanton woman on her way to her lover, a sensual princess who could conquer a rock star's heart. *Marigold's never wrong about clothes,* Crys thought with a slightly hysterical giggle. And she wished that she were on her way to Blade's bed instead of her own.

♥

Crys unlocked the door to the suite she shared with Blade, already half-prepared for what she on some level knew to expect. And indeed, there was Marigold, rising from the couch and putting down her magazine, with a pleased smile as she looked Crys up and down. "You look hot, girl!" Marigold said approvingly. "You're back fairly early, though – how did it go? I trust you put on a good show for our friends in the press?"

Our friends now, are they? But Crys recalled the warm and friendly interest with which the various reporters and photographers had greeted her strategic hints. *Maybe they will turn out to be our friends, at that.* "Oh, I think it went... well," she said, speaking cautiously, hoping to give the right impression without having to actually lie. "It was lovely to have drinks and dinner with Rhys; I'm so glad you brought him in instead of some stranger."

"That was the idea. I did want you to feel comfortable enough to, well, do a good job." Marigold winked, with a slightly salacious curve of her lips. She seemed amused, more than anything. "Poor Blade – I actually think he minded a little."

"Is there anything else, Marigold?" Crys asked, working to keep her voice neutral and polite. "I'm really tired."

"No, we're done for tonight," Marigold said. "Blade's already asleep, okay – I just looked in on him half an hour ago – so don't go waking him or anything. Get some beauty sleep yourself; I think tomorrow's going to be an interesting day."

You don't know the half of it, Crys thought, but she only said, "Goodnight, Marigold."

After Marigold had left, Crys did look for a moment at Blade's closed door. She could hear nothing, and no light shone underneath the lower edge of the door, so presumably Marigold had told the truth about him being asleep. The woman in the elevator mirror would have opened it and gone in, but Crys, unsure of her reception, didn't quite have the confidence for it. So she turned away and opened the door to her own room, realizing that she'd need to turn a light on in there before turning out the lights in the sitting area.

Her hand was reaching for the light switch when she froze, her mind going momentarily numb with shock. It was dark in her room, but the light from the sitting area behind her, combined with moonlight from the window, was enough for her to make out the dark shape of a body lying on her bed – and in another instant she'd recognized the lanky figure and the pale oval of Blade's face as he raised his head to look at her, his lip and eyebrow rings gleaming in the dim light. "Hey, sweetheart," he said softly, his voice deep and raspy with sleep.

"Blade!" she squeaked in surprise. "What...?"

"Shh..." he told her, his voice quietly urgent. "Leave the light off. Just come here." He did not get up, but still lay on the bed, atop the covers and fully dressed. As she moved closer, she realized that he was still wearing his stage makeup, the heavy eyeliner and glitter, his hair still thick with fluorescent blue streaks – and part of his stage wardrobe too, the mesh tank top, the studded leather dog collar, the slashed jeans splattered with glow paint that would pick up black light.

"You're still in your stage gear – what happened?" she asked. She sat down on her bed beside him. Looking down at his face in the low light, she could barely make out the dark lines of his eyebrows, the faint gleam of silver from his piercings, the deeper shadows of his eyes and the curve of his mouth. *Talk to me, love; tell me what happened.* Had he walked out of the arena? Had there been an argument? Had he gone to find more of his personal oblivion? He didn't seem high, but...

"How much do you care about me?" he demanded, his words abrupt and intense as he propped himself up on an elbow and gripped her left hand in both of his. She caught the sweet smell of alcohol on his breath as he spoke.

"I... well, you know I, um, love you..." she said, puzzled. "With... with all my heart – will that do?"

"Is it enough to do something crazy?" he asked. "Enough to take a real chance with a fuck-up like me?" Without waiting for an answer, he jammed something onto her ring finger, and she caught a brilliant sparkle in the light spilling in from the hall. *Oh holy Christ!* "You're mine," he gritted out, "not that actor's. I don't know if I can do this, don't know if I'll be much good at monogamy or shit, but hell, I guess I'm willing to try. So you can wear that, or you can take it off. Your call."

He released her hand, and she looked down in amazed wonder, her thumb almost involuntarily moving to feel the hard metal band around her finger. Even in the semi-darkness, she could see the triad of glittering gems, the flickers of blue-white fire at their hearts. "Was that a...?" She couldn't quite say the word.

"A proposal? Yeah." Even in the darkness, she could feel the burn of his eyes on her. "So are you going to take it off, or are you going to kiss me?"

A proposal. Crys sat there, unable to speak, her tongue flicking at the metal ring in her lip. He was every fantasy she'd ever had, lying there with the studded leather collar around his neck, dressed in ripped denim and mesh, pierced and painted and glittering, her rock star lover. *I can't give you an engagement ring,* he'd said, and yet there it was on her hand. *I thought I already had the only ring he'd ever give me.* What could it mean?

She was quiet for too long, and he rolled on his side, turning away from her. Assuming rejection. "It's all right," he muttered. "You don't have to. It's fine."

"Oh, my love, of course I'll m—" But he hadn't said anything about actually getting married, had he? "I don't want to take it off," she substituted hastily. "I... I'll be proud to wear your ring. It's only that I thought... you told me you'd never..."

"Yeah, well." He still lay with his back to her. "Nothing in life is ever what you think it's going to be... at least you've been a nice surprise for me, sweetheart." He rolled onto his back, and she could see his lips curve in a wry smile. "I don't want to share you."

"You won't have to," she promised. "You didn't need to give me a ring for that, though."

"Well, it'll shut Goldie and Kin up, won't it?" He didn't mention Magus Horton, but he shuddered.

"Is that all this is?" she asked him, holding up her left hand with the ring on it, the three stones softly glittering in the moonlight from the window. She couldn't quite keep the disillusionment out of her voice. "It's always diamonds with you, isn't it – diamonds for hookers, diamonds to say you're sorry, diamonds to fix the mess we're in."

"I thought women were supposed to like diamonds," Blade said in a mocking tone, dark eyebrows arching. And then their eyes met, and she saw something more than mockery in his gaze. Something uncertain and vulnerable, and real. *Are you looking for a sinner to turn saint?* – he'd asked the question in jest when they first met, and now the newly-minted saint was looking out at her from the sinner's body. With eyes full of love.

In awe, feeling powerful and sexy and beautiful all at once – the woman from the elevator mirror: the wanton woman with her lover, the sensual princess who had won a rock star's heart – Crys got up on her knees and put her hands on Blade's shoulders, playfully pushing him flat and pinning him to the bed. "Oh, I like diamonds," she agreed with a grin, wriggling a little so that the barely-there lace of her top threatened to release its hold altogether. And then she paused, playfulness evaporating as she added, "But the ring in my lip means even more to me."

"Good," he said in satisfaction, his hands sliding up her blouse to begin their wicked magic.

♥

Crys woke to sunlight, alone. The pillowcases were smeared and streaked with black and blue and glitter – Blade's stage makeup – and the bed where he'd lain beside her was still warm. Had he stayed with her all night, then? A pleasant half-memory of being wrapped in strong loving arms drifted across her mind, and she smiled.

Hearing a tap running in the en suite washroom, she sat up and looked around for something to cover herself with. Realizing that the hotel bathrobe was hanging in the washroom, she opted for the nearest solution, scooping up her panties and the sexy lace top from the floor by the bed and pulling them on. She padded across the carpet. Blade stood in front of the mirror, his long body completely bare, gazing at himself.

She thought for a moment that he was admiring himself, until she saw his face.

"What's the matter?" she asked him.

"I..." He laughed, an uncertain and hollow laugh. "It's been a damn long time since I've woken up next to anyone. Since I've slept all night with anyone."

Hoping to cheer him, Crys tried for humor. "Um, I hope I don't snore?"

That made him grin, balance restored. "You snuffle a bit, but it's cute," he told her. "You're kind of like a kitten when you sleep, you know – all curled up, making these soft little purring noises."

"I *snuffle*? Now I can never un-know that! You're supposed to pretend I'm a quiet sleeper," she scolded, swatting his bare shoulder gently. He caught her hand and kissed her palm, and she gasped at the tenderness and sensuality of it.

"Hmm..." he said. "You wanna take a shower before we get some breakfast?"

♥

"What happened last night?" she asked him, between mouthfuls of a vast room-service breakfast. The two of them sat companionably on her bed, swathed in fluffy hotel bathrobes, plates in their laps – a cozy and intimate meal, with the door locked to keep Marigold and company out. Because her lip was still tender, Crys had deconstructed her breakfast burrito and scooped small bites of scrambled egg and chorizo and melted cheese out of the tortilla, loading everything up with guacamole and salsa. The food was delicious, and for the first time in a couple of stressful days, she'd found her appetite.

"What d'you mean?" Blade said, pausing with his burrito halfway to his mouth. She couldn't help smiling at the contrast – in the morning light, fresh from the shower and wrapped in a soft white bathrobe, he didn't look much like the half-drunk glammed-up rock star of the night before.

"You'd been drinking, and you were still in your stage gear – what happened?" she repeated.

Blade flushed. "I lost it a bit," he confessed. "Goldie was waiting in the dressing room when we went to get our stuff off after the show, and she wanted to bring some vultures through. Started coaching me on what to say."

"And?" Crys asked with a bit of hesitation.

He sighed. "Hell. I... hell. I guess you'll hear about it anyhow. I broke a mirror, threw some things. Said a lot of stuff I already regret. It... wasn't pretty. Then I left."

"Oh, love," said Crys, reaching out to touch his hand with hers, "oh, love... and did you... did you go find some, um, something to ease the pain?" She didn't want to know – she didn't think he had – but felt compelled to ask.

"Heroin, you mean?" he asked bluntly, his tone almost challenging, and his hand stiffened under hers. Then she heard him release the breath he'd been holding, and she felt him relax. "No, sweetheart, I didn't – it was a near thing, but no. I got a bit drunk instead. I'm done with that evil shit. Done."

"I'm glad. I think... it would have killed you eventually, and I... I couldn't bear that." Even the thought of it made her feel cold. *I couldn't bear to lose you.* Her heart ached at the thought.

They ate in silence for a few minutes.

Out of nowhere, a faraway expression came over Blade's face – some thought across his mind had cast a chill on him. "Did you ever get that morning-after pill, in the end?" he asked idly, but his knuckles were white on the linen napkin he couldn't stop twisting.

A tingle of horror ran down Crys's spine. "Um, no. I... never had a chance." And then she'd been too busy, and had forgotten all about it in the excitement of the bar and the music store and plotting the next day's concert.

He looked down, carefully not meeting her eyes. "If you are... would you want to... end things? I mean, get rid of... you know."

"Would you want me to?" she inquired doubtfully. "I've always thought of myself as pro-choice, but... I'm not sure I..." In the abstract, yes, sure. But to terminate a tiny spark of life that the man she loved might have planted in her? To end the possibility of a baby who might have his eyes and smile, his musical talent even?

"I wasn't a wanted baby, and my parents never let me forget it. Mistake, accident. Hell," he laughed, and the sound was hard and bitter, "all I ever heard was how their lives would have been different if they hadn't blown their birth control. If abortions had been readily accessible back then."

"Oh, Blade – oh, Chris, I'm so sorry! That's awful! To think that..." That his mother would have aborted him if she'd had the option. It sounded almost as though he wished she had. Crys shivered. "Is your family why Smidge uses stage names, why Angel said there were reasons Kin worked to conceal your identities?"

He nodded. "Yeah. My dad especially, he couldn't stand me making it where he'd failed... it's the rock and roll dream, you know – he still lays it on me, on my birth, that he's not the big star. Magus and Kin said he'd bring me down if he could, they had to protect me."

"That's..." *So unfair,* Crys started to say, but then realized how babyish, how futile it would sound. "He doesn't know it's you in Smidge, then?"

"He knows – they both know." Blade laughed, harsh and ugly. "My parents get paid out each month, as long as no one finds out who I really am. Maybe it's the best thing. But... Dice hasn't been home to see his mom in almost three years, the poor kid... and Angel's parents practically raised me – I'd like to be able to see them now and again, maybe have Christmas somewhere other than a hotel room for a change – he misses them too."

"That's ridiculous!" Crys almost screamed at him, she was so frustrated. "Why do you guys let them do this to you? Use your names if you want to; go home for the holidays if you want to."

"Have you ever tried to argue with public relations people?" he pointed out with grim disgust. "They always win."

"Not always," she said. "Marigold told me I'm too direct and need to learn a more subtle approach – she's about to get subtle in spades! Speaking of which, I should really get dressed; I've got a lot to do this morning." Popping the last bite of breakfast into her mouth, Crys got up and fished around in her suitcase for a clean t-shirt and her old cargo pants – the ones Marigold didn't like – to wear for what could be a rough and ready day.

He looked at her, intrigued. "Why? What's going on?"

"You'll see," she told him. She could feel the excitement bubbling up inside herself, and let it spill over with a gleeful giggle. "You're going out with me tonight, okay? So don't make plans. That's all I'm going to say." She wriggled into her pants underneath the bathrobe, but had to drop the robe to finish dressing.

"Cool," he commented, watching her. Did he mean her hinted plans for the evening, or simply the fact that he'd caught an eyeful of her bared torso? She wasn't sure. "You sure looked hot in that thing you were wearing last night – and hey, I never asked you how things went. Are... are the papers going to be really bad today?"

"Bad? I don't think so," Crys said, with an anticipatory smile. "It won't be what Marigold and company expect, either."

chapter

15

*T*HERE WERE ONLY THREE CHAIRS AROUND THE ONE
vacant table at the busy coffee shop, but Sally hunted around
and found a lone student studying with a spare chair at his table. "Can
we take this?" she asked, and when he nodded, she dragged the chair over
just as Crys came back from the counter carrying four enormous lattes.

Shopping had been the excuse. Sally and Erva had two plastic
carrier bags apiece, Crys one, and Kimmy three. The small table was
overwhelmed with shopping bags and purses. Crys handed out the
lattes and sat down with a groan of relief.

"Christ, do I need this!" Kimmy said, taking a huge gulp.

"Um, you may need it even more when you hear what I'm about
to tell you," Crys told her. She'd picked up one of the tabloids earlier,
and now pulled it out of her shopping bag and dropped it on the
table – there on the front page was a picture of her the night before,
in the striped t-shirt, leaving the music store with Rhys and his new
bass. They were laughing in the picture, but there was no hint of the
romance or furtiveness that Marigold had wanted to see. "SMIDGE
GIRLFRIEND BUYS BASS FOR MYSTERY MAN" said the headline.

"Marigold's not going to be too happy," Sally said, with a perturbed
frown. "I thought you were s'posed to be–" And then she stopped
short as Crys took her left hand out of her lap and held it out to show
off her ring.

"Sweet!" said Kimmy.

"Congratulations, dude!" Erva added.

Crys had been hiding the ring all morning, keeping her hands in her pockets, concealing her ring finger with her purse or shopping bag, and had finally found the moment to share her news. "He asked me last night," she said, a helpless joyful smile spreading across her face. "I mean, he kind of put it on my finger and said that I could keep it there if I wanted to, you know?"

Kimmy and Erva laughed, imagining such a Blade-style proposal, but Sally looked increasingly worried. "Oooh, Crys, you're both gonna be in such shit!"

"Marigold's not going to be happy at all," Crys agreed. "But I'm not afraid of her. And you only know what I've done already, not what I'm about to do. What we're about to do, if you're in..." She looked at the three of them, a question on her face. Did they want to hear more, or were they too afraid of possible repercussions to get involved?

For a moment there was silence. They had to think of their jobs, of course – their livelihoods, their reputations in the music industry, their futures. Then Kimmy scratched her cropped hair and shrugged and said, "If it'll make Dice smile, I'm game." All three of the others looked at her in surprise – was she sweet on her drummer, then? She'd never given any sign of it, until this moment when her blush admitted it.

"Dice? I thought you were seeing Ryan," Erva said, and Kimmy's blush got deeper.

"Well, it's not like I'd have a chance with Dice, and Ryan's a nice guy," Kimmy muttered, with a self-deprecating wave of her hand. "But I feel happy when Dice is happy, you know? So, like I said, if it'll make him smile, I'm game."

"It should," Crys told her. "The bar where we're going has a drum kit, but I'm told he'll want his own–"

"Snare and cymbals, yes." Kimmy finished automatically, then what Crys had said clicked in, and the women stared in astonishment. "You're kidding!"

"The... the bar where we're going?" Sally asked, her eyes bright with emotion, but she was slowly nodding. "And Dice will need his snare and cymbals? Are we really... have you...?"

Erva nodded her assent, a wicked grin growing. "Dude! I wouldn't miss it."

"We're going to need to, um, get their amps and stuff somehow too," Crys pointed out, feeling almost shaky with relief that the other women had embraced her plan. "I mean, the bar has some things, but it won't be what they're used to. And what about all the sound equipment, their earpieces and that?"

"I'll talk to Trick and Ruby," Sally offered. "Trick's been with Smidge almost as long as I have; he'll want to be in on this. And Ruby's sleeping with him, so we might as well have them both. And Jed'll help."

"That's probably enough," Erva said. "The more people involved, the more chance the dark side will find out."

"I can get the keys to the van from Mack, no problem," said Kimmy. "Liberating what we need from the trucks will be harder – they're packed and ready to roll in the morning."

"We'll figure it out," Sally assured them, fierce with determination. "This *has* to happen."

"There's one other thing..." Crys rubbed sweating palms on her thighs; one part of her plan called for a higher order of meddling than the rest of it. "Maybe this is wrong of me, but... I don't want to invite Easy to our party – my friend from the tabloids is a bass player, and I thought he could fill in. I know I haven't got any say about the band and things really, but this one time is different. Every time I look at Easy, I think of Blade all doped up the other night... I just don't want that dirtball there."

Erva wrinkled her nose in distaste. "It's such a typical girlfriend thing to do," she said, "but fair enough."

"She's only doing for a night what the boys should do permanently," Kimmy pointed out. "I mean, Jesus-freakin'-Christ, he knew Blade was trying to stay clean! That's next to criminal, far as I can see."

"He'd probably rat us out anyway," Sally said. "Management's golden boy, but he's a horrible pig really. I can't stand him, always looking up skirts and down shirts, and slinking in and out of the women's washroom at bars."

"Gross, yeah," Erva agreed with a shrug. "Bring your friend then, Crys. Maybe the boys'll like him."

Everything seemed to be settled. Crys tipped up her cup and swallowed the last sip of her latte, then fished her phone out of her purse. "I should phone the club manager to confirm," she said.

"Yeah. Look, Crys, you need to stay out of Marigold's sight – between the tabloids and that ring you're wearing, you don't need to cross her path today. Why don't you keep shopping with Erva while Kimmy and I go back to the hotel to get hold of Trick and Jed and the van?"

"I've got to go back to the hotel and change, Sal," Erva protested. "I'm so not dressed for going out!"

"I'll be fine on my own," Crys assured them. "You know what? I'll buy something to wear tonight so I don't have to go back to the hotel at all. Just call me when you're ready to meet up."

"You sure?" Sally asked, but seemed relieved when Crys nodded.

♥

Crys looked at the dress, and bit her lip.

When she'd first mentioned it, the idea of buying something new to wear for the evening had only been to reassure the other women that she'd be fine spending an hour or two on her own. But the more she thought about it, the more Crys realized that nearly every piece of clothing in her hotel room had been provided for her by Marigold – a proper rebellion required a self-chosen, self-purchased outfit. And more than that, a glittery ultra-glamorous rock star's girl had no place at the night's concert; it was meant to be separate from all that, an escape back to the days when the boys had dragged their own equipment around in an old van and played in whatever bars would have them.

She'd started out looking at the kind of thing she might have worn to the campus pub back home – denim skirts, peasant blouses, hoodie sweaters – student clothes. But those now seemed oddly young to her. And cheaply made, after the designer leather and silk she'd been wearing. She looked and looked, but couldn't find anything to suit her, and finally decided to return to one of the shops she'd been to earlier with the other women, where she'd seen a passable floral blouse. That would have to do, and surely she'd be able to find a skirt to go with it. Then, walking through the outdoor mall, she happened to glance at the window display of something called Steampunk Shack – and there it was. *I'll just go in and look at the price tag,* she told herself, eyeing the brown-and-black plaid corset dress on the mannequin.

On closer inspection, the fabric was a very fine wool, soft and slightly rough at once under Crys's fingers, dark chocolate and licorice criss-crossing in the weave. A black lace crinoline puffed out the short full skirt. But...

"Would you like to try it on?" the salesgirl asked.

"I... ah, no... I could never wear something like that. It's beautiful, though..."

The salesgirl looked at her curiously. "Why do you say you could never wear it? Your eyes, the way you touch the fabric – you want to try it on, don't you?"

No, she doesn't. Such a ridiculous lower-class aesthetic. Crys could still hear her mother's voice. *You're not really interested in trying something like that on, are you, Cryssie?* It had been a jacket, not a dress. *No, Mum, of course not.*

"Well, my–" *My mother wouldn't like it? I'm a grown woman half a continent away from her.* "You know what? I *will* try it on, just to see..."

After all, it might not fit. It might not look as good on her as it did on the mannequin.

It was perfect.

She took it off with reluctance, put her cargo pants and t-shirt back on. *I really shouldn't,* she told herself firmly. *Not because of Mum; I just...*

"And how did you make out with that?" the salesgirl asked as Crys emerged from the changing room. "Will you be taking it today?"

Crys opened her mouth to say no, when her phone rang. "Excuse me," she said, and answered the call, still holding the beautiful dress. It was Sally, saying that they had the van loaded up and would pick her up in twenty minutes at the main entrance. She looked at the dress folded over her arm. "I'll take it," she said, and handed over her credit card. With Rhys's equipment already on it, she was pushing her luck and her credit limit.

"You already got the boots to wear with that, hon?" the salesgirl asked. "Or d'you want to look at a pair?" And since Crys couldn't very well wear her sneakers with the dress, she found herself trying on and agreeing to Doc Martens – the exact ones she'd always coveted but never dared to buy against her mother's disapproval. "You know these boots need to be broken in, right?"

"Oh?"

The salesgirl grinned. "Newb. Here, you'll need a pair of *thick* socks, and I'll put some leather conditioner on the boots for you. Just don't wear them more than a couple hours your first time out, okay?"

Crys signed the credit card slip with a determined smile. *Tonight's the thing; I'll worry about the rest tomorrow.*

She asked for directions to the main entrance, and ran as fast as she could, dodging other shoppers and trying not to hit anyone with her shopping bags and purse.

❤

By the time she got outside, the van was waiting in a loading zone with the engine running.

The unmarked white van, general errand vehicle for the Smidge crew, was intended for equipment rather than people. Kimmy sat behind the wheel, with Ruby and Erva on the bench seat beside her; the rest of them were crammed into the back of the van. It was comfortable enough, since the interior was padded to protect the equipment, but Crys – accustomed to seatbelts – felt a bit unnerved, wedged as she was between Sally and Trick, with the side of a speaker case behind her back, and her feet in Jed's lap. Something of her unease must have shown on her face as the van started to move, because Jed winked at her and said, "Kimmy's a very safe driver, Crys."

"I'm such a safety girl," Crys joked, laughing off her discomfort. "Gotta push my boundaries, you know?"

Beside her, Trick nodded approvingly. She'd hardly known him before today, but he seemed a good guy. "Incidentally, congratulations on that ring you're wearing, if it means what I think it does," he said. "Never thought we'd see the day."

"Well, people can surprise you," Crys replied. As Blade had surprised her. And if the proposal hadn't been all that romantic, and if no words of love had been spoken, still it was a declaration of a sort.

The van's interior was cozy and the motion soporific. As she relaxed into the cushioning and the warm bodies of the conspirators on either side of her, Crys found her eyes drifting closed. Not to sleep, but to float in a comfortable state of belonging, contentedly aware of the others' presence around her. Her team, her crew, her friends. Doing this for their band, to whom they all felt connected. In a funny way, the van was full of love.

It came almost as a shock when the van stopped, and a waft of cool air blew in as Ruby opened the passenger door. She hopped out and ran around to open the back doors, and the lot of them piled out into the alley behind the bar, where Luxton himself was waiting. Crys had talked to him on the phone earlier in the day, of course, but now that they were actually there with equipment and crew to make it all real, she had the oddest sense that he had to restrain himself from hugging her in relief. He shook hands enthusiastically with all of them, and personally helped unload the equipment from the van. "We'll have a packed house tonight, I tell you," he assured them, wholehearted in manner and not at all slick. "Anything I can do, just let me know."

Crys was handed a bunch of cables to carry. All around her, the others bustled with the usual process of moving gear, lifting the amps and speaker cases down from the van, the crate with the snare drum and cymbals. "You're the sound guy?" Luxton was saying to Trick. "Call me Frankie. Come this way and I'll show you our setup, if the rest of your guys can manage to shift this stuff in without you? Straight down the hallway."

Crys carried her armful of cables straight down the hallway, following Ruby and Jed with the first of the amps. *It's a good thing those have wheels,* Crys thought, watching the pair guide their hefty black box along. The door marked STAGE couldn't be missed; Crys held it open for the others.

"Bet they're glad those amps are only half-stacks," Sally commented, lugging a pair of microphone stands, Kimmy and Erva behind her with the crate full of Dice's gear.

Trick snickered in amusement as he passed, hands full of wires and bits. "No doubt. By the way, brilliant idea, Sal," he said.

"It was Crys," Sally told him. "Not me. She came up with this – she planned everything. And it *is* brilliant. Our boys need this."

Hearing them, Crys felt all warm and fuzzy inside. *Brilliant.* Was it? Did they really think so? Would it all work out?

Looking into the bar from the small stage, the first thing Crys saw was the poster. Plastered on every pillar, every wall, it featured a black silhouette of a rock band against beaming spotlights and MYSTERY BAND spelled out below. But the distinctive shape of the lettering referenced Smidge's logo as clearly as could be. *Luxton's a genius,* Crys thought – anyone looking would immediately think of Smidge, and yet nowhere did the band's name appear.

As yet the space was almost empty; a couple of afternoon drinkers looked up momentarily as the crew emerged onto the stage, but paid no further interest beyond that – this wasn't a restaurant masquerading as a pub, but a true hard-drinking bar, and the few daytime patrons were only there for the beer.

Sally came through the stage door, shaking her head. "That won't do, Erva," she said with a worried frown. "Goldie'll be looking for her to chew her out about not obeying orders; she's got to stay away from the hotel."

"Sal, we're all needed here. She's not. Standing around holding cables!" This last was muttered and not meant to be overheard, but Crys did hear it.

"Sorry, Erva – I wish I knew how to be more helpful," Crys said, deciding that there was no point in pretending she hadn't heard. She dropped the cables on top of one of the amps. "What did you want me to do instead?"

Sally kicked at the floor in frustration, saying, "You can't go to the hotel, Crys!"

At the same moment, Erva explained, "Someone's got to go and get the boys..."

"Right." Crys had been worrying about that. *You're going out with me tonight,* she'd told Blade, but nothing more, and she hadn't had a chance to talk to Dice or Angel at all. At least Rhys knew to show up at the bar. "Look, I'm fine to go and get them, Sally," she said. "Really. I'll make sure to stay out of everyone's sight."

"Couldn't you just phone them?" Sally suggested, but Crys and Erva both shook their heads.

"The boys are too scared of the dark side to jump by themselves," Erva pointed out with a scowl.

"What if I call them and they don't come?" Crys added. "What then? What if someone stops them or talks them out of it? No – I'll go myself and get them – I want to do it."

Sally sighed. "Just don't run into Goldie, honey," she said.

"I'll get changed here before I go – I bought a dress at the mall – so I can just slip in and out of the hotel, no messing around."

"Coolness. Need any makeup?" Sally always had some bits and pieces for touch-ups in her pockets. She handed over an eyeliner and powder. "You're fine if you just freshen up around the eyes and powder your nose."

"Thanks, Sally. Truly, it will be fine. I'll be back with the boys as soon as I can."

Crys glanced around from inside the taxi before getting out, but didn't see Marigold or anyone from Smidge that she recognized. She'd asked the taxi driver to drop her off at the side of the building, rather than the main entrance. Able to stride out in her new boots – no tottery fragile heels for a change – she marched down the ramp to the underground parking lot and asked the attendant whether she could get upstairs from there. Shortly thereafter, she stepped into the elevator on the P2 level and, swiping her key card for access, was whisked straight up to Smidge's floor.

She didn't dare go to the suite she shared with Blade – if Marigold was lying in wait for her anywhere, that would be the place. Angel's suite, then? She wanted to be out of the hall as quickly as possible, before anyone came along to see her; that was the most vulnerable place, hurrying along the hallway, with nowhere to duck out of sight. She arrived at what she thought was Angel's door and knocked, praying he'd be there. Praying that she had the right room. There was no immediate answer, and she knocked again. Could he be in the washroom? Or asleep?

She heard a rustling noise behind the door, as though someone were there listening or looking through the peephole, and then the sliding scrape of the chain being unfastened. The door opened, and Angel was pulling her inside, closing the door at once and sliding the chain home again. "Thought it was goddamn Goldie looking for you again," he muttered. "Where've you been? She's been making our lives hell about it!" Then he caught sight of the ring on her finger and exclaimed, "Holy shit!" Turning back toward the sitting room, he called out, "Blade, you bastard! You never told me about this..."

And there was Blade, getting up from the couch and moving toward her with a big smile on his face. "Hi, sweetheart," he said softly. "You look beautiful."

"Yeah, well..." Crys replied with a pleased blush. "You know I told you we were going out tonight? I wanted to look good for you, and not like Marigold dressed me."

She'd realized as she'd gotten dressed in the washroom at the bar that she looked different. Different from any way she'd ever looked before. The shy student Crys was gone, as if she'd never existed, replaced by a confident woman with a lip ring and dark eyeliner. And nor was this the glittery rock star's girl that Marigold and Kin had created, all in hard-edged black and ultra-sexy fishnets. *This is just... me the way I want to be,* she'd thought on seeing herself. She was glad that Blade liked what he saw.

"So, where've you been?" he asked her, slipping an arm around her waist.

"Getting stuff organized," she said, with a deliberately mysterious grin. "Are you guys ready to go out?"

"Both of us?" asked Angel in surprise. Blade looked a bit nonplussed at the thought that her plans included anyone but the two of them, which made her giggle.

"Actually, we need to find Dice as well – d'you know where he is?"

Angel shrugged. "Probably in his room," he said, and pulled out his phone to find out. "Yo! Dice! Hop down here, would you?" he said into the phone.

"What about Easy?" Blade asked. His face was neutral, almost stony, and didn't give a clue as to how he felt.

Crys bit her lip. This was, maybe, the worst part – she didn't want them to see her as trying to separate them, wreck the band – as Erva had said, it was such a typical girlfriend thing to do. "Would you guys absolutely hate it if he wasn't invited?" she asked.

But instead there was an almost relieved silence for a moment. "If it's not going to be just the two of us, sweetheart," Blade said slowly, "then I'm glad you're inviting Angel and Dice."

"I've said from the beginning that you see things others don't, Crys Murphy," Angel commented with an approving nod. And Crys felt vastly relieved.

A drum-roll on the door alerted them; only Dice knocked that way. Angel opened the door, then he swore and gestured for Crys to hide as he caught sight of someone else approaching over Dice's shoulder. She scuttled into Angel's bedroom and through into the dark of the en suite washroom. Held her breath and hoped that a cursory glance would suggest the washroom was not in use – Marigold should have no cause to search more closely than that.

But it was Kin's voice rather than Marigold's that she heard, slightly muffled, from the sitting area. "Boys ... heard from Crys at all?"

he asked, his jovial voice booming. "...hasn't been cooperating... poor Marigold... really quite upset..."

She thought she heard "no" and "sorry" from the boys, but beyond that couldn't tell what had happened until she heard the thunk of the door closing, and they called for her to come out.

"So what's up?" Dice asked.

"Apparently we're going out," Angel told him. "Crys won't tell us more than that. Not even what kind of place we're going to, so it's hard to know how to get ready."

"Just, um, dress like you would for a bar," she said. "Whatever you like. You don't even have to change – jeans and t-shirts are fine."

Blade looked down at himself. "I'll just go change my shirt."

"Get your guitar too, while you're there," Crys told him. He raised his eyebrows at that, but nodded.

"Be right back."

Dice said he would change his shirt too, and Crys suggested he fetch his drumsticks, though she knew that Kimmy would have some for him as well.

Angel was shaking his head in wonder as he stepped into his bedroom, to return in a fresh t-shirt and gelled-up hair, with his guitar in its case ready to go. "Do I know what you have in mind for us?" he asked, but Crys just smiled.

"Don't ask, don't think, just come with me," she said.

The others returned. She saw that Blade had put on his 'free love' t-shirt, which reminded her of the first day in Seattle when he'd been detoxing, and she thought how very far they'd come since then. He and Dice had gelled their hair up too, and he'd put on a bit of eyeliner. *I guess he really does like to wear makeup*, Crys thought with amusement and a trace of pleasure. "All right, guys," she told them. "This is it – we're going straight down to get an ordinary taxi from the hotel's queue, and no one is going to stop us, okay? I don't care who it is, we stop for no one. Right?"

♥

The yellow cab pulled up in front of the bar, the driver still in shock at having Smidge in his taxi. It was a cozy fit, with Crys wedged in between Blade and Dice in the back, and Angel up front next to the driver, plus the two guitars. At least Dice's drumsticks didn't take up much space. "Frankie's Bar?" Angel asked, looking out the window at the neon sign above the entrance. He reached for his wallet, but Crys waved him away.

"That's it," she agreed, handing forward some money to pay the driver. "And tonight is my treat to you, okay? Let's go."

They piled out of the taxi and crossed the sidewalk to the double glass doors. The photographer Crys had seen the afternoon before lounged against a nearby wall; had he staked the place out all afternoon? He smiled at her behind the flash, and she waggled her engagement ring at him with a wink. And then they were inside.

"So what's up?" Blade asked her on their way down the stairs. His hand rested on the small of her back. "You going to tell us now?"

"What do you think, love? There's a stage, and you've got your guitar." They reached the bottom of the stairs, and there were Sally and Jed and Trick and Ruby and Erva and Kimmy all standing and applauding the arrival of their boys. Rhys hung back, looking a bit bashful.

"Surprise!" they called out, with huge grins at the stunned looks from Angel and Blade and Dice.

"I brought your snare and cymbals," Kimmy told her drummer with a happy blush for his dumbfounded expression, "and I've tweaked the drum kit so it should be just as you like it."

"I've got your earpieces," Trick added, handing them out. "We can do a quick sound check, okay, then you can hang out backstage and put together your set list for me. Old times, huh?"

"Old times," Sally agreed, hugging each of the boys in turn. "You can thank Crys, you know. This was all her."

"It was everyone," Crys said, waving away the compliments, a huge smile on her face as she saw the joy in all of their eyes. "Just have fun. Be free. Rock out. Oh, and this is Rhys," she added, pulling him forward.

"Blade, you met him before in Portland, but I didn't know he played bass back then."

"Dude," said Angel, looking Rhys up and down and shaking his hand. "We'll see how it goes tonight, but... we may be looking for a bass player."

♥

Crys and the rest of the crew had a front-row table next to the stage, except for Trick who manned the sound board. The small stage looked pretty full with the drum kit and the two big Marshall half-stack amps for the guitars, and Rhys's smaller combo amp for his bass. The microphone stands were way at the front of the stage, right on the edge. Hardly any space up there at all, really.

Luxton had done his job well. All the tables were taken, and the dance floor was full too; it was standing room only and not much of that.

The house lights dimmed, the stage lights brightened, and the band filed out onto the stage: first Angel, then Blade, then Dice, then Rhys. It took a moment for the crowd to recognize Smidge, albeit with a different bass player, and then the screaming started.

Angel stepped up to the microphone and gestured for the crowd to quiet. "Hello, friends," he said in his melting-chocolate voice, when the noise had subsided. "It's great to be playing in a bar again. It's been a long time, and those were good times. So just for tonight, we aren't Smidge, we aren't famous, we're only guys in a band, okay? And just for tonight, don't call me Angel – I'm Andy... Andy Angrath."

"I'm Chris Blakehart," said Blade, stepping up to the microphone next to his friend. "And you know what? I got engaged to my girlfriend last night." He raised his right hand to Crys in salute, with cheers and applause from the crowd – and his two middle fingers were folded down, his thumb sticking out. The horns? But... *With the thumb out like that, it's fucking sign language,* he'd told her once, and Angel had added, *Yeah, sign language for I love you.* Could it be...? The stage lights made it impossible for her to read anything in his eyes.

Dice stood behind his drum kit to another round of appreciative noise and added, "My name's Dylan Satwyn."

"And since the gentleman you all know as Easy couldn't be with us, it's my pleasure to introduce Rhys Davies as our bass player for the night." Angel... Andy smiled, and extended his hand toward Rhys, who ducked his head and waved to the crowd, overwhelmed. "We're changing things up a bit here, so you might want to pay attention to the lyrics – starting with the original dirty version of 'Love Bound'... from before we were asked to clean it up..." And as the crowd roared approval, he turned to his band with a grin and counted them into it.

The house was so full, the servers were run off their feet, and the crush at the bar was ridiculous. A grateful Luxton made sure that the crew's table was well-supplied with pitchers of beer, and the heat made Crys desperately thirsty, but she didn't want to get tipsy and have any moment of this triumphant night blurred away. She decided to order a soda from the bar, but it took her a while to work her way away from the stage and around the fringes of the dance floor.

As she passed the stairs leading up to the street, she felt herself observed, and glanced over at the dark-clad figure standing on the bottom step, maybe half a dozen feet away: a shiver rippled down her spine as her eyes met Marigold's. The public relations woman wore her black leather power suit, and radiated malevolent authority, her eyes holding a frost to rival Magus's. Marigold held out a perfectly-manicured hand and beckoned for Crys to approach.

Crys stood where she was, waiting for Marigold to come to her.

Marigold tapped her toe. Crys didn't move. Above them, the door opened and a cluster of bar-goers headed down the stairs, forcing Marigold to descend and move forward. With stiletto heels and menacing steps, she stalked over to where Crys stood.

Crys didn't give her a chance to speak. "Stay and enjoy the concert or go home, Goldie," she said, her expression cool and uncompromising.

"But don't attempt to ruin the night for any of us. I think you'll find that things have changed a bit, if you try." She smiled, and held out her hand to show off the diamonds sparkling there, adding, "For starters, Chris has asked me to marry him."

"You – 'Chris'? Fuck!" As it sank in that Crys had used Blade's real name, the public relations woman looked explosive.

"Just leave it," Crys suggested, almost pitying her. "They're grown men. Let them be."

Narrowed eyes and a scowl greeted that. "I never chose that dress for you."

"No, you didn't," Crys agreed, waiting.

With no farewell but muttered foulness, Marigold Hendon turned on her heel and stalked up the stairs out of the bar.

That was that, then.

♥

By the end of the night, Crys's feet had blistered in her new boots, and she grimaced as she headed down the hallway to the alley where the van waited. *Carrying cables again.* But it was good. She could hear Blade laughing as he and Dice moved one of the amps, just like any bar band packing up after a show.

The fresh air felt nice after the heat of the bar. Crys passed her armful of cables to Sally in the van, then turned to head back inside for another load.

A hand on her arm stopped her, and Blade's deep voice asked, "Did you like your concert, sweetheart?"

"Mine? It was for you," Crys said, turning to smile up at him, feeling her soul light up at the contentment she saw on his face. "I just wanted you to have a little happiness."

"I sure did. Come here..." He took her hand and tugged her down the alley a little way, away from the van and the lights. He looked away, up at the stars, like a thousand diamond earrings sprinkled across the sky. "Listen, Crys – playing in a bar again was great, but *you* are my fucking happiness, okay?"

She felt oddly like crying, like her heart would burst with something so painfully wonderful it couldn't be real. "Oh, Blade – Chris – what do I call you? I don't even know what to call you."

He laughed at that. "Either is fine. Maybe say Chris when we're in bed, all right? Or when you tell me you love me. That still true?"

"Fishing for compliments, much?" she asked, teasing. Then the serious expression on his face struck her. "I will love you with my whole being until the end of time, Chris Blakehart. You never need to doubt it."

"Good." He held up his right hand, index and pinkie fingers up, thumb out. "You know what this means, right?" *Sign language for I love you.*

Crys nodded, trying not to hope, to be greedy. Trying not to want more than she already had.

"Yeah. That. Anyway, I'm an ass, I have such a hard time saying shit like this, I–"

"It's okay." *He doesn't have to say it. It's enough that he means it, I don't need to hear it.*

"No. I think I... deep down, I've known for a while... I love you. There. Damn." He took her left hand in both of his and looked down at it. The diamonds on her ring finger sparkled, catching streetlights and starlight. "This ring..." he said. "I mean it, you know? For real. Legally wed, till death do us part, all that. I'm a hell of a bad bet, Crys, but I need you in my life, for permanent, okay?"

"You're not a bad bet."

"I'm a heroin addict, sweetheart. For the rest of my life, it's just one damnable decision away. But you make me believe I can be stronger than that – damn, Crys, you make me feel like a god, like I can be the saint you deserve." He grinned, letting go of her hand to grasp her hips and pull her against him. "I want to see you in a wedding dress, and take it off you. I want a honeymoon where we can spend three days straight in bed. I want..." He ducked his head but couldn't hide the wobble in his voice. "I want a family. I want to us to have what Angel's parents have, that thing where it feels like home when you get there."

Crys nodded, too choked up to speak.

Down the alley, the truck's engine rumbled, and Angel called, "Blade! Crys! Come on, we're all loaded up."

"What if I screw this up?" Blade muttered, as though to himself.

"I'm pretty sure we both will, over and over. But then we'll fix it, okay?" She laced her fingers at the nape of his neck and tugged him down so she could reach his lips with hers, delighting in his passionate response – until a peremptory blast from the truck's horn reminded them that it was beyond time to go.

But he stood there looking down at her, as a glorious smile spread across his face like sunrise. "I love you. We're getting *married*. We've got forever to get this right, don't we?"

"Forever, my love," she agreed.

He reached out and caught her hand in his as they headed down the lane toward the truck and their friends. Then, as he saw her wincing with each step on blistered feet, he scooped her up into his arms and carried her.

the end

want more

in your life?

THE STORY OF SMIDGE CONTINUES IN

ROCK GOD IN EXILE

ABOUT EAMONN "EASY" YARROW AND WHAT HAPPENED TO HIM
AFTER THE EVENTS OF ROCK STAR'S HEART.

Is it overreacting to knock someone down for groping you?

*Nell Whelan is a black belt whose self-protective instincts
kick in hard when she's uncomfortable.*

*Then she arrives at her hated day job to find the handsome jerk from the
pub kicking the photocopier, and finds out that he looks familiar because
he's actually the bass player for a famous rock band... but when she asks him
what he's doing working for her boss, he avoids answering.*

*Eamonn Yarrow – known to the rock world as "Easy" – hasn't
always been a good person and he's reaping the consequences,
but maybe Nell is just what he needs to turn his life around.*

Acknowledgments

TEN YEARS AGO, MY TODDLER DAUGHTER SLEPT IN HER stroller while I sat at the Cedar Cottage Coffee House and wrote the first draft of *Rock Star's Heart*. While the initial inspiration had come as a plot fragment long before, the core of the book was formed there: hours of writing, and endless conversations about guitars, performing, the music industry, not wearing your own band's t-shirt, lip piercings, and more – I could not have written this book without the expert knowledge that Tynan, who worked there at the time, shared with me. (Mistakes, of course, are all mine.)

My writing group met at the Cedar Cottage in those days as well. Andy and Jordan supported and pushed me forward from the first line onward. They patiently critiqued the first draft back then, and encouraged me not to give up on further iterations of the story as my writing and plotting skills matured. And there was carrot cake.

I'm not sure I would have dared to take the plunge into indie publishing without the shining examples set by Katie Cross and Katy Regnery – I want to be just like them when I "grow up" as an author. Sometimes watching others who have gone ahead helps us to be brave, and their kindness and encouragement has given me hope.

Unlimited gratitude goes to my fabulous editor, Tanya Oemig, who asked all the right questions to sharpen the story up, found my plot holes and helped me fill them, and kept my adverbs and sentence fragments in check. I'm also thankful for the thoughtful comments from Emily and Katie, who read the manuscript at various stages of its development.

Tiffany, who makes me believe anything is possible, took the gorgeous cover photo, and our adorable model Connor brought Blade to visual life more than I'd ever thought possible. I absolutely love the cover for *Rock Star's Heart,* and they made it happen for me.

My very patient husband has been listening to me talk about this book for an entire decade.

And finally, I have to thank my original core group of Sweethearts – my street team and book chat group – who've been so kindly cheering me on and helping me out through everything.

Writing a book is a solo act, but publishing it takes a whole band and crew, and I'm so very grateful to have all of you.

♥

About the Author

KELLA CAMPBELL CAN USUALLY BE FOUND IN Vancouver, Canada.

She writes mostly romance, because love and relationships are what she finds most interesting about life and in fiction.

She likes tea and chocolate and happily-ever-after endings.

kellacampbell.com